TWISTED JUSTICE

An Oz Garrett Novel

COPYRIGHT

First published by P&J Books 2022

Copyright © 2022 Paul Rix

This novel is entirely a work of fiction. The names, characters, and incidents portrayed in it are the work of the author's imagination. Any resemblance to actual persons, living or dead, events or localities is entirely coincidental.

Paul Rix asserts the moral right to be identified as the author of this work.

Copy Editor: Melanie Underwood

Cover designed by MiblArt.

First edition

DEDICATION

The joy of reading has been with me most of my life. I have my parents and schoolteachers to thank for that.

It is only in later life that I have discovered the joy of storytelling and writing. There are so many influences, I do not know who to thank. I am, however, grateful to everyone who has led me here.

Chapter 1

The deep blue waves sparkled and shimmered, reflecting the late afternoon sun, as the sleek hydrofoil attack craft skimmed the sea at two hundred kilometers per hour. Oz Garrett lay prone, gazing out of the Plexiglas canopy at the horizon. Through his peripheral vision, he was aware of another attack craft riding the waves less than one hundred meters away on his port side.

"Target acquired," said Leela Spicer from the other craft. Although she was a veteran bounty hunter, having chased down dozens of bolters, he could hear the tension in her voice. She had been like a coiled spring most of the day, pacing the dock until they had set sail. He was positive the mission would release that nervous energy.

Assuming everything went to plan.

"Confirmed," came the crisp reply from Naoki Oakes, the third member of the snatch squad sixty-three kilometers away, speeding toward the target from the opposite direction.

A classic pincer movement, as old as time itself. And simple to execute if everyone knew their role and there was clear communication.

Although the mission was going as planned, Garrett knew better than to relax. Success still relied on perfect timing and not a small amount of luck. Although Leela was a seasoned professional, this was only the fifth mission for Naoki. This was the first time Oz had worked with Naoki and he was not entirely content that she was flying solo. It would have made sense for him to have been on the far side of the target. But Leela was driving this mission, and she had made the call. Naoki had jumped at the opportunity like an enthusiastic puppy. Who was he to question Leela's judgment?

For possibly the twentieth time, Garrett checked the weapons and targeting systems. He had piloted similar models of attack craft on countless missions. The pilot interface was almost second nature to him. Whoever owned the three craft had maintained them well, even updating the targeting systems to provide him with one of the most accurate laser sights he had encountered. The four pulse cannons above and below the tiny cockpit could shoot the tip of a man's finger from fifteen kilometers, according to the instructional information. Garrett hoped he would not have to put that accuracy to the test, but it was reassuring to have that capability.

On paper, this extraction was supposed to be fast and relatively risk free. The targets were a couple in their late forties who had embezzled billions of credits from a wealthy shipbuilding organization before abandoning their friends and leaving their two teenage sons to face the music. Because of the sums stolen, the fee for this job was significant, as long as the capture remained private. The organization wanted no adverse publicity. Having a crooked chief financial officer would do nothing for their credibility, especially when bidding for lucrative government contracts.

"Thirty klicks," Leela snapped. "Stay sharp. The target will come into view shortly."

"Which means we will be visible to them," Naoki replied. "Yes, I know."

"Dropping velocity to one-five-zero," Garrett called out, more out of a need to say something. The crafts' synchronized navigational computers maintained a link to each other's location and speed.

The attack craft sank closer to the water at the lower speed as the submerged hydrofoil fought to keep the ride height. Water splashed up, creating thin rivulets of water that ran along the clear canopy like fine silk threads.

The intel on Mindi and Cenobia Lall revealed the couple had been meticulous in their planning. Their crime was not a spontaneous moment of passion or outrage at an unreasonable employer. They had carefully planned it for years, possibly before they had joined the organization. That level of foresight and attention to detail had continued through to the escape and new identities. The level of sophistication was impressive. On reading the file, Garrett had been in no doubt that Mindi and Cenobia were intelligent criminals who left nothing to chance. They had both slept with senior officials within the organization to obtain all the details they needed. And after the almost perfect crime, there was no telling how many millions of credits they had paid in bribes to keep their identities hidden.

Fortunately for Garrett, Leela Spicer was equally dedicated. She had forensically examined all potential evidence as to the whereabouts of Mindi and Cenobia. The couple had moved around for many months, changing planets and their identities like a normal person changes their underwear. Both had undergone extensive reconstructive surgery, but that could only go so far. Parts of every individual are unique and impossible to mask through drugs or surgery.

"Four individuals on the top deck. Weapons visible," Naoki said in a monotone voice. Garrett smiled to himself. She was in the zone and ready for combat.

The surveillance droid flying ninety kilometers above the target provided sharp resolution real-time imagery of the Lall's vessel. It was a two-hundred-meter-long luxury yacht, built for people with more money than sense and which hid an arsenal of defensive and offensive capabilities. The sleek hull and superstructure constructed from a titanium alloy, impregnated with heavy carbon molecules, made it resilient to heat and high-power projectiles. Automated gun emplacements provided a three-hundred-and-sixty-degree ring of firepower.

Below the waterline, the obvious place to attack, was an impressive and deadly set of sonar-guided drones with a range of five hundred kilometers; if they locked onto you, there was no escape.

The three attack craft were stealthy, with silent propulsion units and hydrofoils made from a material that hid them from every kind of sensor except the most sophisticated military-grade equipment.

Garrett glanced at the monitor to his left, gathering all the information he required in a fraction of a second. Two of the people on deck were identifiable as guards, carrying photon rifles and constantly looking out to sea as if expecting trouble. The other two individuals were unmistakably Mindi and Cenobia, laying on floral daybeds in skimpy swimwear, enjoying the warmth of the Sidenvan sun. It was almost a shame to destroy their relaxed afternoon.

The targets remained below the level of the horizon, traveling at a leisurely thirty kilometers per hour with no sudden changes in speed or course. Perfect.

The attack craft slowed their speed to minimize any chance of throwing up spray in their wake. A stealthy approach has the best chance of success and minimal conflict.

Garrett felt his heart rate increase by three beats per minute. He took three deep breaths but reveled in the sensation of adrenalin coursing through his body.

He flicked a switch on the comms panel. "Naoki, I'll take the big guy closest to me. I don't like his shirt."

Oakes laughed. "I thought that was your style, old man. I've got the bald guard in my sights. He's smaller and looks agile. Far more of a challenge."

Garrett groaned aloud. Naoki had continually taken pleasure in reminding him he was old enough to be her father. The sad fact was that she was right.

"No need to remind you both to shoot only to wound. We're not murderers," Leela said.

"I think you did just remind us," Naoki replied.

"Enough chatter, Naoki. Fire in ten seconds."

A magnified image of the target boat appeared in front of Garrett. Using the laser sight to paint a target on the muscular guard wearing a blue and orange patterned shirt, Garrett counted down the time in his head.

The guard was holding his weapon in his right hand. He looked relaxed, except for his constant monitoring of the horizon for anything out of the ordinary. His body language showed he was professional and competent. Garrett figured his black sunglasses contained a scanner and telescopic sight as a minimum.

So why wear a shirt that could be seen from orbit? It was almost as if he was challenging an attacker to target him first.

Garrett's mental count reached zero. Without moving his eyes from the target, he depressed the fire button once, knowing a tiny projectile would fire at almost two thousand kilometers per hour.

A warning must have activated on the Lalls' ship. It leaned sharply to starboard as it altered direction. Water splashed into the air, and white waves churned along the side of the vessel. The man in the blue and orange shirt grabbed hold of a rail to steady himself, at the same time scanning the area for signs of an attack. He was looking directly in Garrett's direction when the projectile struck his right shoulder. The force of the impact knocked the guard to the ground, although his body was now hidden by a low panel

"Target one down," declared Garrett as he altered course.

Naoki replied almost instantly. "Target two down."

Garrett watched as Mindi and Cenobia scrambled for cover across the deck before they descended a set of stairs and disappeared. Not that it mattered. They had nowhere to go and were probably safer hiding away in the bowels of their vessel, which continued to maneuver erratically to throw off Garrett and his colleagues.

It was now Leela's turn to make a move. She gunned her attack craft forward, causing it to lurch out of the water. Within thirty seconds, she was several hundred meters behind the craft for what was going to be the trickiest part.

As she lined her craft up to take a shot, a dozen hatches, only one meter wide, slid open to reveal the ship's defensive cannons, which proceeded to fire high-velocity projectiles.

Garrett flinched as he heard projectiles pounding on his craft's canopy and bodywork. It was a thorough test of the craft's shielding and one that it passed with ease. It was time for retaliation. Garrett returned fire, his eyes focusing from one gun emplacement to the next as he targeted the ship's cannons. In no time at all, he had destroyed three sets of cannons, their targeting mechanisms unable to withstand the onslaught.

"Thanks, guys," Leela said. "I'm going for the engines"

A painfully bright light burst from Leela's craft, enveloping the escaping vessel. The light continued for five seconds until the ship stopped accelerating, its bow dipping into a wave.

The vessel was now dead in the water as Garrett and Naoki's pulse cannons made quick work of the remaining guns on the vessel.

Leela called it. "Oz, Naoki. Time to move in. I'll cover you in case there are more guards than we were told."

Garrett checked the infra-red display, but the vessel's reinforced hull shielded all heat signatures. Boarding the vessel was a risk, but he was well prepared and trained for this type of scenario. He wished he could say the same for Naoki.

Chapter 2

Garrett leaped onto the lower deck, moving swiftly to the wall in case of any unexpected guards. With no immediate visible threats, he crept slowly toward the stern, all senses alert to any movement. Other than the creaking of the vessel as it swayed lazily in the sea swell and the gentle lap of waves against the hull, there was silence.

"All clear," radioed Naoki from her side of the vessel. "Heading to the bow."

"Check," Garrett replied as he reached the rear end of the craft. There was a spiral staircase leading up to the next level through a narrow opening. He spotted blood stains on the handrail and four of the steps. It was fresh.

He activated a small, bird-sized autonomous drone from his backpack. It flew silently upwards, sending a crystal-clear video image to Garrett's heads-up display inside his helmet. The drone swiftly disappeared around a corner, revealing what lay on the upper deck.

All clear.

He spotted Leela's craft one hundred meters away, canopy raised, ready for action.

"I'm in position. Naoki?"

"Thirty seconds tops."

Garrett saw Leela give him a thumbs up. "Remain in contact," she said needlessly.

It was then that the plan fell apart.

"What the—"

Naoki's transmission ended abruptly.

Garrett spun around and sprinted along the deck toward the bow. "Naoki," he called out, but there was no response. "Leela, do you have eyes on her situation?"

There was a two-second pause before Leela replied. "Garrett, stop where you are. There are two armed guards on the deck directly above you. Naoki is down. I'm detecting life signs, but the guards are closing in on her position."

"Give me options."

"Leave Naoki. Go after the Lalls while the guards are distracted."

"That's not an option," Garrett snapped angrily. "I don't leave people stranded."

"Dammit, Oz. Naoki can take care of herself."

"We can argue about why you're wrong later. Get me to Naoki."

Garrett checked no one was behind him before continuing forward.

"Naoki is fifty-three meters from your position. Get up to the next level and you can surprise the guards."

Garrett spotted a narrow metal pillar on the edge of the boat and quickly climbed it, waiting for his drone to confirm it was safe to jump over the low barrier surrounding the higher level. Twenty meters to his left, two muscular male guards were advancing on what had to be Naoki's position behind a storage container. These guards were not the same ones he and Naoki had taken down only minutes earlier.

How many are there?

There was no time to worry about that question now. He aimed and fired his rifle, the electrical discharge hitting the closest guard squarely between his enormous shoulder blades. The effect of the blast was instant and devastating. By the time the now unconscious man hit the deck, Garrett fired at the second guard with the same outcome. With both men incapacitated, he ran toward Naoki, hoping he wasn't too late.

As he reached her position, an angry voice behind him yelled. "Stop!"

Garrett froze, still several meters from safety. He could see Naoki behind the storage container. She was not moving, and it was impossible to see her injuries.

"Drop your weapon and turn around. Slowly."

Garrett did as instructed, finding himself facing the flamboyant guard he had shot only minutes earlier. The man's face was contorted in pain as he held a wide-muzzled pistol in his left hand. Someone had created a makeshift sling for his right arm. The orange and blue shirt was now dotted with spots of dark red blood that had quickly dried in the heat. A random thought entered Garrett's brain, telling him the blood improved the look of the colorful shirt. He kept the opinion to himself.

"What's your name?" the guard asked, wincing and fidgeting.

Garrett held his hands in the air defensively. "I'm here to collect the Lalls. Step aside and let me do my job. No one needs to get hurt."

The guard indicated his shoulder with his chin. "It's too late for that, don't you think? You've ruined my favorite shirt."

Garrett spotted a bloodstained dressing through a rip in the shirt's shoulder. The injury had to be painful, which meant the guard had taken strong medication just to stand there in front of him. However, not only would the painkillers numb the agony, but they would also impair the man's decision-making capability. His left hand was already shaking, either from the pain or the drugs.

"I'm sorry about the shirt. Bear in mind, I could have killed you when I had the chance."

"Unfortunately for you, I don't have the same ethical dilemma." The guard smiled sadistically as he fired his weapon directly at Garrett.

***

Leela eased her craft close to the ship's stern before leaping across the narrow gap. Although frustrated by Garrett ignoring her orders, he and Naoki had created an opportunity for her to complete the extraction. One secret for successful missions was the ability to adapt to quickly evolving situations. Humans were erratic and unpredictable, so flexibility was essential.

Naoki's situation was not ideal but had led to an unforeseen distraction. The Lalls' guards were now focusing their attention at the front of the boat, leaving this area undefended.

Sending her personal drone ahead of her, Leela cautiously entered the rear cabin through the open glass doors. The room was overly decorated in luxurious cream leather from floor to ceiling, including a leather bench seat and a cream table. The only exception was a mirrored wall behind a bar.

"Can I make you a cocktail? I have over one thousand recipes," asked a serving droid, appearing from one end of the bar.

Leela ignored the droid, focusing her attention on the open door in the far wall as she crept silently through the room. On the other side of the door, a brightly lit corridor extended straight along the length of the boat, with numerous closed doors on both sides. Stairs led up to the top decks, as well as down to the bowels of the ship.

Where are the Lalls hiding?

Unlike the ship's reinforced hull, the interior walls were thin, offering no obstacle to the thermal scanners in her helmet. She found three human-sized heat signatures in a room one deck down and near to her location.

Taking the stairs two at a time, Leela found herself in a corridor virtually identical to the one above. The three people were still in the room, only ten meters from her current position. There were no other heat signatures within range of her sensors. Two of the people were sitting on a bed or large chair, while the third was rapidly pacing back and forth, carrying what appeared to be a small weapon, probably a pistol.

Leela took two paces forward, stopping when she heard the floor creak. "Damn," she whispered, raising her gun in anticipation of being discovered.

"Andre?" came a questioning voice from the room. Her sensors showed the pacing individual was now standing motionless by the door. He was the only person between her and the targets. She could not believe her luck when he opened the door and stepped out into the corridor.

His eyes widened as he saw her, too late to raise his weapon before she fired. An electric-blue stream of plasma arced from her rifle, hitting him squarely in the chest, causing his body to spasm. The guard's face contorted in pain as the electrical charge coursed through his body, overloading all of his nerve endings. Unable to scream, the man slumped to the ground, his unconscious body twitching.

Leela stepped over his body and into the side room, seizing the initiative before Mindi or Cenobia could react. However, Mindi was pointing a small pistol, her hand trembling. Cenobia was sitting beside her with an ashen expression.

"I suggest you put that down before you hurt somebody," Leela said calmly. She could sense Mindi was petrified and had likely never fired the pistol in self-defense.

"We're not going with you," Cenobia said, her voice almost a whisper.

Leela lowered her weapon to appear less aggressive. "Mindi, Cenobia. You don't have a choice. I've found you. I am not going to walk away, and I don't believe you really want to kill me and have murder added to the list of charges."

This time, it was Mindi who spoke. Her voice sounded stronger than Cenobia's, more assured. "We cannot go back. They'll place us in jail for life."

"You stole millions of credits from the Khans. What did you expect?"

"Luxury and freedom," Mindi quickly replied, not fully grasping the seriousness of her situation. "We had it until you arrived."

"You were living a lie. Both of you were. You've burned through a third of what you embezzled. The credits would have run out within five years."

"Not true. We had some expensive investments to create this home, but we were curbing our outgoings."

Ignoring the pistol that was still being pointed at her, Leela continued. "It's a shame you spent so much. The Khans may have been more lenient if you could repay what you stole. It is going to be much harder for you to find their considerate side."

"They don't have any compassion," Cenobia snapped. "They will kill us."

Leela shook her head. "There are laws preventing that. You have rights, despite the list of offenses you both committed."

"But we've tasted the lifestyle we dreamed of. You can't take that from us." There were tears in Cenobia's eyes. Leela had seen this dozens of times. Bolters were nearly always remorseful when captured. Usually, because they had grown complacent and the shock of being found gave them a swift reality check, forcing them to face up to the consequences of their actions. There was almost a playbook of emotions that bolters went through, and she knew the next move was coming.

"How many credits are you getting for this job?" asked Mindi. "We can double it. Simply walk away and say you never found us. Better still, tell the Khans that we're dead."

Leela resisted a smile at this last desperate act. "I can't do that."

"We'll triple it," blurted Cenobia. "In fact, name your price. Everyone has a magical number they can retire on."

Mindi nodded in agreement. "You can't enjoy what you do. Bounty hunting is a risky business. Surely, you'd prefer an easier life. Think about what you would rather do than chase individuals across the galaxy. We've not harmed anyone. Okay, we took some credits from the Khans, but it's not as if they can't afford it."

"The answer is still no. Tempting though your offer is, I wouldn't be able to live with myself. You may be able to justify your motives to yourselves, but what you did was wrong, and the Khans are still victims. Please, Mindi, can you drop your weapon? You're making me nervous."

Mindi stared at her gun as if she had forgotten she was holding it. She began to lower it, but then found her resolve and pointed it once more at Leela's head. "Please. Whoever you are. Leave us. I promise we will lead good lives. I don't want to shoot you, but I will."

"I don't think you're a murderer," Leela replied, outwardly showing a level of calm she wasn't feeling. A few more seconds and she would be forced to take measures into her own hands. Her preference was always for bolters to come peacefully. Unfortunately, that was not always possible, and in those cases, someone invariably ended up wounded. Or dead. "My colleagues will not be happy if they find me dead."

"She's right, Mindi," said an anxious Cenobia. "We're not murderers. I couldn't live with myself if we caused someone's death. Please put the gun down. You know it's over for us." She put a hand on Mindi's arm.

Mindi looked pleadingly at Cenobia before lowering the gun onto the bed. Leela breathed a sigh of relief as the two women hugged each other and began sobbing uncontrollably.

Chapter 3

Although Garrett's body shield absorbed most of the energy from the projectile, the force still knocked him violently from his feet. He relaxed his body as he hit the ground, rolling over on his shoulder and finding safety behind the storage box next to Naoki.

He sensed another bullet hit the wall less than one meter above his head as the storage box vibrated from the impact of a third bullet. The wide spread of bullets was evidence the guard was not using his dominant hand to shoot. While that was a minor consolation, it didn't mean the guard wouldn't get lucky with his next shot.

As he decided on his next move, Garrett took a closer look at Naoki. She was on her back with her eyes closed, her open mouth making a gurgling sound. Whatever had struck her had overpowered her body shield and thrown her helmet from her head. A thin stream of blood trailed from her mouth down the side of her face, pooling into a crimson puddle on the deck.

Damn!

He could see no obvious external injuries, but it was obvious Naoki was in a bad way. He guessed fractured ribs and pierced lungs were likely contributors to the blood and labored breathing. There was no telling what other internal damage she may have suffered; they were way beyond Garrett's level of expertise to diagnose and treat. All he could do was roll her on her side and inject her with a double dose of ketamorphine from his field medikit.

"Leela, I've located Naoki. We need to evacuate her immediately," Garrett whispered, keeping an eye out for a further attack.

There was no response.

Where is she?

There was no time to find out. The mission priorities had changed. Garrett knew he had to overpower the guard as quickly as possible and get Naoki to the nearest medical facility before she bled out. Difficult when the closest port was at least four hundred kilometers away.

"Hey," he shouted, keeping his head down. "My friend here is dying. Let me take her for medical help."

"That's not my problem," the guard shouted back. "You'll be joining her soon enough."

Garrett pulled his pistol from its rear holster, at the same time re-establishing the connection to his drone. It was hovering a couple of meters from the edge of the ship, giving him a clear tactical view. The two guards he had shot were still unconscious, but he could now see a woman, crouched close to the man with the terrible taste in shirts. She was wearing full body armor and aiming a lethal snub-nosed rifle at Garrett's hiding place. He knew from her posture that she was military-trained, unlike her colleagues. Which made him wonder why she was working with them.

"I don't have time to argue. Do you really want our deaths on your hands?"

"It's what I'm paid to do. No one will find your bodies out here and the Sidenvan authorities won't waste their resources on missing off-worlders. I suggest you—"

Garrett didn't let him finish the sentence. He slid two stun grenades along the deck, waiting for them to explode before diving from his position and firing four shots at the hidden woman. His new position was behind a low wall, away from the line of sight of the woman. He doubted any of his shots had hit the target, but they had done what he intended; prevent her from firing at him.

The drone imagery showed she was slowly retreating, keeping her rifle pointed in his direction as she edged toward an open door behind her. The security guard was on his knees with his hands over his ears. He was screaming loudly. Garrett leaned around the corner of the wall, taking aim at his chest and firing an electric charge that instantly silenced the man.

When he looked for the woman, she had disappeared through the doorway. The feed from the drone couldn't locate her on any of the decks, but he was sure she was finding a new location that would benefit her.

Which meant there was no way he could get Naoki off the ship until she was found and neutralized. Carrying Naoki in both arms, he could not defend himself from an attack.

Where is Leela?

This simple mission had quickly turned south. If Leela was injured, or worse, it left him with a tough decision where he may have to leave Naoki behind after all.

"Leela? Can you hear me?"

His concerns were allayed at the sound of her voice. "Garrett, I have the Lalls. State your position."

"Naoki is down and bleeding out. There is a female security guard close by. Military type. I can't get back to my attack craft with her in the vicinity."

"Okay. I'm coming for you."

Garrett returned to Naoki. Her breathing was increasingly shallow and ragged. More worryingly, the pool of blood on the deck was growing. "Help is on its way, Naoki. Hold in there."

The feed from the drone suddenly cut out; the guard must have found a new observation point. Garrett cursed for allowing himself to be cornered and for losing the advantage.

He tried to put himself in her mind. The obvious place to gain an advantage was to reach a higher deck. It gave her better visibility and offered protection. He leaned around the corner of the storage box, glancing up. At the sight of movement two decks above, he pulled his head back just in time to see an ugly black scorch mark appear on the deck just in front of him.

That was too close.

"I'm on deck two, Leela. Pinned down by someone on deck three or four."

"Copy. I'll be there in thirty seconds. Keep your head down."

What else am I supposed to do?

He fired a couple of shots toward his attacker. There was little chance of actually hitting the target, but it may keep her distracted long enough to allow Leela to catch her off guard.

"There's no one here," Leela called out from somewhere above.

At the same time, Garrett heard a loud splash, followed by the roar of a powerful engine.

"Whoever it was has thought better of it. I'll come down to you."

Leela's face turned ashen when she saw the slumped body on the deck. "Naoki. What were you thinking?"

Garrett effortlessly picked up the limp body. "I'll get her to the medics before meeting you back at the spaceport."

Leela nodded. "Thanks, Oz. Take good care of her."

Chapter 4

Garrett spotted the ambulance waiting dockside as his craft entered New Rotterdam harbor. He didn't care that he was traveling faster than the speed limit, or that the wash from his craft was causing others to bob up and down on their moorings.

By now, he was struggling to detect Naoki's shallow heartbeat. He had done his best in the last forty-five minutes to make her comfortable, setting up a saline drip and keeping her as warm as possible. However, her skin was cold and pale. During his time in the Marines, he had seen soldiers with similar symptoms and knew her chances of survival were slim if she didn't soon receive professional treatment.

"What is the medical emergency?" asked a medi-droid as he pushed open the canopy and gently lifted Naoki out.

Great, he thought. *Where are the real medics?*

"Naoki Oakes. Twenty-eight years old. She has suffered severe internal trauma after being shot at close range. Pulmonary hemorrhage and irregular heartbeat. I've given a double dose of ketamorphine and one liter of saline."

A second medi-droid rolled forward next to Garrett's craft, pulling a metal gurney.

"Please place the patient on the gurney. I will conduct a full examination and administer the necessary treatment."

Garrett followed the instructions, ignoring his distrust of medi-droids. Although they were efficient, he disliked their insensitivity.

"Step away," ordered the first medi-droid as a variety of needles and scanners emerged from sections of the gurney. An oxygen mask slipped over Naoki's nose and mouth.

A small crowd of onlookers had now gathered on the dockside, trying to satisfy their morbid curiosity. "What are you looking at?" Garrett snapped as the medi-droids continued their diagnosis. Those at the front of the crowd averted their eyes and ambled away, leaving only two people with the nerve to ignore Garrett's anger. He glared in their direction before returning his attention to Naoki.

"Can you save her?"

"This patient has suffered multiple organ damage and has lost a lot of blood. The lungs have been punctured in two locations. Her heart is under a high level of stress, bordering on cardiac failure."

"I didn't ask for a diagnosis. Is she going to survive?"

"We will take her to New Rotterdam Hospital. The patient requires urgent surgery. We will do our best to keep her stable until then."

The medi-droids wheeled the gurney toward the ambulance, a small white vehicle with an illuminated red cross on the side.

"Take me with you. I have to know she's safe," said Garrett, following close behind.

"Passengers are not permitted. You do not require medical treatment."

"I don't care about rules, you tin can. Let me ride to the hospital."

"You may make your own way," the medi-droid replied, sliding Naoki into the rear of the ambulance. As the door slid closed, the two droids attached themselves to the side of their vehicle without further explanation.

Garrett watched in angry frustration as the ambulance lifted into the darkening sky and quickly flew off in the city's direction. Turning once more to the onlookers, he asked, "How do I get to the hospital?"

The two men looked at each other, smiling, before walking away.

Standing alone on the dock, Garrett cursed his luck. He hoped Leela was having more success with her prisoners.

***

The air taxi landed in the designated unloading area in front of the hospital. Garrett sprinted the short distance to the entrance and quickly found a nurse. A human one.

"I'm looking for a friend. Naoki Oakes. She was brought in by ambulance about twenty minutes ago with internal trauma."

The nurse had a sympathetic smile. "Let me check our records," she said, tapping the screen of a small computer strapped to her wrist. "Yes, I've found her. She is undergoing emergency surgery in theater number three. There is a waiting room along there," she said, pointing along a wide, white corridor.

Garrett watched as the nurse scurried away before trotting along the corridor, fearing the worst and feeling weary. As he reached the waiting room, he remembered why he detested hospitals. It was the antiseptic smell. The unmistakable odor reminded him of death. While in the Space Marines, he had visited too many of his squad members who had been injured or mutilated in battle. Many had not survived, the deathly efficiency of weapons no match for human frailties. He had lost count of how many dead soldiers he had identified. Good men and women losing their lives for someone else's cause. Some of them were unrecognizable but never forgotten.

He had visited too many hospitals and medical facilities. The only constant was the antiseptic smell and the genuine sympathy expressed by the dedicated medical staff.

He realized he must have dozed off in his seat because a doctor was suddenly standing over him. "Any news?" he said.

"I'm Dr. Dowling. Ms. Oakes is out of surgery, and we have placed her in an induced coma."

"Will she live?"

The doctor shook his head. "Honestly, it is too early to tell. Her injuries were severe. We had to conduct an emergency heart transplant. It is likely she will also need a new kidney in the next few days. As she's young I give her a seventy percent chance of pulling through."

That was something! Garrett had expected to be told that Naoki was dead. Any news to the contrary was a bonus. He had seen more than enough death in his lifetime, and she was too young to be yet another victim.

"Thanks, Doc. I can't tell you what a relief that news is."

"She has you to thank for getting this far. I'm told your initial actions have given her a fighting chance,"

Garrett shrugged his shoulders. "Any idea how long she'll be here?"

"Two weeks. Maybe three. Can I ask how Ms. Oakes sustained her injuries?"

"Of course, Doc. We were apprehending a couple of bolters who have to be returned and answer for their crimes. Unfortunately, they had hired some trigger-happy security guards. Her armor failed to protect her, so I'm guessing they must have shot her at point-blank range."

The doctor frowned. "That explains the injuries. I would say there were two attackers. One in front and the other behind. There were deep burns on her chest and between her shoulder blades."

"Damn, that's cowardly," Garrett said, clenching his fist.

"It's all too common. Sidenva has become a haven for Nestan mercenaries who like to drink too much and bully the locals."

"We should have dealt with them in the war. Weak politicians caused this situation to happen."

The doctor blinked at him. "No prizes for guessing you were a Space Marine."

Garrett nodded. It didn't take a genius to guess from his size and physique that he had spent a long time in the military. "I was a Lafayette Gunnery Sergeant." He pointed his finger upwards. "I led my squad during the final attack on your moon, Kaplan," he said bitterly, remembering what a disaster it had been. Forty-five men and women had died that day and, despite the passage of time, he could still recite their names and serial numbers.

"Of course. I saw you on the Saratoga after the battle. Back then, I was a junior medic working for Dr. Stravinsky. There were two other survivors, as I recall."

"You have an excellent memory, Doc," Garrett replied with a wry smile.

"Yes. Emanuel Canning and Gideon Wang."

"That's right. Where are they now?"

Garrett's expression darkened. "Both dead," he said. His tone warned the doctor not to ask any more questions.

There was an awkward silence, broken by the sudden arrival of Leela Spicer, who was still wearing her fatigues. Seeing the expression on Garrett's face, she immediately put her hands to her face. "Oh, my God. I'm too late!"

Garrett put a consoling arm around her shoulders. "Not yet. Naoki is a fighter. She's out of surgery."

"The next seventy-two hours are the most important," said Dr. Dowling. "If her body doesn't reject the new heart, we can bring Ms. Oakes out of her coma. I am quietly optimistic, but I don't want to make false promises. My patient is very sick."

"Thank you so much, Doctor," Leela said, reaching out to shake his hand. "Can we see Naoki?"

"I'm sorry. She is in isolation to avoid infection. Come back in three days."

Leela glanced at Garrett and then back at Dowling. "We need to drop some people off first. But we'll be back for her as soon as we can."

"Fine. I will inform you if there is a change in Ms. Oakes' condition. It's been a pleasure to meet you, but I must return to my other patients."

"Thank you again, Doc," Garrett called out as Dowling left the room. He then turned to Leela. "I can take the Lalls back if you want to remain with Naoki."

Leela shook her head. "I'm no good at waiting around. Naoki is going nowhere for some time and she's in capable hands. Let's get out of here. I hate hospitals."

Chapter 5

After a two-day journey from Sidenva, Leela Spicer's ship, the Novak, slowed as it approached Destiny Station. The immense artificial transit hub located in deepest space was one of three gateways acting as a waypoint for travelers as they made their way across the Stellar Cluster. Hundreds of years old and continually expanding, Destiny Station could accommodate tens of thousands of people. Travelers, traders, and commodity haulers passed through its hundreds of levels on a daily basis, stopping only briefly to stretch their legs or buy gifts before boarding a spacecraft to their next destination.

For almost two thousand people who serviced the various needs of the visitors, the station was home. They remained for decades, with the occasional person spending their whole life on the transit hub. For others, Destiny Station became an unintentional stay as they became addicted to the multitude of gambling establishments and bars.

For Garrett, Destiny Station was nothing more than a convenient location to base himself. It wasn't a permanent home for him, and he doubted it ever could be. But dwelling on his future was not something he was ready to consider.

However, the size and complexity of the transit hub, and others like it, never ceased to amaze him whenever he got this close to it. Destiny Station was truly a symbol of humanity's engineering prowess.

As the Novak approached its berth on one of the lower docking rings, Garrett paid attention to the variety of ships already latched onto the station. There were several he recognized from previous visits. He knew the crews from half of them and made a mental note to catch up with two or three of them.

The one omission was Levi Murphy's ship. He had not seen his old friend for over six months and had quietly hoped to find him on Destiny Station.

Leela must have noticed Garrett's search.

"He's not here, Oz. Last time I checked, Levi was on his brother's farm. It's become a regular haunt."

"Do you keep tabs on all your former lovers?" Garrett asked as he continued to stare through the glass viewing dome on the side of the Novak's control deck. In honesty, Murphy's absence was a relief. It avoided any awkward explanations.

"Only the talented ones," she laughed. "He's supposed to be your best friend. Why don't you keep in touch?"

"There's no need to when we have years of comradeship to fall back on." Even to Garrett, his excuse sounded lame.

"So, you've not told him you're working with me."

Garrett turned his attention to the controls in front of him, even though Novak's docking processes were completely automated. "I thought it would complicate matters. You know how jealous he can get," he said.

"One of the many reasons we are no longer together."

He nodded, keen to steer the conversation away from Murphy. "Any news from Dr. Dowling?" he asked, already knowing the answer.

"It's only been two days. Dowling said Naoki would be in a coma for another day at least." Leela rubbed her eyes as if to ease away any tension she felt about Naoki.

Garrett knew Leela was tormenting herself over decisions made back on Sidenva. She had already admitted that Naoki should have remained with her for the extraction. He had tried to convince her it was only bad luck that had caused the young woman to be in the wrong place.

"Naoki is young and physically strong. Dowling is a talented doctor. She will be okay. No news is good news in my book. It means she is stable."

"I guess so," Leela replied, her voice lacking any conviction.

The sound of the docking clamps scraping against the Novak's hull brought them both back to the present and caused them to flinch. It sounded as if the hull plates were being peeled back. Garrett was grateful this wasn't his ship.

"Someone is going to pay if I see any scratches," Leela snapped. "Grab your things, Oz. I'll meet you at the airlock with the Lalls."

***

Carrying his kit bag and weapons over one shoulder, Garrett helped Leela escort Mindi and Cenobia from the ship. The Lalls had been subdued during the journey, but as they now walked along the narrow corridor from the No-vak to the transit station, they began once more to cause a fuss.

"It's not too late to let us go," Mindi pleaded. "You have access to all our accounts. How many millions of credits do you want?"

"That's right," added Cenobia, struggling to free her hands from the re-straining bar wrapped around her wrists. Her hair had not seen a brush in days and the dark rings around her eyes revealed how much sleep she'd had. "You can have it all. We can disappear and you will never see us again."

Garrett looked knowingly in Leela's direction. "Don't you think we al-ready considered that option? If we wanted to take those credits, we wouldn't want either of you walking around to tell the Khans that we had them. I would have pushed you out of an airlock somewhere between Sidenva and here."

"That's right," added Leela. "I wouldn't want any witnesses. Loose lips from either of you and I would soon find myself on the run. I can't tell you how close I was to agreeing to Garrett's plan. I just don't think I'm desperate enough. Perhaps there's still time, though. We haven't informed the Khans that we have you."

Mindi stopped walking. "Now, there's no need to be so hasty. You have our word that we will tell no one. All we want is our freedom."

Leela laughed. "Excuse me for doubting your reliability. You'd do any-thing to save your lives. Carry on walking."

"Of course we want to live. Have you any idea what the Khans will do to us? Do you want our deaths on your conscience?"

Cenobia began to sob.

"I know they won't kill you," said Garrett. "We would not have taken this job without assurances regarding your safety. They can't hurt you. Not severe-ly at least."

"And you believed them? How stupid are you?"

Leela nudged Mindi forward with her hand. "Not as stupid as you for stealing their credits in the first place. Or for getting caught."

Mindi and Cenobia looked at each other and fell silent. Garrett noticed their shoulders and heads droop in a subconscious acceptance of their plight.

One hundred meters further on, the group reached a bank of transit tubes. The tubes comprised a vast network of vacuum tubes that enabled fast access to all levels of the vast transit station.

"I can take them from here," said Leela, turning to Garrett as they waited for a pod to arrive. "I'll meet you at the Lodge in two hours. If you get there first, order me my usual drink."

Garrett smiled as he accepted her offer. Two hours would be long enough to return to his digs and decompress. In any case, he hated completing all the administration of checking-in bolters.

Chapter 6

Garrett stepped from the transit tube and into a familiar, well-lit corridor. He turned right and walked past brightly colored walls depicting the wilderness from a planet within the Stellar Cluster. From the size and deep orange color of the sun, he guessed this was a live feed from Tau Aros.

I hate that planet. Actually no, I only hate the people.

With no one else nearby, he called out, "Change image to Lafayette."

The images on the wall flickered and changed to show snow-capped mountains. "That's much better," he said aloud, recognizing the unmistakable profile of the Alps, a range of mountains only twenty minutes' flight time from his family home on Lafayette. The thought of home filled him with momentary regret. It was far too long since he had returned there.

The only thing keeping him away was his brother. Or was it his pride? Either way, Garrett knew he had said too much the last time he had seen Seth. A reconciliation was out of the question.

Despite the passing of time, he was not prepared to apologize. And he was sure that Seth would never back down. He was a powerful political figure and trained to show no outward signs of weakness. An apology would destroy the persona Seth and his entourage had meticulously nurtured over thirty years.

Garrett's thoughts returned to the present as he stopped in front of the door to his room and waited for the computer to confirm his identity. There was the faintest of clicks before the heavy door slid open, allowing him to step inside.

The room was a standard rental unit. Fundamentally, it was nothing more than a square box, four meters on each side, with a small bathroom built into the corner containing a shower and toilet. His bunk was folded up against the rear wall, allowing for more floor space, although he didn't really need it.

The room came with a food replicator built into the wall on his left. It was an older model but functioned almost as reliably as newer ones, delivering his favorite food and drink. Its main failing was the inability to deliver

26

the perfect coffee, but he had learned to accept the black liquid it served instead.

On the opposite wall, Garrett had installed a large black cabinet to store the weapons he had collected over the years. Although not permissible under the terms of his lease, he was not willing to leave his collection of guns, knives, and grenades in the public arsenal. There was comfort in having his spoils of war close by. They were a constant reminder of the good he had done over the years. He had helped to ensure the owners of those weapons were imprisoned for their crimes, unable to torment any more victims.

The room was otherwise spartan. Garrett did not believe in owning many possessions. They only weighed him down and there was no telling how long he would remain in this unit. The three months he had lived there seemed long enough, but he had no plans to be anywhere else. And having a base on Destiny Station was convenient for picking up the occasional mission. He knew many of the bounty hunters that passed through, and they were often happy to have someone of his experience join them.

Garrett placed his kit bag on the floor in front of the cabinet. "Coffee. Extra hot," he said, walking over to the replicator. The glass mug he had left on the replicator pad filled with a black steaming liquid. Before grabbing the mug, he pulled his bunk down, sitting wearily on it and rubbing his left shoulder.

Grimacing in pain, he removed his top to get a closer look at his arm. Normally, it was impossible to see where his artificial arm connected to his shoulder. That was not the case today. His skin above the graft had become pink and inflamed, contrasting with the neutral tone of the artificial skin. No wonder it's unusually itchy, thought Garrett, using all his willpower to not scratch his shoulder.

Instead, he pulled a glass vial from his pocket, broke the seal, and swallowed the clear liquid it contained. He scowled at the taste and reached for his coffee, emptying half the mug despite the scalding liquid.

He closed his eyes and leaned back on his bunk until his shoulders were resting against the cold, unforgiving metal wall.

After five minutes, he drained the rest of his coffee and sat back up. The inflammation in his shoulder had subsided. He moved his left arm in small circles, testing the shoulder joint and flinching as the pain continued, but to a lesser extent.

"Computer, make an appointment with Dr. Aisling Cassidy. As soon as possible."

Five seconds later, the disembodied voice of the computer replied. <You can see Dr. Cassidy at two p.m. tomorrow.>

Garrett sighed, regretting he hadn't contacted Dr. Cassidy sooner, although it would have been difficult to do so from the Novak without alerting Leela. And he wanted no one to know he was not at his best. The infection was affecting his coordination. He'd known on Sidenva that his arm was not quite right. He had put it down to rustiness at the time. After all, he had not been on a mission for several months. But it was now clear his arm was a problem he could no longer ignore.

If anyone could resolve the matter, it was Dr. Cassidy. She had fitted the artificial arm and had since installed upgrades and minor modifications. There was no one else he trusted to take care of whatever problems he now faced.

Checking the small clock on the wall, he calculated he had plenty of time for a shower. He reckoned he needed to freshen up. It was likely going to be a long session in the Lodge.

As he undressed, he looked at the image of Mercy on the wall above the bunk. It was his favorite photo of her, perfectly capturing her beauty and confident attitude. He knew the exact moment they had taken it on the planet Vadia. It was when they had found the spot where they would build their home together. The distant mountains behind Mercy had been the final clincher, along with the remoteness of the plot.

The open spaces and fresh clean air were light years away from his current accommodation.

"I know you think I'm not taking care of myself," he said. "You always were the practical one. To be honest, I'm finding it difficult to raise any enthusiasm. The mission on Sidenva ended up being a shitshow. We captured the bolters, but one of the squad nearly died. Naoki Oakes. I don't think you met her. A good girl, but possibly overly confident. You'd like her."

He disappeared into the bathroom, to take a quick shower. As he dried himself and decided what to wear, he held up two shirts. "What do you think, Mercy? Green or tan?"

He chose the tan-colored shirt. "I so want to talk with you again just to hear your voice. But life goes on. That's what you would want me to do. So, I'll go out and celebrate with Leela and get drunk with the gang. And we'll raise a glass to you and the colonel."

Tucking a pistol into the rear of his trousers, Garrett turned off the lights as he stepped back out into the corridor, knowing that Mercy would still be there when he returned. She always was.

Chapter 7

It had been almost a month since Garrett last visited Hunters' Lodge, the favorite haunt of bounty hunters across the Stellar Cluster. Researching and locating the exact position of Mindi and Cenobia Lall had taken longer than Leela promised. Fortunately, the Khans had offered a very generous bounty that more than compensated for the additional week's effort.

As soon as he stepped through the front doors, he could hear Leela's raucous laughter over the talk of the other people in the bar. Garrett made his way toward the noise, along the way greeting two bounty hunters he barely recognized. He found Leela standing next to a table at the rear of the bar. From the number of empty glasses already on the table, he knew she had been there for a while.

As often happened, Leela was holding court and basking in the glory of her successful capture of the Lalls. Today it was to two people he knew very well, Keisha Dennis and Toru. Garrett had worked with both of them at one time or another. Keisha was a similar age to him, maybe a few years younger. She had worked in law enforcement on Constance IV but had become discontented with the bureaucracy. He admired her because she was a quiet and thoughtful person who enjoyed the thrill of the chase, especially picking up the trail of bolters.

Keisha was also a very good drinker of spirits. Garrett had once made the mistake of accepting a drinking challenge where it had taken three days to recover sufficiently to eat food without throwing up.

Never again, he thought. But he knew this night could turn into a long one if she decided to hang around.

Toru could not have been more different. If he had a surname, he had kept it a secret. No one knew his exact age, but Garrett guessed he had to be in his mid-seventies. He had known him for over ten years and, throughout that time, Toru had frequently claimed he was going to retire after the next mission. Yet here he was, still one job away from retirement.

He was also one of the most opinionated people that Garrett knew. There were plenty of others who came close, but none had the sharp tongue that he did. And there was no point arguing with the old man because he insisted on always having the last word.

Despite his sometimes abrasive nature, Garrett had a genuine fondness for Toru, although he did sometimes wonder if he was slowly turning into the old man.

"Ah, you made it," Leela said, smiling and holding up a half-empty glass in a mock salute. "I did order you a drink, but I think one of us may have drunk it in the excitement."

"No worries. I wanted to speak to Bernardo anyway. Keisha, Toru. Can I get you anything?"

Keisha smiled. "Thanks, Oz. You know what I like," Keisha said with a smile and a cheeky wink that made him slightly uncomfortable.

"I won't say no, young man," added Toru.

Garrett nodded. "And the same again for you, Leela?"

"Like you need to ask."

Garrett pushed his way through the crowd to get to the bar. Although some regarded it as old-fashioned and less efficient to have human bartenders, Garrett preferred it this way. He didn't know a single bartender who didn't have a good story or information to share. Hospitality droids were cold and devoid of customer interaction however advanced the AI software was.

Bernardo was the owner of Hunters' Lodge and had been for longer than anyone could remember. Toru claimed Bernardo had been tending the bar when he had first visited the Lodge over forty years earlier. Yet, despite his advancing years and only having one good eye, Bernardo's memory could recall conversations and events from years past. Garrett had quickly realized Bernardo must have a vast network of contacts because he seemed to know what was occurring across the entire expanse of the Stellar Cluster.

"That was unpleasant business on Sidenva," he said as Garrett walked up to the bar.

"We ran into some bad luck," acknowledged Garrett, unsurprised that four drinks were already lined up and waiting for him. He downed his ale in one go, enjoying the cold, satisfying flavor.

Bernardo stared at him with his single eye. "We both know that blaming failures on bad luck is just an excuse for poor planning. I expect better of you, Oz."

Garrett shrugged his shoulders. "It was not my mission. I will not stand here and blame Leela for what went down. The important thing is that Naoki is alive. And we captured the Lalls."

"You're saying the mission was a success?"

"I'm saying there were some variables that were not fully addressed. The plan was adapted and we came away with an acceptable result."

"Hmmm," replied Bernardo, unconvinced by the reply. "Are you aware that Leela has had similar accidents in the past? Each time, she has put it down to bad luck. I say they're lapses of judgment."

Garrett knew Leela's history only too well. Bernardo had taken pleasure in telling him before he accepted Leela's offer. "On the return journey, we discussed areas for improvement. No mission is perfect and I'm sure she listened to what I had to say."

"But she's no Colonel Lane."

Garrett flinched at the name of his long-deceased friend. "The colonel was the most capable person I've worked with in my entire career. But he made errors, as we all do. We debriefed after every mission to learn from our mistakes, both large and small. Leela needs more experience under her belt. That's all."

"Are you going to be the one to teach her?"

"Do you think Levi would approve?"

Bernardo laughed. "Stranger things have happened. To be honest, you surprised me when you went away with Leela, bearing in mind her history with Levi."

Garrett could understand why but was not prepared to make excuses for his actions. "It came along at the right time, and it was easy money. Or at least should have been. I've got nothing against Leela."

"Is that how you explained it to Levi?"

"I've not told him. He's with his brother and I don't want to interrupt their time together. They're building bridges."

"Maybe you should do the same with your brother."

"When I need family advice, I'll ask for it. But not from you, old man." Talk of Seth always unsettled him. He had grown used to pretending he had no family. It was easier that way, particularly after he had lost his bounty hunting family. Yet he immediately regretted snapping at Bernardo, who was only having some fun with him. "I'm sorry, Bernardo. You know I get cranky when someone digs up my past."

Bernardo gave Garrett a sympathetic smile as he refilled his glass. "No need to apologize. I've grown a thick skin standing behind this bar for so long. I've seen that family ties matter. Whatever happened between the two of you, don't leave it too late to make your peace."

Garrett scooped up the four glasses in his hands. "I'll bear that in mind," he said, before turning and making his way back to where Leela was standing.

"About time," Toru said, taking his drink. "We're dying of thirst here."

"That is one thing that will never happen to you," Garrett replied. "Cirrhosis or a jealous husband are far more likely to kill you."

Toru grinned, revealing half his teeth were missing. "Please make it a jealous husband catching me in the act with his young wife."

"Toru!" exclaimed Leela and Keisha together

Holding up his hands in self-defense, Toru was unrepentant. "An old man can dream."

"Of course, you can. Provided your dreams remain private," said Leela. "None of us want to imagine your wrinkled old body writhing away on some helpless young girl."

"Don't knock the benefits of experience," Toru continued.

"Enough," snapped Keisha, pretending she wanted to throw up.

Garrett missed this type of banter. He had grown up with it in the Space Marines when no subject was off limits. There was always a character, similar to Toru, who would push the boundaries of decency. Usually, it was all an act, designed to hide some underlying insecurities. They were all talk and no real action.

Colonel Lane had encouraged banter within the squad, but it was a healthier level of fun, always maintaining respect for each other and never overstepping the line that could embarrass someone.

"As I was saying earlier," Leela said, holding up her glass. "We wouldn't be celebrating today if it wasn't for the actions of Osiris Garrett. First, he provided a distraction, allowing me the opportunity to locate and extract the two bolters. Second, and more importantly, his quick thinking saved the life of our dear colleague, Naoki Oakes."

Garrett felt his cheeks blushing. He was uncomfortable that Leela was making such a big issue of what had happened on Sidenva, but Keisha and Toru were staring at him, waiting for his response. "Thank you, Leela," he said. "I did what any of you would do in the same situation."

Keisha raised her glass in a similar salute to Leela's. "Don't be so modest, Oz. Learn to accept praise when it's rightly given. I know Naoki will want to thank you as soon as she can."

"That is definitely something to look forward to. She was in a bad way when I found her. I don't know how she stayed alive long enough for me to get her to the medical help she needed. Naoki is the actual hero here, along with the medical team in the hospital."

"Well said," said Leela. "Here's to heroes everywhere." She gulped the contents of her glass, encouraging the others to do the same.

Toru didn't need any encouragement as he slugged his drink back.

"To heroes," Garrett muttered before swallowing his ale and placing the empty glass on the table. As he did so, he heard muted toasts from the bounty hunters at the surrounding tables, only increasing his level of discomfort.

Leela had been half right. The most important part of the mission had been to walk away without losing Naoki. But he knew deep down that the situation should never have arisen. Good fortune had played a major factor. They had been lucky the Lalls' guards were not the most skilled, the one exception being the mystery woman who had escaped. If the guards had been halfway decent, Keisha and Toru would be holding a wake instead of a celebration.

But the night was not one to be morbid; it was one to kick back and enjoy the company of his fellow bounty hunters.

***

Six hours later, the Lodge had emptied with only a handful of people left, drinking the night away. Garrett was feeling the effects of countless rounds of drinks. He could not remember how many people had bought him drinks.

It was more than he normally drank, and the amount of alcohol dulled his senses. He knew he would pay for his overindulgence in the morning.

Even though Keisha had drunk far more than him, she looked as though she was still on her first drink as she sat nonchalantly on her chair, chewing on some dates.

How does she do that?

It was a mystery Garrett thought he was unlikely to solve. But at least he was in a better state than Toru, who had fallen asleep with his head resting on the sticky tabletop. The old bounty hunter had given up trying to stay awake thirty minutes earlier. At least his breathing was reassuringly strong and regular for someone of his age.

Leela looked as if she wanted to drink all night, but her body was betraying her. Whenever she spoke, her arms swung violently through the air, and she had to sit to avoid falling over.

"We need to have these nights more often," she said for maybe the twentieth time.

Keisha laughed. "You guys are lightweights. I expected more from Toru. Oz, you drink like my grandma."

Garrett was not sure if her remark was supposed to be a compliment. He decided it was and raised his glass. "Here's to grandmas."

Leela joined him in the toast, but Keisha merely rolled her eyes. "You're proving my point."

Garrett thought about Keisha's words but could not understand what the point was. What he did know was that it was time to return to his bunk. He was tired and way too drunk for his own good. His glass was still half full, but, looking at the amber liquid, he decided he could not drink any more.

Slamming his glass on the table, he got unsteadily to his feet.

"Where are you going?" Leela asked, putting a firm hand on his shoulder that forced him to sit back down.

"I need some sleep. I'd rather get back to my room than join Toru on this table."

"But I've not finished." Leela leaned her head in so close to Garrett's that he could smell the alcohol on her warm breath. Waving her arms at nothing in particular, she continued speaking. "Look at us, Oz. All four of us. We're good together. I have had a wonderful idea. We should pool our resources and form a super squad."

Garrett was not sure he had heard her correctly. "You want the four of us to form a unit?"

Leela grinned. "I think it's a brilliant idea. We could take on bigger jobs. Maybe include Naoki when she's recovered. We could be the 'Fantastic Five'. What do you think?"

Although he admired her enthusiasm, Garrett had enough sense to know how bad the idea was. His dilemma was how to let her down gently. Fortunately, Keisha was not afraid to share her opinion.

"That's your second-worst idea ever. Dumping Levi remains your absolute worst. We're a bunch of misfits. You would make a terrible leader and I've never had you as a team player. As for Toru, who knows how many more years he has in him? Oz spends half his life in mourning for his murdered wife and can't get over it, bringing down the atmosphere in any room he enters."

That is definitely not a compliment!

"I resent that statement. I'm doing my best to lead a normal life. If you had known her better, you would understand."

Keisha gave him her best scowl of disbelief. "I was a bridesmaid at your wedding. Mercy chose me!"

Garrett could not recall if Keisha's statement was true. Alcohol really does kill brain cells, he thought. Pointing in her direction, he said, "If you say so. But don't blame me. You gave reasons for the others too."

Leela looked deflated by Keisha's blunt pushback. "I'm a natural leader. You're only jealous. Do you think you could do better?"

"I'd make sure all my team came back after every mission," Keisha replied defiantly.

Garrett could see the argument was about to spiral out of control and wanted no part of it. "Ladies, I think we should discuss the matter when we're sober. We need to take a break. You know where to find me."

"So, you would consider teaming up?" Leela asked hopefully.

"I didn't commit to anything. But good try." Garrett swayed as he left the Lodge, waving to Bernardo along the way.

What a crazy night!

Outside in the thoroughfare, life in Destiny Station continued as normal, with people going about their daily business and rushing to their next destination. Garrett paused to concentrate on the route to his room. As he made his way toward the closest transit tube, he failed to notice someone paying him close attention.

Chapter 8

"You look rough," were Dr. Cassidy's first words as Garrett walked into her office and slumped heavily onto the seat offered to him.

"Is that your professional medical opinion, Aisling?" he replied. He felt worse than rough. It had been a long time since he'd drunk so much alcohol in one night. It was only that morning, when he'd woken late, that he remembered why he didn't like to drink.

Dr. Cassidy laughed. "It's a simple observation. Have you been trying to keep up with the young bucks?"

Garrett shook his head slowly. Even that movement was enough to make him nauseous. "It was a quiet night in the Lodge with colleagues that got out of hand. Before you say anything else, yes, I should know better. My head is pounding, your lights are too bright, and I somehow woke up on the floor of my unit hugging one of my sniper rifles."

"Ouch. Maybe you need a psych assessment rather than my help." Dr. Cassidy's response lacked any sympathy, although he had not expected any.

"Pimping out your husband for business again, Aisling? I'm shocked. I was actually hoping you had something to ease the pain?"

"Other than advice to not drink?" She reached into a drawer and pulled out a small bottle containing a green liquid. "Drink this. It will replace the electrolytes and minerals you pissed away in the night."

Garrett gratefully took the bottle and swallowed the entire contents, almost choking as the liquid hit his taste buds.

"I forgot to mention that it tastes foul," said a smiling Cassidy.

No kidding! Fighting the urge to retch, he put the glass on the table. "What is in that?" he said in disgust.

"You don't want to know, which is why you can't widely get it. You're very lucky I keep a supply."

Garrett didn't feel lucky. But it was worth trying if it made him feel more like his usual self. After all, he had no one to blame but himself for the state he was in. Leela, Toru, and Keisha had only encouraged him to drink. He could have always said no. Never again, he promised himself.

"So, Oz. I assume you didn't have the foresight to book the appointment because you knew you would need a hangover cure. What can I help you with?"

Whatever was in the green liquid was having an immediate effect. The pain in his eyes was less intense and his headache was easing. "It's my arm again. This time the pain is worse."

Dr. Cassidy began typing notes into her desk pad. "Can you describe the symptoms?"

"Other than the intense burning sensation where the arm grafts onto my shoulder? I've lost a small degree of sensation in my fingers and there are some coordination issues."

Dr. Cassidy paused her typing to look at him. "We wondered when this would happen, but it is far sooner than I expected. Have you damaged it or done anything out of the ordinary?"

Garrett smiled. The side-effects from the previous night's overindulgence had almost worn off. No more nausea or pounding headache. He felt like a new man ready to face any challenges thrown his way. "What do you class as ordinary? Someone shot at me a few days ago from close range. My body shield protected me, but the shot still packed a punch."

"What type of weapon?"

"An old-style explosive projectile pistol. Not a lot of energy, but highly effective at close range."

"That wouldn't have caused the issues you're describing. Remove your top. I want to inspect the graft."

Garrett did as she asked him and sat motionless as Dr. Cassidy took a close look at his arm and shoulder. "You've gained a few contusions since I last saw you," she said, noticing the dark blue and purple bruises, about the size of a man's fist, that crisscrossed his chest.

"It would have been far worse without my body shield," he said as if this was a normal occurrence.

He flinched as the doctor brushed her hand across the inflamed area of skin on his shoulder. Although it was the lightest of touches, it felt as if she had stabbed him with a dagger.

"Can you clench your hand tightly?" she asked. "Thanks. Now stretch out your hand. And repeat."

"What's your prognosis?" he asked after repeating the exercise a dozen times.

"I have an idea but need to run a series of tests to confirm. I think you're suffering from nano-regression."

"Is that as bad as it sounds?"

She shook her head. "It is treatable if that's what you mean. And not life-threatening, if you're worried. Stay there and I'll get my diagnostic equipment."

Garrett heard the squeak of wheels behind him on the metallic floor of Dr. Cassidy's surgery before a squat droid stopped on his left. This machine had various instruments hanging from the side of its body, as well as a horizontal tube on top of its head. The robot's styling made him think it must have come from a child's nightmarish imagination. He looked at it skeptically, wondering how it could help.

Dr. Cassidy must have noticed his cautious expression. "Come on, Oz. Stick your arm into the tube as far as it will go and then relax."

"Easy for you to say."

They must have designed the tube for someone far smaller than Garrett. The aperture was only just large enough to allow his forearm to squeeze through, let alone his biceps. But after a few seconds, the tube expanded until he could fit his arm in all the way to his shoulder.

"Good, good," said Dr. Cassidy, typing more notes. "Simply relax your arm and your body. This won't take more than five minutes."

Garrett closed his eyes and took a series of deep breaths. Initially, he felt nothing other than the cool, smooth metal of the tube. Then he could feel a mild tingling sensation, beginning in his fingertips but spreading along the full length of his arm.

"How does that feel?" Dr. Cassidy asked, glancing up from the screen she was monitoring."

"Strange. Like I'm being tormented with the lightest of feather touches."

"Good, good," she said, before tapping on the screen.

The intensity of the tingling sensation increased for thirty seconds, causing Garrett to squirm in his seat. And then all sensation vanished from his hand.

"Can you clench your ball into a fist again please, Oz?"

He tried but did not know if his hand had reacted or not. "How's that?"

"Good, good," Dr. Cassidy replied, still staring at her screen. "Now open your hand again. Really stretch those fingers."

Once more, Garrett could not be certain his fingers had responded to his mental command.

"Thanks, Oz. You can remove your arm."

He did so, surprised to see his arm in one piece with no marks. "Well?" he asked.

"As I suspected. Nano-regression is isolating your nerve endings, preventing electrical commands from your brain reaching their destination. It's a progressive condition. At the moment, there are multiple nerve pathways. If one route fails, then the electrical signals try to find another way. That is what's causing your coordination issues. It's taking microseconds longer than it should for your brain's commands to reach your artificial hand, making you think your timing is out."

"You said it's progressive. That implies my arm will become useless."

"Yes, if left unchecked. The remaining nerve pathways will eventually close down. You won't be able to control any of your arm's motor movements."

"You don't seem overly concerned. Does that mean you have a solution?"

Dr. Cassidy nodded. "A full arm replacement. The infection around the skin graft means your body is rejecting this arm. Your antibodies are effectively at war with the nanotech. It's very unusual to occur in someone as fit as you."

Garrett frowned at the news. "I can't afford a new arm. Not one that is as good as this. Surely there is another way. Nano-blockers or medication that will heal the infection."

Dr. Cassidy shook her head. "It doesn't work that way, Oz. The interface between the artificial arm and your immune system has corrupted. No amount of nano-technology can repair what's happening inside your shoulder. When you can no longer control the arm, it will be just a dead weight, a useless appendage. If left unchecked, the infection could spread to the rest of your body, and you will die."

"That's a cheerful prospect, Aisling." When Dr. Cassidy had originally installed his artificial arm, it had taken months for Garrett to adjust to it.

However, he had since learned to treat it like any other part of his body. It did everything he had always done, and more thanks to the high-grade alloys, polymers, and technology. He wasn't sure he was ready for the trauma of losing his left arm for a second time. But if the alternative was death, did he have a choice? "How long have I got to decide?"

"Difficult to say. Less than six months. It could be six weeks. I understand if you need time to consider your options."

Garrett stood up. "Sounds like I have no genuine option. I get a new arm, or I die."

"Or we can simply remove the arm and deal with the infection."

"I won't be any use as a one-armed bounty hunter!"

"Don't underestimate your skill, Oz. And remember, you'll be even less use if you're dead."

"Point taken, Doc." It didn't take a genius to understand what he needed to do. If only he had the credits for a replacement. "Thanks for your time today. I'll let you know when I'm ready to give you an answer."

Garrett left Dr. Cassidy's office with confirmation of the facts he had been denying for weeks. But even the Lall bounty was not enough to cover the cost of a new arm and the surgery. Maybe it was time to go back to his brother and claim a slice of his legacy.

No! There has to be another way.

Chapter 9

Levels East Thirty-Six to East Forty were designated fitness zones. These levels comprised open spaces, allowing for a variety of sports and fitness activities, catering for many people, from the casually curious to the most dedicated athletes.

Level Forty was where Garrett often went when he needed to clear his mind. A series of running tracks meandered through an artificial backdrop of trees and shrubs, to give a sense of being planetside. It was only when you reached the outer regions of the level that the view through the full-length glass walls reminded you of your location, with the stark blackness of space and passing spacecraft often shocking people back into the present.

He went running directly from seeing Dr. Cassidy. After changing into his running gear, he took a steady pace around his favorite course that looped through the very center of the level, past a small lake. He had always intended to come here as a method of excising the toxins in his body, but the consultation with the doctor had given him more to think about.

His running goggles provided him with a holographic running partner. Today, as he often did, he had selected Mercy to run alongside him, acting as a silent pacemaker; there was a comforting reassurance to think that an element of her was with him.

For almost an hour, Garrett lost himself in the running, placing one foot in front of the other and maintaining a rhythmic tempo. During his time on Sidenva, there had been no opportunity to exercise; a fact his muscles and lungs quickly reminded him of. However, focusing only on his breathing and Mercy's long legs, he pushed through the pain barrier.

"Thanks for the company, Mercy," he said, pulling up at the end of his run and removing his goggles. Breathing heavily, it disappointed him to see he was two minutes short of his best time. His heart rate was also elevated, but he put that down to the previous night's overindulgence.

I really must get back into shape.

The large communal shower area was only half full, allowing him to take his time to cool down and rinse the sweat from his body. As he stood with his eyes closed, feeling the powerful water jets on his head, back and shoulders, his thoughts returned to the conversation with Dr. Cassidy. The run had caused the dull ache in his shoulder to return.

The only viable option was a replacement arm with similar, if not better, functionality. The artificial arm was a necessity rather than a luxury and had helped him out of several scrapes. Its strength and durability, together with a compartment in his forearm large enough to conceal a weapon, were now second nature to him. Yet the cost was prohibitive.

Returning to Lafayette and requesting financial help from Seth was his least favorite solution. Garrett had lived most of his adult life being self-sufficient, turning his back on the fortune his family had amassed. The thought of Seth's smug 'told-you-so' expression was enough to know it wasn't really something he wanted to pursue.

He briefly considered the option of loan sharks, but the thought of being in debt to a crook was as dangerous as it sounded.

That left continuing with what he was best at; bounty hunting. Going it alone would mean he kept all the bounty, but it limited the number of bolters he could chase down. So many bolters hired security to protect their freedom that it was virtually impossible to capture them single-handedly.

He wondered how serious Leela's drunken offer had been. Maybe she wouldn't remember it in the cold light of day. Although she had her faults, Leela seemed to have the best contacts with access to the most lucrative jobs. If he could persuade her to enter a partnership with a fairer split of any bounties, a new arm was possibly within reach. He convinced himself the arrangement would not need to be forever. A couple of well-paid jobs in the next few months could be sufficient. Maybe they wouldn't need Keisha or Toru.

Drying himself off, he was sure he knew where to find her.

***

Garrett strode along the thoroughfare with a new sense of purpose. Taking a transit pod, he went directly to the lower docking ring where Novak was berthed, only to find the ship sealed. He pressed the comms button but there was no response. Leela was either sleeping off her hangover or, more likely, she had returned to the Lodge.

Frustrated, Garrett retraced his steps to the closest transit tube. As he waited for the pod to arrive, he had the sensation he was being watched. It wasn't the first time he had felt it over the past day, but there was no one within sight.

He had survived so long by trusting his gut and it was telling him he was being discreetly observed. He would bet his life on it. There were countless reasons he could think of why someone would spy on him. The problem was none of those reasons had a positive motive or outcome for him. Bounty hunters occasionally attracted unwelcome interest, especially from disgruntled associates of recaptured bolters. Garrett figured this was the most likely scenario.

He asked himself who he had recently upset, why they had decided now was the right time, and what were their intentions?

Although he did not appreciate being spied on, the situation intrigued him. If someone wanted to check on his whereabouts, then he expected to know the reason. The only sure fact was the person paying him close attention was a professional who knew how to remain hidden.

Until now. As Garrett entered the transit pod, he was determined to discover who was tracking him. He wanted to become the hunter. Being the hunted made him uneasy.

He instructed the pod to stop three levels below Hunters' Lodge, on a thoroughfare Garrett knew was relatively quiet. This level consisted primarily of maintenance workers and construction droids who used it for moving equipment between facilities. If there was someone following him, then they would be conspicuous. Garrett spotted an open service door only fifty meters from the transit tubes. An ideal location to spy on whoever was stalking him.

Ten minutes passed with no one arriving who didn't appear to belong.

Maybe I'm getting jumpy in my old age, Garrett considered, reluctant to believe his senses were betraying him.

After waiting for one more minute, he moved out from his hiding place and returned to the transit tubes. Before he had the chance to request a pod, the door in front of him slid open. A man was standing in the pod, almost as if they were waiting for him. Garrett knew instinctively from his body language and shocked facial expression that he had not expected to be discovered.

In one swift motion, Garrett pulled the pistol from his rear holster and aimed it at the head of the newcomer.

"Don't shoot," screamed the man, raising his hands in a defensive posture. "It's me. Andron!"

Chapter 10

Garrett slowly lowered his weapon. The young man standing in the pod was quivering, his eyes wide in fear.

"Andron! What the hell are you doing stalking me around Destiny Station?" Garrett could not hide his shock at recognizing this face from his distant past. Andron was the last person he had expected to see.

Stepping shakily from the pod, Andron looked as if Garrett had given him the death sentence. "I am sorry, Mr. Garrett. Several days ago, I thought I saw you walk past me. I have been trying to find you since then so I can thank you for saving me."

"But you have been following me around for days. There were plenty of opportunities to speak with me. You were on the docking ring earlier, weren't you?"

The young man nodded. "I wanted to be sure it was you and not one of the Brotherhood."

"Why would the Brotherhood be after you?"

"Because I finally ran away six months ago. They don't tolerate deserters. I know they have sent hunters out to return me to Eminence Zaen."

"Is that twisted old bastard still alive?"

"He was when I left. I have been hiding from him while trying to start a brand new life in the Stellar Cluster."

"Good for you, Andron. I'm proud of you." Garrett knew the young man had suffered growing up under the Brotherhood's domination. A religious cult, the Brotherhood had cut themselves off from the rest of the Stellar Cluster and controlled their population with an iron fist. Andron had been treated appallingly for most of his life. His master, Eminence Zaen, had sexually abused the boy to a point where he had thought it was normal behavior.

When Garrett had given Andron the chance to free himself years earlier, the boy was so institutionalized that, to Garrett's disgust, he had remained with his master.

Andron glanced nervously along the corridor. "Can we talk somewhere?"

Garrett smiled. "Of course. You look hungry. I know the perfect place."

***

Chow's was a culinary secret, well away from the busy levels frequented by the casual visitor. In Garrett's opinion, this family-run restaurant made the tastiest authentic noodles on Destiny Station.

"Good evening, Mr. Chow," Garrett called across the counter as he entered the busy restaurant. "I've brought a friend. Do you have a table for two?"

Mr. Chow grinned as he looked up from his wok, sweat running down his wrinkled face. "Mr. Oz, it is so good to see you." He barked some orders at three junior cooks in the cramped kitchen and walked across to greet his new customers, wiping his pudgy hands on a dirty cloth tied to his waistband. He was a big man, almost as tall as Garrett and carrying a lot of extra weight from enjoying his own food too much.

"And who do we have here?" he asked, inspecting Andron, who shrank behind Garrett.

"This is my old friend, Andron. We've not seen one another in several years. Where better to catch up than here?"

Chow nodded enthusiastically. "You speak wise words, Mr. Oz. The young man looks as though he has not eaten in months. We must do something about that. I have two tables at the back. Take your choice."

Andron blushed but said nothing.

The aroma of spices, roasting meat, and sizzling fish reminded Garrett he had not eaten since the previous day. His stomach grumbled, urging him to order food. "Can we have two bowls of your special and a couple of beers?"

"Of course. Take a seat and I will bring it to you shortly."

Garrett decided on the table in the corner, as it meant no one was sitting behind him. After he sat down, he asked, "What do you think?"

Andron looked around at the people in the restaurant, reassured to see they were all either eating or in conversation with their companions. "I have experienced nothing like this. I thought everyone ate food from replicators."

Garrett suppressed a laugh. It was not the young man's fault that he had limited knowledge of the Stellar Cluster. The Brotherhood would have been feeding him propaganda since he was a young child. "Replicators are convenient, but they don't compare with proper cooking. Your taste buds are going to be in a for a pleasant surprise."

"There are no replicators back home. We cook our own meals, but they are mainly vegetables and grains. They only permitted meat for special religious festivals. Or for senior members of the Brotherhood."

"Such as your former master?"

"Yes. Eminence Zaen had a personal chef to prepare and cook his meals."

"I imagine the chef had to taste each meal before Zaen would eat it," Garrett said, half joking.

"Yes, he did," Andron replied, with no sense of irony. "I think there have been five different chefs in the time I have served the eminence. Three were poisoned at their own hands and Zaen executed two others for crimes against the Brotherhood."

"Wow! The man is a fussy eater." Garrett laughed at his own joke, but Andron stared blankly back at him.

Fortunately, one of Chow's staff delivered the food and beers, breaking the awkward silence. Chow had filled the bowls with a generous mountain of steaming noodles, beef, and a colorful array of peppers, chili, and vegetables.

"Here's to your successful escape," Garrett said, raising a glass to his lips.

Andron looked uncertainly at his glass of beer. "I've not drunk alcohol before, either. It is forbidden at home. Can I have water?"

"This is your new home, Andron. You don't need to follow the rules you grew up with. Live a little and try the beer. You might like it."

Andron took a sip of the amber liquid in the glass before pulling a face of disgust. "How do you drink this?"

Garrett smiled. "Dedication and years of practice."

Again, no reaction. *Does Andron have a sense of humor?*

Andron picked up a fork and clumsily scooped up a few noodles. Garrett looked on, interested in seeing his reaction. "This is fantastic," Andron said, chewing on a mixture of noodles and beef. He took another mouthful and then another. There was nothing wrong with his appetite.

Garrett tried his own bowl of noodles and had to agree with Andron's sentiment. It didn't take long for the food to be eaten. Garrett downed the rest of his beer. Andron took a few more tentative sips, but clearly, beer was one step too far for him.

"Thank you for this meal. I have never tasted so many flavors in one bowl. I don't know if I can pay you for it."

"No need. Think of it as a gift. You wanted to talk. I would love to know how you escaped from the Bevas Sector. And why now?"

The meal had settled Andron's nerves. His eyes had stopped darting around the room, looking for unseen dangers.

"I planned my escape over a year ago. After I returned to Drani IV, Eminence Zaen never forgave me for my part in your capture of him. He said I should have done more to overpower you, even kill you."

"That's ridiculous. I'm a trained soldier. You never stood a chance."

"That didn't matter to the eminence. As far as he was concerned, I failed him."

Although Garrett had only spent ten days with Andron, he had initially worried for the young man's safety when he had decided to return to Drani IV with Zaen. He now regretted not having done more but, back then, he had been hurrying to save his wife and the rest of Colonel Lane's squad. "I'm so sorry to hear that happened. You showed your devotion to Zaen."

Andron shrugged as if it no longer mattered. "Eminence Zaen ordered me to work in the fields. It nearly killed me. I had always worked inside his palace. My body was not ready for physical activity, outdoors in all weathers and having only five hours' sleep each night." He paused, his eyes becoming unfocused for several seconds.

"It was a difficult time for me. I could not reconcile my punishment when I was sure I had done as much as I could to protect my master. After all, he was alive and living back in his palace. Eminence Zaen's treatment of me challenged my faith. Fatigued and ill, I was told this was the gods' way of showing displeasure for my weaknesses."

"And you believed it?"

"I knew no better. We are all taught that the Brotherhood are benevolent and act as interpreters of the gods' laws for mortal men. We cannot challenge their decisions and motives."

Andron's dire story confirmed what Garrett had heard about the autocratic regime within the Bevas Sector; the Brotherhood was evil. He had briefly experienced their harsh hospitality and had no intention of ever returning. It was a wonder that the central government continued to turn a blind eye to the suffering of the Bevas population.

There was one question that sprang to mind on hearing Andron's tale. "What changed for you?"

"My time with you!" Andron immediately replied. "You gave me a glimpse of an alternative path that was contrary to the Brotherhood's teachings. You showed determination and mercy I had never witnessed from Eminence Zaen. The people on this transit hub showed me compassion. Back then, I was too young and naïve to appreciate it. But I never forgot. Every night, before I fell asleep under my tarp. I would remember my short time with you. Over time, I realized I had made an enormous mistake, and the Brotherhood was not what they claimed to be."

"How did that make you feel?"

"Angry. Resentful. Manipulated. They built my whole life to that point on lies, manufactured to allow the privileged few to control the masses. The fact it had happened for hundreds of years was of no satisfaction. I was worshipping false gods. Suddenly my eyes were opened to the truth."

Garrett noticed Andron becoming more animated as he recounted this. The young man was visibly shaking with outrage at being misled for so many years. It came as no surprise. Having the basis of your faith wrenched apart must have been painful. He recalled how fervent Andron had been when he had first encountered him. This was an entirely different man sitting in front of him. He couldn't help but be impressed by Andron's courage.

"You still haven't told me how you escaped."

"There were six of us in my work unit. We would talk as we ate our meals at night. Gradually, I shared my opinions. It was dangerous. They could have charged me with blasphemy, so I was cautious. The entire work unit could be at risk. The unit leader was Viktor. It amazed me to discover his views aligned with mine, as did the other members. Viktor knew someone who worked at the Drani IV spaceport, loading fresh produce onto transports. The transports regularly dock with a Stellar Cluster vessel on the border of the Bevas Sector and a trade occurs."

The news intrigued Garrett. "What goods do they trade?"

"Mainly medical supplies. Also spares for our failing and ancient technology." Andron seemed dismissive of the Brotherhood's disdain for technology.

During his short but unforgettable time in the Bevas Sector, Garrett had witnessed firsthand how basic and run-down most of the equipment was. Even the spaceships were older models that had been retired decades earlier in the Stellar Cluster. Whatever riches the Brotherhood were sitting on, it certainly wasn't being spent on what most people took for granted.

"Five months ago, Viktor and I concealed ourselves inside a packing crate surrounded by tons of wheat. We created a small chamber within a transit container. It was only just large enough for the two of us, an air supply and water. The rest of the work unit loaded the wheat, covering the chamber."

Garrett could only imagine how challenging the escape attempt must have been. "How long were you hiding?"

"A good question," Andron replied, gesticulating with his arms. "We had expected only three days. One day to move the container to the spaceport and load it onto the transport. A further two days for the transport to reach the rendezvous point and exchange cargoes. In reality, we waited at the spaceport for almost two days before being loaded. I remember the fear that they had discovered our plan."

"And your supplies?"

"Water ran out on the journey to the rendezvous. The air supply was running dangerously low. Our monitors were showing dangerous levels of carbon dioxide. After the transfer was completed, we waited less than thirty minutes before opening the access panel, allowing us to breathe fresh air. We were close to suffocation."

"How did you explain your presence to the crew of the new ship? They must have been shocked to discover you in their hold."

"They were good men. We said we were seeking asylum. The captain was doubtful at first and considered returning us. But when we told him the Brotherhood would kill us, along with the other four members of our work unit, he let us stay. It was a genuine act of kindness I will never forget."

It astounded Garrett the escape plan was a success. So many elements could have gone wrong, and it only took one person to tell the authorities for

Andron and his friend to be captured and punished. The Brotherhood were not known for their forgiveness. "Did the captain bring you here?"

"No. He was going only so far as Nesta. He dropped us there and directed us to one of his cousins, who took us in. We are good workers and found casual employment on a coffee plantation. The work was simple after our time on Drani IV. We learned to control the machines that collect the coffee beans and we had warm meals every day. We were quick learners, and this was the life we had talked about."

"If that was the case, how did you end up here. And where is Viktor?"

Andron's expression darkened. "The Brotherhood! They sent out a search party. Apparently, Eminence Zaen was not finished with me. We had been living on Nesta for maybe one month before they found us. Three men were waiting for us when we returned home after work. Viktor entered the room first. They took him, but not before he warned me to run. I ran for my life through the streets, eventually finding a disused basement. For five days, I stayed hidden before going to the spaceport. I knew Nesta was no longer a safe place for me. I got passage on a ship that brought me here. Viktor is dead or back on Drani IV."

Garrett nodded in appreciation of Andron's resourcefulness. "How have you taken care of yourself?"

Andron shrugged. "There are always jobs that people do not want to do themselves. Maintenance and cleaning jobs where a droid isn't the best option. I also discovered that tourists pay well if you take care of their baggage or their kids while they enjoy the bars."

"That sounds tough, kid." Garrett had never considered the various subcultures operating within the transit hub. His friends and fellow bounty hunters frequented similar restaurants and bars, never wondering what else was happening around Destiny Station. The exception was the seedy gambling establishments in the lower decks where he used to find Murphy.

"It is a good life. I can afford to pay for my room, and I eat most days."

That hardly sounded like a good life. Garrett was conflicted by Andron's story; while thrilled the young man had escaped the misery of life under the Brotherhood, he was barely existing.

"Do you have any friends?"

"If you mean people I speak to regularly, then no. I have little in common with anyone here. And I am afraid that Eminence Zaen is still searching for me. That's why I learned to live in the shadows."

Garrett nodded. "And that is why you didn't reveal yourself sooner."

"I had to be sure you weren't with Zaen's team or being monitored by them. I can't go back to the Bevas Sector."

The plea was heartfelt. Garrett could see the fear in Andron's eyes. Capture by Zaen's team would be a certain death sentence for the young man.

"You have done a fantastic job getting this far, Andron. But you cannot spend the rest of your life hiding and living in fear. You may as well be back on Drani IV. You're not a criminal and deserve a better life."

Andron visibly relaxed at the words, his arms resting on the table. "The Brotherhood have spies everywhere. They will find me one day."

"Not if I have anything to do about it. I can find you steady work. Something more fulfilling than you're doing now."

Andron's eyes opened wide at the prospect. "Staying here on Destiny Station?"

"No, it's not safe for you here. Too many strangers pass through daily. Zaen's spies are likely to be among them. We need to get you to a planet, Somewhere strangers stand out."

Andron leaned forward and grabbed Garrett's hand, vigorously shaking it. "Thank you so much. That would be truly amazing. Maybe you are my first friend."

Garrett felt his cheeks redden at Andron's enthusiastic display. "I'm sure you'll make plenty more friends, given the right opportunities. You're a likable young man and a hard worker."

"You are too kind, Mr. Garrett. You are nothing like the person Eminence Zaen says you are."

Sliding his hand from Andron's clammy grasp, Garrett's mind was racing. "Give me two days. Let me see what I can find for you." He moved his chair back and stood up, ready to leave. He had seen Mr. Chow hovering nearby and did not want to overstay his welcome.

A disappointed Andron stood and followed Garrett from the restaurant.

Back on the concourse, Garrett turned and smiled. "Meet me here the day after tomorrow, same time. I'll have some news for you."

"Are you leaving?" Andron looked as if he was about to burst into tears.

Garrett patted him on the shoulder. "I have people to see. But it was a fantastic surprise meeting you again. I will ensure you have a safe place to live and grow old. Stay safe."

"Thank you, Mr. Garrett. I will see you in two days."

"And no more spying on me. That isn't what friends do."

Andron's head dropped a few centimeters. "I promise."

Garrett walked toward the transit tubes, thinking through the conversation in his mind. Andron was a strange young man. Broken and awkward. It was hardly a surprise having grown up where he did. The mental scars must run deep. But there was no denying his courage. He deserved Garrett's help.

Chapter 11

Garrett found Leela with Keisha in Hunters' Lodge ten minutes later. The pair of them were sitting at a table, talking quietly. Definitely a more subdued atmosphere than the previous day.

Leela looked up and winced as he approached. "I hope you're feeling as rough as I look."

She looked as if she had not slept all night. Her eyes were dark and sunken, her long hair tied in an untidy knot, with random strands hanging down. He was sure it was the same outfit she had been wearing the previous night, with maybe just a few more creases. "You look great," he lied. "I don't know how you can drink all night and still look so fresh."

Leela smiled at the compliment

Keisha glared at him but, unusually for her, kept quiet.

"Can I get you ladies another drink?"

"Pineapple and mango for me," Leela said. "And a double Nestan vodka with orange and ice for Keisha."

"Hold the orange and ice," Keisha sneered.

Bernardo watched him carefully as he walked up to the bar. "Are you trying your luck with those two again?" he asked, pouring three drinks before Garrett had placed the order.

"Depends on what you mean. If you think I'm after some horizontal action with either of them, then think again."

"I've seen stranger events happen in here."

"How can you see so much with only one good eye?"

Bernardo laughed. "Imagine what I'd see with two eyes. It's just I've never seen you spend so much time with Leela. And she normally goes for the younger men. Ones she can dominate."

"And then along came Levi! I don't think he falls into either category."

"True," the elderly bartender admitted with a snigger. "Maybe she now has the taste for the older, more experienced man."

"That may be so, but I can assure you she's not my type. I've stopped mixing business with pleasure"

"So why are you sniffing around? Do you want another chance for her to get you killed?"

Garrett sighed. Bernardo had a way of getting to the core of the matter. "Yes, I'm considering an offer she made to work with her. I'm still weighing up my options."

"I can see your dilemma. A man with your range of skills must have plenty of offers on the table. Must be a great feeling to be in demand."

"Mock me all you want. I need the credits for one of these," Garrett said, raising his artificial arm.

Bernardo rubbed his stubbly chin. "That's very expensive kit. You should make do with what you have."

"Not an option." Scooping up the three glasses, Garrett said, "Wish me luck."

"What was Bernie saying about me?" asked Leela as he approached the table.

"Oh, he was agreeing with me how remarkable you look. He says you have more stamina than most of his customers. Except Toru and Keisha, of course."

"You talk some shit, Oz."

Garrett grinned, taking a seat opposite Leela.

Keisha continued to sneer. "Why are you in such a good mood?"

He shrugged. "Life occasionally comes up with surprises, It makes you realize flowers can bloom in the most inhospitable of places."

"Have you been taking some of Murphy's special medication? I've never taken you for a romantic."

Blushing, he replied. "I just bumped into an old acquaintance from a previous life. He has somehow turned his life around. I want to help him secure his future."

"So now you're a charity worker."

"Keisha, have you no compassion running through your veins of chilled vodka? The young man has escaped the clutches of the Brotherhood."

"You're wasting your time," Keisha replied. "They'll come for him."

"They'll have to find him first. He helped me after I lost my arm on Drani IV. I owe him."

"Does that mean you're retiring from our business?" Leela asked.

Garrett shook his head. "I have years left in me yet. In fact, I came here to see how serious you were about the offer you made last night."

"Remind me. My recollection of last night is hazy."

He was sure Leela knew exactly what he was talking about. Although she had been very drunk, she had still been lucid. "Forming a super squad. You were adamant you would amount to nothing without my finely honed skills."

She raised her eyebrows. "That doesn't sound like something I would say."

"Alcohol makes us speak the truth," Garrett replied, somehow able to keep a straight face. "Keisha was there. I'm sure she remembers."

"I recall getting this black eye," said Keisha, turning her head so he could get a good view of her swollen and purple right eye. "I've forgiven Leela for this. But I don't recall her being so drunk that she would ask an aging former Space Marine to be the backbone of her crack new squad."

"My bad," he said.

It was Leela's turn to crack a smile. "Your timing is actually immaculate. I was telling Keisha about a new job that will be posted in two hours unless I claim it first. Keisha says she's in. Toru will be in, although he doesn't know it yet. Which leaves only you."

"Where, who, and how much?"

"Five hundred thousand credits!" She paused to let the amount sink in.

Most jobs were around only one hundred thousand credits. Garrett knew this bolter had to be exceedingly high profile or extremely dangerous. But assuming the terms were the same or better than Sidenva, the payday would more than cover the cost of his replacement arm.

"I knew you'd like that," said Leela. "It gets better. The target is hiding out on Lafayette. You're going home."

That is an unnecessary complication, thought Garrett. While it would be interesting to return to the planet of his birth and formative years, Lafayette possessed too many unresolved issues for him. Which was the main reason he had stayed away for so long. "You want to use my local knowledge? You'd be a fool not to."

"Exactly. Do you have any reliable contacts there? Would you consider asking your brother to help us?"

"The answer is no to both questions. I never hunted bolters on my home planet. I communicate occasionally with old military comrades who might know the right people. But no promises. As for Seth? He is off limits."

"Think about it, Oz. Any help will increase the chances of success and get the job finished quicker. This will be easy credits. Plus, you'll have time to meet up with your old buddies. Perhaps your brother has mellowed over the years. It could be time for a family reconciliation."

Garrett's heart beat faster at the mere mention of his brother's name. "I have a family and Seth isn't part of it. That's all you need to know."

"Okay, I respect that," said Leela. "I won't raise the subject again."

Keen to change the topic, Garrett asked. "Who is the bolter and what have they done?"

"I'm sorry. That is confidential until they make the award public. There are at least two individuals. You don't want to know their crimes. Suffice it to say, they abused positions of power to benefit financially, and pursue the sickest of fetishes. I don't yet know the specific details, but I understand young children were involved. I'm sure you agree that's plenty of motivation to catch them."

Garrett sighed. Leela's need for secrecy was frustrating and didn't speak to the arrangement being an equal partnership. However, she clearly had access to a senior official. How else could she get such a fantastic opportunity?

"Nice guys! I'm in. But don't expect any family reunions. When do we depart?"

"Two days. I booked the Novak in for minor systems upgrades tomorrow, otherwise, I'd be leaving as soon as they post the job."

At that moment, Toru shuffled lazily up to the table, collapsing onto the chair next to Garrett. "You'll turn into me if you're not careful."

"Just the person we wanted to see," Leela said.

Toru glanced suspiciously at the three gathered around the table. "What have you signed me up to this time?"

Chapter 12

As Garrett arrived at Chow's, he spotted Andron pacing up and down the concourse.

"Is everything okay?" he asked.

The young man forced a smile. "Yes, it is now. I get anxious when waiting around in the same place for too long. I'm scared they'll find me. And I wasn't sure you would return."

"Hey, kid, I keep my promises. The last thing I want is for you to feel unsafe."

"You are too kind, Mr. Garrett. I do not deserve your generosity."

"It's no problem, Andron. Genuinely, I want to help. You have so much potential. And I have some good news for you. Let me buy you another meal in here and I will tell you all about it."

Andron shuffled his feet as he stared at Chow's shop front. "You're doing too much already. I want to show my gratitude and have prepared a meal in my room. It is not as flavorsome as this restaurant but you will honor me if you accept my invitation."

Garrett briefly considered Andron's earnest offer. The young man was unlikely to possess culinary skills or the credits to purchase quality produce. But if Andron had created a meal, he would have cooked it from the heart. It would be rude to refuse.

"I'd be delighted to."

The bright expression on Andron's face was enough to show he had made the correct choice.

"Thank you," Andron said, grabbing Garrett by the arm and leading him away from the enticing smells of Chow's.

***

Fifteen minutes later, Andron enthusiastically led Garrett along a narrow, dark corridor. This part of Destiny Station looked as though it should have been condemned years earlier. Garrett guessed it had to be one of the oldest sections of the transit hub on the lower levels and close to the external skin of the massive structure.

How does anyone live down here?

The corridor walls were caked in grease and grime accumulated over hundreds of years. Graffiti in a variety of languages and colors was the only thing that brightened the area. Soiled clothing, half-eaten food, and general trash littered the floor. Garrett tried to ignore it as he stepped over insect-infested piles of rubbish.

As for the smell! Maintenance of the air purifiers was long overdue. There was a clammy, noxious stench that stung his eyes and clung to the back of his throat, making him feel nauseous. It was one of the worst smells he had experienced, and he had been to some pretty messed up dives in his time. His senses felt as if they were being bombarded. No one ought to live like this. Garrett wondered how the hub's administrators had allowed sections of Destiny Station to fall into such disrepair.

"Do you pay to live down here?"

"Yes. Two credits per seven-day period," he replied proudly.

Garrett thought the amount was daylight robbery but kept his opinion to himself. This was probably still a vast improvement on Andron's living conditions on Drani IV.

Andron stopped in front of a rusty door, sliding his delicate fingers into a small gap. Grunting with the effort, he slid the door open and grinned widely.

"Welcome to my home, Mr. Garrett. Please come in."

Garrett hesitated before accepting Andron's offer, asking himself if there was some way he could take them both to an alternative venue without causing offense. From Andron's excited expression, the answer was clearly no. He would have to suffer this atmosphere for at least the next hour. "No need to be so formal, Andron. You can call me Oz like my other friends do."

Andron frowned, deep creases forming on his forehead, making him appear ten years older. "I'm not sure that would be right."

"It is. And I insist on it."

Garrett entered the room, pleasantly surprised that it was far cleaner than the corridor. Nothing was out of place, and Andron had scrubbed the floor and walls hard enough to make them presentable. The room itself was roughly half the size of Garrett's own unit, nothing more than a sleep capsule. Sufficient for anyone who was working all day trying to earn enough to stay another night.

If he thought his own accommodation was frugal, Andron had taken it to another level. The only furniture was a table and two chairs, none of which matched and which a sane person would have discarded years earlier. The bed was only a roll of thin felt. There was no sign of any blankets or any other clothing. The only item was a clear plastic box containing food and plates.

"Well, this is nice," were the only words he could think of saying. It was a hellhole. He had visited military prison cells that were more hospitable. "Where is your bathroom?"

"There is a communal toilet thirty meters down the corridor," Andron replied, standing by the door and pointing to his left. "Do you need to use it?"

"No, I'm good. I was simply trying to understand what you have here. No replicator in the room either."

"There is no need. I prepare my food. It is healthier and more nutritious."

Garrett didn't really have an appetite. There were so many details to absorb, none of them great. At least he could console himself with the knowledge he would soon get Andron away from here.

"Please, take a seat, Mr. Garr—, I mean, Oz."

"See, I told you it was easy." Garrett looked at the chair, doubtful it was strong enough to take his enormous frame. Easing himself gently onto it, he confirmed the chair was as uncomfortable as it looked. And, although the chair creaked whenever he adjusted his position, it showed unexpected strength.

Andron placed the food box on the table, removed the two plates, and began assembling the strangest salad Garrett had ever seen, comprising an onion, a handful of lettuce leaves, a colorful collection of peppers, a handful of spices, and what looked like a sweet potato.

Have I come all this way for this?

"You didn't need to go to so much effort."

"It is the least I can offer when you are helping me."

Garrett thought back to his younger days, training to be a Space Marine. There had been several exercises where he and his fellow cadets were dropped into the wilderness to forage on berries, leaves, and whatever wildlife they could capture. There had been a few rough nights when he had only the most basic of provisions. This meal prepared by Andron was only a slight improvement on those.

"I've been wondering, Andron. Did you intentionally seek me out?"

Andron paused what he was doing. "Of course not. I prayed to the gods that I would encounter you again. They must have heard me. Why do you ask?"

"I believe in coincidence as much as I believe in divine intervention. Of all the destinations within the Stellar Cluster and the hundreds of millions of inhabitants, I am astounded that our paths crossed again."

Andron smiled, nervously. "That is because you have no faith. Tell me how you think I could possibly track you down. After all, you're the one who hunts people for a living."

Garrett did not have an answer. Perhaps it was destiny that had brought the two of them together, however unlikely that was. And if Andron was lying, where was the harm? Garrett was likely the only person he knew in the Stellar Cluster.

Andron finished arranging the food and sat on the other seat. "I only have water," he said, filling two glasses with clear liquid. "I did not realize how expensive beer is until I tried to purchase it."

"Water is just fine. I drink too much ale, anyway. More than is healthy."

"Eat. Please." Andron gestured at the plate in front of him. It wasn't appetizing, but the young man had presented it as well as he could. At least the food was fresh.

"You're very enterprising," Garrett said, taking a mouthful and realizing Andron had sprinkled a generous amount of pepper and chili powder, no doubt to provide extra flavor. It was overpowering and Garrett drank the water to avoid choking.

Andron was grinning so much that he did not notice Garrett's discomfort. "Are you going to tell me what you have arranged for me?"

Garrett had almost forgotten the reason he was there. But explaining his plans would allow him time to work out how to finish the meal without destroying his taste buds. Andron's sense of taste must have been numbed by years of consuming spices, as he did not seem to be affected by the intense flavors.

"Yes, of course. Tomorrow I am heading out on another mission. This time, it means going to my home planet, Lafayette. There is a huge agricultural community there. Although I don't know the leaders, I can contact them. There will be plenty of work for someone like you."

"Is Lafayette far from here?"

"Four days."

"Will you leave me on my own when you have completed your mission?"

Andron's forlorn expression struck Garrett. "I will once I am sure that you are settled and safe. The people on my planet are caring and hardworking. It won't take long for you to find friends of your own age."

"If Lafayette is so good, why have you spent so much time away from it?"

Good question, kid!

"Mainly work," he lied. "There is not a lot of calling on Lafayette for a man of my skills."

"Do you think you could teach me?"

Garrett almost choked. "To be a bounty hunter? I don't think so. We deal with some scummy people who can turn violent. You must be able to handle yourself and know your way around weapons. That takes years of training. You have had a sheltered background and, to be honest, I wouldn't want you to witness some of the things I've seen. It would change you."

"Do you think I am not strong and should be protected?"

Garrett chewed on some more food. The spices made it hard work and he could feel his tongue swelling. "Basically, yes. You have faced enough hardship in your life and suffered because of the Brotherhood's methods. It's time you realized there are plenty of good people in the universe. You don't need to be corrupted by killers, fraudsters, and cheats who think they are above the law."

Andron nodded. "You may be right. I am just a simple acolyte. What would I know about bringing people to justice?"

Garrett drank some more water. He was feeling hot, either from the spices or the inadequate ventilation. He didn't know how Andron looked so chilled. "My uncle always said I should swim in my lane if I wanted to be successful. It was some of the best advice I had."

Seeing the confusion on Andron's face, he added. "He didn't mean it literally. He was telling me to stick with what I'm good at and not try to be something I'm not. The same applies to you. Stay with farming or something similar. And be happy that you are skilled at it."

Andron poured more water into Garrett's glass. "Ah, I see. You are guiding me rather than instructing me. It is something I should get used to."

Garrett wiped sweat from his brow. "How do you cope with this heat? It's unbearable." He stopped eating. The spices were making him light-headed.

"I have never noticed. Are you feeling okay?"

No, I'm not.

A sudden wave of nausea made him almost throw up, the taste of bile burning the back of his throat. He gripped the edges of the table to steady himself as the room spun. Something was definitely wrong.

He noticed Andron staring from across the table, looking quizzically at his discomfort. Why wasn't he more concerned and trying to help?

Garrett glanced down at his plate of food. Had he been poisoned? His arms and legs were becoming heavy. His fingers were struggling to maintain their grip.

He knew he had to escape and find fresh air. "Help me," he gasped. Andron continued to stare at him.

Why?

Garrett's attempt to stand failed as his knees buckled beneath him. Losing his balance, he hardly felt his head crash into the metal deck plate. He was focusing all his attention on the simple act of breathing. Panic set in as he finally accepted someone had poisoned him.

Is this how it ends? This was his last thought as his eyes lost their ability to focus and the room went dark.

Chapter 13

Keisha ducked her head as she stepped through the hatch onto the bridge of the Novak. Leela was already there, sitting in her captain's chair, keying coordinates into the navigational computer.

"You do realize this is the forty-ninth century," Keisha said. "The master computers are more than capable of taking us to any point in the galaxy with no manual intervention."

Leela glanced up from the screen. "Call me old-fashioned. I like to personally check before I rely on a machine to fly me at close to light speed. You're far too trusting, Keisha. Anyway, I have time to kill."

Keisha could not have looked less interested in the explanation. "I came to let you know the Q-droids have loaded all provisions and stowed the requested equipment. Replicators are also fully replenished. Toru is in the galley checking them out as we speak."

"So where's Oz?"

Keisha shrugged her shoulders. "This isn't like him. He's always punctual. Maybe he's reconsidered your offer or found something better."

"At the very least, he should inform me of a change of plan. I know he was reluctant to visit his brother on Lafayette, but I believed we had resolved that matter."

Keisha nodded. "Oz wouldn't have changed his mind without telling us. That's not his style. Perhaps he's just running late. Have you considered something may have happened to him?"

"It crossed my mind," said Leela. "I've checked with all the medical facilities on the hub. There are no admittance records for anyone fitting his description."

"That's dark," Keisha said. "Your first thought when Garrett is late is that he could be injured or dead? Have you seen the size of the man? You would have to be brave or stupid to take him on."

Leela knew Keisha was right. Although Destiny Station was full of lowlifes, Garrett was more than capable of dealing with violent scenarios. Murphy had told her enough stories about Garrett's various heroic acts over the years. Chasing medical facilities so soon was extreme, but she couldn't ignore a gut feeling that something was wrong.

"Maybe he's just having drinks with his old pals and forgotten the time. Oz is liked by many in the community."

"I don't believe that any more than you. For a start, he wouldn't have deactivated his comms device."

"How long do we wait?" asked Keisha. Now that the hunt was officially on for the bolters, she was eager to start the pursuit. Patience had never been a strength.

Leela studied the bolters' details on her digital device one more time. She was also reluctant to wait for too long. Each minute of delay increased the risk of the targets changing their location, through fear or common sense. For the moment, she was confident they were still on Lafayette, but it could take weeks or months to find them again if they moved off-planet.

But Garrett's welfare also had to be considered. Keisha was right; it was not like him to disappear without notifying them, yet she had exhausted all known options. Even Bernardo had not seen him since the previous day.

If it was Levi Murphy, she would not have waited. How many times had she found him in an illegal gambling room or seedy bar on the lower decks? And although Murphy had promised he was a reformed character, she had seen him relapse before. Garrett was not like Murphy, though. He enjoyed his ale, but not to excess, and was a creature of habit, drinking usually in Hunters' Lodge or occasionally in one of the countless bars on the tourist promenades.

So where was he now? It was as if he had completely disappeared. Although not impossible on a transit hub the size of Destiny Station, it was difficult to hide one's location. It was something you intentionally had to do by removing your comms and staying away from the areas under constant surveillance. Garrett's absence was out of character.

Her gut told her that something was wrong. Her head kept telling her she was overreacting and that she would kick herself when he finally appeared.

"How long?" Keisha repeated, this time more insistently.

Leela sighed. "Thirty minutes. If Oz is not here by then, we leave without him. He knows where we're going, so can always catch up on the next transport. Although he'd best have a damn good explanation. Can you check on Toru? I don't want him drunk before we leave Destiny."

"It may be too late for that," Keisha replied, happy they would soon be on their way. She ducked back out of the room, leaving Leela to glance at the clock as she continued to second-guess where Garrett may be.

Chapter 14

The bitter smell of rotting vegetables combined with the sweet aroma of incense seemed an odd combination to his senses.

Garrett awoke with a start, sitting up quickly. It was a mistake, and he spent the next minute vomiting, his stomach dry-retching until his throat felt as though he had swallowed broken glass. But the pain was a positive sign.

I'm alive!

Garrett's first instinct was to take stock of his surroundings. Metal restraints held his wrists together, limiting his movement. A wise precaution, as he swore to himself he was going to teach a lesson to whoever had done this.

With his head throbbing, he lifted his hands to his face, finding a large lump above his left temple. He flinched as his fingers touched it. Gently probing around the lump, he discovered blood, now dried, had run down his face and matted his hair. He doubted the wound was bad enough to cause a concussion, but it would explain the dizziness.

He was relieved to discover his captors had not bound his legs. But, as he stretched his knees and ankles, they ached from the long spell of inactivity. He also noticed someone had removed his boots.

The only other pain was to the ribs on his right side. They didn't feel broken but were severely bruised as if someone had kicked him hard.

Where am I?

He knew he was on a spacecraft. A rhythmic vibration, and low-level hum, told him one of the propulsion generators was out of phase. Aligning the generators was a simple fix and would increase the efficiency of the engines. Any engineer should have picked up on it.

The room he was in was nothing more than a small box, less than three meters on each side. An emergency globe on the ceiling offered barely enough light to see. The room was bare except for the cot he had been lying on. A series of scrapes and scratches on the metal walls indicated years of storing heavy objects, likely transit containers. The double doors on the other side of the room looked solid and were, undoubtedly, locked.

Garrett swung his legs around so that he was sitting on the edge of the cot. Carefully avoiding the splatters of vomit on the floor as best he could, he slowly stood up. Feeling light-headed, he shuffled forward to inspect the door. As he suspected, his captors had sealed the door. It was a solid piece of smooth steel, except for a niche that had been cut out at the same level as his shoulders, the niche's rough edges and irregular corners a sign it had been added quickly by an unskilled technician. From the shape and size, Garrett suspected this was an inspection hatch. The back of the niche was probably a flap to allow visibility into the room.

Or cell!

He knew banging on the door or shouting out was pointless. Whoever had kidnapped him knew he was there. He was better off saving his energy and waiting for his captor to reveal himself.

Garrett flicked open the panel in his forearm, expecting to find his small utility knife. The compartment was empty. His captors had done their homework thoroughly; few people were aware of his arm's capabilities.

Curling himself back on the cot, he closed his eyes and forced himself to rest, knowing there was nothing he could do but wait it out.

***

The sound of metal on metal alerted Garrett to the fact he was being watched from the far side of the room. Keeping his eyes closed, he kept his body relaxed. Hopefully, his captor would enter the room to check on his health. The only hope was that his foe would make a mistake. A single chance was all that Garrett needed.

"Stand up," said a man's voice. It had an authoritative tone; this was someone used to giving orders.

Garrett didn't stir.

"I said stand up," the man repeated, with more insistence. "Don't play games with me, Garrett. It won't end well."

Garrett maintained his silence, controlling his breathing and readying himself to pounce if anyone entered the room. There was no advantage to responding to any command.

"Have it your way!"

Garrett felt a sturdy object bounce off his shoulder. A few seconds later, a metal cup hit him on the side of the head, a cold liquid covering his face. Still, he didn't move.

He could hear a mumbled conversation on the far side of the door but could not make out the words. It sounded like a disagreement. But then the sound of metal on metal signaled the end of the conversation.

After one minute, he opened his eyes. The hatch was closed, and the room looked as it had been minutes earlier. The cup was leaning against his head and the liquid, which tasted like water, had run down his face and was now soaking into the mattress. He cautiously leaned over the edge of the cot and saw the first object thrown was a food wrap; thin bread that had contained a mixture of salad items. It was now spread across the congealed pool of vomit.

Missing out on a meal was not an immediate issue. He didn't have an appetite, anyway. But he regretted not having more water to drink. His mouth was dry. And dehydration would make his reactions slower.

But he had learned a few facts from the brief encounter. The food and water meant his captors wanted to keep him alive. Whoever had ordered his capture wanted him for some other purpose. Whatever that purpose was, however, had caused him to be kidnapped against his will. Which meant it was unlikely he would have gone willingly if he had known what he was letting himself in for.

Second, there were at least two captors on the ship. This didn't come as a tremendous surprise. It would have taken more than one individual to load him onto the ship. Andron, if he was involved, certainly did not have the strength. But was Andron a willing participant?

Finally, his captors feared him. They had not entered the cell despite him feigning death or injury. Maybe they were simply following orders. If that was the case, he may not get the opportunity to overpower them before reaching their destination.

For the time being, it was nothing more than a waiting game. He would have to save his energy and hope an opportunity presented itself, allowing him to show how he felt about being held against his will. The one certainty was he would ensure that whoever was responsible would pay.

***

Several more hours passed. Whether it was two or ten, Garrett did not know.

This time he was sitting on the corner of the cot with his back leaning on the wall when he heard the hatch open again. The silhouette of a head appeared, backlit by a bright white light.

"Good. You've stopped playing dead." It was the same voice as earlier.

"Who are you? And why have you kidnapped me?" Garrett's voice rasped.

"My name is not important to you. I am taking you to face the justice you ran from."

Confused, Garrett asked. "What justice? I have committed no crimes. Are you sure you have the right man?"

"There are no mistakes. You are former Gunnery Sergeant Osiris Garrett, are you not?"

"That was a long time ago. What crimes have they charged me with? And who has made them?"

"Make yourself at home, Mr. Garrett. You have a long journey ahead of you."

Garrett held his hands up to reveal the bindings. "I don't appreciate being locked up like an animal. Can you take these off me and release me from this cell?"

The man at the door laughed. "No. Those measures are in place for safety reasons. Yours and mine."

"This is inhumane. There are rules on how to keep prisoners."

"They are not our rules."

The response confused Garrett. Who were his captors? Had they no sense of probity?

"How do you expect me to take a piss?"

"There is a bucket under your cot. You should have used it when you threw up."

Great! Now you tell me.

"How about a drink and some food?"

"I provided you with rations on my last visit. But I am not without mercy. Here is more water. I suggest you don't spill it this time." The man placed a small flask on a ledge below the niche before the hatch slid closed once more.

Frustrated by the conversation, Garrett retrieved the flask and took a sip of the water. Although it had a strong metallic taste, he could not detect any unusual flavor, but that meant nothing. His unknown captor could have easily added drugs. His choice was simple. Death by thirst or by poisoning.

He drank the contents of the flask.

Chapter 15

Garrett felt, rather than heard, the thrusters firing. Deck plates rattled and the artificial gravity generators took a fraction of a second to react to the sudden change in velocity.

He had lost all concept of passing time in his tiny cell. The beard on his face was the only clue. It had turned from prickly stubble to soft hair he could run his fingers through. Approximately ten days was his best guess.

The bare minimum amounts of food and water had been provided by his captors, but his constant fatigue convinced Garrett he was being drugged with a sedative. He slept more than he normally would, and he found it increasingly difficult to concentrate for long periods.

The cramped conditions in his cell, together with his hands still being bound, meant that exercise was limited to stretching and sit-ups. He could not recall ever being as unfit as he currently felt.

The skin on his shoulder continued to itch. Being unable to scratch it was maddening. The best he could manage was to rub his shoulder on the sharp edge of the shelf. He was thankful for the rough workmanship that had left sufficiently unfinished edges. Yet however much he rubbed his shoulder, the sensation never disappeared. He longed for medication to ease the discomfort.

Annoyingly, he had learned nothing more from his captor so far during to journey. The routine whenever the hatch opened had become monotonous. Garrett still didn't know the man's name, the crime he was charged with committing, or the ship's destination.

The firing of the thrusters was a definite sign this stage of his ordeal was over. The ship was rapidly slowing its forward momentum, presumably to enter a planet's atmosphere for landing.

The time alone in his cell had allowed Garrett plenty of time to reflect on his plight. And it was looking more ominous by the moment.

The time taken from Destiny Station, assuming it was roughly ten days, ruled out those planets that were within seven days of the transit hub. That ruled out Lafayette, Nesta, and Sidenva. After that, it depended on the average velocity of the ship. Based on his limited experience of his cell, he was sure this was an older vessel. He knew the engines were poorly maintained and so its cruising speed would be slower than modern vessels.

Even so, there was still enough time for the ship to have reached the Bevas Sector. And the Brotherhood! It was his best guess, as well as a logical conclusion, especially when factoring in Andron. Eminence Zaen was finally enacting his revenge. If that was the case, Garrett regretted not killing Zaen when he'd had the opportunity.

The sound of air rushing past the hull confirmed the ship had entered an atmosphere. Deck plates creaked and groaned under gravitational stresses as the ship's thrusters exerted more power to reduce its momentum. For several seconds, he feared the ship may not hold together.

Three minutes later, the ship landed with a considerable jolt. Garrett cursed as the force bounced him off the cot onto the floor, where he landed heavily.

Someone needs to teach the pilot how to fly!

As he climbed back to his feet, the hatch slid open. "Put this hood on," the man said, throwing a black cloth bag onto the cot.

"And if I don't comply?"

"You stay in here until you do. No more rations while you decide."

Garrett knew if he held out for several days, he would be weaker than he was now, and he would still end up wearing the hood. Although the odds of escape were already small, it made no sense to reduce those odds further.

He placed the hood over his head as ordered. It was made from a thick, coarse material that blocked out all light. It also smelled strongly of stale cabbage.

The door creaked as his captor opened it and, almost instantly, Garrett felt a firm hand on each shoulder, forcing him forward. Unprepared for the sudden movement, he lost his balance and feared he would fall on his face, but the hands kept him upright.

"Next time, we let you fall," his captor snapped.

His captors manhandled Garrett around several corners before leading him down a shallow decline that he guessed was a ramp. The hood muffled sounds, but the backs of his hands could feel a cool breeze. After fifteen paces, he stepped from the ramp onto a solid surface that felt entirely different underfoot. The hands guided him to the right and urged him to walk for a fur-ther sixty-seven paces.

As the hands released their grip on his shoulder, the same voice barked, "Stop there."

He did as he was told and waited in silence. He could sense people walking nearby, although none of them were speaking. As he waited, Garrett subtly adjusted his weight from one foot to the other, keeping the circulation flowing. In the unlikely event there was an opportunity to escape, he had to be ready to take it.

If he was on Drani IV, that meant he was at the spaceport he had flown from on his previous visit years earlier. He tried to recall the layout, but one spaceport was very much like another in his memory. He remembered it was smaller than most, with only seven hangars and very little infrastructure. His best chance of escape would be to re-board the ship he had arrived on and hope he could overpower the crew. Although his hands were bound, give him a blaster and he would be formidable.

The chance never came. Instead, he heard a motorized vehicle approach and stop close by. A solid fist in the middle of his back urged him forward a dozen paces, before the voice called out, "Step!"

Garrett cursed as his shin crashed into a solid object.

"Step up," the voice repeated.

Taking the hint, Garrett climbed three steps before he found another level surface and moved forward. Once more, firm hands on his shoulders guided him until he felt something solid against the back of his legs.

"Sit"

He nervously crouched down until he was sitting on a narrow bench. More restraints were placed around his waist and secured tightly. He felt people on either side of him.

They're taking no chances.

The vehicle shuddered before accelerating slowly away, rounding a series of bends and bouncing over something hard. Soon, Garrett felt it traveling at speed.

They must have been traveling for at least an hour before Garrett felt the vehicle slow and perform further maneuvers. As soon as the vehicle stopped, the guards released the restraints, and he was bundled outside. Sharp pieces of gravel bit into the soles of his feet as he was hustled forward. He gritted his teeth, sure that his feet would be a bloody mess.

After a short distance, an abrasive, concrete-like surface that was easier to walk on replaced the gravel. After being ordered to climb a flight of steps, the cold feel of marble beneath his feet was a welcome change.

"Wait there." Still the same harsh voice.

Garrett heard the echoing resonance of boots on marble. At least eight individuals. There was no hope of overpowering all of them as long as they kept his hands bound.

He wasn't expecting the hood to be removed so quickly. The bright light stung his eyes. He clamped them shut before slowly opening them again, blinking tears away. It took several seconds for his eyes to adjust and focus on what was around him.

"I cannot tell you how much pleasure it gives me, seeing you helpless in front of me. How times have changed."

Eminence Zaen was standing ten meters in front of Garrett, flanked by twenty guards in combat gear who were holding photon rifles. Zaen had chosen his best finery, a long robe lined with gold and gray fur. Zaen had aged since the last time Garrett had seen him, his hair grayer than before and his face more wrinkled, but the cynical sneer was unmistakable.

Garrett glared back at him. "I should have known the Brotherhood never forget."

"Or forgive! Why should we when forgiveness is a symbol of weakness?"

"And you're all about demonstrating strength and power. I can see that from the grandeur of this room and the dozens of followers and guards in this room. Is all of this spectacle just for my benefit?"

Zaen waved his arms with an exaggerated flourish. "This is to demonstrate that, despite what you did to me, I still have power and respect."

"I'm pleased for you. I really am. But now that you've displayed your power, can you release me?"

Zaen laughed out loud. "You're not stupid enough to think that this is all I wanted you for. Or did you believe your previous crimes would go unpunished?"

"You know the Stellar Cluster government will not tolerate their citizens being snatched in this way. You cannot simply kidnap me. If you believe

I committed an offense, there are procedures to follow. Forcing me here against my will is breaking many long-standing protocols."

"Protocols designed to ensure the protection of your people from the Brotherhood," Zaen snapped, spittle flying from his mouth and briefly glistening in the sunlight streaming through a large window. "I would never have received adequate justice if I had taken that path."

"And where is my justice?"

"I recall you had no such qualms when you and your squad of bounty hunters invaded the Bevas Sector."

"A traitor led us into a trap. You cannot compare those events with what you are doing."

"I can do whatever I like."

Garrett realized someone was missing. "Where is Andron?"

There was movement somewhere to his right. Several soldiers parted to allow Andron through. He walked up to stand in front of Eminence Zaen, a smug expression on his face. "I proved I am superior to you. You were so desperate to see the good in me and to help absorb me into your culture. Not once did you consider I was playing you."

Garrett knew it was true. Whether it was guilt or compassion, it had swept him up in the moment. He had honestly thought he could help Andron. Although the young man had been very convincing, he had been too eager to accept the story. "I made it too easy for you. But everything I told you was true. I would have done my best to ensure you had a safe life."

"Why would you think I could have a better life than I do here? You are a fool. The eminence designed the plan. He knew you were weak. People like you are so arrogant."

"It's not arrogance," said Garrett, still furious at himself. "Many of the Stellar Cluster would have done the same as I tried with you. We encourage people to grow. That's the difference between us and the Brotherhood."

"Simplistic propaganda!" Zaen's voice boomed around the chamber. "Do not stand there and judge us. Not when it is you who have sinned."

"You haven't told me what I'm accused of."

"That is remiss of me. How could I think you would understand? Your charges are an unlawful escape from detention, multiple homicides, kidnapping, theft of Brotherhood property, false imprisonment, and my attempted murder. It is rare for us to have such a prolific and unrepentant sinner in our midst."

Garrett had to admit Zaen was diligent with the list of offenses. Most of the events had occurred during his daring escape from the prison hospital and had been necessary. "I don't remember trying to kill you, Zaen. You were alive when I left you. And I promise you, if I had wanted you dead, you would not be here now."

"I feel you're not taking this matter seriously. Do you think I'm being overly zealous?"

"Damn right I do. I'm seriously pissed at the whole situation. A lot of water has passed under the bridge since then. I lost my arm, my best friends, and my wife. It has taken me a long time to recover. So don't stand there pretending to be the victim. If you think I committed any crimes, I can assure you I paid for them. And then some."

Zaen began an ironic clap. "Those sad events were karma for the misdemeanors you instigated. That is not justice. Have you ever thought about what you did to me? The consequences of your actions."

"Whatever they were, you clearly survived and prospered."

"You destroyed my reputation, Mr. Garrett. When you left me on your artificial world, I would have died if it were not for the bravery of my loyal apprentice, Andron. He was the one who ensured my safe return to the Bevas Sector."

Zaen placed his hand on top of Andron's head, eliciting a self-satisfied smile from his devotee.

"After I returned here, I was regarded as a laughing stock for a long time by the Elders. They lacked empathy for my situation, taken against my will across the expanse of space. Something you are now familiar with. They stripped away my privileges and returned me to the ranks of the Brotherhood. It took me a long time to once again prove I was worthy of being an eminence. Something deep within me was convinced this was a challenge I had to overcome. The gods had sent you to test my faith. And I passed. I am now stronger and more powerful than I could have dreamed."

Garrett was sure Zaen was mad or, at the very least, a narcissist. The man's rambling went far beyond religious fervor. He was delusional and dangerous. Maybe there was an opportunity to use religion against him. "If you believe I am a tool of the gods, then how can I be a sinner? Aren't you defying the very gods you venerate?"

Zaen sneered. "I knew you would not understand. What I am doing now is closing the chapter on the gods' games. Convicting you and taking your life will show them where the genuine power lies and that I will no longer be their servant. A new order will rise where gods are the Brotherhood's servants."

Garrett thought he saw a moment of doubt cross Andron's face. If so, it disappeared as quickly as it arrived. He glanced around the room at the soldiers standing at attention as they stared straight ahead. He recognized elite troops when he saw them. These were highly trained, and the relaxed attitude in their shooting arms was enough to convince him they were ready to kill if he made any false moves.

"What happens now? Are you to be my judge and executioner?"

"If only I had that right," Zaen said wistfully. "The Brotherhood has a defined legal system. You will face a trial prior to your conviction."

"So my guilt is a foregone conclusion. That hardly seems like a fair trial."

Zaen nodded. "There is no dispute about your guilt. Your sins are apparent for all to see. But there are still processes to abide by. The trial will be shown to the people in the Stellar Cluster. They will see for themselves what happens when you cross the Brotherhood. Your conviction will act as a deterrent to keep the inquisitive away."

Garrett was strangely relieved. "I know you won't kill me now. You want to humiliate me."

"Of course. Know that any humiliation you feel will be insignificant compared to the ignominy I suffered. Your punishment and death, however, will be adequate restitution."

There was no reasoning with Zaen. He had waited years to exact his revenge and had carefully laid out a scheme to ensnare him. Garrett was angry at himself for being caught so easily. Now, he faced the direst situation in his life. One that he could not talk his way out of.

Zaen motioned to the guard closest to him. "Take the prisoner away. I'm done with him."

The guard stepped forward with another on his flank.

"Where are you sending me?"

He didn't like the evil expression in Zaen's grin. "Your trial has yet to be scheduled. In the meantime, your new home will be an instruction camp. You will have time to contemplate your sins. Maybe you will come to accept your weaknesses. Assuming you live long enough."

The two guards on either side of Garrett turned him around and forced him back to the vehicle he had arrived in. After being restrained once more in the rear cabin, Garrett began the long journey to his new temporary home.

Chapter 16

After he had triumphantly watched as his guards marched Garrett away, Eminence Zaen stepped down from his dais and dismissed his guards.

"Come with me, Andron," he said, as he began walking the length of the chamber toward his private garden. Andron fell in step three paces behind.

"Your Eminence, everything you told me was correct. People in the Stellar Cluster lack faith. Even those who profess to having their own religions. They may talk as if they believe, but their actions lack conviction. It is good to be back where I belong."

Zaen nodded his head once. "You have done well, Andron. The task I gave you had its unique challenges, but I knew you had the talent to succeed. You could not have made me prouder of you."

"Everything I do is to serve your purpose, Your Eminence. It has been my greatest honor to return Osiris Garrett to you. Failure would have left me forever shamed."

Zaen smacked a fist into his hand. "That man has been the biggest thorn in my side. The fact he is a non-believer makes his actions most unbearable. I will ensure he suffers for his sins."

The pair of them continued to walk in step, their footsteps echoing along the long corridor. Andron was quietly in awe of the ornate furnishings and tapestries. In all his years of service, he had never been in this part of the eminence's palace; it was a private space, normally reserved for proctors and other senior officials. He wondered what this might mean for him. Was he finally going to be rewarded for his years of dedication?

Zaen entered a quadrangle surrounded by high windows. A single fruit tree in the center of the space was heavy with purple plum-like fruit. Surrounding the tree in concentric circles were three rows of wooden benches.

Andron knew this space simply as 'The Cloister', an area reserved for only the worthiest, allowing time for quiet contemplation. Not in his wildest dreams had he imagined he would ever stand here.

Zaen picked one of the plumpest fruits, took a large bite, and sat down on the first row of benches. "Andron, you have served me diligently for many years and I look at you as a father proudly looks at his son. You have studied hard, memorized large passages of scripture, and never given me cause to question your devotion. And, through all those years, you have asked nothing of me in return. Now that you have fulfilled my quest to return the architect of my torment, I feel it is the right time for your efforts to be recognized. Tell me, what does your heart desire?"

Andron's heart beat faster as he listened to Zaen's words, but he did not forget his breathing exercises. It was important to maintain a calm exterior whenever engaging with the eminence. Especially so on this occasion. Zaen had never asked Andron what he wanted, and he would never be so bold as to voice his desire.

"Your Eminence, you do me a great honor. I have always striven to serve you to the best of my abilities, ever since you took me into your home as an eight-year-old. My time with you has allowed me to experience wonders and benefits that most people never see. And I am grateful for your guidance. After all these years, there is only one thing I request for my obedience. And that is my freedom."

Zaen frowned before suddenly throwing his half-eaten fruit across the open space. The fruit hit a window in the far wall with a soft splash, purple juice slowly running down the glass and onto the ancient brickwork. "You disappoint me, Andron," he said, standing up before pacing past the tree. "Despite all that I have done for you, your first thought is to leave my service. This is a betrayal. You pledged a life of service to me."

Andron stood open-mouthed, his legs unable to move. "Your Eminence. I did not wish to offend you. Of course, I will always be your servant. But I have performed many tasks for you to ensure you return to your rightful position. I thought that, by returning Garrett to you, I had completed more than my fair share of duties."

"You have spent too much time with them," snarled Zaen. "Your presumption of my decision and your own worth shows an arrogance I have never witnessed in you. If it were anyone else, I would have them taken away and punished for daring to speak to me in such a brazen manner. I was going to reward you with a larger apartment and an increased status within the palace. Now I wonder if you deserve a reward at all."

Andron lowered his eyes to hide the tears of frustration and sorrow that were bursting to cascade down his face. He'd had no intention of offending

Eminence Zaen. He would never do that, he told himself. Yet part of him felt he was being treated unfairly. He had committed unspeakable atrocities on behalf of Zaen, not once questioning that the actions were wrong. How many times had Zaen lain with him, or called him to his bedchamber in the middle of the night?

While he had never complained about his treatment, Andron had always assumed Zaen would release him from his duties at some point. He had heard of other eminences rewarding their most trusted servants, freeing them and allowing them to live in relative freedom, and even procreating to support population growth. His dreams of managing a team of workers on a smallholding were dashed. He now faced a life sentence, serving Zaen's every need.

For a fraction of a second, Andron felt pure hatred for Zaen. The novel sensation burned deep within him until he swiftly snuffed it out. Ashamed, he kneeled on the ground and, with his palm facing down, he held his hand up, hoping Zaen would kiss it as a sign of forgiveness. "I am truly sorry, Your Eminence. I do not know what came over me. With my life, I pledge my absolute loyalty to you and beg for your forgiveness. I know you have the wisdom to see the honesty in me."

"I have the wisdom to know when a trusted servant has overstepped the boundaries. I am ashamed of your behavior. Go to your quarters and pray for the forgiveness of the gods. I will pray for you as well, my son. I will pray for the goodness in your heart to return."

Andron jumped to his feet for fear of upsetting Zaen further. Perhaps the eminence was correct and his time in the Stellar Cluster had tainted his essence. Since his meetings with Garrett, he'd had new thoughts and feelings.

Garrett had been prepared to accept him for who he portrayed himself to be. Although he was only playing a role, there were elements of his fictional character he had based on his true desires. Garrett's description of life on Lafayette had stirred an emotional resonance he had not expected. For the briefest of moments, there'd been an alternative path for him that appealed to his sense of freedom.

Andron had completed the mission with a sense of empowerment he had never experienced. Perhaps it was learning the citizens of the Stellar Cluster were not much different from him; they were certainly not the evil monsters that the Brotherhood were so fond of describing.

And after years of listening to Zaen's ranting about how evil Garrett was, it had come as a shock to find the man actually had a kind and generous heart.

Eminence Zaen is wise and compassionate, Andron recited. But, for the first time in his life, his emotions were conflicted. More confused than he had been in his life, he stalked the palace's corridors back to his tiny room.

Chapter 17

The drive from Zaen's palace was uneventful, although the road was bumpy, often disturbing Garrett's attempts to sleep. The two guards sitting with him said nothing throughout the trip, even when he attempted to start a conversation. They simply stared coldly ahead, refusing to even make eye contact with him.

It didn't take a genius to know someone had warned them he was dangerous, as they spent much of the time nervously caressing their weapons.

Garrett's view outside the vehicle was through two small rectangular openings, covered in a fine mesh rather than glass. It meant a chilly breeze, as well as rain, continually swept through the back of the armored transport. The terrain they passed through was mainly an overgrown jungle. All Garrett could see was dense undergrowth and a bleak charcoal mountain ridge in the distance.

It was almost dark as the transport rumbled up to a high metal fence. Garrett peered outside and saw a sign in bold black letters—'INSTRUCTION CAMP 4'. He heard a brief conversation before the vehicle lurched forward for about one hundred meters.

More conversation, this time longer, before the rear doors were opened from the outside. Two men in black uniforms glared briefly at Garrett before closing the doors again.

The transport carried on its way again for five minutes. As it slowed for the third time, Garrett saw they were entering what looked like a small compound. The vehicle stopped, killing its engine. The sound of a heavy gate sliding behind the vehicle hinted that this may be the final destination.

He heard the harsh sound of boots on concrete before the rear doors opened one more time.

"Out," a voice boomed.

The two guards eased Garrett from his seat, allowing him to stand. He stretched his legs, feeling the circulation return to his feet, before being nudged toward the door.

Stepping out, he found himself in an enclosure surrounded by five-meter-high steel walls topped with razor wire. No doors, only enormous gates at either end of the enclosure. Two rows of spotlights cast a harsh glow across everything within. As well as the two guards and the vehicle's driver, he counted eight other guards, all heavily armed and wearing helmets and body armor. No one was taking any chances with him.

"Stand where you are. Legs wide apart."

Garrett complied. Outnumbered and trapped, he had little choice.

"Hold your hands out in front of you."

He raised his arms. A guard, several centimeters taller than the rest and wearing gold insignia on his collar, stepped up in front of him. The man was stocky, and from his bulging triceps, liked to work out. Garrett eyed him up, confident he could beat the man in a one-on-one fight.

He silently hoped he got the chance to find out.

The guard produced a long, curved blade from his tunic and, in one swift motion, sliced through the bindings on Garrett's wrists.

Garrett rubbed his right wrist to recover the circulation in his hand. Angry red welts on his skin showed how tight the ropes had been.

"Thank you. Can I get a drink?" he asked the man. His last taste of water had been back on the spaceship, more than half a day earlier.

"You will refer to me as Instructor Darr," replied the guard.

Garrett pursed his lips. "Instructor Darr, may I have a drink?"

"Remove your clothes," Darr replied, ignoring Garrett's request, his booming voice echoing off the walls of the enclosure. Garrett drew back at the man's foul breath. Personal hygiene was clearly not one of his priorities.

Glancing at the rest of the guards surrounding him, he could see the anxiety in their body language as if they were waiting for something to happen. He would have expected nothing less from his own men back in the day. His first lesson on day one of field training had been to always be ready for the unexpected.

If only I had followed my own advice, he thought.

If only I had a squad of Space Marines now.

He removed his top and pants. After living and sleeping in them for the previous ten days, they were not as fresh as he was used to. But they were still preferable to standing naked in the chilly open air in front of these nervous guards.

Despite the smell, his rancid clothes were infinitely better than the long orange robe that was thrown at his feet. He looked questioningly at Instructor Darr.

"This is the only garment you need. Put it on."

Garrett picked up the robe. Like everything else on the planet, the material had an almost overwhelming odor of rotting vegetables. This particular robe also had brown streaks of dried blood running down the front. From the size and location of the hole, someone had stabbed the previous owner in the heart. Garrett could see where the blade had penetrated the robe. Not only was there a round brown patch about the size of his head, but also a poorly repaired gash in the fabric.

As he pulled the robe over his head, Garrett tried not to think about how many previous owners there had been. It wasn't a matter to dwell on.

"Follow me," Darr said, walking past Garrett toward the inner gate. Garrett did as he instructed, encouraged by six guards who walked into him, urging him forward.

The large gate slowly trundled open on rollers, shocking Garrett that such antiquated machinery still operated. He wondered why the Stellar Cluster allowed the Brotherhood to continue their reign of terror. It would have been easy to send in a few battalions of highly trained soldiers with advanced weapons. The resulting conflict would be over in a matter of days, freeing the masses from the Brotherhood's oppression.

As they shepherded him through the gates, the ground turned to soft mud that splashed up between his toes. The area on both sides of the path was depressingly barren. Garrett had never been inside a prison, but what he could see now was a fair approximation of what he imagined one to be like.

What else should there be? It's a prison!

Ahead, he could see a low, single-story concrete building. The well-worn path he was walking along went directly to a single black door. A high wall ran from the corner of the building, stretching into the distance in both directions.

"Are these walls for keeping people in or out?" he asked the guard walking next to him. His attempt at humor fell flat with the man maintaining a steady gaze ahead.

Escape was going to be difficult. But it was something he was going to have to try if he wanted to survive. All he had to do was find a weakness. He suspected the Brotherhood's aversion to technology could benefit him. Humans were weak and unpredictable. It was simply a matter of singling out the guards open to bribes, or the ones that were overly fatigued or complacent. It was just a matter of time.

Something he wasn't sure he had much of.

***

The inside of the building proved to be one long shower block. Down one side of the building, showerheads hung down from the ceiling in a neat now. Garrett estimated there had to be over twenty of them. Unsurprisingly, the shower heads were caked with limescale. He was learning that nothing on Drani IV was well maintained.

He also noticed there were no shower screens or cubicles.

"I suggest you clean yourself. This will be your last taste of cleanliness for a very long time. Keep your robe on." It was not a request, but an order. Garrett's initial thought was Instructor Darr and most of his men could do with a spell under the showers.

He soon realized why they didn't as freezing cold water rained down on his head. As he shivered under the deluge, he noticed a strong smell of disinfectant. His eyes stung and his skin itched.

All that water and none of it fit to drink, he said to himself.

When Garrett tried to step from the shower, three of the guards beat him back with a series of sturdy blows from their rifle butts. Garrett raised his arms in defense but could not force his way out

The water stopped after two minutes, leaving Garrett shivering and feeling weak. His saturated robe clung to him, draining any residual body heat. He knew there was a risk of hypothermia if he stayed like this, not that the guards cared.

"Follow me," Darr said again.

"I need a drink?" Garrett called out, standing his ground.

The response was a painful jab in the small of his back from a rifle butt. Garrett spun round angrily, ready to retaliate, but the four guards behind him had their guns raised at his head.

Darr shouted, "You'll get water when processing is complete. Don't make it harder for yourself."

How can it get worse? I'm already facing a show trial and certain death!

There was another solid steel door at the far end of the shower block. Darr opened a series of locks with an old-fashioned key, the likes of which Garrett had seen only in historical files.

He wanted the experience to be over. A freezing wind was blowing through his damp robe. By now, his teeth were chattering. He knew he had to find somewhere warm, and fast.

At the opposite side of the yard, an open door beckoned the group. This time, he didn't wait to be commanded to move. Inside, he found himself in what had to be the processing area. Another guard sat behind a desk, filling out paper forms. The seated man wrote something on a document before handing it to Darr.

"Through that door," Darr said, pointing to a wooden door to the side.

Garrett was surprised to see that only Instructor Darr followed him in. He was further surprised when the guard closed the door behind him. The room itself was small and bare, with lime-green walls. No furniture or windows, just the one door in and out.

"We all know who you are," Darr said, leaning in close to his face.

Garrett turned his face away to avoid the halitosis. "I guess there aren't many secrets in a place like this."

"Eminence Zaen insists you receive no special treatment. He wants you alive for your trial, and they have tasked me to ensure he gets what he wants. I have seen your personal record in the military and know how dangerous you are."

"That's all in my past."

"Just as well. Because you have no future. My instructors have orders to wound you only, unless you provoke them, or they feel threatened by you. You'll know, of course, that humans make mistakes. It takes only a split second to accidentally kill instead of maiming. I therefore strongly recommend you be a model prisoner during your temporary stay here."

"Thank you," Garrett replied, as his shivering subsided. "Is there anything else I should know?"

Darr sneered. "No one has escaped this instruction camp. The sinners accept there is no chance of success. If you're one of those guys who has an irrational belief that they can be the first, then think again. If you made it through the barriers, you would still have to cross the terrain. You saw when you were driven here. Thick jungles and swamps, with fish and animals that want to kill you and feast on your sorry corpse."

Garrett nodded silently as if accepting his fate. This was just the standard warning to make prisoners more compliant. Escape is futile, so don't even consider making an attempt. Of course, that did not mean he would not be trying to find a way out.

"If you follow instructions and cause no trouble, your life will be easier. You will receive adequate sustenance and shelter. Failure to comply will see a range of punishments. The warden does not tolerate insubordination. Neither do I. Do you understand?"

"Yes," Garrett replied, his head bowed.

"Yes, what?"

"Yes, Instructor Darr."

Darr looked at him with suspicion. "I thought you'd be a tough guy with no brains. Maybe you have enough common sense to stay alive long enough for your trial. I think it's time for you to acquaint yourself with where you're going to spend the rest of your life."

Garrett resisted the urge to attack Darr. Although he wanted more than anything to resist entering the facility, overpowering the instructor would be unproductive, with the array of guards waiting on the other side of the door. His moment would come if he was patient.

It had to!

Chapter 18

For Leela, it was yet another frustratingly slow day in Celeste, the capital city of Lafayette. The planet's wet season was ending, but this year had seen record amounts of rainfall. Great news for the farmers. Less so for the rest of the population, who were dealing with an explosion of mosquitoes and a range of other flying insects. Each trip outside meant fighting off a frenzy of tiny critters, wearing down everyone's patience.

Leela looked out of the cockpit window at the growing puddles on the landing pad. Listening to the drumming sound of heavy rain on the upper hull of the Novak, she wished she had paid extra for a bay inside one of the voluminous hangars. Three days of persistent rain and being stuck inside her ship were making her edgy.

How do the locals cope?

The slow progress Keisha and Toru were making on locating the bolters was not helping her mood either. Five days of research and still no firm lead. The trail was stone cold. She was beginning to doubt if the bolters were still even on the planet. But with no other destinations to explore, continuing the research on Lafayette was the only option.

It wasn't Keisha's fault. She was doing her best with the limited assets at her disposal, avoiding official local resources. That route was too obvious and likely to be compromised. If only Garrett was with them. Despite his claims to the contrary, Leela was convinced he had some contacts he could call up-on.

The only positive news had been Naoki Oakes' release from hospital on Sidenva. She was now en route back to Destiny Station for rehabilitation and was eager to get back to work. It had taken all of Leela's powers of persuasion to convince Naoki to not come directly to Lafayette. Even so, Leela was thankful that Naoki had survived her injuries.

Thoughts of Garrett raised another concern in her mind. *Where is Oz?* It was twelve days since she had spoken with him. That was the last time anyone had spotted him, as far as she had determined. His whereabouts were as big a puzzle as that of the bolters. She had reached out to everyone within the bounty hunter community, all of whom committed to letting her know as soon as Garrett reappeared.

There was, however, one person she had not yet contacted. Someone she had avoided reaching out to for fear of dragging up old emotions. But she could see no other option if she wanted peace of mind. Reluctantly, she connected the quantum communications system to the Confederacy matrix and waited for a response. Ten minutes later, she was rewarded with a quiet chime. When a three-dimensional holographic image of the person materialized above the console in front of her, she silently acknowledged to herself it was good to see him again.

"Hi, Levi. I wasn't sure you would answer," she said, unable to hide her happiness.

Levi Murphy returned her smile. He was clean-shaven and neatly groomed. She could not recall him looking so smart or so healthy. "Leela, your request intrigued me. You said you never wanted to speak to me again."

"Never is a long time. And I was angry."

"We were both angry, Leela. I know I'm not the easiest person to be around. My brother is helping me to overcome my issues."

"Whatever he's doing, tell him it's working. You're looking great," Leela said, surprising herself at how much she meant it.

"What can I help you with?" Levi's curt response brought Leela's emotions crashing back down.

That's why we're not together, she said to herself, feeling foolish.

"I was wondering if you've seen or heard from Oz recently?"

"Not for several months. Why?"

"He was supposed to join me on a mission. The last time I saw him was in the Lodge almost two weeks ago. The following day, he failed to show up on the Novak. I've reached out many times, but he is not answering my messages. I've tried everyone else I know. It's as if Oz has simply vanished."

"You've come to me as a last resort?" Leela detected annoyance in his voice.

"Levi, you're his best friend. If anyone knows his possible whereabouts, it's you."

"If he was my best friend, he wouldn't be working with you," snapped Levi.

This was the reaction Leela had expected and the reason she had not contacted Murphy sooner. Part of her was angry at Garrett for not informing his friend they were working together. "I wanted his local knowledge. The current job is on Lafayette, and it's highly lucrative if we can locate the bolters. I thought he could help with the intel and contacts here."

"He didn't have to accept."

"I don't have time to argue with you, Levi. I'm genuinely concerned about Oz's safety. You should be too. Has he done anything like this before? Do you know where he could have gone?"

Levi was quiet for several moments. "Oz had a rough time after Mercy's death, but he's had several years to get over that. If he committed to joining your latest excursion, he wouldn't have let you down. The fact he's not responding means he must be in trouble, or worse."

"That's what I'm afraid of."

"How was he when you last spoke with him? Was he worried about anything?"

"No, nothing that I was aware of. He had been for drinks with me, Keisha and Toru and seemed in good spirits. In fact, he was helping a man he had met on one of your old missions."

"Do you know who it was?"

"No, Oz didn't give a name, but he seemed excited about giving this friend a new start. Do you think that's why he's gone silent?"

"Definitely not. I would understand if it was me. I've lost months of my life where I didn't know where I was and didn't want to be found. But that isn't Oz."

Leela was out of ideas. She had hoped Murphy's connection with Garrett would open up some new avenues to investigate. Perhaps this was one mystery she couldn't solve. Yet, the one lesson Garrett had taught her was to leave no one behind. She could not simply forget about him now and hope for the best.

"Have you tried his brother?" Murphy asked.

"No. Oz was adamant he had not spoken to Seth in years and had no intention of reconciling. He made it clear that the subject was off limits."

Murphy nodded. "It's a long shot but reach out to him. I see you're calling me from Celeste. There's the Garrett family ranch on the outskirts. Go speak with Seth. Even if he hasn't heard from Oz, he is a senior political figure. He'll have contacts he can call upon."

"Okay, thanks, Levi. I'll do that."

"Let me know how you get on." Murphy cut the connection before Leela could say anything else.

She sat looking out of the window once again, staring into the distance. The conversation with Murphy had only increased her anxiety levels. She was now surer than ever that Garrett was in serious trouble. There had to be clues she was missing; ironic with her reputation for finding people who did not want to be found.

She keyed the comms panel again. "Keisha, any updates?"

"Other than this weather is pissing me off? No. We're chasing up another lead, but I'm not optimistic."

"Thanks. I'm coming into the city and will catch up with you in two hours. I need to make a stop on the way."

"Okay. You may want to bring some credits with you. These contacts are becoming more expensive."

"Great!" Leela replied, cutting the link.

Where are you, Oz?

Chapter 19

As the heavy barred gate closed with a resounding metallic crash behind Garrett, he figured it was safe for him to remove the hood. He regretted the decision almost immediately as his senses threatened to be overwhelmed by the stench of stale human sweat and excrement. The atmosphere was warm and fetid; like entering a sewer.

So this is the inside of an instruction camp, he thought as he fought the urge to gag. The smell was far worse than anything he could imagine and confirmed his worst fears; that Zaen kept his people in far worse conditions than he probably kept his pets.

The room itself seemed unremarkable; a large open space roughly twenty meters square hewed out of rock. The roof was less than three meters high, rough with the marks of whatever tools had been used to create the space. A series of low-powered lights barely lit the room, with two of the corners in deep shadow.

A row of benches was stacked along one wall. An empty alcove on another wall had a set of rails embedded into the floor. Garrett followed the track with his eyes; it ran around the edge of the room and along the corridor through which he had just arrived before disappearing under the heavy barred gate.

Looking further around the room, he saw the words 'LEVEL ZERO' had been hand-painted in white. Underneath it, in smaller untidy letters, someone had painted 'Penitence Will Heal Your Soul'.

Finally, on the far wall, he detected movement in the shadows. Stepping closer, he saw what appeared to be a vertical conveyor belt with wooden plates placed at regular intervals, about three meters apart. One side of the belt was moving upwards, disappearing through a small aperture in the roof. Separated by a series of continually turning spindles, the other side of the belt came back down through a second hole and continued its journey to what Garrett could only guess were lower levels.

He had seen nothing like it, except in historic data files. Ancient history data! The entire apparatus looked unsafe and in dire need of replacement. As he stared closer, he could see the belt itself was a patchwork of leather and other material. It was a miracle it worked at all.

With nowhere else to go, Garrett waited for the right moment to step onto one of the wooden plates before it descended into the bowels of the instruction camp, ready to leap off at the first hint of the belt snapping. To his surprise, the plate held. As he disappeared into the rock face, he entered complete darkness for several seconds before coming out into a tunnel.

Before it took him further down, Garrett jumped from the conveyor belt, landing lightly on the rocky ground. On the wall in front of him were the words 'LEVEL ONE-A'. The tunnel itself was narrow, maybe two meters wide, and as dimly lit as the level above. And seemingly just as empty. Cables ran along the roof from light to light. He could also see a tube, no wider than his arm that, he presumed from the faint breeze, was for ventilation.

Garrett was beginning to wonder if he was the only inmate in this Brotherhood prison when he heard a scuffling noise somewhere along the tunnel. The sound stopped almost as soon as it began, and he had to strain his ears for several seconds before he heard it again. Whatever the sound was, it was too loud to have been caused by a rat which made him wonder what indigenous animals inhabited Drani IV. He had not given it any thought until now.

Taking two steps forward, his bare toes discovered a thick layer of mud coated the floor. At least he hoped it was mud, although the powerful smell of feces hinted it could be something else. Putting the thought to one side, Garrett peered into the gloom before detecting the sound of hushed human voices. After three more paces, he finally spotted people sitting on either side of the tunnel. The nearest were only ten meters away, but it was difficult to see their features in the low light.

He continued walking slowly before he could confirm two women and a child kneeling at the side of the tunnel. It was impossible to tell how old they were or what they looked like from the dirt that was plastered on their faces and matted hair. They were rubbing their robes with a rock although Garrett did not understand the purpose. He thought about speaking with them, but they paid him no attention as he walked past.

Further along, he spotted recesses dug into the walls on either side. They were spaced out fairly evenly but were different depths, from one to three meters. There were small brown piles in most of the recesses, but he could not discern if they were people, blankets, or supplies.

After one hundred meters, he came to the end of the tunnel; a blank wall where the diggers had decided they'd had enough. Garrett was about to turn around and retrace his steps when a gruff voice behind him called out.

"What do you think you're doing?"

Garrett stepped away from the wall before turning to face four men standing three meters away. They were all wearing robes, similar to the one he was wearing, except these were covered in mud and dirt. And each of the men was carrying a crude hammer.

The welcoming committee!

He held his ground, pushing out his chest to stress his size. The men in front of him were all shorter than him, with wiry frames. Garrett knew that his height was not necessarily an advantage. What the men lacked in size, they possibly made up for in speed and agility.

"I'm new. Only arrived a few minutes ago. I was hoping to find someone to show me around."

The man on the right of the group took half a pace forward. "Are you a spy?"

"Do I look like a spy?"

The man shrugged. "You don't look like one of us. And you don't sound like one of us. Where are you from?"

"Well observed. I'm from a planet in the Stellar Cluster. I promise you, I am a prisoner. The same as you."

"Why would an off-worlder be sent to an instruction camp?"

"You ask a lot of questions, my friend."

"You have entered our home. If you want to survive the night, you would do well to prove who you say you are."

"Okay, let's start again. My name is Osiris Garrett. Who are you?"

The man looked unsure. He was supposed to be asking the questions. "You can call me Sylwester."

"Well, Sylwester. Many years ago, I offended Eminence Zaen. Apparently, he's held a grudge ever since then. So much so that he had me kidnapped and sent here. There's going to be a trial but I'm sure the result is a foregone conclusion."

Sylwester glanced at his companions and laughed. "Are you the off-worlder who took the eminence against his will and tortured him? We heard you performed numerous acts of brutality on him."

"If that is what you've heard, then it's a lie. I stole his ship, and he was unfortunately on it. At no time did I harm or torture him. That is not my way."

"Shame, I like the original version," another prisoner murmured.

Sylwester lowered his hammer. "Eminence Zaen is not popular in this camp. We are all here because of him. I should have known he had lied about his encounter with the beasts of the Stellar Cluster."

Garrett noticed the body language of the other men relax, even though they continued to clasp their weapons. Countless other prisoners suddenly appeared behind them. He also heard movement from the recess to his left, although no one appeared. Nonetheless, his peripheral vision was on alert for any unexpected movements from close by.

"I assure you, we are not beasts and we do not treat people like the Brotherhood mistreat their own."

"We believe you. But that information will do you no good here. You are lucky to have a trial. They have condemned each of us for impurities with no trial. We are in this camp for our souls to be cleansed."

"I read the sign on the way in. What is an instruction camp?"

"Don't trust him," someone in the dark whispered.

"He's a spy," murmured another.

"Silence," Sylwester said. We will give him a chance. If he is telling the truth, then he deserves our sympathy. If not, then we all know what happens to spies."

Garrett looked around him. He figured he could take down at least a dozen before he was overwhelmed by the sheer weight of numbers. But he didn't want to do that. These people had suffered enough.

Sylwester took another small pace forward. "An instruction camp is where sinners are sent to rediscover their faith in the Brotherhood and the gods. We're here because of improper thoughts or for voicing our doubts. The instructors allow the lucky few back into the population, but only once they prove their repentance."

"I was told that no one has escaped."

"That is true. You saw the barriers and the guards. Ridiculous really. This entire planet is one large nightmarish prison. There is nowhere safe to hide outside of this camp. Yet we all live a lie. Especially those who choose to surrender to the Brotherhood's lies so they can return to their families."

Garrett spotted women and children in the growing crowd. "How many live here?"

Sylwester shrugged. "I don't think we've ever counted. One hundred? Possibly more. Numbers change daily with new arrivals or deaths. We have generations of families here."

"How long have you been in the camp?"

"Does it look like we have calendars?"

Garrett realized it was a dumb question. "What happens here?"

"You really don't know, do you?"

"I didn't know of the camp's existence until a few hours ago. It seems more than a simple prison."

"It's hell," a voice yelled out from the crowd. "The Brotherhood have damned us."

"My friend Caylan is right," said Sylwester. "The Brotherhood have crafted a hell. They tell us they built these facilities to save our souls, but they lie. We're supposed to study the scriptures as we look at our inner beings, searching for redemption. In reality, we're slave labor. I spend thirteen hours each day digging out rock, twenty-eight levels down. There is a seam of precious metals running diagonally at that depth. Using only hammers and pickaxes, we hack away at the rock. That's one pleasure for you to discover."

Garrett was in no hurry for that treat. He wanted an escape route.

"Where are the guards? Surely they supervise you."

Sylwester shook his head. "You don't see the instructors down here very often. All instructions are provided during mealtimes. They class most of the instruction as 'self-reflection'. Instructor Darr is a bastard. He tries to set us against one another by appointing foremen. He picks random names, but he knows what he's doing. Anything to undermine the stability we have down here."

Garrett found that interesting. How could Darr select the right people to cause the maximum disruption? He filed that away in his brain for further thought. He had other, more important, considerations.

"What about eating?"

"They provide food once a day. The next level up, where you entered the camp, is what we call the kitchen. That's a loose description. A vat of stew is delivered once a day. The guards dish it out to us and withhold it from those they deem not worthy. As you can see from our physiques, the portions are not large."

Garrett could imagine the quality and quantity of the food. Almost certainly, it would consist only of vegetables.

Another experience to look forward to.

"And sleeping?"

"Sleep is easy. Find an empty recess and a blanket and they're yours. No one will trouble you. These will be your only possessions in here. No one will take them from you. We respect one another enough to know that the smallest things in life are precious. Darr hates it. He would like nothing more than for us to start a riot."

"So he can be seen as a hero when he stops it? I've seen it before."

"I think so. He wants to see his men in action with us. Men with body armor, shields, and projectile weapons against a rabble of unprotected country folk. Hardly a fair fight, but it would enable him to move up the ranks."

Garrett had experienced similar individuals across the Stellar Cluster. Men like Darr were bullies, building their careers and reputations through intimidation. The irony was that most of them were cowards, racked with insecurities. Once you uncovered their weaknesses, they swiftly lost their control.

"I forgot to mention. Sleep periods are two hours at a time. Sirens will sound to let you know it is time for quiet contemplation."

"So that you can consider your sins?"

"Exactly. Broken sleep takes time to get used to. Some people never do. You'll soon learn who those people are and to steer clear of their short tempers."

Yet another way of breaking the spirit of an individual. Garrett had studied the effects of long-term sleep deprivation on the human psyche. That, combined with the living conditions and poor nutrition, turned the population of this instruction camp into compliant sheep, probably with underlying mental and physical conditions that required expert help. Help that would never be provided to this wretched group.

The Brotherhood had a lot to answer for.

Garrett looked behind the mob of men. "What will I find if I go down on that conveyor death trap?"

Sylwester shrugged. "Two more levels like this one. Below them, the mine begins. That's where we spend most of our day."

"How deep does it go?"

"I don' think anyone knows. This camp has existed for hundreds of years. Maybe longer. The shafts run deep. Many levels have become abandoned or collapsed. Sometimes when we dig new tunnels, we come across the old ones."

"And do you all contribute?"

"If we want to be fed, then yes. We exchange what we dig for food. The women and children help to carry the minerals up to the kitchen."

"And for anyone too weak to work?"

Sylwester's dark expression answered the question.

Chapter 20

The rain had stopped by the time Leela's robo-cab landed at the imposing Lafayette parliament in the center of Celeste. A golden shaft of sunlight burst through the clouds, bathing the marble facade of the colonial-style building with a warm hue.

Leela had been to similar buildings across the Stellar Cluster. The people inside often had access to valuable information that was not available to the public. It never ceased to amaze her how so many politicians and elected officials had such a sense of grandiose self-importance that they had to work in quasi-palaces. There was an element of striking reverence into the hearts of commoners who dared to visit, but Leela was neither impressed nor awestruck by politicians' shows of decadence.

As she strode through the main lobby, a large holographic information screen confronted her. "Please state your name and purpose," it said with a polite, gender-neutral voice.

"Leela Spicer. I'm here to meet with Senator Seth Garrett."

"Thank you for your response. Do you have an invitation?"

"Yes," she lied. She had decided not to call ahead for fear of being turned away at the mention of Oz Garrett's name.

"I do not have you listed in the system," the screen replied, still being polite.

Leela placed her hands on her hips. "That must be your mistake. I spoke with Seth less than an hour ago. We're old friends and he invited me for a drink in his office."

"The senator has not registered your appointment."

She shrugged. "I guess he didn't want to publicize it. This is an informal catch-up rather than official government business."

The screen froze for several seconds before replying. "This is most irregular. Senator Garrett knows he must enter all gatherings within this building to maintain a sense of propriety. I will contact his assistant."

"You do that. But I'm running late. I'm going to his office while you update your records."

"Please wait while I—"

Leela began striding down a long corridor to her left, shutting out the computer's protestations. The problem was, she did not know where Seth Garrett's office was located. Eventually, after hassling a busy-looking young intern for directions, she found his office on the third floor at the end of another long corridor.

As she arrived, she was pleased to see the wooden doors to the office were open. Without breaking her stride, she stepped into a large area, nearer the size of a lecture room than an office. Yet there was only one desk and several chairs gathered in small groups around the room.

Behind the desk was a distinguished man in his fifties, with a neatly groomed beard and a black tunic. His sharp angular nose and inquisitive eyes left Leela in no doubt that this was Garrett's brother.

He stared at her in confusion as he stood. "I believe there has been a mistake. The administration system informs me you believe we have a social appointment. Can you explain yourself?"

Leela stopped several meters in front of the desk and smiled. "Senator Garrett, if you can spare me five minutes of your valuable time, I will explain to you why I'm here."

"I'll give you sixty seconds before I call security," he replied, his eyebrows knotting into a deep frown.

"Okay, I can work with that," Leela said. "My name is Leela Spicer. I'm here because of your brother, Oz. He suddenly went missing almost two weeks ago, and no one has been able to contact him since. I know the two of you aren't close, but I hoped you may know his whereabouts."

"Osiris?" murmured Seth softly, as if he hadn't spoken that name in a long time. He sat back down in his chair and casually indicated with his hand that Leela should take a seat on her side of the desk. "What is your relationship with my brother?"

"Purely professional. We've worked together on a couple of missions. Oz was due to board my ship on Destiny Station, but he never showed up. He didn't even leave a message."

"Has he done anything like this before?"

"Not that I'm aware of. Do you have any suggestions?"

Seth rubbed his chin thoughtfully as he stared out of the window at some tall trees swaying in the breeze. "I don't know what Osiris may have told you about me. Neither of us is an innocent party to the breakdown of our relationship. Unfortunately, I cannot see a resolution soon even if he turns up safely. Which means I'm the last person he would contact if he were in trouble."

Leela feared as much. Garrett's current situation was more mysterious than that of the bolters she was chasing down. Seth Garrett had been a long shot, but she had given it a try. Garrett's case was stone cold; somewhere in the Stellar Cluster was all she had.

"Is there anyone else on Lafayette that may have a clue to his whereabouts?"

"I can't think of anyone," said Seth. "Maybe you can search his military records. There could be a name hidden in there, but I assume you know it's been many years since Osiris was a member of the Space Marines."

"He often mentions his time in the Space Marines with pride. But I think all his friends from back then are dead." Leela paused for a moment, unsure whether to ask the next question, but decided she had no choice. "Senator, I know it is an imposition. Is there anything you can do to request President D'Angelo's government search for Oz? There must be a special agency that deals with missing persons. The more resources looking for Oz, the better chance we have of finding him."

"I admire your persistence, Miss Spicer. My brother must mean a lot to you."

Leela blushed with anger. "Not in the way you think. Oz taught me we don't leave people behind. No one else is looking out for him."

"My apologies if I caused any offense. I will make some inquiries on your behalf. The central government established a task force to search and retrieve dignitaries and VIPs, usually when a kidnapping for ransom is involved. They're an elite tactical unit. I'm not sure a missing bounty hunter falls into their remit."

"Try it. Please. Surely you can argue he's your brother. Perhaps someone kidnapped him to put pressure on you."

Seth sighed. "We both know that's not true, as there have been no ransom demands. However, I will do all that I can. He is my brother, after all."

Leela stood, feeling she had done as much as she could without overstaying her welcome. "I would really appreciate that. You can contact me on the Novak, currently parked at the spaceport."

Seth typed a quick note onto the screen in front of him. "I assume you're on a mission, Miss Spicer."

"Yes, we're trying to locate several high-profile bolters. I had recruited Oz for his local knowledge. Without him, we're struggling to pick up their trail." Leela didn't feel it necessary to add that Garrett had been reluctant to return to his home planet.

"Most unfortunate. If you send me the details of these miscreants, I will get my staff to offer their help although, I cannot promise they will be more successful than you have been."

Leela reached forward to shake his hand. "That is a very generous offer and one that I will take up. Thank you again for your time. I hope I've not offended you."

Seth smiled. "Thank you for bringing this matter to my attention. You've made me consider if it's time to bury the past." His expression changed to a frown as he added. "Assuming I'm not too late."

Leela left the office with mixed feelings. While Seth had made a commitment to help her search, Garrett was no closer to being found. It was becoming harder to ignore the knot in her gut that told her he was already dead.

Chapter 21

Garrett was starving but had to make do with half a flask of water passed to him by a stranger. The water was warm and had a unique aftertaste, but he didn't care. His throat was the driest it had been since a training mishap in the Space Marines when his squad was almost killed from overexposure to the sun. With his thirst quenched, he found an empty recess halfway along the tunnel on level three.

He had been asleep for only a few minutes when a siren resounded throughout the camp. Garrett remained where he was, quietly watching people walk past toward the end of the tunnel. Interested to know what was happening, he followed the last group.

Everyone on the level was kneeling on the ground, facing the conveyor belt. As the siren ceased its ear-shattering screech, silence filled the tunnel. The crowd looked weary. Some of the younger children were lying half asleep on their parents' knees.

Garrett expected someone to speak to the crowd. He knew enough about religion that there was always a preacher to lead this type of event. But it quickly became apparent the people were silently praying or whatever they did to prove they were seeking redemption.

With nothing to see and an apathy toward all religions, Garrett went back to his recess and was soon dreaming about food and ale. He awoke suddenly, aware of movement around him, but it was too late for him to defend himself against a vicious kick to the ribs. He groaned in pain, rolling over to avoid the next kick and bringing his arm up to protect his head.

Fortunately, the kicks had no force behind them. Bare feet were no match for the boots he was normally kicked with. Four men were standing over him, masks covering their faces.

"Stinking spy!" said one of them, lashing out once more with his foot. This time, Garrett was ready. He grabbed the foot and was able to unbalance the man, who fell backward with a yell of surprise.

Using the momentum, Garrett rolled to his feet, towering above the remaining three men. "Do you want to continue with this? I don't want to hurt any of you, but I will if you make me defend myself."

One man pulled out a crude hammer. "Stay back," he said, his voice quavering with fear.

Garrett glared at him. "Put it down before you get hurt. I don't want any trouble."

"You're an off-worlder. Why should we believe you?"

"That's your choice. As it is to walk away with no broken bones. So stand down and let's all calm down."

The fourth attacker rose to his feet, also brandishing a hammer and looking incensed. He was ready to attack Garrett when Sylwester appeared behind him.

"This is no way to treat a new guest. Where are your manners, boys?"

"He's a spy, Syl. You know he is. He'll be telling Darr all about us."

Sylwester quickly reached forward and snatched the man's mask down. "Why the need for this, Don? And the rest of you? You're paranoid. Go back to your recesses and allow us all to get some sleep."

The men looked uncertainly at one another before drifting away into the darkness.

"Thank you," Garrett said.

Sylwester frowned. "That was for their benefit, not yours. They won't be able to work with broken limbs. Which means no food for them. If I had left you to defend yourself, their deaths would be on my conscience."

"Very perceptive. I have been known to crack bones in my time."

Sylwester shrugged. "They won't come at you again. Get some sleep while you can."

As Sylwester walked away, Garrett lay back down on his blanket and stared at the roof. This time, sleep was harder to find. His mind was racing through options for his one priority.

Escape.

Chapter 22

As had been the custom most of his life, Eminence Zaen awoke one hour before dawn, his body clock rousing him, not servants. He turned over in his bed, pleased to see the two young men had vacated the room silently during the night. Not all supplicants were as accepting of their position. Merely because he welcomed them into his bedchamber didn't mean they were anything other than a physical attraction to satisfy his needs.

Not every acolyte realized that, thinking they would become a permanent addition to his inner circle and enjoy the associated luxury. Instead, they would swiftly discover an impatient Zaen ordering their immediate dismissal back to a commune.

The one exception was Andron. The young man had been more than a transitory interest. There was something different about him that sparked emotions within Zaen. It wasn't merely Andron's angelic looks and childlike innocence. Zaen had taken years to understand the reasons for the difference and it had shocked him to realize it was Andron's unadulterated love for him.

While the other supplicants would try their best to accommodate his sexual desires, none of them had put their heart into the exercise. Zaen had known that and was usually indifferent to their feelings. He was interested in their bodies, not their sensibilities. Whether they enjoyed the encounter was immaterial. It was their duty to him.

Andron had shown promise soon after joining the palace staff. Zaen had noticed him the first time he served food at a banquet. Private scripture lessons soon became a regular habit. Andron had a questioning mind and was eager to learn from the eminence.

It had been Andron who rescued him from the clutches of Osiris Garrett. And it was the young man's loyalty and unflappable faith that had maintained his belief during his darkest hours when his confidence was challenged as never before.

But Andron was now proving to be a liability, with unseemly expectations.

As Zaen showered, he considered what he should do. He suspected it was partly his own fault. He had allowed Andron too much freedom over the years. The young man had become too familiar, his latest display of arrogance proving the point.

It was a shame. Andron had done well to bring back Garrett. But all he had done was to execute the eminence's plan to the letter. Zaen could not recall any time when he had intimated he would reward Andron with his freedom.

It was a dangerous precedent that would undermine the carefully crafted reputation Zaen had painstakingly built since his kidnapping.

Damn you, Andron!

Zaen threw a bar of soap at the wall, cracking two antique tiles. This day should be one of celebration. Garrett was safely inside Instruction Camp Four, awaiting his trial and execution. Andron's presumptuous request had almost ruined the moment.

***

Zaen's mood had still not improved by midday. He had sat through calls to prayer and his regular weekly meeting with the junior proctors with an air of indifference.

At the end of the meeting, the proctors dispersed except for Chief Proctor Chan, his most senior adviser. The sixty-year-old had held the position for six years without feeling Zaen's wrath, able to navigate a successful path through the eminence's contrary emotions.

"Your Eminence, if you don't mind me saying, you do not seem yourself today. What is troubling you?"

Zaen rose and walked to the window, staring at the distant mountains. Storm clouds were building, a sure sign of rain later that day. He didn't share his innermost thoughts with anyone. But he recognized Chan might be exactly the right person to enact his wishes. The old proctor had limited ambitions and was satisfied with his role as head of the palace. He was the least likely person to use personal information to further his own agenda.

"I am troubled, Chan. I may have compromised my position and showed too much compassion to an individual."

"Andron?"

Zaen spun around to face Chan, surprised at the man's insight. "I have allowed him to become too intimate with my affairs. Although he has served me well, it is time to let him go. Why am I finding that decision so difficult to make?"

"Your Eminence, only you know the answer. I suspect you understand the truth, otherwise, you would not be voicing this to me now. Are you seeking validation?"

"Am I?" Zaen wasn't sure. He had never sought approval from anyone, even his parents and the Elders. He had always been certain of the decisions he made, never giving them a second thought. On the rare occasions he had made mistakes, he had owned them, or, more correctly, found someone to shoulder the blame. And he'd learned from his errors, making him stronger and wiser. The doubts he was now feeling were new and unwelcome. He wanted them gone.

"You owe nothing to the supplicant. You have favored him for many years and he has had a good life serving you. Perhaps it is time to release him from your service."

Zaen nodded. "That is my thought. Certain emotions exist and they should not. Yet I would regret not feeling them again."

Chan walked anxiously up to Zaen and lowered his voice. "This young man has infiltrated your mind. You should not be expressing these feelings aloud to anyone. It is not proper for someone of your standing to have an attachment to a supplicant. I beg you to keep this confidential. Get rid of Andron before he destroys you."

Zaen nodded his head. "Thank you for your counsel, Chan. I apologize for sharing such a burden with you. But you have clarified what I must do."

Chan bowed. "I am honored to serve, Your Eminence. I know you will make the correct decision."

Zaen returned to staring out of the window. "I respect your wisdom and your discretion. You may leave me now."

Chan coughed nervously. "There is one other matter. A delegation has arrived from Province Ninety-Eight. They traveled overnight to speak with you personally."

I don't need this now, Zaen thought. "Is it something you can handle?"

"One of the junior proctors assured them they could speak with you. He thought the matter serious enough to deserve your attention."

Zaen slammed his fist against the wall. "Is the proctor part of the delegation?"

"He chose to remain in the province to oversee production."

"Have him returned here. I want to meet whoever is arrogant enough to think they know my mind."

"As you wish," said Chan. "What about the delegation?"

"I suppose you should send them in. But inform them they have only five minutes of my precious time."

As Chan left the room, Zaen sat back on his throne and took five deep breaths to calm himself. Dealing with commoners was a tiresome but necessary part of his role as eminence. He had a reputation to maintain after all.

Chan returned several minutes later, ushering two men and two women to the center of the room, twenty paces from Zaen's position. He looked down at them from his throne with an expression of disdain. The four commoners looked to be in their mid-thirties and dressed in their standard work overalls. One of his staff must have cleaned the group because Zaen could smell disinfectant wafting across the room.

The four of them stood in a row, nervously fidgeting and glancing at one another.

"Is one of you going to speak?" Zaen boomed, already wishing the meeting over.

One man took a tentative step forward and bowed his head. "Your Eminence, thank you for listening to us. I know you must be very busy."

"I am busy with important matters. So get on with whatever you are here for."

"Yes, of course. Proctor Crouch said we must speak with you. The river flooded our village eight days ago. Since then, we have had no power and the crops continue to be underwater. We fear the floods have destroyed them for this season."

Zaen recalled the mention of flooding being discussed in his previous meeting, but had paid little attention to the details. So this was the province. "The gods control the weather. What are you asking of me?"

"Your Eminence, we request you permit our commune to relocate to another province. One that is not flooded."

"And what about your existing homes?"

"We will return when the waters subside. We cannot stay there now or we will starve. There are seventy-eight others in our commune. Some of them are already sick."

"Where do you think you could go? Other communes are already delivering the required production targets."

"I understand, Your Eminence. This is only a temporary solution. We could assist other provinces with their workload."

Zaen rubbed his chin. "As I understand it, you are telling me your production has been non-existent for many days and is unlikely to recover soon. You want me to allow you to diminish the work of your fellow commoners without increasing production targets. Why would I do that?"

"As you said, the floods were not our fault. We will starve and die if you do not help us."

"I won't go against the will of the gods. They sent floodwaters to your commune as a punishment. What are your sins?"

The spokesman stared with his eyes open wide as his companions shuffled behind him. "We have committed no sins. Our commune is faithful. We pray every day and have always met our targets."

"So you're now accusing the gods of making a mistake. That is blasphemy."

"No! I meant no disrespect to the gods. We are here to seek your mercy. Our children and old people will surely die without your benevolence."

Zaen stood up, surprising the delegation. "My decision is final. You shall remain in your current location and do all you can to return the land to its arable nature. If anyone dies, then that is the will of the gods and I won't challenge it."

One woman wailed loudly, irritating Zaen further. "Chief Proctor Chan, please remove these people. This audience is concluded."

"No!" shouted the spokesman. "You are sentencing us to die."

"Do not question me again," Zaen shouted, his voice echoing around the room above the noise of the wailing woman. "I am your eminence and you will respect me. Now go."

Zaen didn't wait for a response before storming out of the chamber. *Time to deal with Andron.*

Chapter 23

The sound of the siren broke Garrett's sleep three more times that first night. For the first and second times, he stayed in his recess thinking what a pitiful life the camp's inmates led. The Brotherhood professed it to be a correction center, offering a glimmer of hope to the inmates that, if they corrected their ways, the Brotherhood would allow them back into society to plow the fields and work hard on the farms. How was that a reward? In reality, this camp was nothing more than a labor camp, where the majority lived and died in appalling conditions. He was yet to see what was being mined in the camp but knew the Brotherhood used the precious metals for their own benefit. Probably trading with planets in the Stellar Cluster.

He wondered if the governments of the Stellar Cluster would act differently if they knew the source of the minerals or the conditions the people had to work in. His cynical side thought it unlikely. Even though slave labor was outlawed across all planets, he knew of instances where senior officials turned a blind eye when it suited them.

On the third sounding of the siren, a stranger leaned into his recess. "Offworlder, it's time for roll call in the kitchen."

Garrett stood up, slowly. His muscles ached from lying on hard rock all night. He performed a few quick stretches, noticing his left shoulder was tender. He pushed the irritation to the back of his mind. There was nothing he could do to ease it and, in reality, it was the least of his problems if he couldn't find a way to escape.

There was a short queue at the end of the tunnel, with people waiting patiently to step onto the conveyor belt. Small family units chatted to one another, although Garrett noticed everyone kept a healthy distance from him. He could not blame them and would be just as suspicious of a newcomer.

Eventually, it was his turn to step carefully onto a wooden plate and travel up three levels to the large room he had first entered only hours earlier. It could hardly be called a kitchen, but he guessed someone with a warped sense of humor had christened the room many years earlier. People were now shuffling forward in parallel lines between rows of wooden benches that had been unstacked overnight.

Garrett's additional height allowed him to see the front of the queues where three of Instructor Darr's men were handing out hand tools to each adult. The process was calm and efficient, with the guards carefully listing the names of each person who collected a tool. They limited the options to a hammer or a pickax. As far as Garrett could see, the choice was down to the individual.

He reached the front of the line, acutely aware he was being watched by several instructors. From nowhere, Darr stepped up and stood directly in front of Garrett.

"I trust your fellow sinners have treated you well," he sneered.

"They're a friendly group," Garrett replied, maintaining eye contact with Darr. He was well aware the instructor was trying to gain a psychological advantage, but Garrett was not one to be intimidated.

It was Darr who eventually looked away. "You'll be working on level nineteen," he said, handing Garrett a small hammer that looked like a child's toy in his hand.

"Don't I get the choice of a pickax?"

"Not until you've earned the right. Return the hammer at the end of your shift if you want to be fed."

Garrett decided not to argue, turning his back on Instructor Darr. In the same motion, he scanned the rear of the kitchen and spotted the corridor he had entered through. The vast heavy iron gate was currently open as guards carried another crate containing tools.

"There's no escape that way," Sylwester whispered in his ear.

"Has anyone tried it?" Garrett replied as he waited to return down the conveyor belt. He had failed to notice Sylwester's approach and was annoyed at himself for his latest lapse.

"Why would we try to escape?" said Sylwester with a confused expression on his face. "We have been sent here as a punishment. The only hope is that the gods will judge our penitence to be genuine, allowing us to return freely to our communes."

"But the conditions here are squalid. Why wait for the gods when you could force your way out?"

"You have strange thoughts, even for an off-worlder. They show disrespect for the gods and the Brotherhood."

The answer did not fill Garrett with hope for his escape attempt. "If you're adamant on remaining, why are there so many guards and locked gates?"

The expression on Sylwester's face made it clear he had never considered the matter. After a few seconds, he cautiously replied. "Perhaps it is to protect us from beasts on the outside. Certainly not to keep us here."

"Duly noted." Garrett was not ready to give up on his plan of escape just yet, even if the inmates showed no inclination to leave the camp. It was possible he could see opportunities that Sylwester and his fellow inmates had never considered. He told himself that someone designed the camp for the compliant inmates, not a resourceful Space Marine who had trained to be self-sufficient.

As the queue shuffled forward, Sylwester asked. "Which level are they sending you to?"

"Nineteen."

He nodded. "That makes sense. It's the most dangerous. At least four men have died in that tunnel since I arrived."

"What do I have to do down there?"

Sylwester laughed. "You dig! All day. The end of the tunnel has a thick seam of rock that is lighter in color than the tunnel walls. Dig there and you'll discover the metals that will feed you tonight."

"I don't understand."

"Fill as many baskets as you can with rocks. Then fill one bin that you'll find here." Sylwester pointed to the alcove where the rails ended. "The older children will carry the baskets for you throughout the day."

By now, they were almost at the front of the line for the conveyor belt, with people stepping onto the wooden planks in pairs. It surprised Garrett how efficient the process seemed to be, despite the old-fashioned and simplistic machinery.

"I assume the more rocks I deliver, the bigger the portion of food?"

"Exactly. I knew you'd understand. Even though you are an off-worlder. It is a fair system. But beware on level nineteen. The rocks can crumble and cause cave-ins."

Garrett followed Sylwester onto the conveyor belt and began the long, slow descent. He doubted Zaen would be happy if he knew his star prisoner was being put at risk before the trial. "Where do I find a child to help me carry the rocks?"

"Let me ask around. There may be families who are happy to divide work between their children. It's up to you how much of the food you share as payment. Remember, they won't return tomorrow if you don't sufficiently reward them."

Sylwester stepped off at level nine, leaving Garrett to continue his journey into the darker and warmer parts of the mine. As the conveyor belt rattled, his only thought was how he could escape this hellhole.

Chapter 24

Level nineteen was almost at the bottom of the conveyor belt shaft. By the time he reached it, Garrett was the only person left. Everyone else had climbed off at various levels well above this one. He had noted the different tunnels, all of which seemed similar to one another, as the conveyor belt slowly completed its descent. Only two levels seemed to be non-operational, with the tunnels hiding in thick, impenetrable darkness.

The air at this level was uncomfortably hot. Touching the walls, Garrett could feel the heat emanating from the rock. He estimated he was at least one hundred meters underground, so the geothermal heating came as little surprise. But, as he began his walk along the tunnel, he could already feel the trickle of sweat down his back.

"No wonder no one wants to work down here," he murmured, anticipating a tough day ahead.

The tunnel initially seemed to be no different from others he had seen. Lighting and ventilation pathways were installed along the roof and the walls' rough finish revealed the original miners had given less attention to this level compared to those where most of the inmates slept.

As he moved further along the tunnel, the rhythmic thrum of metal on rock from elsewhere in the camp slowly diminished. The near silence gave him a greater sense of isolation. Although he was happy with his own company, he did not enjoy the fact that his only escape route was so distant. He was still unsure whether he would get any help from the inmates who seemed resigned to their fate, making the instructors' lives incredibly easy.

He soon discovered the tunnel was not very long; only fifty meters. As he neared the end, the roof sloped down until it was barely above his head. The ground here was dusty, with piles of small dark gray rocks stacked on the side. The closest light was five meters from the tunnel end, leaving the rock face in near darkness.

Garrett walked up to the end of the tunnel, lightly rubbing his hands over the coarse surface. His eyes caught the occasional glimmer of metallic or crystalline substances. But he was no geologist and had no clue what elements the rock contained. Whatever it was clearly had some value to the

Brotherhood, although why they didn't use more efficient processes to extract the precious metal was beyond him.

He stepped away from the wall, hammer in hand, deciding if he should help the Brotherhood amass further wealth by doing their work for them. After all, they were going to convict him and sentence him to death in a few days if Zaen got his way. Refusal, however, would mean no food. Having barely survived on the rations aboard the ship that had brought him to Drani IV, plus the fact he had not eaten in over twenty-four hours, he was not at his strongest. And he would need all the strength he had if he was to complete a successful escape.

So, after a deep sigh, he began swinging his hammer at a spot on the wall that seemed to gleam more than other parts.

Several hours into his labor, Garrett heard a scuffling sound behind him. He stopped hammering away at the rock face and turned to see a small child, no more than ten years old. The child looked like a girl, but the grimy face and chopped brown hair made it difficult to be certain. Garrett leaned over and smiled. A wooden basket was hanging over her shoulders by two straps.

"What is your name?" he asked gently, deciding the child was, in fact, a young girl.

"Mercedes," the girl replied, with no hint of fear. "Sylwester said you needed my help. I brought you water."

She held out a flask, which Garrett gratefully took. "Thank you, Mercedes. It is a pleasure to meet you. How long have you lived here?"

The child looked quizzically at him. "I was told not to answer any of your questions. You must speak with Sylwester."

"I'm sorry. I only wanted to know more about you."

"There is no more. You know my name and that I live in this camp."

Garrett shrugged. "Okay, would you like to ask me any questions?"

"How much will you pay me?"

He smiled at the girl's directness. "I don't know. What is the going rate?"

Mercedes frowned as she looked at the small pile of metallic ore on the ground. "You will starve if you cannot dig more. I want half of any food you get."

"Half? That's pretty steep, kid, when it's me doing the hard work. I was thinking more like a quarter."

The child looked confidently up at him. "This is one of the lowest levels, so it will take me longer to transport the rocks to the kitchen. And I will be hungry if I get only a quarter of your reward. I will eat better elsewhere."

Mercedes turned to walk away.

"Okay, half," said Garrett. "But I'll review the rate tomorrow."

The child smiled and sat cross-legged, watching him. "Agreed."

Garrett smiled to himself. The child was smarter than many of the adults he had encountered in the camp.

"My name is Osiris."

"Yes, I know."

"You can call me Oz if you'd like."

Mercedes shrugged, seemingly unimpressed by his name or what to call him.

He returned to hammering the rock. It was hard work in the confined space of the tunnel. With little air circulating at this end of the tunnel, he was already bathed in sweat with his robe sticking to his back. Although the water Mercedes had brought had been a blessed relief, he could have easily drunk the same amount again.

"You need to swing more with your shoulders," Mercedes observed after five minutes.

"What?" he asked, sweat dripping down his nose.

"You're tapping the rock like an old person. Brace your feet and swing through the strike with your shoulders and upper body. That way you will loosen larger pieces than the flakes and pebbles currently flying off."

Now I'm getting advice from a ten-year-old!

Keeping his opinion to himself, Garrett stood as Mercedes suggested, tentatively striking the rock face with increasingly longer swings and more force. It did not take long for him to be rewarded with a fist-sized chunk falling to the ground with a resounding crunch, just missing his left foot.

"Is that better?" he scowled.

Mercedes nodded her head. "It's a start."

He turned away from her so that she could not see the grin on his face. This girl had more of an attitude than he'd had at her age. It was a shame she was confined to the instruction camp. She deserved better.

Garrett picked up the rock and turned it over in his hands. A silvery seam, the width of his finger, ran through the middle of it. Weirdly, the sight of the metallic ore gave him a moment of pleasure. Until he remembered it would end up benefiting the Brotherhood.

Cursing silently in front of Mercedes, he angrily tossed the rock into one of the baskets before once more using his hammer to loosen more rocks.

Chapter 25

During the rest of the day, Mercedes left Garrett on four occasions, taking the rocks he had collected back to the storage area in the kitchen. Each time, she returned with a flask of water that he thirstily drank while she looked on impassively.

He had never considered how back-breaking the work could be. By the end of the day, he ached all over, especially his arms and shoulders, and longed for a hot bath to ease his tired muscles and to wash away the rock dust. He imagined the only way to rinse away the dirt would be if it rained during his exercise period outside. Even the cold shower he had experienced only a day earlier would be welcome.

But the monotonous physical activity had allowed his mind to work on the options for escaping. He felt more alert than he had in days and realized that Andron and his associates must have sedated him more than he had known.

From what he had seen of the inmates, they seemed overly compliant. That could be a cultural attitude, helped by a poor diet and hard labor that would leave anyone feeling physically weak. They didn't need to be drugged to keep them in line. And, while they might not assist him with his escape attempt, he had the impression they were unlikely to hinder him either. In fact, they would probably think of his plans as a curious distraction or the mad ramblings of an off-worlder, assuming he earned their trust.

Yet he knew the chances of successfully escaping without their help were zero. If he somehow got past the instructors, the locked gates, and as far as the perimeter, where would he go? The camp was in the wilderness, hidden on the edge of a jungle and bordered by a sheer rock face.

Garrett had never reviewed maps of Drani IV. How was he supposed to find his way back to the spaceport and steal a spaceship?

He was a long way from having all the answers. Or any of the answers. The first step was to find the right people who could give him some information that would make sense. Sylwester appeared to be one of the senior inmates and had not been afraid to speak with him. Perhaps he would share his knowledge.

"It is time to finish," Mercedes said as she finished loading her basket for the last time that day.

Garrett lowered his hammer, using his forearm to wipe the sweat from his forehead. "What happens now?"

"You present your daily load to be weighed by the instructors. That will determine how much food the instructors give you. And then you give me half before you eat it all."

Garrett looked at the rocks inside the basket. Crystalline structures, like tiny veins, crisscrossed their way through the rock, glinting in the weak over-head light. "Do you know what this is?"

"I know the Brotherhood value it."

The rocks were a mystery to him too. Geology was not a core subject at the Marine academy and the deficiency had never been an issue for him. Un-til now. "Are these rocks the same on each level?"

Mercedes shook her head. "There is gold on levels eleven and twelve. I think that is what it's called. The other levels have different minerals, but I do not know their names. You will have to ask the old men. They will tell you what you want to know."

She turned and skipped back along the tunnel, with Garrett following behind.

Mercedes was waiting for him when he finally arrived at the kitchen, his shoulders and back screaming from the day's exercise. Looking around the large room, no one else seemed to be as breathless as he was. They were stand-ing around in small groups or, for the children, sitting patiently on the bench-es, presumably waiting to be fed.

Fewer people were staring at him this time. Garrett searched the room for Sylwester, hoping to grab an immediate word, but he was nowhere in sight.

Through the crowd of inmates, he saw Mercedes enthusiastically waving at him with both arms. She was standing next to a waist-high wooden bin, one of many lined up near the wall next to the track. He estimated there had to be close to forty bins, none of which had been there at the start of the day.

"This bin is yours," she said as he ambled up to her.

He glimpsed inside, disappointed to see the bin was less than a third full. Compared to some of the fuller bins nearby, it wasn't an impressive return for his day's labor. "I see what you mean," he said, resigned to remaining hungry.

"You did alright, Oz. For your first day. Some of these bins are for families where more than one person has filled it."

"Where is your family's bin?"

Mercedes' expression darkened. "My family is dead," she said coldly, wiping away a single tear.

"I'm sorry. Who takes care of you?"

"Everyone," she replied, pointing around the room. "There are two other orphans like me. We help whoever wants it."

Garrett looked at the room of people with a newfound sense of respect. Despite the conditions they found themselves in, they had a strong bond and a sense of wholesome goodness that he sometimes found lacking in the Stellar Cluster. It was refreshing to witness. He doubted he would be as resolute if he were there for years. Luckily, he would never find out.

It was then that he saw a pair of instructors heading toward him. His body tensed, waiting for them to attack him or try to take him away. The inmates stepped back, creating a path through the kitchen.

"Stand to the side," the first instructor ordered, looking up at him.

The instruction briefly confused Garrett until Mercedes said. "He wants to read the scales. They're behind you."

He hadn't noticed the bins were standing on low plinths. Feeling stupid, he saw a display on the plinth but could not decipher the symbols.

The instructor copied the symbols onto a piece of thick paper and handed it to Garrett before moving on to another bin.

"What now?"

"Give that number to the instructors at the front. Make sure you ask for two bowls."

As Garrett moved through the throng, the slightly better aroma of food replaced the stale smell of body odor. His stomach rumbled at the prospect of eating; it had been several days since his last meal. He spotted a large cast-iron vat with two more instructors standing next to it, measuring out food portions to a short queue of people.

Two minutes later, he was standing in front of an instructor, handing over the slip of paper. The instructor looked at the symbols before staring back at Garrett. For several moments, he wondered if this was another pun-ishment and the instructors wanted him to miss out on the meal.

"Is everything okay?" he asked, ready to fight for his dinner if he had to. He had to eat. Plus, it was unfair to punish Mercedes after her help.

"Hand over your hammer," the instructor replied, his monotone voice cold and dripping with disdain.

Damn hammer! He had forgotten he was still holding it. Handing it to the second instructor, Garrett was relieved to see the first one picking up a carved wooden bowl and scooping out a measure of stew from the vat.

"Can I have a second bowl for my helper?" he asked, taking the full bowl from the instructor.

"Did you say something?"

"Yes, I had a helper today. I need a second bowl so that I can share my meal."

"You need to learn some respect, off-worlder. When you speak to me or my fellow instructors, you will refer to us as sir."

Another authoritarian, Garrett thought. He knew the drill though. He had seen it too often. At any other time, he would have picked up the man and thrown him across the room. But now wasn't the time for knee-jerk re-actions.

"Of course. I'm sorry, sir. Please, may I have a second bowl? Sir." The em-phasis on the last word was stronger than he had intended, but he knew an apology would only make the matter worse.

The instructor glared at him for several seconds before handing him an-other bowl.

"Thank you, sir," Garrett said, before taking the food to Mercedes, who was now sitting on a table next to Sylwester.

"Any trouble?" Sylwester asked.

He shrugged. "A simple misunderstanding. Thanks for sending Mercedes to me today. She has been a godsend."

He passed the bowls to her so that she could share the food, smiling as he noticed she left him with more than half the stew.

Sylwester finished his own meal. "The instructors are paying you close at-tention. I have not seen them this way with anyone else."

That's interesting, Garrett thought. He had assumed their level of apprehension was normal. "How many instructors are there at any time?"

"Six," Sylwester replied without hesitation. "There are twelve in total, on rotation."

Garrett thought that sounded about right for such a compliant population. Through years of conditioning, riots and escape attempts were not risks to be worried about. That was good news for him. "Where do they stay when not on duty?"

"There are barracks on the way to the main entrance. You can see it from the exercise yard. There's also a warehouse and a garage for the vehicles."

"Anyone else? A cook?"

Sylwester shrugged. "Not that I know of. We've only ever seen the instructors. Oh, and Warden Stagg."

"There is one more thing on my mind. Last night, you and your friends were holding tools. Did you steal them?"

"The instructors are not as smart as they think. Over the years, inmates have retained the odd item. The hammers are not the best quality and would break if used to break rock."

"Then why do you have them? None of you are planning a prison break."

"It's good to break the rules occasionally, don't you think?"

Garrett smiled. Maybe the inmates weren't quite as compliant as he had thought. He glanced down at his bowl of food, thinking the variety of vegetables was maybe more appealing than he had realized. The first mouthful soon put paid to that illusion, but that didn't stop him from thinking more positively about his chances of escape.

Chapter 26

Eminence Zaen was resting in the cloister when Chief Proctor Chan politely coughed to make his presence known.

"Your Eminence, Warden Stagg is waiting in the main hall."

Zaen continued reading his book for several more seconds before resting it face down on his lap. "Tell him I will be with him shortly."

Chan bowed and departed, leaving Zaen to his thoughts. The cold air made his bones ache, despite the thick layers of clothing he had chosen for his morning meditation. He knew these were the twilight years of his life and recognized that more days were behind him than in front. Which was why every hour was precious and why it thrilled him to know Osiris Garrett was going to face justice within a matter of days. With Garrett's imminent death, his revenge would be complete, allowing him to focus entirely on fulfilling his ambition of becoming Chief Elder.

Pieces of the puzzle were falling into place and, with it, an inner calm he had not felt for many years.

His closest contacts had advised he was being considered for prominence, having proved his tenacity and thirst for greatness. The power and respect the Elders wielded were what he yearned for. And, as he reminded himself each day, what he deserved. While he never considered himself to be one of the most devout members of the Brotherhood, he was adamant there was no one more zealous at meting out the religion's doctrines and punishments. That was what made him the outstanding candidate, he told himself.

Zaen waited a further ten minutes before walking back inside. It felt good to make the warden wait. Stagg may be in charge of Instruction Camp Four, but he was a nobody in this palace. Having to wait in a drafty hall would be a suitable reminder of his position within the Brotherhood. And of Zaen's absolute authority.

He met with Stagg in his throne room. Zaen had decorated it in lavish velvet with gold inlays and high ceilings painted with depictions of scenes from the Bible. It was a stark contrast from the instruction camp and a symbol of the disparity in the warden's stature to the eminence.

As a final touch, Zaen ordered a servant to bring him a tall glass of necta, his preferred alcoholic refreshment. The very exclusive drink had a strong, unique aroma that he knew would swiftly fill the room.

Two minutes later, Chief Proctor Chan entered the room, followed closely by Warden Stagg. "Your Eminence, as requested, I present Warden Stagg," Chan pronounced, stopping ten paces in front of Zaen.

Stagg took one more step and bowed. "Your Eminence."

Zaen looked down from his throne at the two men. "Thank you, Chan. You may leave us."

"As you please," he replied, slowly retreating before closing the immense paneled doors behind him.

Zaen continued to study Stagg and was pleased to see the warden looking both uncomfortable and irritated.

"Thank you for coming at such short notice, Warden Stagg."

Forcing a gracious smile, the warden said, "How can I refuse such an honored request from Your Eminence."

"Quite so. I assume you know why I asked you here today."

"Garrett?"

Good, the man isn't as stupid as they warned me. "Precisely. Any signs of trouble since he arrived three days ago?"

"Nothing out of the ordinary for a new prisoner. He is asking the inmates many questions, wanting to know how the camp is guarded."

"No doubt planning an escape. Of course he is. He knows our courts will sentence him to death extremely soon. He has nothing to lose."

"I assure you, he will not be successful should he try to escape."

Zaen nodded his head. "I have the utmost faith in you and your men. More than I do in the Elders' ability to act with any haste." Zaen took a long drink of necta to calm his temper. As he felt the warm, soothing liquid slide down his throat, the aroma threatened to overpower his senses.

"Your Eminence, I take it you don't have a trial date set."

Zaen sighed loudly. "The Elders, in their infinite wisdom, are refusing to prioritize my request. It may be another few days before I have all the pieces in place. I want this trial to be magnificent. After all, it is going to be shared with those fools in the Stellar Cluster. This is going to be the ultimate show trial. They will know my name across the entire human population. And those savages will know not to cross me or the Brotherhood."

"Of course they will. The Stellar Cluster will learn to fear Your Eminence."

Zaen stared thoughtfully at Stagg, unsure if the man was being ironic. It was difficult to tell.

"Has Garrett made any friends since he arrived?"

"My men have noted he is often with the same group. We identify none of them as troublemakers."

Zaen thought for a moment, rubbing his chin. "Perhaps he is also mixing with other factions within your camp without your knowledge."

"No one else in the camp has ever caused any trouble. There is the occasional fight among the sinners but my instructors have never seen the need to intervene." Stagg stood straight, proud of his history.

The warden's pompous attitude riled Zaen. He knew Stagg must have heard the tales of violence and unrest from other camps and wanted to prove his superiority.

"Do you think maybe you are too easy on your sinners?"

Stagg looked puzzled. "They work up to fourteen-hour days, every day, on one meal a day. Yet they consistently exceed their ore quotas. My camp is the most profitable one you have. What more would you have me do?"

"Drive them harder, of course. Have you considered you're becoming too complacent?"

"Your Eminence, I would welcome a visit by you to see what I have achieved. Perhaps you could use us as a model for other instruction camps. Particularly the ones failing to hit their targets."

Zaen smiled. "That sounds an excellent idea. I will have one of my proctors arrange it." He had no intention of going near such a despicable place as an instruction camp. It was full of foul-smelling sinners, most of whom were beyond redemption. But he enjoyed the brief look of horror that passed across Stagg's face.

"I would be honored," the ashen warden replied through clenched teeth.

"In the meantime, ensure that Garrett stays unharmed. I've no use for a corpse. When he appears in front of the Elders, I want him looking wretched. Ideally, I would like a confession out of him."

Stagg nodded vigorously. "Garrett will be in perfect condition for the trial. You have my word."

"That's all I wanted to know. You may leave now."

Chief Proctor Chan suddenly reappeared at the far end of the room. Meanwhile, Stagg looked up at Zaen. "Was that all you wanted from me?"

"I hope you're not questioning why I asked that I see you in person."

Stagg quickly recovered his poise, realizing he had overstepped the mark. "No, of course not, Your Eminence. I am most grateful that you could spare your valuable time with me." He bowed before turning and allowing Chan to show him out.

What a strange man, Zaen thought to himself. Although it pleased him to put the warden in his place, there was something about the man's arrogant attitude that unnerved him. Was Stagg too complacent? Zaen briefly considered if maybe he was losing his own nerve; the importance of Garrett's trial had not gone unnoticed inside the palace.

Each additional day waiting for the trial was a wasted opportunity. There was nothing in his schedule that was more important, and he would not rest until he had witnessed Garrett's execution.

Chapter 27

It was early evening when Warden Stagg arrived back in his office. The last hour of his journey back from Zaen's palace had been completed in darkness and heavy rain, far from ideal conditions on the unforgiving and badly maintained road, which had only increased his bad mood.

The day had been a complete waste of his time. Although a private audience with the eminence was highly prized by many, Stagg was not a fan of Zaen. He knew too many unsavory truths about the man who regarded himself as the shining example of what the Brotherhood stood for. Stagg had utter faith in the religion but could not comprehend how, if the gods used the Brotherhood to spread their word, could they allow such a twisted, corrupt sexual deviant to be in a position of power?

Stagg slammed his fist down hard on his desk. The lecherous old man had made him go to his palace. Refusal was never an option. Not if he valued his career and his life. It was a ridiculous abuse of power.

"I heard you had returned," said Head Instructor Darr, turning up in the doorway. "Did the eminence show his appreciation for your loyal service?"

Stagg beckoned him into the office. "Hardly. The old fool treated me as nothing more than an errand boy. An eight-hour round trip to be told something he could have told me over the radio. He thinks we are all at his beck and call."

"We are," Darr said, with no hint of irony.

"The advantage of privilege," Stagg muttered under his breath. While he was grateful for his position as an instruction camp warden, he had never fully bought into the trappings associated with the senior Brotherhood officials. Their exploitation of the masses through religion was palpable and corrosive. Yet their grip on power was absolute. At least he wasn't working in the fields like so many others.

"What did he want? Has he discovered what we're doing?"

"No need to worry about that. Zaen is only concerned about Garrett and his precious trial. He ordered me to ensure Garrett is ready to face the Elders whenever they are ready."

Darr rolled his eyes. "What does Zaen think we're going to do with him?"

"I don't know. I get the impression he believes we are underestimating the ingenuity of the man. Zaen is worried Garrett will escape or die trying, either of which will void a trial. He's staking his reputation on this moment."

"That's ridiculous. I hope you told him."

"Darr, you don't tell the eminence anything he doesn't want to hear. I reminded Zaen of our record compared to the other instruction camps, but I don't think that changed his mind. The pompous fool even had the audacity to tell me how to do my job. He thinks we're too soft on the sinners."

"I hope he's not thinking of replacing you," said Darr, leaning in close. "That would screw our plans entirely."

The thought hadn't crossed Stagg's mind. But something in Darr's words rang true. What if today's audience was a statement by Zaen that his role as warden depended on getting Garrett to court in one piece? He knew what failure would mean. An execution squad if he was lucky, or a life sentence in his own instruction camp.

"Do we have any worries about Garrett?"

Darr scratched the top of his head, deep in thought. "He's up to something. I'm sure of it. The fact he's acting as a model sinner is an obvious sign. Since he arrived, he has not put a foot wrong. He is already smashing his daily production targets and has challenged none of the instructors."

Stagg looked confused. "Isn't that good? Perhaps he has accepted his fate."

"A possibility, but unlikely. He isn't like our people. I've seen his record. He's a soldier and a leader. Garrett will not lie down and die without a fight. My best guess is he's lulling us into a false sense of security while he probes our instructors for a weakness. I guarantee one month's salary that he will attempt an escape in the next week."

Stagg knew to trust Darr's instincts. "We simply can't have that. Garrett might be killed in an escape attempt. I cannot have a situation where we lose control of his actions."

"No need to worry. I can arrange a small demonstration for Garrett. Just to let him know we're watching him."

This was the news Stagg wanted to hear, lifting his mood after a depressingly wasteful day. Of course, there was no need to know the specifics. Darr would see to that. "Very good. You know what's at stake. Keep Garrett in line so that Zaen can have his day in the spotlight. I want no harm to befall our star guest."

Darr stood, ready to leave. "Very good, sir. I'll let you know when the message has been delivered."

Left alone once again, Stagg leaned back in his chair, feeling at ease with life. He knew he had been lucky to find a kindred spirit in the chief instructor. Only another six months and their own plan would come to fruition. No one was going to screw it up.

Chapter 28

After the daily meal, Sylwester rode the conveyor down to Level Five, making sure that Garrett was not following him. While he had grown to admire the off-worlder, it was time to share the information he had obtained from the man with strange ideas.

Level five was the least occupied area of the camp. The tunnel went on far deeper than any other level and, uniquely, snaked its way through the bedrock rather than remaining straight. Almost two hundred meters along, the tunnel forked in two directions. The tunnel to the left was only ten meters long and barely wide enough for two people to stand side by side. Whoever had created it in the distant past realized there was nothing worth digging and had abandoned the effort.

But that didn't mean the tunnel was empty.

This was Rosa's domain.

Sylwester walked past a small group of men and women, talking wearily to each other. He knew them all and waved hello without needing to stop and chat with them. Their topic of conversation was bound to be the newcomer.

He slowed as he entered the smaller tunnel. The lighting was not as good as the main tunnel, and he did not want to trip over a misplaced foot or leg in the semi-darkness.

"Good evening, Syl. I was wondering when you would come to me," a voice called out from the shadows.

Sylwester stopped. "I'm sorry, Rosa. The man isn't a simple person to understand, or to slip away from. It has taken me longer than I expected."

"Come and sit with me. You can tell me all about him."

He edged forward until he saw Rosa sitting on a pile of blankets in her recess. As always, she had tied her hair up in a strange fashion none of the other women copied. Her eyes sparkled despite the meager lighting, and she had a kindly face.

As he sat down cross-legged next to Rosa, he offered her a small bowl. "I brought you some stew. I had a productive day in my tunnel."

She took the bowl from him, sniffing the contents. He knew it was a habit of hers; the stew never changed.

"Thank you, Syl," she said, before taking a mouthful. "Vegetables! What a pleasant change."

"You will be first to know if the instructors learn to cook anything else."

Rosa smiled. "Tell me about the new man, Garrett. Is he who he declares himself to be?"

"If Oz Garrett is a spy, then he is an excellent actor. He is definitely an off-worlder. It's clear he's not used to manual labor, and he constantly talks about his beloved life in the Stellar Cluster. I've only met one other person like him."

"Be cautious, Syl. He may be an off-worlder, but that doesn't mean he's not a paid mercenary. All men have their price and Zaen has more than enough credits to offer a reward sufficient for the most scrupulous of people to move in here."

"I honestly don't think he's looking for you if that's your concern."

"But you don't know for sure. None of us do. I trust your judgment though."

Sylwester nodded in acceptance of the compliment. "If he is lying, he will give himself away, eventually. No one can keep up the pretense for days on end in these conditions. We're observing him constantly."

"What does Mercedes think?"

"The child? She speaks honestly. She says Garrett is a fool, but she likes him. He looks after her and treats her fairly. I've never seen Mercedes take to another person like she has with Garrett."

"Interesting. What is Garrett's excuse for being here?"

"Eminence Zaen's revenge. Several years ago, Garrett was part of an illegal mission on Drani III. He was captured and brought to this planet where he later escaped. He stole Zaen's spaceship, realizing too late that the eminence was aboard. Zaen recently sent a snatch squad into the Stellar Cluster to kidnap Garrett so he can face trial by the Elders."

Rosa nodded. "I vaguely recall rumors of a senior Brotherhood dignitary turning up on a transit hub. The Brotherhood suppressed the stories, so the truth was never made public. Perhaps that was Zaen."

Sylwester's expression was blank. "I would be surprised if Eminence Zaen allowed himself to get into such a position. Although Garrett's account is convincing, how can one man kidnap such an important person?"

"I like your skepticism, Syl. Never lose it. Does Garrett believe he is going to die?"

"He knows what his fate will be when there is a trial. I wouldn't say he's accepted it."

"In what way?"

"He is asking way too many questions about the camp and the instructors. It's as though he wants to escape."

Rosa laughed out loud. "Of course he does. Assuming he is telling the truth, he's not going to simply wait around for the inevitable to happen. I guarantee he is plotting his way out of here as we speak."

"Isn't that selfish?"

"Absolutely. I don't think he will have considered the collateral damage. Whether he succeeds or fails, there will be repercussions."

Sylwester shuffled nervously on the blankets. He had not considered the effects of an escape attempt. Privately, he was excited at the thought, even if it was doomed to failure.

"Bring him to me tomorrow. It's time I finally met the man and tell him how it is in this camp."

"And if he refuses to accept our ways?"

Rosa grinned. "As you said, he is only one man. I'm sure you and your friends can persuade Garrett. We can't have him risk what we have established."

Sylwester made his way back along the tunnel, his mind churning with possibilities at the prospect of Rosa interrogating Garrett. Although Garrett's story had convinced him of the man's truth, Rosa would uncover any lies. Frowning, he considered the options if she found Garrett to be a spy? It had not ended well for the previous man sent in by the warden.

Chapter 29

Garrett's day was not going well. The infection in his left shoulder had flared up again during the night due either to the increased physical activity or the humid conditions of the mine. A quick look at his shoulder, and the angry red inflammation, told him all he needed to know. It was a matter of time before Dr. Cassidy's prediction came true.

An escape attempt within the next week was essential. Any longer and there was now a real danger of the infection leading to a fever, or worse, his arm ceasing to operate. However, he still hadn't formulated an effective plan to get out of the camp.

He was confident he could overpower the instructors to gain a key to get him through the first heavy gate. After that, he did not know how to reach the vehicle compound without alerting the instructors. He cursed himself for not paying more attention during his arrival. The hood had not helped, but he was determined to learn more if he ever had another opportunity.

He knew he could not succeed on his own. As well as additional intel on what lay beyond the first gate, he was going to need a distraction. That required help. Although Sylwester had shown the occasional hint of a rebellious side, Garrett wasn't sure the man was willing to put his life at risk. And even if Sylwester did help, that still wouldn't be enough. The task seemed almost insurmountable.

That didn't mean escape was impossible.

He had attempted to speak with Sylwester when collecting his hammer earlier that morning but had noticed the instructors were paying him more attention than usual. The conversation would have to wait for the privacy of the tunnels after the daily meal. Assuming his arm did not get worse in the meantime.

"You don't look well," said Mercedes as she collected the latest batch of rocks in her basket.

Garrett paused to wipe sweat from his forehead. "It's nothing," he lied. Sleep deprivation was not helping. He now fully appreciated how disruptive the two-hourly siren was. His body felt heavy and slow, and he suspected he was far more irritable than normal.

"I'll bring you more water," she said, strapping the basket to her shoulders.

"Can you find Sylwester and let him know I have to speak with him?"

Mercedes cocked her head to one side. "You can talk to him at mealtime."

"I know. But I want our conversation to be private. The instructors have been watching me in the kitchen. They must see that I talk with him all the time."

"Yes, I have noticed too. I think the instructors are scared of you."

"And so they should be. But I really do need to speak with Sylwester. It's urgent."

Mercedes nodded her head. "Okay. I will let him know."

"Thank you."

Garrett palmed the hammer in his right hand and smashed the rock in front of him once more. The loud thud reverberated along the tunnel, making his head ache. In fact, his whole body hurt. Blisters on his right hand had not had time to heal and although the skin on his artificial left hand was incapable of blistering, the pain in his shoulder was almost unbearable.

A while later, Garrett heard movement behind him. Expecting to see Mercedes or Sylwester, he turned to face three instructors holding axes and looking menacing.

"Is this part of the formal induction?" he asked, squaring up to them. Instinctively, he knew he was in a vulnerable position. Trapped at the end of a tunnel. The three instructors knew what they were doing, keeping a sufficient distance from one another to allow each of them to wield their weapon should Garrett decide to attack.

"You could say that," the middle instructor sneered. Garrett recognized him as the one who recorded the weight of the bins every evening. The other two were the instructors who served food. He had not attempted to learn their names.

"What can I help you with?"

"We've been watching you. And to be honest, we don't like your attitude."

"Is it because I shouldn't really be here? You all know this is a dreadful mistake. I'm innocent."

The three instructors glanced at each other and laughed. "All sinners say that when they first arrive. It can take up to several years for them to confront their sins and accept the way of the Brotherhood."

"I don't think I have that long."

"We have heard you don't attend the mandatory prayer sessions," said a second instructor.

"Religion is not my thing. But if you want to believe in almighty gods, then I will not stop you."

As the three instructors moved closer, Garrett crouched with his hammer above his head, ready to defend himself.

The lead instructor raised his ax. "That attitude will not help you, off-worlder. We demand nothing less than complete compliance from all the sinners in this camp. What we don't want is anyone causing unrest. People can get hurt."

Garrett decided there had been enough talking. The instructors still had not made their intentions clear, but he wasn't about to let them maintain their advantage. And he wanted to test how proficient they were with their axes. Confident they didn't have instructions from Zaen or Darr to kill him, he lunged for the lead instructor.

Keeping low, Garrett swung his hammer in a long arc, catching the instructor's knee with a glancing blow. The instructor froze for a fraction of a second, the unexpected attack taking him by surprise. Yelling in pain, he brought his ax down, but it was too late. As the sharp ax head bit into the rocky floor, Garrett was already rolling and moving onto the second instructor.

The years of Marine training came flooding back to Garrett. But, although everything around him appeared to be happening in slow motion, he was only too aware his reflexes were not what they used to be in his youth.

However, he could still rise and strike a blow to the instructor's ribs. The resounding cracking of bones was almost drowned out by the man's screams. Garrett was too busy focused on the third instructor to take any notice.

This man had seen what was happening and had assumed a defensive pose. Garrett rushed forward, swinging the hammer with all his might. This time, the instructor's reactions were quick. He used the handle of his ax to block the blow, knocking the hammer from Garrett's hand. The hammer flew down the tunnel, crashing into the wall well out of reach.

Cursing, Garrett ducked to his left, hoping to catch the instructor off balance, but again, the man was too fast. Garrett had to use all his agility to dodge the ax swinging toward his legs.

The second instructor sank to his knees, coughing up blood and dropping his weapon. Garrett saw it in his peripheral vision. This was exactly what he needed.

Ducking under another blow from the third instructor, Garrett moved to his left and reached for the fallen ax. However, a heavy kick from the lead instructor was enough to knock him off balance. Rolling over, his hand just failed to grab the ax.

Getting back to his feet, he squared off once more against the remaining two instructors. Rage filled their faces as they stalked toward him.

"This is why you need to be taught a lesson," sneered the first instructor.

Garrett took two deep breaths to remain calm. There was an element of fear in the men's eyes. They had probably never faced off against someone with advanced military training. He had seen the look of bullies who were great at dishing out beatings, but unprepared to accept them. It was what he had suspected. And what gave him some hope.

Impaired by his injured leg, the lead instructor held slightly back. "Take him out, Gabe," he yelled.

The second instructor immediately attacked, his movements quick but erratic. Garrett stepped back, out of reach of the flailing ax, causing his attacker to scream in frustration. The instructor sped forward, intent on landing a heavy blow. This was the moment Garrett had been waiting for. Allowing the ax to miss his head by centimeters, he rushed in. The momentum of the swing took the instructor off balance, leaving his right side exposed. Enough for Garrett to use his left hand to deliver a devastating uppercut to the man's jaw.

The effect was instant, with the man dropping to his knees, dazed and unable to continue the battle.

But the move had left Garrett temporarily exposed. The lead instructor wielded his ax, hitting Garrett firmly on his right side, just below his ribs. Garrett gripped the ax handle, gritting his teeth to deal with the pain coursing down his side. He threw one punch, hitting the instructor firmly on the chin before his legs buckled and he sank to his knees.

The instructor reeled backward, harshly pulling his bloody ax from Garrett's side.

"You weren't supposed to kill the bastard," Garrett heard the third instructor's voice.

"He's not dead."

"For now, maybe. That wound will not heal itself."

"What was I supposed to do? I was acting in self-defense. It was him or us."

"Is that what you'll tell Darr?"

"It's the truth, Gabe. You saw what happened. I expect you to back me up. I just saved your life."

Garrett heard the voices as a distant echo. Delicately touching his side, he felt the sticky warm blood on his clothes and immediately understood how much trouble he was in. With the intense pain, he knew he was going to pass out. A sharp blow to the side of his head, however, saved him from further pain as he slumped to the floor, unconscious.

Chapter 30

Mercedes had been emptying her basket into Garrett's bin when she spotted the three instructors marching through the kitchen and stepping onto the conveyor belt, one after another. It was a rare event for any instructor to venture into the tunnels. There was something about their deliberate strides and tense body language that told her she needed to tell somebody.

Sylwester was digging in his normal plot on level nine, about two hundred meters from the conveyor. A knee-high pile of rock was already waiting to be collected by his helper for the day. As he heard someone sprint up behind him, he stopped mid-swing, allowing the pickax to drop to his side.

"Mercedes, what's wrong?"

Mercedes waited a moment to catch her breath. "I saw three instructors take the conveyor to the lower levels," she panted.

Sylwester didn't need to guess which level they would be targeting. Whenever the instructors made an unannounced inspection, it never ended well for those involved.

"Who were the instructors?"

"Gabe, Cylus, and Melf. And they looked angry."

Three of Darr's most trusted instructors. Sylwester had witnessed several occasions when two of them had taken a sinner to one side, only to inflict their own type of justice. He had never seen three of them act together. But then, Garrett was bigger and stronger than anyone else in the camp. The instructors would want to ensure their superiority.

There was nothing he, nor anyone else in the camp, could do to prevent what the instructors were going to do with Garrett. Intervention of any kind would only result in punishments for those stupid enough to defy the will of the instructors. All that Syl could hope for was that Garrett survived.

"Thanks, Mercedes. Stay with me for now. It's safer for you here."

She nodded and sat cross-legged, rocking slowly back and forth.

"Syl, will Oz be okay?" Mercedes asked as he was about to take another swing at the rock face. "He wanted me to tell you he needed to speak with you urgently."

"What about?"

"He didn't say. But I know it was important"

Sylwester rubbed his chin. Three against one were never fair odds, but Garrett had shown he could handle himself. How good a fighter he was had yet to be determined. And what was the instructors' intent? Was this just a warning or something more serious? Cylus was one of the meanest instructors, second only to Darr himself.

He smiled kindly down at Mercedes. "I'm sure Oz is perfectly safe. He's a big, tough fighter."

"He told me he used to be a soldier. In the Space Marines, they taught him how to kill the enemy with guns and knives," she replied excitedly.

"There you go then. I told you he can look after himself."

"But what about the instructors? We will all be in trouble if he hurts one of them."

"Oz knows that. I'm sure they will just be having a talk. No one will be harmed. You did the right thing coming to me though."

The answer seemed to placate Mercedes. She continued rocking back and forth, humming a random tune under her breath while Sylwester pondered what he should do. He knew he couldn't go straight down to level nineteen. The instructors would not accept any intervention from the sinners. He would only make matters worse for everyone.

"Mercedes, can you go hide near the conveyor and watch out for the instructors to return? Come straight back here once they've passed. Then I can go have that talk Oz wants."

She skipped away along the tunnel, leaving Sylwester to contemplate informing Rosa. She would surely want to know the instructors had invaded their space. If Garrett was attracting unwanted attention, it may only be a matter of time before the instructors accidentally stumbled on Rosa's location.

And he knew that would be bad for everyone.

Chapter 31

Garrett stirred, vaguely aware he was lying on his back, and that the pain had eased. In fact, his whole body felt numb. Startled by the realization, he opened his eyes, expecting to see the instructors standing over him, waiting to finish him off.

Instead, he found himself in one of the family recesses, although it wasn't the one he had been using to sleep in. Sensing movement to his right, he slowly turned his head to see who was with him. At the same time, he tried and failed to lift an arm to defend himself. The best he managed was a strangled grunt.

"Lay still," a woman's voice commanded from the shadows.

"Who are you?"

"Your savior, Mr. Garrett! I'm halfway through sewing up the hole in your side. If you want me to finish, do as I ask. There will be plenty of time for questions."

The woman leaned forward to get a better view of his wound. Her face was now visible in the low light of the recess. The woman's graying hair was pulled tightly away from her face and tied neatly in a bun. From the wrinkles around her eyes and on her forehead, he placed her at around fifty years of age, give or take ten years. Dirt, malnutrition, and living in permanent darkness had played havoc with her skin.

Garrett had known enough medics to know this woman had received medical training. He was also aware not to argue with anyone pulling a needle through his skin. Forcing himself to relax, he stared back up at the rough ridges of the roof, the tool marks clearly visible. He tried to recall if he had seen the woman before, but her face was not familiar. How many other people had he not seen in the camp?

He briefly wondered if the instructors had sent her in to keep him alive for Zaen, but she was wearing the same drab clothing as everyone else. Except maybe her robe was a little cleaner. Hopefully, she would stay around to answer his questions.

Five minutes later, the woman sat back up, moving away from him. "Okay, Mr. Garrett, I'm done. I think you'll live," she said, with no hint of self-importance. "I would suggest you stay there for a while to recover and allow the effects of the anesthetic to wear off."

He doubted whether he could stand anyway. His limbs still felt leaden. "Thank you. You know my name. What is yours?"

"Rosa Palma."

"It's a pleasure to meet you, Rosa. And thank you for saving my life."

"You have Sylwester to thank for that, Mr. Garrett. I only patched you up."

"Thanks anyway," Garrett replied, making a mental note to thank Sylwester at the earliest opportunity. "You have a familiar accent. Where are you from?"

She frowned. "Like you, I'm originally from the Stellar Cluster. From a small village on Nesta, actually."

Garrett flinched. He had been in the Lafayette army that had battled Nestan forces for many months. It had been a bloody war where he had lost too many friends and recruits. There had been no winner in the end. But that was many years before, and most people on both sides had learned to forgive.

"You must have a story to find yourself here. I thought I was the only off-worlder."

"It is a long story," she replied. "Not one I'm prepared to share with you at this time. I want to know what happened to you."

"Today or prior to me arriving in this hellhole?"

"Today will do. You can start by telling me why Cylus and his fellow instructors attempted to kill you?"

"I don't know. They took me by surprise."

"They must have said something to you. Unless you provoked them."

Garrett recalled the fight, remembering the string of events and what the instructors had said. Although the fight had lasted a matter of seconds, it seemed like it had taken place in slow motion. Walking it through in his head, he felt he had done the best he could have against three men with better weapons.

"I think it was supposed to be a warning. To quash any ideas I had of escaping the camp."

"Some warning! That wound in your side is deep. It's a miracle the blade missed all of your internal organs. You could easily have died."

"Are you a doctor or nurse?"

Rosa sighed. "In a former life, I was an army medic. So no need to worry. I know what I'm doing. At least I'm not dealing with severed limbs or shrapnel wounds."

"How did you take care of me down here? Where did you get the medical supplies?"

Rosa shrugged her shoulders. "The children are very resourceful. They have been collecting supplies from the instructors' stores. Don't ask me how they get inside. And you will find that some of the instructors can be bribed with gold nuggets or favors of the flesh."

Garrett raised an eyebrow.

"Don't be surprised. The Brotherhood's followers may be religious zealots, but they're still human. It does mean I've been able to accumulate a wide range of medical supplies while I've been here. It's a good job too, otherwise, you'd be dead."

He knew he could not dispute the fact. He had believed the pickax blow was fatal. "I've not seen you in the kitchen. Do you always remain down here?"

"I'm lucky. The people here accepted me quickly. When they knew I could treat their medical issues, we came to an arrangement. I don't enjoy digging for rocks." She held up her hands. "These are delicate. Manual work will harm my fingers. So I act as a one-person hospital in return for provisions. Each person takes turns to provide food, so it's a minor inconvenience for them."

The symbiotic relationship she had established with the prisoners impressed Garrett. "How long have you been here?"

Rosa shrugged. "I honestly don't know. You'll get to appreciate the passage of time is relative down here. Every day is the same."

Garrett shook his head. "If Zaen gets his way, I won't be around for long."

"I heard what you did."

"Which version?"

"The Brotherhood's."

"I thought as much. I'm sure you're smart enough to not believe everything you hear."

"What's your version of the truth?"

Although the events had happened several years earlier, Garrett could remember them as if they had occurred only a week earlier. Recalling them never lessened the pain. "My squad was in this sector on a covert mission. We knew it was illegal, but we were here to apprehend a criminal from the Stellar Cluster. There was a large bounty on his head and so we bent the rules."

"Is that what you normally do?"

"Only when I have to," he replied with a wry smile. "This time, we were misled. It was a mistake. People died, and I lost my arm."

"I thought you had lost that in battle. The tattoo on your right shoulder gives you away as a Space Marine."

Garrett wondered how much he should share with Rosa. She was a stranger, after all. But how could he make matters any worse for himself?

"To cut a long story short, I escaped this planet in Eminence Zaen's spaceship. I didn't know he was aboard and, once I discovered him, there was no turning back."

Rosa burst into an unexpected fit of laughter. "I would have loved to see his face. That was unlucky for you though. Why didn't you kill him when you had the chance?"

"That's not my style. Zaen was an innocent party to my escape. I released him when we reached a transit hub. That now feels like one of the biggest mistakes of my life. Followed closely by being captured and kidnapped by one of his sycophants."

By now, the effect of the painkillers was wearing off. Although sensation was returning to his limbs, a sharp pain was spreading down his right side. There was also a dull ache returning to his left shoulder. Rosa must have noticed his discomfort.

"Do you need more pain relief? I assume you know the graft is infected. The drugs I've given you will help for a while."

"I wouldn't say no."

"I'm sorry I don't have neuro-blockers. The Brotherhood has not developed sophisticated medications. At least not for the general population. In fact, my stock is probably better than you'd find in most communes."

Garrett felt a needle in his side, followed by a warm, numbing feeling spreading through that area of his body. "Is that a syringe?" he asked in disbelief.

"I told you it was old school. Crude but effective. It's the same with the stitches. I've no skin-grafting nanotech, so you will have an ugly scar."

"It's a small price to pay for staying alive."

Garrett suddenly felt weary. There was a brief realization that Rosa had injected him with more than just a painkiller before his eyes closed and he fell into a deep sleep.

Chapter 32

The three instructors looked woeful as they stood unsteadily in front of Chief Instructor Darr in the instructors' mess hall. Cylus was virtually standing on one leg, eager to avoid placing any weight on the knee that Garrett had smashed. Melf was wheezing as he clasped his ribs, his clothes splattered in dried blood. Gabe had come off best but was tentatively rubbing his aching jaw.

"So, who is going to tell me what happened?" Darr demanded.

Cylus coughed nervously. "We did as you asked. Garrett was alone. We confronted him to pass on your message. And it was then that he attacked us. It was unprovoked."

"That's exactly what happened," Gabe added. "That man is deranged. He went berserk before Cylus could speak. We were lucky to escape with our lives."

"I'll decide how lucky you are," Darr sneered. His emotions were a mixture of anger and confusion. The three instructors were the toughest men under his command, with the most experience of controlling dangerous sinners. Yet here they were, with severe injuries after barely overcoming a single individual. Worst of all, they had overstepped their remit. How was he going to tell Warden Stagg that Eminence Zaen's prized prisoner was lying dead over two hundred meters underground? Heads will roll this time, he told himself.

Zaen's anger and ferocity were legendary. Darr had heard plenty of stories where communes had been eradicated at a whim, of officials disappearing in the night, and of a laboratory that experimented on humans. The eminence ruled by fear where any hint of dissent or failure was not tolerated.

It was time for damage limitation. Darr had known Stagg long enough to know there was no loyalty other than to himself. When shit went down, and it most definitely would, Stagg would do his utmost to shift the blame elsewhere. Anywhere. All Darr had to do was ensure he was not the sacrificial lamb. He had too much invested in his venture with Stagg.

"Are you sure he's dead?"

Cylus held up his pickax. The blood had dried halfway along the blade, revealing how deep he had driven it into Garrett's side. "No one is going to survive that. If he doesn't bleed out, then the infection will get him." There was no hint of remorse in his answer.

Darr considered sending more instructors to retrieve Garrett. If the man wasn't dead, then he desperately needed medical attention. Perhaps it would be possible to save Garrett's life and recover the situation. But that assumed Garrett was still alive, and that seemed increasingly unlikely from the report given by Cylus. In any case, how could Darr explain the knowledge that he was critically injured?

"Get yourselves cleaned up. I'm taking you off the roster until I resolve this mess. Do not speak to any of the others about what happened."

"What are you going to do?" Gabe asked nervously.

"Protect our asses. That's my job. Now get out of here all of you."

Darr spent the next minute cursing to himself as he paced up and down. The instructors didn't fully understand the severity of the situation. The decisions he made in the next few hours could decide the fate of many people, including himself.

That meant someone was going to have to take the fall for the mistake. He would make damn sure it wasn't him.

***

"They did what?" Warden Stagg screamed, banging both of his fists down hard on his desk.

The reaction was no less than Darr expected. He had felt exactly the same when Cylus told him what had gone wrong. The fear was still there, giving him indigestion. "They didn't expect Garrett to react in the way he did. Before they knew it, he was lying on the floor, bleeding out."

As the gravity of the situation sank in, Stagg's eyes opened wide in fear. "We're all dead. You know that. As soon as Zaen discovers what's happened, he'll send a cleansing squad to punish everyone in the camp. Your men's actions have given us all a death sentence."

"It doesn't have to be like that," Darr said in a calm voice.

"Of course it does. Why didn't Cylus bring Garrett to the surface? We might have been able to save him. Save us."

"He panicked! He should have known better. Maybe—"

"Don't make excuses. Your men were incompetent. Eminence Zaen will not listen to whatever argument you or I have."

"Yes, they failed, and I will deal with them accordingly. But if we remain calm, there may be a way out of this."

Stagg glared at Darr. "Remain calm! Do you understand this is the end for us? Zaen was planning to make an enormous political statement with Garrett's trial. It's all about promoting his own interests. Do you think he's going to be forgiving when I tell him the trial is off?"

"I know only too well that we're both in the firing line. But no one currently knows Garrett is dead. Zaen told you the Elders have yet to confirm the trial date. That gives us some breathing space to plan our exit. We can be off-planet before the news leaks out."

Stagg considered the idea for a moment before shaking his head. "Zaen will come after us. Running is as good as accepting responsibility for Garrett's death."

"It's an opportunity," Darr replied. "You said it yourself. If we stay here, Zaen will hold us responsible and we'll definitely be dead."

"It's an opportunity to survive a few months longer, I suppose. Living in fear every day that a snatch squad will catch up with us. Is that how you want to spend your remaining days?"

"Of course not. Do you have a better idea?"

Darr waited in silence as Stagg paced nervously behind his desk. He knew exactly how the warden was feeling. After all, they were both struggling to find a way through the dire circumstances. Stagg was right though. Simply running away was not a viable option, and he had been naïve to think it was.

A maximum of one week's head start on Zaen's snatch squad was insufficient. Neither he nor Stagg had any reliable contacts in the Stellar Cluster or any firm idea of where or how they could find a haven on any of the planets. As strangers, with no knowledge of the local culture, they would stand out when all they wanted to do was blend in.

Stagg sat back in his chair, muttering and cursing to himself. "Maybe the one good thing your imbeciles did was leave Garrett down there after all. It means we don't officially know his situation. We can continue to act normally for the next few days. Then we report we noticed Garrett was missing from mealtimes and had stopped digging for ore. We say we carried out a detailed search of the tunnel complex and discovered his fellow sinners had killed him."

"How does that help us? Zaen will still want to take his vengeance out on someone."

"Yes, I admit the plan needs more work. My initial thought is we give Zaen some sinners and claim they are responsible for Garrett's untimely murder. I'm sure you can round up a suitable group of ten. Maybe we include your three guards. Multiple executions may placate the eminence."

Darr could hear the fear and doubt in Stagg's voice. He was grasping for a solution. "Do you really want to be around to see if that plan works? If Zaen's wrath is as ferocious as they say, then he will still look for more extreme punishments."

"True," Stagg reluctantly admitted. "The key has to be spinning Garrett's death positively. Unfortunately, I'm not a politician."

Darr was all out of ideas. His specialty was dealing with sinners; not with the inner workings of the Brotherhood elite. "Do you want me to leave you alone? Maybe give you time to think of something?"

"Oh, no! You're not dumping this problem on me and expecting me to work miracles in order to fix your screw-up."

"It's our screw-up, Stagg. Remember whose suggestion it was?"

"I gave explicit instructions, which you and your instructors failed to follow. You're staying here until we have a workable solution. I don't think I could sleep tonight, anyway."

Darr sighed loudly as he leaned back in his chair. It was going to be a long night.

Chapter 33

Garrett awoke to the uncompromising sound of the siren calling everyone to prayer. Opening his eyes, he found himself in the same recess as earlier, with Rosa still sitting next to him. She was reading a book, which she put down as soon as she saw him stirring.

"How long have I been asleep?" he asked, feeling less pain than he had previously. There was a dull ache in his injured side, but it was bearable.

"I would estimate about five hours. How are you feeling?"

Garrett cautiously stretched his body, rolling from side to side to test his injuries. "Much better. Whatever you did to me has worked."

She smiled, looking less reserved than the last time they had spoken. "It's good to see I still know what I'm doing. I've not dealt with many traumatic injuries down here. You can try to sit up."

Garrett didn't need to be asked twice. Although the movement caused the pain in his side to become more intense, it quickly eased as he found a comfortable position to sit. As Rosa handed him a flask of water, he realized how thirsty he was.

"Do you want some cold stew?"

He nodded, and she handed him a bowl that was half filled with the standard rations; a mixture of coarsely cut and almost raw vegetables in a watery gravy. Although not hungry, Garrett began eating the unappetizing meal.

"You've not bought into the prayer rituals?" he asked between mouthfuls as Rosa watched him eat.

"I'm a long way from being a convert, Mr. Garrett. The Brotherhood is cruel and barbaric. If I could remove them from power, I would."

"Is that why are you here? You attempted a rebellion?"

Rosa was silent for a moment as she decided how much to share. "Personal reasons. My son, Mikel, came to the Bevas Sector to research the culture. I warned him not to come. In fact, I pleaded with him as a loving mother. But he and his friends were in their early twenties. They all thought of themselves as invincible. Mikel fell into one of the religions that had become fashionable on Nesta. I can't even remember its name. Anyway, the group he associated with had the urge to help and convert others to their ways. They thought they could come here and help the locals by spreading the word of God."

"That's ridiculous. Did they not know what the Brotherhood are like?"

Rosa shook her head. "They knew. That's one of the reasons they felt compelled to come here. I remember Mikel telling me not to worry and that God would take care of them. He couldn't stand by knowing millions of people were suffering under the regime here. He accused me and the Stellar government of being complicit. His friends had idealistic intentions of freeing the people here by showing them a better alternative. They didn't care that the Brotherhood had been in place for centuries."

"You should have tried harder to stop them," said Garrett, instantly regretting the accusation as he saw her fighting back tears. Rosa was a mother; she would have used all rational arguments to prevent her son from leaving.

"I think that every minute of the day. It's my biggest regret. The other mothers begged their children not to go. We had no support from the church minister, however, and he had more influence on their decision. In the end, Mikel left without even saying goodbye."

Rosa stopped talking and wiped away tears.

Garrett placed the empty bowl on the ground next to him. "When did this occur?"

"What year is it?"

"AD 4891. June."

Rosa gasped. "As long as that? Mikel left almost four years ago. I never heard from him again. His friends' parents were in the same situation. I spoke with government officials, thinking they could ask questions of the Brotherhood. Or at least do something useful. But they claimed it was a private matter and there was nothing they could do because no diplomatic relations exist." She stopped again, shaking her head at the recollection of many fruitless meetings with vapid bureaucrats.

"So you came here alone in search of your son."

"Not just me. There were four other interested parties. We hired two guides who had their own ship. A husband and wife. They promised they had contacts in the Bevas Sector. People they traded with. They guaranteed they would find our children and help us return them to safety. I still remember breaking orbit from Nesta, full of hope and optimism. All I wanted was to hug Mikel and tell him how much I loved him."

"Of course, that wasn't to be. After ten days traveling through space, we arrived on Drani IV and were arrested almost immediately. The authorities also took the two guides. Apparently, their contacts weren't as loyal as they believed. There was no trial. We were all separated and taken to different instructional camps. I've been here ever since and do not know if anyone else survived."

Garrett felt profoundly sad for Rosa. She had endured terrible loss at the hands of the Brotherhood. Not only had she lost her son, but she was also going to live out the rest of her days hidden away underground. All for the love of her son.

"How long have you been down here?"

"From what you just said, three years and two months. I hadn't realized how long until you told me the year. I could have sworn it was only about half that."

"Has the warden or any of the instructors offered you hope of leniency?"

Rosa's laugh was bitter. "How can you even ask that? You've had experience with the Brotherhood. They hate outsiders from the Stellar Cluster. They have no capacity for compassion, which I find impossible to understand for a supposedly religious society. The best I could do was hide down here and allow the instructors to think I had died."

Garrett felt dumb for asking the question. He'd had more than enough experience through Eminence Zaen to know the Brotherhood did things in their own unique way. Tolerance was an entirely alien concept to them. He had lost close friends because of them and now they also wanted to take his life in the most epic example of revenge.

Listening to Rosa's story fired up a rage within him. This poor woman had done nothing wrong other than love her son. She did not deserve to be here. Her mental fortitude to remain alive in such surroundings was nothing more than miraculous. Even now, he could hear the hope in her voice that she would one day be reconciled with Mikel, however improbable that seemed.

Without fully knowing the reasons, Garrett felt compelled to help Rosa. Once he had formulated an escape plan, it would have to include her. Yet escape seemed a remote possibility, especially with his latest injuries.

"I assume you've not been here all this time without learning about the camp and instructors."

"Do you mean have I been working on an escape plan?"

He nodded. "You didn't come all this way to save your son, just to end your life in a hole."

"I spent the first few months here trying to understand everything I could. Just like you've been doing since you arrived."

Garrett nodded. He could hear people along the tunnel, returning from their prayers. With less than two hours until the next siren, they would be keen to grab whatever sleep they could.

"What did you learn?"

"Well, Mr. Garrett. I can tell you the residents here will offer little help."

"Yes, I gathered that. The instructors have conditioned the people to be compliant."

"That isn't a result of their time in the camp. I've seen plenty of newcomers since I arrived and spoken to everyone here. The Brotherhood is thorough. They teach children from the age of two that they must abide by the Brotherhood's doctrines or face harsh consequences."

Garrett had witnessed enough to confirm Rosa's observation. They had effectively brainwashed the Bevas Sector population over tens of generations. The methods were brutal. What he did not understand was what the Brotherhood's beliefs were founded on. He had never expected the subject to be important; in fact, he had done his best to block out his brief contact with Zaen and his colleagues.

"I guess you're an expert on the Brotherhood, thanks to Mikel. Can you tell me why they have created this society?"

Rosa sucked in her cheeks as she decided where to begin. "I was probably the same as you for most of my life. Aware that the Brotherhood existed but ignorant of what they were doing here. So, when Mikel and his friends first started talking about the Brotherhood, I thought their stories were just propaganda from the government or zealous religious leaders."

Garrett nodded at the familiarity of her experience.

"It was only after three months of preaching from Mikel that I took the Brotherhood seriously and carried out some research of my own. The history of the religion goes as far back as Earth. A religious order called the 'Covenant of Brothers' funded two of the Exodus Arks."

He raised a quizzical eyebrow. "How was that possible? They always taught us there was a strict selection process."

"Money talks!" replied Rosa grimly. "I imagine Grand President Trask was open to bribes like any other person. Maybe he wasn't as perfect as history portrays him, despite saving the human species."

Garrett kept quiet, knowing only too well how imperfect Trask had been. For all his vision, Trask's thirst for power had been his real motivation. Thankfully, fate had stepped in to prevent what could have been a disaster.

"Anyway, the Covenant of Brothers were against so many things they regarded as leading to Earth's downfall. Technology, capitalism, political corruption. The list goes on. They had millions of global followers. Their leaders wanted to create a new community in the Stellar Cluster that did away with all of those human failings."

"Ironic, when the Covenant of Brothers exploited all of those activities in order to reach the Stellar Cluster."

"Very true. But when you're a fanatic, the ends always justify the means. I guess the Covenant's leaders felt a compulsion to ensure their religion continued. The Brotherhood's core belief is that they don't want to repeat the same mistakes that led to Earth's demise."

"By turning their back on technology and everything else that makes our lives bearable."

Rosa nodded. "Within four hundred years of arriving in the Stellar Cluster, the Covenant was shunned. Humanity was discovering new worlds to populate. It was the age of ultra-development. These planetary systems in the Bevas Sector were a long way from the rest of humanity, and not the most hospitable. Feeling alienated, the several thousand members of the Covenant volunteered to move here. It was sold as a new beginning."

"And they changed their name to the Brotherhood. Sounds more like a rebranding," Oz said with a smile. That was about as far as his knowledge went though.

"The governments in the Stellar Cluster were relieved by the move, and quickly turned a blind eye to what the Brotherhood were doing. And little has changed in almost two thousand years."

That did not surprise Garrett based on the fact the two factions barely spoke to one another. "What else should I know?" he asked, interested to discover the culture he was up against."

"Whatever you've heard about life here is nothing compared to reality," said Rosa, standing to perform a series of stretching exercises. "The Brotherhood rules with an iron fist. It's a very hierarchical system run by a handful of Elders who are elected by their peers. There are countless levels of officials, such as Eminence Zaen and the proctors who perform day-to-day administration of the population. As for the masses? They have a miserable existence not much better than the inmates in this camp."

"I find that hard to believe."

"Really? Here are some hard facts. Seventy percent of the people on this planet have limited access to electricity. Those same people plow the fields and tend the crops in order to feed the masses. The eldest son is transferred to a Brotherhood academy at the age of six, never to see his family again. They regard women only as workers or to increase population numbers. Food incentives are available for any family with over five children. Which is harder than you think when you discover the mortality rate. It's truly appalling."

Garrett was understanding the reasons for Sylwester's compliance; it had been drilled into him and his ancestors. But he couldn't help but wonder if the inmates, and the general population, harbored a deep-seated resentment that could be fired up into an uprising. He needed that to be true.

Rosa sat back down. "So, you understand why you'll get no help. And in a way I'm glad."

The comment took Garrett by surprise. Surely Rosa had been in the camp long enough to want to taste freedom again. "It's not you that is going to be facing the death sentence in a matter of days. I have to escape."

"It's not just about you. If by some miracle you succeed, everyone in this camp will be punished. Some or all of them will die. Even if you fail, Warden Stagg will carry out some atrocity as a deterrent. Do you want that on your conscience?"

He was about to respond but stopped himself as he thought through what Rosa had said. Annoyingly, he knew she was right. He wouldn't be able to live with himself in the knowledge that innocent people had died because of him.

"Would you prevent me from escaping?" he eventually asked.

"I would do anything to keep these people safe. They are my friends."

He grudgingly accepted the fact. There had to be another way where no one had to die. His escape plan now took on extra significance and was going to be far tougher than it already was.

Chapter 34

An official government transport flew Leela and Keisha from Celeste's spaceport to the private ranch of Senator Seth Garrett, fifteen kilometers from the city.

As the craft gently descended onto the front lawn of the property, Keisha could not help herself. "Oz left all this behind to be a bounty hunter? The Garretts must be one of the wealthiest families on Lafayette."

Leela knew Keisha would have conducted a detailed background search of the Garrett finances so her astonishment was nothing more than an act. Despite that, there was no disputing the family ranch was gigantic, its fields disappearing into the distance in all directions.

"For some people, there's more to life than credits," said Leela, although the words sounded hollow.

"That's what someone who isn't rich says," scoffed Keisha. "If I had millions in the bank and this much property, you wouldn't find me crawling across the Stellar Cluster putting my life in danger so that I can apprehend scum."

"Is that so? I think you'd get bored quickly, squander your credits on booze and men and then return to chasing bolters. I know you enjoy it really."

"Hmmm!" Keisha muttered as the transport landed on the lush carpet of grass.

A smartly dressed woman with long, flowing blonde hair over her shoulders came walking down the front steps of the house to greet them with a warm smile.

"My name is Gemma Garrett. It is so nice of you to visit. I've not met any of Oz's friends for so long," she said.

Leela stared at Gemma's dress, instantly deciding she should have made more of an effort than wearing a clean set of fatigues and polishing her boots. But, although dressed in a similar fashion, Keisha seemed to have no qualms at being underdressed as she reached out a hand to Gemma.

"I'm sorry it could not be under better circumstances," was all Leela could say.

"Oz has never mentioned you," said Keisha, making Leela cringe.

Gemma's smile changed to an expression of disappointment. "Oh, really?" she said. "I guess it's been many years since the boys had their fallout. What should I expect?"

"Oz tends to live in the moment," said Leela, trying to recover the situation. "He's been through a lot of pain in his life. Like most men, he bottles up his emotions."

Gemma nodded her head. "Yes, of course. Seth can be like that too. Anyway, please follow me. Seth is in the study, finishing a conference. He won't be long."

***

It was a further thirty minutes before Seth finally appeared. By then, there was an awkward silence in the room as Leela and Keisha found they had little in common with Gemma. After sharing a few of Garrett's exploits, which Gemma had gratefully listened to, even asking several questions, Leela had run out of things she felt capable of sharing.

Seth entered with his friendliest politician face. "Ladies, I am so sorry for keeping you waiting. Some of the junior finance ministers simply don't know when to stop talking. It is quite frustrating."

"That's quite okay, Senator Garrett. We understand you're a busy man," said Leela. She shot a glance at Keisha who was drinking her third vodka cocktail while staring out of the window at four horses in the adjacent paddock.

"That's no excuse for poor manners. And please, call me Seth. You're in my home now as my guests. No need for formalities. I trust Gemma has kept you entertained."

"Your robo-waiters make superb cocktails, Seth," said Keisha, with extra emphasis on his name.

"This is my associate, Keisha Dennis," Leela said by way of introduction, and explanation. "She's an expert on tracking down the most determined of bolters."

"In that case, I may have something of interest for you," said Seth, reaching into an inside pocket of his jacket and revealing a data cube, which he handed to Keisha.

She immediately placed her drink on the floor next to her boot before inspecting the cube. It was a standard issue, only two centimeters on each side, yet capable of holding a zettabyte of compressed data. As Leela watched with interest, Keisha pulled a datapad from her hip pocket and attached the data cube to it.

"The data's encrypted," she said, staring at the rows of unintelligible symbols scrolling across the screen.

"Forgive me," said Seth, waving his own datapad across Keisha's. "None of us are supposed to possess this information. I called in a few favors with the security office."

Keisha's screen changed to a clear image of the bolters she had been trying to track down for days. She nodded at Leela.

"How old is this information?" Leela asked.

"Four hours," replied Seth. "The coordinates are detailed next to the image."

"Is it far from here?"

Seth checked the details on Keisha's screen. "It's the port of New Cannes, located ninety minutes flight time from Celeste. It's a refuge for the wealthy who want to throw their credits away on crass experiences."

"Have you been there?" Keisha asked. Leela considered if it had been wise to bring her to this meeting but it had been impossible to keep Keisha away when she was in charge of tracking.

"For business, not pleasure," Seth replied.

"Your business?" Keisha continued.

"I think what Keisha is trying to say is we are most grateful for this information. It makes our job easier and I'm relieved to know the bolters are still on Lafayette. Is there anything we should know about New Cannes?"

"Only that it is full of immoral people," said Gemma, surprising everyone in the room. "I don't know why the government doesn't regulate the place. It's a cesspit of sin."

"Sounds like my type of place," said Keisha with a mischievous smile.

Leela cringed once more, hoping neither Gemma nor Seth were offended by Keisha's flippant remark. "We'll follow up as soon as we return to Novak. Is there any news on Oz?"

This was the question she had been desperate to ask since arriving at the ranch. Seth's focus on the bolters, though welcome, did not fill her with any confidence that Garrett had been found.

Seth shook his head. "Osiris's whereabouts truly are a mystery. My department has been in contact with the central government as well as the administrators on Destiny Station. There are no records of Osiris from the date you told me. That includes records of him leaving the transport hub and arrivals at all major spaceports across the Stellar Cluster."

"Could he still be on Destiny Station?" Leela asked, hoping there was at least one clue to help her.

"No. A full biometric scan was completed earlier today. While it uncovered some illegal human smuggling activities, there was no sign of Osiris."

"You mean they couldn't find his life signs."

"Keisha!" Leela screamed. "There's no need."

"I'm only interested in clarifying the facts," she replied with no hint of remorse.

"Biometrics would have picked up signs of his DNA, even if he'd been dead for several weeks," said Seth. "It's safe to say he is not on Destiny Station."

Disappointed by the lack of new information on Garrett, Leela felt it was time to leave. She was also fearful that Keisha would say something that could have them evicted from Lafayette. Seth had been extremely helpful and was not the man she expected from Garrett's description but the last thing she needed was for Keisha to ruin the goodwill she had established.

"Thank you both for your hospitality. It has been a pleasure to meet Oz's family and to see your wonderful home. I'm sorry you were unable to find him."

"Me too," replied Seth. "Let me reassure you I have not given up on Osiris. No one simply disappears. I will extend my endeavors until we locate him. And good luck with capturing your bolters."

Leela had to virtually drag Keisha, a drink back in her hand, through the front door to the waiting transport. "We'll let you know when we have the bolters in our custody. And, of course, if Oz turns up we'll share the information immediately."

"We'll meet again soon," Gemma shouted with a wave as she remained at the top of the steps.

After climbing into the transport, Leela took an envious look at the Garrett ranch house, wondering what it must be like to call it home. She then turned to Keisha. "I can't believe you sometimes. Do you have no respect for people's feelings?"

Keisha shrugged, looking out of a side window as the transport rose into the early evening sky.

Chapter 35

Oz spent the following day recuperating and talking with Rosa, getting to understand her better and gradually opening up parts of himself that he rarely shared with close friends, let alone casual acquaintances. He found her easy to talk to and noticed that her attitude slowly softened as she got to know him better.

His injuries were healing well, although far slower than he would have liked. He could not blame Rosa for that. She had performed a miracle by merely saving his life with the sparse medical resources at her disposal. There were limits to what she could do, and he simply had to be patient.

Despite the pain subsiding, the toughest part was physical movement. The tiniest amount of stretching would cause him to wince as the stitches holding his wounds together threatened to break under the strain. An escape attempt was still out of the question and would be for several more days.

Yet Garrett was overly aware that time was a factor for him. Each hour, he wondered what Zaen had planned for him and how soon the court would be convened.

"Maybe Zaen thinks you're already dead and has moved on to his next act of vengeance," Rosa suggested on the morning of the second day since his attack.

Oz shook his head. "The warden hasn't informed him of my attack."

"How can you be so sure?"

"Because he has not sent any instructors to retrieve my body. I saw the hatred in his eyes. If he had any suspicion I had been killed, he would want proof."

Rosa frowned, idly scratching the back of her head in thought for several moments. "Would he order us all killed if he thought you were dead?"

"It's a possibility. He's been plotting his revenge for a long time. The trial is a demonstration of his power over me. Without it, he has nothing but anger and frustration, which he will want to vent in any direction he can."

"But the people here have done nothing wrong. They're already paying a high enough price by being here."

"That won't matter. You were right; if I die or escape and Zaen doesn't get what he wants, I fear he would wipe out this entire camp."

"That's crazy. How can a civilized society allow people like Zaen to flourish?"

"It's as you told me. Centuries of domination and crushing the will of the population. The Brotherhood have had their power for so long that most of the people do not know there is an alternative."

The conversation was interrupted by an anxious Sylwester hurrying along the tunnel, bringing a flask of water.

"You're looking much better," he said to Garrett, who nodded in return.

"Do you have any news today?" Rosa asked.

Sylwester handed her the flask while standing over the pair of them. "The instructors are asking questions about Oz. I heard them ask several people if they had seen him. Of course, no one could confirm or deny his presence."

"How did the instructors react?"

"They weren't happy. They said they expect to see him in the kitchen tonight, on the pretense that Oz should not be shirking his work duties. But you can see in their eyes that they're nervous."

"Is that a normal request?" Garrett asked.

"I've never known it before," replied Sylwester. "Provided we deliver the quota of ore and metals, the instructors don't care who supplied it. If anyone doesn't turn up to eat, they assume that person is too ill to work. Or dead."

"So, if I don't show up later, they'll believe I am dead?"

"No. They threatened to search every level to locate you. It's unheard of. The news has upset everyone."

Garrett adjusted his position as Rosa passed him the water, instantly regretting the decision as pain spiked down his right side. He gasped but still took the water, taking several long sips while he thought. The instructors were clearly desperate after two days of absence. But did this latest interest mean that the court date was set? Or was this merely a way to reassure Darr and the warden that he was not dead?

As if reading his thoughts, Rosa said, "This could be a trap. Darr may want to torture you more."

"That's a distinct possibility. But if I don't prove I'm still alive, then the instructors will make everyone's lives more miserable than they already are. And they'll find me, anyway."

"As your doctor, I really don't think you're fit enough to get yourself to the kitchen, let alone confront Darr. Those stitches could rupture and I'm only just able to control the infection in your left shoulder."

Garrett smiled. "Thanks for your concerns, Rosa. But I don't have any choice. I can't hide here and allow the instructors to bulldoze their way through the camp. And I'm sure you want to maintain your privacy down here."

"It has to be your decision," Sylwester said. "Whatever you decide, the people here will support you."

"That's a kind gesture, Syl. You have all done more than enough for me, and I doubt I will ever be able to return the favor. But it is time for me to reveal myself."

Sylwester's shoulders relaxed at Garrett's response and a smile crossed his face. "Thank you. I will escort you there myself. Rosa, I promise I will look out for him."

With that, he disappeared back down the tunnel to continue his day's graft.

Garrett noticed Rosa's deep frown.

"What else can I do?" he pleaded. "These are good people."

"Yes, I know. But you can't even stand, let alone make your way to the kitchen."

"Don't worry about that. They make Marines from stern stuff. I'll survive."

"Remind me how long it is since you left the Space Marines," she replied with a wry smile.

Spurred on by Rosa's misgivings, Garrett grabbed the rock wall next to him and maneuvered himself around. Through gritted teeth and with regular gasps of pain, he gradually raised himself onto one knee. He paused for a moment, taking deep breaths.

Rosa sat watching him, stubbornly refusing to offer any assistance. If he wanted to ignore her advice, he was on his own.

With renewed effort, Garrett continued to straighten his legs until he was standing upright, looking pale and with beads of sweat on his forehead. Holding onto the wall with one hand, and with his legs looking as though they would buckle, he stared challengingly at Rosa.

"Do you still believe you're ready to face the instructors?" she asked.

Garrett took two more deep breaths. "Of course," he said, before vomiting onto the ground.

***

Garrett wasn't feeling much better when Sylwester came to collect him later that day. Rosa had provided as many painkillers as she was willing to share, dulling the pain in his side. She had also wrapped a bandage tightly around his torso which, while restricting his movement, provided enough pressure on the wound to prevent any further tears. He had walked up and down the tunnel several times and was steadier than he had been. But he knew he would be hopeless in a fight. The meager rations, as well as the injuries, had sapped his strength.

"Are you sure about this?" Sylwester asked, genuine concern etched across his face.

"Let's get on with it," Garrett said. He was not sure how long the painkillers would last.

"Good luck," Rosa called out as they made their way carefully along the tunnel toward the shaft. Garrett was grateful that Sylwester said little along the way; he was too busy concentrating on not tripping on the uneven surface.

As he stepped onto the conveyor, it felt like a lifetime since he had last ventured onto the ancient contraption. The bumpy ride did nothing to ease his discomfort as he steadily passed the different levels on his journey to the kitchen.

Arriving in the kitchen, he carefully timed his jump from the conveyor to minimize the impact of the landing. To his relief, most people were still in the room, eating their stew or talking with friends.

Mercedes surprised him by running over from the bins, carrying a small sheet of paper. "I emptied your load for the day," she called out, loud enough for the instructors to hear. "That must be your best day ever."

Garrett was briefly confused, until Sylwester whispered, "Everyone contributed a modest amount. I thanked them on your behalf."

He took the paper from Mercedes and walked to the queue for food, sensing many pairs of eyes looking at him. As he drew closer to the front of the queue, he smiled as he saw different instructors were serving the stew. However, Darr was still hovering around and reached the giant cauldron of food just as Garrett arrived.

Darr snatched the slip of paper from him. "I was hoping you'd show up. You had us worried you had given up working."

Garrett held his gaze. "Are your instructors still in the infirmary? I heard they had a nasty fall."

Darr smirked. "You look like shit. Are the sinners not treating you well?"

Garrett leaned forward to whisper. "We both know what happened. Is that what Zaen ordered you to do?"

"I don't know what you're talking about, off-worlder. As far as I'm concerned, you're just another scummy sinner. It's no concern of mine if you can't take care of yourself down here."

"In that case, why were you so desperate to see me tonight."

Darr shrugged. "I think you're mistaken." Turning to the instructor next to him, he ordered, "Give this sinner his allotted rations," before walking off toward the door leading to the rest of the camp.

Carrying his bowl of steaming stew, Garrett found an empty bench and gently sat down, using all his willpower not to grimace at the pain in his side.

Mercedes quickly ran up and sat next to him, a huge smile on her face. "It is so good to see you again, Oz."

Garrett guiltily realized he had forgotten a second bowl for her. It was not as if he had earned any of the food in front of him. "I'm told I have you to thank for saving my life," he said, passing the bowl to her.

Mercedes held up a grime-stained hand and pulled out a small bowl from her tunic. She deftly scooped out a handful of food, splashing it into her bowl. "Syl says you need food to recover your strength. You should eat."

The acts of kindness from the surrounding people continued to surprise Garrett. The Brotherhood had taken their lives in the most brutal manner, yet they were still filled with compassion, even for a stranger.

He ate a few mouthfuls of the warm stew, feeling the heat course through his body. "Mercedes, you're one of the smartest people down here. You notice things that the adults miss. What have you heard while I've been recovering?"

The young girl sat up straight, her face beaming. "Yes, I think I'm smart too, even if I cannot read or write. The instructors were worried. They talked about you and also the three instructors that are injured. There are rumors there was a fight, but no one believes it. The instructors rarely fight among themselves."

"None of the instructors know I was attacked?" He found that fact interesting; Darr or the warden were containing the information. So not all the instructors were trusted.

Mercedes shook her head. "Will you teach me how to fight?"

Garrett burst out laughing, stopping quickly as he noticed the look of anguish on Mercedes' face. "I'm sorry, Mercedes. I'm not laughing at you. I admire your guts and think you would make an excellent soldier. But I doubt I'll be here much longer."

"That's not fair. I want to be strong enough to put three instructors in the infirmary like you did. How did you do it?"

Garrett finished his stew and placed the bowl on the bench before wiping his mouth on his sleeve. "I tell most people that it's years of training. But the secret is to control your feelings. Ignore the fear. Ignore the pain. Focus on your opponent's weakness."

Mercedes nodded slowly as she considered the advice. "How do you know what that weakness is?"

"Ah, that's the secret. Pay attention to their eyes and how they stand. No one likes to lose. And everyone knows their own flaws. So watch how someone stands. Do they favor their left leg or right arm? Are their fists raised or lowered? Are they waiting for their friends to make the first move?"

The young girl stared open-mouthed, memorizing every single word he said. He knew she was too smart to be locked away in this camp forever. There was too much inquisitiveness within her to be constrained by her current circumstances. Garrett regretted he could not spend more time with her. There was so much he could teach Mercedes, and he was sure she could have been one of his best pupils. That was saying a lot after all the elite Marines he had trained in his younger days.

As the prisoners left the kitchen and returned to their recesses below, Garrett allowed Mercedes to return the empty bowls to an instructor. Aware that it was still likely he was being observed by one of Darr's men, he stood as normally as he could manage and walked slowly to join the queue of people waiting to step onto the conveyor. It was only once he had descended out of sight that he allowed himself to gasp at the pain in his side.

He hoped Rosa was ready to give him more pain relief.

Chapter 36

A bank of dark rain clouds was approaching from the distant mountains as Eminence Zaen's convoy approached the Produce Collection Facility next to the spaceport. Occasional bright shafts of sunlight cut across the dense forests, casting brief spotlights on the green vegetation before sliding on to a new target as a strong northerly wind carried the clouds.

The grim weather reflected Zaen's mood as he continued to wait for the Elders to confirm a court date for Garrett's trial. He knew there was no point in approaching them directly; they would regard his impatience as a weakness and unseemly for a man of his standing. While the trial was an important personal matter, closing a miserable chapter on his life, Garrett was insignificant to the Elders. The old men of the Brotherhood were not known for acting in haste, or for being influenced to make decisions.

Which was why he had tasked Proctor Chan to see what he could discreetly achieve behind the scenes. The experienced Chan had a strong network of influential contacts. To date, Chan had always learned valuable information. Garrett's trial, however, was proving more problematic.

However, Zaen had another distraction to deal with today that could easily jeopardize his ambitions.

The Produce Collection Facility was fundamentally an immense warehouse, one of many located across Drani IV, built to store the harvests collected by the communes. This facility, though, had an additional function. It stored and received items traded with planets in the Stellar Cluster. Although the Brotherhood denied their limitations, they were reliant on technical expertise that they had turned their back on centuries earlier. They, therefore, traded the ample fresh produce grown on Drani III and Drani IV in return for medical supplies, equipment spares, and the occasional luxury goods. A proportion of the precious metals mined at the instruction camps was also used to pay for the more expensive items, such as secondhand spaceships and black-market weapons.

Unlicensed smugglers carried out most of the trade, with officials on both sides of the border turning a blind eye. The arrangement suited all parties, but the Stellar Cluster government could never officially acknowledge it;

that would mean condoning the abysmal atrocities performed by the Brotherhood on its people.

The entire process had been running for longer than anyone could remember and usually went smoothly. Today, however, supply issues had caused trading to come to an unceremonious halt.

The small Drani spaceport was less than two kilometers from the facility and Zaen scowled as he spotted the offending freighter resting motionless on its landing pad next to a hangar on the edge of the spaceport. There should have been plenty of activity, with goods being unloaded and transferred to the Produce Collection Facility. Normally, there would be a continuous convoy of trucks, ensuring the freighter was on the ground for no longer than necessary. Yet this one had arrived two days earlier and was still waiting to be unloaded.

Zaen would have to have to report the delay to the Elders, and he was going to make damned sure that they could not hold him responsible for any failures. Strong, decisive leadership was necessary to demonstrate he had control of the situation and although he believed his record as eminence spoke volumes as to his character, he realized how churlish the Elders could be. While that was an issue for him now, he would regard that behavior as an honored privilege once he achieved that position.

As his convoy rolled up to the main entrance of the facility, two men in suits came running out to greet him.

How undignified, Zaen thought as he recognized the facility's director. The middle-aged man had been in his role for five years and, until now, had proved reliable. But, as the man came to a halt ten feet away, Zaen could see a strained expression on his face.

Proctor Chan opened the vehicle's door, allowing Zaen to step out into the humid air. The director and his assistant bowed their heads.

"Eminence Zaen, it is an honor to have you visit our facility. Apologies that we were not prepared for you. If your proctor had notified us, I would have ensured a more pleasing welcome parade."

Zaen strode past the director toward the vast green warehouse. "Walk with me, Director Koenig."

The director jumped at the request, quickly catching up with Zaen and walking exactly one pace behind.

"If I had wanted you to know I was arriving, I would have let Proctor Chan communicate ahead. The fact you didn't expect me to visit is troubling, considering the grave situation here."

"The situation is under control, Your Eminence. I don't know what you have heard," the director stammered.

Zaen stopped and spun round to confront Koenig. "Are you accusing my most trusted advisor of overreacting?"

The director was visibly sweating, and not from the humidity. "No, that is not what I meant," he said, casting a nervous look toward Chan. "The matter is under control and I will have it resolved in the next few days."

"Totally unacceptable!" Zaen said, continuing his way to the warehouse. "Why is there a freighter waiting to be unloaded at the spaceport?"

"The ship's captain refused to allow us to board until we confirmed we had all the listed products to trade. I am still waiting for a delivery to arrive from PCF Seven."

"When I appointed you as director, I expected you to take orders from me, not from an off-world captain. Did I make the wrong choice?"

"Of course not. And I do not believe I have ever given you the opportunity to regret your decision."

"Until now."

"As I said, Produce Collection Facility Seven's incompetence has let me down. Director Brown is the person you should be questioning."

"Are you telling me how to do my job?" Zaen's voice boomed for everyone to hear, causing Koenig to cringe.

"No, Your Eminence. I would never make such a presumption."

Zaen walked through the main entrance, into a large gathering space used for prayer times. "I want everyone here within five minutes."

Koenig turned to his assistant. "Jaques, round everyone up as Eminence Zaen requests. Now!"

Jaques swiftly scuttled out of sight around a corner, clearly eager to be out of range of Zaen's anger. Director Koenig wasn't feeling so fortunate.

"Your Eminence, may I provide you some refreshment after your journey?"

Zaen glared down at him. "Stop being a worm. All I want is a satisfactory explanation. You can start with telling me why you have not unloaded that freighter."

"As I said before, the captain—"

"No!" Zaen roared. "I'm not here for excuses. This is our planet. Off-worlders abide by our rules."

Koenig shrank under the intense gaze. "The freighter is heavily armed. When we get close, they point the automatic cannons at us. Captain Dreyfus refuses to open his cargo doors without confirmation we have the goods to trade."

"So you accepted being spoken to like that? How long do you plan to be held to ransom?"

"I don't see it that way. We still get the supplies; it just means there's going to be a delay. It's all Director Brown's fault."

Zaen noticed some of the facility's staff nervously enter the room, standing in small groups near the wall, hoping to not incur his wrath. He ignored them, acknowledging to himself they could do with a show of strength to encourage their efforts.

"Again, you're blaming others. Do you hold yourself accountable for any of this fiasco?"

Koenig looked anxiously around the room, becoming increasingly uncomfortable with his situation. He was not used to being spoken to in such a manner, especially in front of his employees. But this was the eminence and the best he could now hope for was damage limitation. Running away was not an option, even as he spied two of Zaen's guards standing next to the main entrance.

From deep within, he found a small amount of composure. Standing slightly straighter than he had only moments earlier, he said. "I have spent many hours in communication with Captain Dreyfus, assuring him we always honor our agreements and there is no need for his crass actions. I have also spoken with Director Brown daily. He has failed to offer a good excuse for his failure, but he committed to making the delivery next week."

"I think I've heard enough," an exasperated Zaen replied, circling the hapless director.

Jaques ambled back into the center of the room. "Your Eminence, every-one is here, as you requested," he said in a low voice, before taking several paces back.

"Excellent timing," said Zaen. He looked around the room at the small groups of men and women staring in wonderment at him. They look a wretched bunch, he thought. Most of them looked as though they hadn't washed in days, and their overalls had seen better days. Ignoring the pungent smell of rotting vegetables, he beckoned them to move closer.

"Come here, my children. There is no need to be afraid of your eminence. You are nothing but loyal and hardworking." None of the people looked con-vinced by his words, but they gradually took three or four paces forward. Za-en decided that was close enough.

"I am here today to offer my support to you all by weeding out the in-competence. Director Koenig has failed you as much as he has failed me. He has forgotten the lofty standards demanded by the Brotherhood to make Drani a better world. I cannot allow that to continue."

Koenig, with fear in his eyes, began to creep slowly away from Zaen. "You're mistaken, Eminence Zaen. I have always done my utmost to satisfy your expectations. Even now."

"If this is your best, then clearly you are the wrong man for the job. I here-by fire you."

For a man of his age, Zaen had incredibly fast reflexes. His right hand withdrew a small firearm from a hidden pocket in the left sleeve of his robe. Before Koenig could react, Zaen raised the weapon, aiming it at the direc-tor's forehead and firing two shots in rapid succession.

There was an audible gasp from everyone in the room as the back of Koenig's head exploded, sending fragments of blood, brain, and bone flying into the air before spraying the floor in a red, sticky mess. His corpse slumped lifelessly to the ground in a crumpled heap as two women screamed.

Zaen turned to look at Koenig's assistant. "Jaques, I'm promoting you. Don't disappoint me."

Jaques was staring at the bloody remains of Koenig, his eyes filled with disbelief. For a few moments, he was silent. "Th-thank you, Your Eminence. You can rely on me."

"Good man. I hope you learn from your predecessor's mistakes." Zaen glanced around at the others in the room. "I may be harsh, but only when I need to be in the Brotherhood's name. Everyone back to work and may you prosper under your new director."

None of the assembled staff needed to be told twice. They quickly filed out of the room, back to wherever they spent their working days.

A quivering Jaques wasn't so fortunate. "You're coming with me," Zaen said to him, leaving no room for debate.

***

Thirty minutes later, Zaen's convoy pulled up two hundred meters from the enormous interplanetary freighter. A rain shower had passed through only minutes earlier, leaving the ship's hull plates glistening, though Zaen could see reddish-brown streaks of rust on some of the lower parts.

It incensed Zaen to see the freighter's cannons train their sights on his vehicles. He would ensure that Captain Dreyfus never piloted a mission to the Bevas Sector again. The man was obviously arrogant, with no respect for the office of eminence.

The newly appointed Director Jaques was sitting next to him, fidgeting uncomfortably. "Introduce me to this insolent captain. I want to explain to him who is really in charge here."

As Jaques opened the door, Chief Proctor Chan expressed his concerns. "Your Eminence, is it wise for you to put yourself in danger? Let the new director prove himself instead."

Zaen, still buoyed by the recent execution of Koenig, was feeling invincible. "Thank you, Chan. I need to show Jaques what I expect from him. Also, I want to teach a lesson to the freighter's captain."

Chan nodded as Zaen stepped from the vehicle and began walking toward the freighter's cargo bay door that was resolutely closed. As his boots splashed through shallow puddles on the cracked concrete landing pad, Zaen sensed Jaques walking several paces behind him.

Ahead, he could see a pair of deadly cannons tracking his steady walk closer to the ship.

How pathetic, he thought.

Pausing twenty meters from one of the freighter's enormous landing legs, he said. "Director, bring the captain to me."

Without hesitation, Jaques strode up to the ship and pressed a comms panel next to the cargo bay door. Zaen watched on impassively as Jaques had a protracted conversation with someone on board. After several minutes, a hatch opened outwards on the edge of the cargo bay door, releasing a set of stars that extended to the ground.

A middle-aged man in blue trousers and matching shirt descended the steps. He scowled at Jaques and walked slowly toward Zaen.

Jaques quickly caught up with the man and declared. "Eminence Zaen, this is Captain Dreyfus."

Dreyfus was about ten centimeters taller than Zaen and looked down at both men, seemingly unimpressed with his invitation.

"Do you know who I am?" Zaen asked in his most commanding voice.

Dreyfus lazily nodded. "I've heard of you and I know of your reputation."

"Then why do you choose to defy me and point your weapons in my direction?"

"Where is Director Koenig? He can explain the situation to you. I am only doing what I have been authorized to in this situation."

"I have replaced Koenig. And as a guest of the Drani System, you should not have to be reminded that my authority is absolute. Therefore, if one of my directors instructs you to unload your cargo, you can be assured they have my delegated authority."

"I will gladly unload the contents of my ship as soon as someone confirms your supplies are ready. That is how trade works."

"Your lack of trust offends me."

"I have my orders."

Zaen was quickly losing patience with the man. He would execute anyone else on the spot for daring to speak to him in such a manner. While that was still an option for this off-worlder, it would cause further problems that Zaen could do without. "I do not care about your orders. You will unload your cargo now and await delivery of our supplies."

Dreyfus stared back at Zaen, folding his arms. "I can't do that."

"Do you want me to impound your ship?"

The captain shrugged. "I'd like to see you try. As you can see, my ship can defend itself."

"You really don't want to be starting an interplanetary incident. The trading agreements have gone on for centuries."

"Look, Your Highness, just give me your products. That's all I need to get out of your hair and we can put this misunderstanding behind us."

Zaen clenched his fists and took two steps toward Dreyfus, who didn't flinch. "Listen, off-worlder. You have my word and that of the esteemed Brotherhood that the products will arrive within the next few days. If you continue with your insolent attitude, I will ensure you're delayed here for another month, wasting money and letting your freighter rust. Is that what you want?"

Dreyfus thought for a moment. "I think maybe we can come to some sort of arrangement. But no tricks."

"I don't play games, Captain."

Zaen turned to face Jaques. "Director, you heard the man. Make it happen, and instruct Chan when the unloading is complete."

He returned to his vehicle, leaving Jaques and Dreyfus staring at one another in silence. Now to deal with Director Brown.

Chapter 37

Zaen arrived back at his palace in the late afternoon. Although he had slept for most of the journey, he felt tired and irritable from the day's activity. Dealing with petty squabbles was beneath a man of his standing, but it seemed almost impossible to find people he could trust to carry out work to his standards.

As he entered through the large, ornate doorway into the impressive entrance hall, Chief Proctor Chan informed him that Director Jaques had confirmed unloading supplies from the freighter was underway.

Zaen simply nodded. He had expected nothing less.

"You'll find me in the cloister. Bring me some refreshment."

"With pleasure, Your Eminence."

Zaen walked through the empty corridors, his shoes echoing on the marble floors. A servant bowed as he opened the large glass door.

This was Zaen's place of contemplation. The sweet smell of the large fruit tree and surrounding flowers, together with the melodic sound of birdsong, allowed him to find inner peace. As he got older, he visited this place on an increasingly regular basis, preferring his own company to that of his subordinates. It was rare that any of his peers visited the palace, not that he had anyone he could call a friend.

He slumped into his favorite seat and closed his eyes. Resting his hands on his lap, he took several deep breaths, finding an inner calmness. The day had been unnecessarily tedious, but those feelings disappeared as his mind cleared.

At the sound of the door opening and closing, Zaen opened his eyes expecting to see Proctor Chan carrying a tray of food and a goblet of wine. Instead, he was disappointed to see Andron walking toward him with a satisfied look on his face. Zaen silently cursed that he had not yet ordered the removal of the young man from his palace. This latest intrusion was yet another reason Andron had to go. The young man clearly had not learned that he could no longer be so familiar.

"Andron, get out. Return to your duties."

Andron's smile momentarily dropped at Zaen's harsh tone. "Your Eminence, please spare me one minute of your time. I have good news for you."

"I have Chief Proctor Chan to provide me all the information I need."

"This news is fresh. It's personal. It's about Osiris Garrett's trial." Andron could hardly contain his excitement.

While it intrigued Zaen to discover when the court trial would take place, he would have preferred to hear it through formal channels. Andron's bursting into the cloister had the feeling of idle gossip being shared. It cheapened the moment for what should be the culmination of his revenge.

"Go on. When is it?" he snarled, barely containing his anger.

"Tomorrow!" Andron grinned excitedly.

The news did not cheer Zaen. Although his preparations were almost complete, he had expected the Elders to provide more notice, if for no reason other than respect for his seniority. There were several logistical challenges he had to resolve, including the time to transport Garrett to the trial.

His technicians also had problems with synchronizing the quantum communications equipment that would transmit the trial across the Stellar Cluster. He needed it to be fully functional. After all, he wanted as many people as possible to see Garrett's ultimate humiliation. And for billions of people to know who Eminence Zaen was.

"Are you sure? How did you find out?"

Andron fidgeted nervously. "I was passing the propaganda center when I overheard the news. Please accept my apologies for my unseemly entrance, but I thought you should know immediately. I understand more than anyone how much Garrett's execution will mean to you."

"So you decided this news sufficient to override my instructions to you?"

Andron grinned. "Yes, of course. I have been with you all the way through the indignity you suffered at Garrett's hand, then the years of shame you endured. I saw you at your most vulnerable and am inspired by your tenacity and wisdom. The trial will be a moment of glory for you. I thought you would like me to convey the wonderful news to you."

"Andron, you're mistaken. You are a part of those painful and shameful times in my life. I cannot cast my eyes upon you without remembering the awful events. Why do you think I shun you from my presence?"

Andron's eyes began to water as his bottom lip quivered. "Your Eminence, no one has been more loyal than I have. Have I not delivered everything you asked of me?"

"You think any of that is important to me? That I owe you some kind of debt of gratitude? I'm the eminence. I owe nothing to anyone, least of all a lowly servant. You served me because that was your duty. Nothing more."

Andron bowed his head and whispered. "I understand, Your Eminence."

"I'm not sure you do," Zaen continued. "It's best that you leave this palace and never return."

Andron's complexion turned ashen at the words. To his credit, Andron chose not to beg, knowing it would be a wasted effort. He did, however, have one request. "Your Eminence, thank you for the clarity you have provided me. I will cherish all the years I have served you. There is one final request. Please let me attend the trial. I would like to witness Garrett's face when he receives his sentence."

There was something about Andron's eyes and soft skin that Zaen had secretly found difficult to resist. It was such a shame the young man had overstayed his welcome. He considered the request for several moments. "You may attend the trial as a spectator. You can enjoy my triumph before you depart for your new life. But you have spent your last night here under my roof. Find yourself some lodgings close by, or perhaps the stables."

At that moment, Zaen was grateful to see Proctor Chan arrive with a tray of refreshments. Chan's face had a shocked expression as he saw Andron. "I'm sorry, Your Eminence. I did not know he was here."

"It's okay, Chan. Andron knows he made a mistake and is leaving."

His bottom lip still quivering, Andron glanced from one man to the other in silence. After one long pleading gaze at Zaen, he spun around and ran to the exit.

Chan delicately placed the tray on a small table next to Zaen. "I have news about the trial."

Zaen held up his hand to stop Chan. "I know. Andron felt he had a duty to tell me first. Contact Warden Stagg and tell him to prepare Garrett."

As Chan departed, Zaen took a small sip of his drink before once more cursing the Elders and Andron. Feeling unsettled by the events of the day, he hoped the trial would return order to his life.

Chapter 38

As Garrett queued up in the kitchen with the others to collect a hammer, he was still unsure how much work he could perform. He'd had a restless night, unable to get comfortable or ignore the pain in his side and shoulder. Because she was quickly using up her supplies, Rosa had had no choice but to reduce his medication.

He had not argued with her decision. The prisoners had already done enough for him; it wasn't right that he also took their medication, especially when he was likely to be dead within the month anyway.

Distracted by lack of sleep, Garrett didn't notice Darr walk up to him.

"You're coming with me today," the head instructor said in a low, menacing voice.

"Why?" Garrett guessed the answer but was in no mood to leave.

Darr grinned, revealing his brown-stained teeth. "It's your moment of fame. Your trial is happening today. Eminence Zaen requests your attendance."

"I don't suppose I can decline? I do have a busy day ahead."

"Move toward the door." Darr nudged him in the side with enough force to send Garrett in the desired direction.

Garrett cursed his luck as he hobbled toward the door leading to the rest of the camp. He was not ready for the trial. Not that it made any difference. He already knew the outcome. The entire event was staged for Zaen's benefit. Garrett was in too much discomfort to offer any resistance.

This was the first time he had passed through the door since his arrival, although he had looked along the length of the corridor several times, wondering what was beyond the reinforced gate at the far end.

This was the only access point. Today could be his one chance to discover the camp's weaknesses.

Garrett stopped by the locked gate, waiting for Darr to unlock it and let him through.

"Hands behind your back," Darr commanded.

Slowly, Garrett did as he was told. This wasn't a battle worth fighting. He immediately felt the cold steel of handcuffs snap around his wrists.

"You can never be too careful," Darr whispered in his ear.

Garrett didn't respond. He stood silently, watching as Darr used an old-style key to unlock the heavy padlock. Simple but effective.

Beyond the gate, the tunnel continued for another ten meters. White paint covered the rough walls, helping to make the space seem brighter than the kitchen or the mine. He was still underground. The tunnel curved slowly to the right until another heavy metal door blocked the way. Darr quickly unlocked this door and urged Garrett forward.

But what grabbed Garrett's attention was the rack of rifles hanging next to the door. Five laser assault rifles, an old model but still deadly. He knew they would be highly effective in the close confines of the cave complex. Each rifle was charged and ready to use, with a spare power unit on a tray at the bottom of the rack.

Maybe there is hope!

The door slowly swung open, its hinges creaking. Garrett was met with his first view of the outside in more than a week. Gray clouds rolled overhead, threatening rain. He stepped out, breathing in the fresh, cold air. After the fetid air of the tunnels, the smell of pine trees and damp ferns was a welcome relief. He stood for several moments, taking in slow deep breaths, savoring each one as if it was the first time he had smelled such an abundance of aromas.

With a start, he realized he was close to the exercise area, but not in it. The rails that had run all the way from the kitchen continued thirty meters to a single-story, metal building. It was nothing more than a rusty shack, neglected and showing the effects of the local climate. Steam burst from a chimney on one edge of the flat roof.

Garrett smiled as he spotted two more instructors waiting for him. Darr was wise to be cautious of him. They walked either side of him, with Darr staying at the rear, guiding him along the side of the building.

Beyond was another building. This one had many windows and was painted a dull gray color. Garrett suspected this was the living quarters for the instructors. It looked better cared for than the first building and its location made sense. Plus, it looked almost identical to the barracks in which he had spent most of his military career.

So far, Garrett had spotted no security cameras or watchtowers. This was as he had hoped. The instructors were complacent. Hardly surprising after centuries of minding over such a compliant group of inmates, with no thoughts of escape. The locked gates were hardly essential.

Ahead was the shower block he had arrived through. In front of it stood a short man in a dark, badly fitting suit. The man was gazing at him as the instructors shepherded him forward.

"Where are your manners, Garrett?" said Darr. "Say hello to Warden Stagg."

Garrett stopped ten paces in front of the warden, who took a small involuntary step back. "Good morning, warden. May I compliment you on running such a tight camp?" He thought the warden looked incredibly nervous for someone in charge.

Stagg rubbed his hands together as he turned to Darr. "This man looks a mess and his smell offends me. Get him clean and presentable for Eminence Zaen." He then turned and walked toward a separate building.

Garrett knew the drill. They marched him into the shower block and forced him to stand under a stream of freezing cold water. This time, however, he was grateful for the experience. It washed away the dust, sweat, and grime that had accumulated on his body and clothes and the icy water invigorated him from his sense of malaise.

The instructors marched him back toward the arrival compound, shivering but feeling very much alive. It looked different from the outside, less robust. A series of steps ran up to a gantry that circled the top of the compound, providing a perfect vantage point for the instructors.

The group silently passed three armored vehicles and a large truck, all of which were protected from the elements by a canvas sheet, pulled taut between a series of metal poles. The vehicles were all old models Garrett had thought were museum pieces. They did, however, look as if someone had maintained them.

An instructor opened a door to the compound, where two more armored vehicles waited for him. Garrett saw Warden Stagg climb into the cab of the front vehicle just before they led him into the rear of the second vehicle. After being chained to the side bench, Garrett relaxed his body. This would be a long day, and he wanted to be ready for any opportunity to escape. He knew he was unlikely to get a second chance.

With an instructor sitting opposite him, Garret heard the motor fire up before the vehicle lurched forward. After bumping through the gates, the vehicle quickly picked up speed. With the steady drone of the engine and the rocking motion as the vehicle navigated the poorly maintained roads, Garrett soon fell into a light sleep.

The same could not be said for the unfortunate instructor who sat tensely alert for the entire journey, shifting his position frequently without ever giving Garrett an opportunity to make a move.

Chapter 39

After arriving at the courthouse, Garrett found himself hooded and unceremoniously bundled along a corridor, barely able to keep his balance. Steered around a series of corners and up two flights of steps, he was quickly disoriented, a tactic he recognized from his military days to confuse and intimidate prisoners. He had experienced it twice during training exercises, but it didn't compare with the real thing.

Eventually, he felt powerful hands on each shoulder, directing him to stand still. Several seconds later, the hood was removed roughly. His eyes blinked at the unexpected light.

After a few moments, he was able to focus on the room, which was empty except for himself and the two guards standing on either side. The room itself looked like any other courtroom he had seen across the Stellar Cluster. Whether judicial or military, all courts seemed to follow the same basic design, with a raised judges' bench looking down on a space for the lawyers and witnesses, and the defendant's box to one side but also raised, as if on display.

The only significant difference from the courts he had attended was the builders had constructed this from timber panels that had been well maintained over the intervening years. Red wood still glowed, enhancing the intricate patterns of gold inlaid around the borders. They had saved the most lavish details for the impressive three judges' chairs. They reminded Garrett of regal thrones he had seen in the history books from back on Earth when kings and queens ruled over certain nations.

As he had done in Zaen's palace, Garrett wondered how so few people could attain such fortunes and surround themselves with finery, while letting most of the population live in squalor. Were the elite oblivious to their double standards, or was there a sense of entitlement? He suspected a bit of both. But he could understand why Rosa's son and his friends had felt compelled to help, even if their mission had been misguided.

If the inmates back at the camp were representative of the entire population, then they deserved better lives.

Movement in the courtroom interrupted his thoughts. A door on one side opened and Eminence Zaen strolled in, his eyes fixed straight ahead. As he walked toward one of the legal benches, his crimson robe billowing behind him, two men carrying scrolls followed him. Garrett had to admit this role was made for Zaen.

On the far side of the room, Garrett spotted Warden Stagg and Andron enter through another door and quietly sit on a bench near the wall. Andron's complexion was ashen as he stared in Garrett's direction. Garrett thought he looked miserable and could not help but wonder why. Surely this was what his deceit back on Destiny Station had been all about.

Zaen remained standing, finally turning to face Garrett, a look of triumph in his eyes. Garrett shrugged and stared back impassively, not willing to react and increase Zaen's satisfaction. The trial was going to be a complete farce, and there was no point in getting angry. The important matter was avoiding the punishment being inflicted. Time and opportunity were quickly running out.

There was a commotion on the far side of the room. Garrett broke his gaze with Zaen to see three elderly gray-haired men in purple robes slowly enter the room. The three of them could hardly walk and he wondered how old they must be as they unsteadily reached their seats. Everyone in the room, including Zaen, stood stiffly to attention until the middle of the three judges rapped his gavel three times on a wooden block. As the noise echoed around the courtroom, the three men sat down while everyone else remained standing.

In a steady voice that surprised Garrett, the judge on the left called out. "The Superior Court of Drani IV is now in session. Elder Stokes presiding, supported by Elder Della and Elder Sweeny. Eminence Zaen, we are here to listen to a case you have requested be brought before us."

Zaen nodded. "May it please the Elders, this trial is being transmitted across the Stellar Cluster using their quantum communications network."

The judge, who Garrett assumed was Elder Sweeny, nodded. "We read your request and accept that it is in the interests of the Brotherhood for the defendant's people to see our form of justice is transparent."

The revelation shocked Garrett. He had not fully appreciated how much Zaen wanted to use the trial as a propaganda exercise. This was more than just securing his status in the Bevas Sector. The events of today would send a coherent message to everyone in the Stellar Cluster, confirming the fears of the government that the Brotherhood was uncompromising.

At least my friends will now know where I am, he thought wryly. Not that it would do him any good. He wondered how the Brotherhood had acquired the quantum communications equipment and for what other purposes it was used.

The presiding judge rapped his gavel again. "Eminence Zaen, please can you detail the charges against the defendant?"

"It will be my pleasure. The defendant, Osiris Garrett, is from the planet Lafayette, in the Stellar Cluster. Three years ago, he and a group of fellow mercenaries unlawfully invaded the Bevas Sector, landing on Drani III intending to kidnap one of our honored guests who was providing valuable work for the Brotherhood. Fortunately, our highly efficient peacekeepers intercepted the attempt, killing most of the mercenaries and capturing Mr. Garrett."

Zaen paused for effect. Garrett stood stiffly, Zaen's account bringing back the events of that fateful day when Colonel Lane died as a result of being lured into a trap.

"As Mr. Garrett had received serious injuries, the humane thing to do was return him to our finest medical facility here on Drani IV. Our best medical staff worked on him for many hours and, despite his critical injuries, saved his life. In such circumstances, you would expect some show of gratitude. On the contrary, like a coward, Mr. Garrett took his first opportunity to overpower and kill medical personnel in order to escape the medical facility. He then proceeded on a killing rampage on his way to the spaceport. Once there, he stole my personal shuttle, taking myself and my assistant hostage. For the next ten days, Mr. Garrett subjected me to humiliation and starvation, imprisoning me in a small cubicle where I feared for my life. Once he realized our teams were closing in, he abandoned me at an outpost located deep within the Stellar Cluster. He then made his escape thinking he was safe from Brotherhood justice."

Garrett fought back the urge to scoff. Zaen's version of events was a misrepresentation of the truth. And while he had taken Zaen against his will, it had been an inadvertent kidnapping. At no time had Zaen been a victim.

And neither had he killed as many people as Zaen implied in his opening statement.

Elder Stokes cleared his throat. "Thank you, Eminence Zaen, for your eloquent yet brief summation of the crimes. I am sure it must be painful for you to recount something that caused you so much anguish."

Zaen nodded. "Thank you, Elder Stokes. This was by far the darkest moment of my life. If it wasn't for my devout faith in the gods, and the support of the noble Brotherhood, I don't know how I would have survived."

"Oh, please!" exclaimed Garrett.

As one, everyone in the room turned to glare at him.

Elder Sweeny, his wrinkled face frowning, held up his hand. "The defendant will remain silent unless answering a specific question."

"Do I have to listen to the incorrect shit that Zaen is spouting?" Garrett replied defiantly. If this trial was being transmitted, then he didn't want to be seen to accept Zaen's twisted version of events without some defense.

Elder Stokes used his gavel to silence the murmurs circulating the room. "Another outburst like that, and I will order the guards to gag you. Is that clear, Mr. Garrett? This is our courtroom and you will respect myself and my fellow judges."

Garrett shrugged silently. He had made his point.

Zaen smiled. "Elders, as you can see from his unwarranted outburst, the defendant has no respect for our ways. As is our experience with many off-worlders, he shows an arrogant disregard for the ways of the Brotherhood. Our ways have ensured peace for centuries; more than can I can say for the peoples of the Stellar Cluster."

The three Elders slowly nodded their assent.

"Back to the reason we are here today. Because of the heinous nature of the crimes, I am requesting the Elders impose the maximum punishment available to them."

Garrett looked on in resignation as Zaen took his seat. This trial was going exactly as he had expected. It was nothing more than a farce. Although he was the defendant, in reality, he was nothing more than a spectator, watching the ultimate demonstration of propaganda. The result was a foregone conclusion. He wondered if the court would allow him to defend himself. After all, there was no one else representing him.

Elder Della, who until this point had remained silent, cleared his throat with a gravelly cough. His voice was weaker than his fellow Elders as he said. "Eminence Zaen, we have read your written submissions, which concur with your verbal summary. It is most regretful that you suffered in such a way at the hands of this off-worlder." Della pointed a scrawny finger in Garrett's direction. "I understand the personal guards who allowed this situation to get out of hand have been dealt with."

Zaen jumped to his feet. "That is correct, Elder Della. Their incompetence was punished efficiently and justly when I returned to Drani IV. Mr. Garrett is the last person to face justice. He has evaded it for many years but, I hope, now accepts that no one can run from Brotherhood justice forever. My most sincere wish is that this case will be a lesson to others and prevent similar travesties from occurring."

"Well said," murmured Warden Stagg, loud enough to be heard around the courtroom. It warranted a dark look from the Elders, but they refrained from a verbal rebuke. Stagg blushed at his impetuous outburst.

"I believe the facts are clear-cut," Elder Stokes said. "The truth of Eminence Zaen's testimony is not in question, and there is no doubt in my mind that he suffered undue hardship and embarrassment through no fault of his own. The sole perpetrator of the despicable episode is the defendant. If he had not unlawfully trespassed into our space, I am convinced that none of the events would have transpired as they did." He paused and turned his attention to Garrett. "Although I can think of no valid excuse for your actions, the Supreme Court of the Brotherhood is a fair and just institution. Therefore, is there anything you would like to share as mitigation before we pass sentence?"

Garrett stared open-mouthed at the judges. They had clearly already made their decision; they were always going to believe the word of one of their most senior officials against an off-worlder. Nothing he could say would change that. Yet, saying nothing would be a clear admission of guilt for all the crimes listed. "Thank you, Elder Stokes, for the opportunity to speak. While most of the facts recounted by Eminence Zaen are true, he has taken them out of context. When I stole his ship, my intent was solely to make my way back to the Stellar Cluster. It was not until we were in space that I realized Zaen was on board. I was as shocked as him. I didn't need any hostages and would have preferred to be on my own. But I released Zaen and his servant at the earliest opportunity and ensured they were taken care of. At no time were they in danger."

Garrett stopped speaking, noticing the Elders appeared unimpressed by his words. There was no point extending this charade any longer. Whether or not he ultimately escaped, he was sure those in the Stellar Cluster would understand this was a no-win situation.

The three elderly men conferred with one another for several minutes before returning to their positions. Elder Stokes rapped his gavel twice in quick succession, sending Zaen and his assistants to their feet. "Thank you, Mr. Garrett, for your confession. It is a shame you have not also felt the need to apologize to Eminence Zaen for your appalling actions. With the facts presented before us, we see little alternative but to accede to the eminence's request and apply the maximum punishment. Mr. Garrett, we find you guilty of trespass, multiple homicides, kidnapping of a senior Brotherhood dignitary, and theft of Brotherhood property. The sentence for your crimes is death by execution squad, to be carried out in two days."

It was no less than Garrett had expected, but hearing the words made his situation more real. Particularly how little time he had to live came as a shock. Instead of years, he could now measure the rest of his life in hours.

A triumphant Zaen could not help but smile at Garrett, before restoring his composure and facing the judges. "Thank you for your wise handling of this dark blemish on my life. I pray I may now live out my life as a worthy servant of the Brotherhood."

As the three Elders rose unsteadily to their feet, everyone other than Garrett bowed their heads. It was not until the three old men had left the courtroom that people felt able to move. Garrett watched as Zaen walked over to where Stagg was sitting. "Warden, bring Garrett to my palace the day after next. Execution will be at midday." Zaen's voice was intentionally loud enough for Garrett to hear.

"By your command, Your Eminence," Stagg replied, his attitude reeking of self-importance.

Garrett noticed Andron about to speak, but Zaen walked away, ignoring his young accomplice. He couldn't help but wonder what had happened between the two of them and guessed that Andron, having fulfilled his task, had outgrown his usefulness to Zaen.

"Make the most of the time available to you," Zaen called across, interrupting Garrett's thoughts. "May I suggest you use your remaining hours to find peace with all the sins you have committed in your lifetime? It is never too late to allow the instructors to guide you down the path of forgiveness."

"The only thing I will pray for is your premature demise," Garrett replied. "You know your actions today will only further alienate the Brotherhood from the Stellar Cluster's government."

Zaen grinned, baring his stained and rotting teeth. "I hope that is correct. Your people are morally corrupt and should not interfere with the business of the Brotherhood."

"You've done the right thing by ordering my execution. It is the only way of ensuring I don't kill you."

"Brave words, Mr. Garrett. You got close to me once. I would never allow that to happen again."

Having said his piece, Zaen left the courtroom. Feeling bemused by the events of the previous ten minutes, Garrett let the two guards lead him from the courtroom. As they escorted him back to the waiting transport, only one thought occupied his brain.

Escape this damned planet.

Chapter 40

Leela was asleep in her cabin on the Novak when the persistent chime of her comms channel disturbed her dreams. Cursing at whoever was daring to call her in the middle of the night, she wearily reached out her left arm, her fingers fumbling for the controls next to her bunk.

"Yes?" she said, not hiding the irritation in her voice. Her pet grievance was being woken early.

"Leela? It's Seth Garrett. I assume from your tone you've not seen the news."

She sat up, turning on the soft cabin light and switching the comms channel to holographic mode. "Hi, Seth. I've been asleep for the past..." she checked the ship's clock. "Three hours." *Is that all?*

"In that case, let me update you. Oz has turned up. He's on Drani IV in the Bevas Sector. The Brotherhood shared his trial via a quantum comms channel," Seth replied, his tone anxious.

This was too much information for Leela to grasp while half asleep. Questions filled her mind. What was Oz doing in Brotherhood territory? Why was he in court? And how was the case transmitted when the Brotherhood did not possess the technology?

"You need to tell me more," she said.

Seth recounted the main events from the transmission, culminating in his brother's death sentence. By now, Leela was fully awake and dressed.

"Is there anything you can do, Seth? Perhaps a diplomatic solution?"

Seth shook his head. "There are no formal diplomatic channels in place. I've already spoken with the Lafayette government, as well as President D'Angelo's representatives. They are going to register formal complaints within the hour. That's the most they can do, but I doubt the Brotherhood will respond. This was a show trial, the live transmission designed to demonstrate their absolute power in that region. If they back down, it would be a sign of weakness."

"You can't just stand by and let your brother die. You're a senior politician in the Lafayette parliament. Surely that means something."

"I wish it did, Leela. I promise you I am doing everything in my power to save Oz. But it's only fair to not raise your expectations of success."

"How about a trade?" Leela asked in desperation. "Surely there must be something the Brotherhood needs. I know we do business with them."

Seth sighed heavily. "I am looking at all alternatives with my advisers. I will let you know if we have any success."

"What about a rescue mission? Send in Marines."

"Ignoring the tensions that would cause, we simply don't have enough time to get our forces close to Drani IV before the execution is due to take place. In any event, no government officials would ever sanction an extraction mission."

"So, if Oz's cause looks hopeless, why are you telling me?"

"It was something you told me a few days ago. You made me realize Oz has people who care about him. Just because my relationship with my brother is beyond repair doesn't mean I can abandon him. Perhaps there are 'unofficial' ways that you can help him."

Leela grunted, unsure what she could achieve that a planetary government could not. But she was grateful for Seth's faith and for not giving up on his brother. "Let me check with my colleagues. I'll let you know."

"Thanks, Leela. And good luck."

Seth cut the comms link, leaving Leela to stare at the blank screen as she figured out if she had any options. The Novak remained parked at Celeste's spaceport as the net closed on the bolters she was chasing down. Keisha and Toru were working their magic, but the pair they were hunting down were smart, changing their identities and location every few days. That meant the bolters were eating through their credits like a laser through steel. It was only a matter of time before their pace would slow and they made a mistake. Leela estimated it would be another week at the most before they apprehended the pair.

She briefly considered making a dash for the Bevas Sector, but Drani IV was over six days away. With the engines at maximum thrust for the entire journey, which was unwise if she didn't want to have to replace the propulsion manifolds, Garrett would be long dead. Even if she could get there in time, she doubted she could invade a planet single-handedly, then locate, rescue, and return Garrett. She told herself she was a bounty hunter, not a superwoman.

Her comms link chimed again. This time it was Levi Murphy.

Good news travels fast, she said to herself as she opened the link. Murphy's holographic face appeared in front of her. "You heard the news then," she said before he had a chance to speak.

His nostrils flared, a sign she knew meant he was unimpressed by her forthright greeting. "The trial explains why Oz disappeared so abruptly. The Brotherhood's goons must have snatched him."

Leela cursed as she remembered her last encounter with Garrett in the Lodge. "Dammit. The day before we left Destiny Station, Oz told me he was helping a young man, a young man who had escaped the clutches of the Brotherhood."

"Holy crap! Did you get the man's name?"

"No, but Oz mentioned the man had helped him when he lost his arm."

"Andron! Yes, I remember Oz telling me about him. He was one of Zaen's disciples, or chosen few, I think. It's more than a coincidence that Oz turns up in court facing accusations raised by Zaen. The man must have been convincing to have fooled Oz."

"A mistake he will soon regret unless we can do something."

"What are you suggesting, Leela?"

"I just finished speaking with Seth. He didn't offer any positive solutions to retrieving Oz alive. Diplomacy is a long shot, and he's ruling out official military action."

"So Oz is being left to die? Hardly brotherly love."

This time, it was Leela's turn to scowl. "That's unfair. Seth has promised to try every avenue. He's simply being realistic."

"We can't let the Brotherhood get away with this. They kidnapped Oz from our region of space."

"I'm sure there will be repercussions. None of which will help Oz." She paused, allowing a crazy thought to develop in her mind. "Where are you right now?"

Murphy cocked his head to one side. "Why?"

"How soon could you get to Drani IV?"

"You must think I'm crazy."

Leela grinned, the first time she had smiled at Murphy for a long time. "I know you're crazy enough to do anything to save your best friend."

He looked away from Leela for thirty seconds. "The navigational star charts say I can get there in three days."

"Damn, that's still too long."

"What exactly do you expect me to do? Break him out from wherever he's being imprisoned? The Brotherhood will expect such a move."

"Levi, I don't know. It just feels wrong giving up on him."

She saw him sigh. "I know. Which is why I've plotted in a course for Drani IV."

"You never cease to amaze me," she said, sensing her eyes tearing up.

"I thought I had," he replied with a wry smile. "Maybe the Brotherhood will delay Oz's execution. Or we come up with a cunning master plan in the next forty-eight hours. Can you reach out to all the bounty hunters we know?"

"I'll get on it straight away. And thank you, Levi."

"Thank me when we rescue Oz." He winked as he cut the connection.

Now fully awake, Leela made her way to the Novak's bridge. She had some calls to make.

Chapter 41

By the time Zaen returned to his palace, Proctor Chan had already received seven representations from different government officials located in the Stellar Cluster.

"I judged their reaction perfectly," said Zaen as he strode purposefully along the hallway toward his private quarters. "Those arrogant fools will remember my name and will fear me."

"Surely you mean they will fear the Brotherhood," Proctor Chan replied, without thinking. "After all, it was the Elders who—"

Zaen stopped in his tracks. "The Elders agreed with my actions and acknowledged the trauma I have suffered. Sometimes you forget your place, Chan. Remember who it was who arranged Garrett's return. Now everyone knows that nowhere is safe from my justice."

Chan bowed his head. "My apologies, Your Eminence. I meant no offense."

"I'm wondering if I sometimes retain my staff for too long. Some of you are becoming far too familiar. Perhaps it's time for a reshuffle."

Chan squirmed. "There's no need to be hasty, Your Eminence."

Zaen grunted and then continued his steady march through his palace. "Has there been any response from the Elders?"

"Yes. They have sent their wholehearted congratulations. Your performance today was flawless and they too could not have asked for any more." Chan moved closer to Zaen and lowered his voice. "As you know, I am not one to repeat gossip, but I hear the Elders are considering filming more trials. The prompt and angry reactions from those scum in the Stellar Cluster have impressed them. There are more of their citizens imprisoned in camps across the Bevas Sector who could now go to trial."

"One of many changes I will make once I become an Elder. The old men may be wise but they need to find new ways of getting their message to the populous."

"Despite the use of technology to achieve it?" queried Chan.

"If used in the right way, as you have seen today, technology can be an immensely powerful tool."

Despite his bravado, Zaen knew he had to choose his words carefully. The Brotherhood shunned overreliance on machines and technology. They feared humans would become servants to the machines; it had ultimately undermined society on Earth and could not be repeated. Zaen took a more progressive view that was not shared by all of his peers. Perhaps because he was more widely traveled, he could see the advantages of exploiting what others feared. He was confident, given time, that he could convert enough of the Brotherhood to his way of thinking.

At that moment, he was feeling invincible.

Zaen and Chan reached his personal quarters. This part of the palace was the most lavish, with expensive tapestries on the walls, rich fabrics, and the largest bed on the planet. The full-height glass doors opened onto a balcony overlooking his beloved cloister's garden. In the room's corner, a sunken marble bath, large enough to accommodate eight people currently sat empty, waiting for his orders for it to be filled.

He eyed the bath and felt like celebrating his victory. "Chan, please arrange for the bath to be filled and three acolytes to be sent to me with an excess of my finest wines and a selection of fruits."

Chan's face remained impassive. He had suspected the eminence would feel like partying. "I will make the arrangements. Before I depart, however, have you given any thought to the manner of Mr. Garrett's execution?"

By now, Zaen was having his formal robes removed by two young male servants. "Chan, you know full well I have had years to decide how I would like to see him suffer. It has to be slow and painful, which rules out hanging, firing squad, and lethal injection. In my research, I discovered hundreds of ways to kill a person, most of which I hadn't heard of. The human mind is the most creative and marvelous instrument. And the older methods from ancient Earth are some of the most brutal I could find."

He paused while his servants removed the rest of his clothes and dressed him in his standard evening attire, all while Chan stood patiently, awaiting his instructions. Once dressed in a long shirt that hung down to his knees, he continued.

"There is one punishment, in particular, that is most fitting for Garrett. Crucifixion." He let the word linger in the room for a long moment, shutting his eyes as, not for the first time, he imagined Garrett being nailed to a cross and dying slowly over several days, either from blood loss or thirst. "The concept has such strong religious connotations. Can you see the irony of Garrett, a self-proclaimed non-believer, living his last hours hanging on a cross?"

"I can, Your Eminence. A very bold, yet correct, choice."

Zaen took Chan's words as a compliment. He had researched the subject thoroughly and had been surprised to discover no record of a crucifixion for thousands of years. It was time to bring it back.

"Where would you like the cross located?"

"You can decide. Somewhere I can see it without having to listen to his screams at night. Not too close that I can smell his rotting flesh."

Chan's lips moved as he made a mental note of each of Zaen's demands. The method of Garrett's demise had come as somewhat of a shock. He was going to have to carry out his own research to uncover how to construct a cross that would be freestanding and sturdy enough. As this was another event Zaen had requested wanted to be shared across the quantum comms network, there was no room for embarrassing failures.

"Is there anything else, Your Eminence?"

Zaen shook his head. "I grow weary. I will have a short sleep to recover my energy. Delay the acolytes and wine but begin the filling of the bath."

After Chan had left the room, Zaen was left with the two junior servants. In his younger days, he would have used them for his pleasure but, to his dismay, all he wanted to do was lie down and rest. As he placed his head on a pillow, he cursed his body's age for failing him.

Within several minutes, however, he was dreaming of Garrett howling in agony as he hammered long nails through the man's hands and feet.

Chapter 42

"How did it go?" Rosa asked, genuine concern etched across her face as Garrett stopped outside her recess.

Garrett was tired and sore. The road to and from the courthouse was bumpy, and the vehicle had only limited suspension. His whole body felt bruised by the experience, but that was the least of his concerns. "As expected, it was nothing more than a show trial."

"The Brotherhood are adept at doing that," Rosa replied, offering him a flask of water. She must have sensed his thirst. He had gone the whole day without food or drink.

"The only surprise was the Brotherhood filmed the trial. They even transmitted it over the QC network for everyone in the Stellar Cluster to witness. The Brotherhood and Zaen are determined to make my misery complete. And send a warning they are prepared to do whatever they want."

"How the hell did the Brotherhood lay their hands on quantum communication equipment?"

Garrett shook his head. "I've been wondering that too. Especially for a culture so averse to technology. My guess is they've been spying on our comms traffic for years. Perhaps they have a network of agents on planets across the Stellar Cluster. The more I think about it, the more sense it makes."

"What is this quantum system you speak of?" Sylwester asked.

Garrett patted him on the shoulder. "Something your masters should not possess. It's a method of instantaneous communication across vast distances of space. People can speak to one another as well as link computers to data cores, allowing you to access any information in real-time. We're talking highly advanced technology that makes the universe a smaller place."

"You sound like one of the company's salesmen. Wasn't that one of their tag lines?" Rosa said, breaking the tension.

Garrett forced a smile. "Damn, I think you're right."

Sylwester was frowning as he tried to grasp the concept. "You have seen our lives here. The Brotherhood teach us that technology is bad."

"They tell you what it suits them to. The Brotherhood use whatever they want whenever they want. They're not stupid."

"That is wrong."

"No shit, Syl," Garrett snapped, his anger bubbling to the surface. "I'm sorry, that wasn't aimed at you. There is so much wrong with this culture and it frustrates the hell out of me that the Brotherhood get away with it."

"You still haven't told us about your sentence," interrupted Rosa.

Garrett sighed. "What is there to tell? I'm to be executed the day after tomorrow."

Rosa's jaw dropped. "How can you be so calm about it?"

He shrugged. "I plan to escape before then."

"That is not possible," said Sylwester. "The security here is too much. The instructors will stop you."

"That is what they have brainwashed you to believe, my friend. The instructors are poorly trained and complacent. The last thing they expect is for anyone to make an escape attempt because you're all so compliant. That's their first mistake."

Rosa frowned. "Even if you're right about the instructors, there are gates and barriers to overcome, as well as the fact we're in the middle of a jungle. How do you plan to effect your getaway? I assume you have to get to the spaceport and away from Drani IV."

"Again, minor obstacles."

Garrett's flippant reply did not convince Sylwester. "If they catch you, they will kill you. Then they will kill us."

"I'm going to die in less than two days anyway. The worst that can happen is I shorten my life by a few hours. But that will not happen. And all of you will remain safe, I promise." Garrett wasn't as confident as he sounded, but he needed to convince those around him. He was going to need their help. A fact that Rosa appeared to have already grasped.

"What is it you want us to do?" she asked.

Garrett took a moment to compose his thoughts. He had spent most of the journey back to the camp thinking through an escape strategy. While there were still several elements to clarify, he thought his plan had a reasonable chance of success. Cautiously, he sat on a pile of blankets, ignoring the pain from his wounds. "I realize it's selfish of me to make a solo escape. The conditions in this camp are inhumane. Syl was correct when he said there would be consequences if I escape. And I can't allow that to happen. Therefore, what I plan is a mass breakout."

Garrett paused, waiting for a reaction from either Rosa or Sylwester, but they merely stared back at him. "Thoughts?" he asked.

"I think you're mad," Rosa exclaimed, a look of disbelief on her face.

He shook his head. "I'm not willing to leave people behind to suffer whatever Stagg and Darr have in store. There is more chance of success if we use our superior numbers against the instructors. There are enough vehicles in the compound to take everyone. With luck, we can make it to the spaceport before the officials know we have escaped."

"And then what? You have one hundred people trapped in the open, hoping there is a spaceship ready to take them to a new world?"

"Basically, yes."

"That is insane!"

"I agree with Rosa," Sylwester said. "You have seen the people in here. They are not ready for such an adventure. While the conditions are not perfect, we get fed once a day and have clothes to wear."

"You're being exploited, living in squalor and ordered to work long hours in appalling conditions for the Brotherhood to profit from your labor."

"We are atoning for our sins."

"You've not committed any sins. The Brotherhood have convinced you that you need to be better. But what have you actually done wrong to deserve this treatment?"

Sylwester shook his head. "You cannot question the laws of the Brotherhood when you do not understand our religion. They interpret the words of the gods."

"I doubt your gods want their representatives to live in luxurious palaces, flaunting the rules they put in place for you and your kind. Somewhere within, you must realize that inequality is unfair."

Rosa shook her head at Garrett. "You're wasting your time. I've had this argument countless times with Sylwester and his friends. It's almost as if they do not want to be saved."

Frustrated, Garrett knew Rosa was partially right. "I'm not sure that's entirely true. I've seen a fighting spirit here. Sylwester has helped me several times. Rosa, the people here help you by keeping you safe. They're defying the instructors daily. Then you have the likes of Mercedes. She has an inquiring mind and wants more from life."

"She's only a child," protested Sylwester.

"With the whole of her life ahead of her. Is it right she spends it living in these awful tunnels?"

"Why should existence be any different for Mercedes or her friends? This is how life has been for generations."

Unexpectedly, Rosa stood and put her hand tenderly on Sylwester's shoulder. "What Oz is trying to say is don't you want something better for your children? A life that's fair and allows you some freedoms?"

Garrett looked worriedly at Sylwester, aware that he was making radical suggestions. Sylwester was one of the more open-minded inmates in the camp. If he could not be convinced, then no one could. After centuries of repression, any form of uprising would be a tremendous leap of faith.

"Trust me, Syl. I can get everyone out of this camp and off-planet. This could be the one chance you get to change your lives."

"You ask so much of me," Sylwester replied. "Let me sleep on it. I will give you my answer in the morning."

Garrett was hoping for a more immediate response, but Rosa signaled with her eyes not to pursue the debate. She had been here far longer than him, which meant her instincts were probably right. He watched as Sylwester slowly disappeared back along the tunnel to wherever his own recess was located.

"You can't push these people," Rosa said. "I understand it's frustrating, but you're pushing back against centuries of repression. You can't expect that to change overnight."

"I don't have the luxury of time," Garrett replied. "The escape attempt has to be tomorrow night."

"Sylwester is a good man. He'll give your plan a lot of thought. Remember, you're asking a lot of him and the other people in here. For some, this camp is the only life they've known. There are going to be many scared people. You're asking them to risk their lives and to accept a new, uncertain future on a distant planet among an entirely alien culture. Something none of them have ever considered."

Garrett nodded. "I get it. And I meant what I said. This escape isn't just about me. It's an opportunity to help these people lead a better life. A life that isn't dominated by fear."

"I'm glad to hear that, Oz. I think you now see what I do and I commend you for offering to do the right thing for these people."

"You don't seem overly excited about my plan."

Rosa smiled. "I wouldn't exactly call it a plan. At the moment, it's an ambition at best. I'm reserving judgment, waiting to see Sylwester's decision. If he decides not to join you, I will remain here. These people need me and I can't desert them."

The words shocked Garrett. He had been positive that Rosa would want to return with him to the Stellar Cluster. This was her one chance to escape the camp; she wouldn't get another opportunity. "You'll die here."

"Maybe so. But I'll be making a difference to these innocent people. I couldn't help my son, but I know I can help inside this camp. That means more to me than running away."

Her reasoning was hard to argue against. It aligned with the reasons he wanted to take the prisoners with him. He couldn't save the entire planet, but transferring one hundred souls would be a start.

As long as Sylwester thought the same way.

"You've not told me how you plan to get through this camp's defenses," Rosa said, diverting the conversation.

"The trip to court today filled in several gaps for me. The tough part will be the first few minutes. If I can get through the interior gates, there are a handful of laser assault rifles. They look old, but they are still effective. I can fight my way past the instructors by catching them by surprise."

"Fine. How do you plan on getting through the gates?"

Garrett smiled. "Something you said the other day. The two women that make nightly trips to the instructors' quarters. They hold the key, literally, to the plan. All they have to do is find something to wedge the gate open when the instructors let them through."

Rosa looked puzzled. "Don't the instructors lock the gate from the far side?"

"That's what I thought. This morning I watched Darr. He used his key to unlock the gate, but once we were through, it slammed shut behind us.

There must be a simple locking mechanism that clicks into place when the gate is closed, together with a spring to ensure the gate swings shut. A small rock, dropped in the right place, could be enough to wedge the gate open just enough to prevent the locking mechanism from engaging."

Rosa pursed her lips. "That sounds risky. What if the women get caught?"

"They won't. The instructors are lazy. There are so many rocks in this place that the women can deny any knowledge. Who can prove someone did not accidentally kick it?"

"You're assuming the women will agree."

Garrett shrugged. "Very true. Which is why I need Sylwester on side."

"Walk me through the rest of your plan. Maybe I can offer some suggestions."

Raising a quizzical eyebrow, he said, "You're a medic, not a strategist."

"I'm also the only person on this planet who will understand what you're trying to do. And I know these people and what they're capable of."

"Good point," he replied. "But first, can you give me another painkiller?"

Chapter 43

Warden Stagg leaned back in his chair, relieved the day had gone as smoothly as it had. Eminence Zaen had almost been pleasant to him. And, most importantly, he still had his job.

He pulled a half-empty bottle of vodka from his drawer, pouring a generous measure into a battered glass, its rim chipped. He drained the glass, not realizing how much he needed alcohol, and refilled it. This time, he left it on the desk in front of him as he stared at the darkness out of his window.

"Do you have a second glass, sir?" Darr said, walking into the office. "It's no fun celebrating on your own."

Stagg scowled as his head instructor took a seat without being asked. He didn't like Darr's attitude or the fact his head instructor never supplied his own vodka. Rummaging through a drawer, he found another glass. There was a thin brown residue resting in the bottom, although he couldn't recall what it was. Not that he cared. With a wry smile, he poured a small measure and slid the glass closer to Darr.

"What a week!" Darr exclaimed before downing the contents of his glass. If he had noticed the glass was dirty, he said nothing. "Only two more days and Garrett will be out of our way for good."

Stagg let out a sigh as he leaned back in his chair. As always, Darr had a knack for stating the obvious. But the prospect of Garrett's imminent execution filled him with a sense of satisfaction. The man was a potential liability. Stagg had suffered from several restless nights as the weight of Zaen's expectations played heavily on his mind. The end of the drama was now almost within touching distance.

"I hope you've not given your men any instructions to rough him up again," Stagg sneered.

Darr was looking enviously at the remaining contents of the vodka bottle. "I've warned all instructors to treat him with kid gloves. If he dies before the execution, it will not be because of anything we do."

"I'll let you explain that to Eminence Zaen if the situation arises. I'm sure he would understand." Stagg picked up his glass and drained it for a second time. He slammed the glass back down, harder than he meant to. Darr grabbed the vodka and filled the two glasses until the bottle was empty.

"You need to have a more positive spin on life. Nothing bad is going to happen to Garrett. Not until his execution at least." He began laughing at his own joke as Stagg continued to frown.

"It's no laughing matter, Darr. Your idiots almost got us both killed a few days ago."

"And I have sent those three to different camps. You won't see them here again."

"Good. I don't want instructors who don't have enough common sense to understand the orders they're given. When do the replacements arrive?"

Darr took another sip of his drink, this time savoring the rough, burning sensation at the back of his throat. "The three new instructors arrive in three days. Because of the 'incident', we're currently short-staffed. I've had to adjust the roster to cater for the personnel changes, but we'll still be able to cope without the three I let go."

"I hope you're right," Stagg replied, anger building within him. "I'm thinking we should cut our losses. We have a sufficient stockpile of heavy metals to retire on. Why continue chancing our luck?"

"Are you planning a quiet retirement?" mocked Darr. "We may have enough to live on, but I want to do more than sit in a home watching the video channels as my savings slowly diminish. Have you lost your nerve?"

Stagg considered Darr's question. Perhaps he was being excessively paranoid. Ever since Zaen had dropped Garrett on him, he had felt the pressure of increased attention from the eminence and his proctors. Having listened to the facts raised in court, he now understood Zaen's obsession with bringing Garrett to justice. That Garrett had almost died under his watch did not bear thinking about. Zaen's fury would have been swift and brutal. News of Director Koenig's failure and death had permeated across the planet. He did not want to be next.

He stared angrily at Darr once more. This was the man who had brought them within an inch of disaster. The instructor had already lost a female off-worlder somewhere in the tunnels, presumably killed by the sinners. Fortunately, she had not been important.

"Darr, I don't want to live fearing that the next day will be my last. You've become reckless lately. That fact worries me."

"One mistake makes me dangerous?" Darr emptied his glass and set it back on the desk next to the empty bottle.

"How many mistakes do you want to make? How many will Zaen tolerate? I need to get away from this place with what we have. We can start a new life and invest whatever credits we make from selling the ore. It may not be as much as you want, but at least we'll be alive."

Darr frowned, causing Stagg to feel anxious. "Another six months, Warden. That's all I ask. I can work the inmates harder. We can skim off a larger share and give us a healthy contingency fund."

Stagg sighed. His nerves would not survive that long. "Three months. Work the inmates like dogs. I'll make the arrangements to get us off-planet."

Darr nodded, a grim expression on his face. "Deal. But you need to relax. With Garrett gone, the heat is off." He stood up and left the room without another word.

Stagg resumed staring at the darkness outside, wishing he had as much confidence in the plan as Darr did. With Eminence Zaen's actions becoming increasingly unpredictable, he was conscious of the risk of failure.

Not for the first time, Stagg considered going solo. If he could escape Drani with *all* the ore, it would minimize any chance of capture or being discovered. What could Darr do about it? He could not follow or acknowledge that he was part of the scheme.

Retrieving a fresh bottle of vodka from his bottom drawer, Stagg spent the rest of the evening working out the logistics of betraying Darr, his mood lifting at the prospect of an early exit on his own terms.

Chapter 44

Oz woke with a start before realizing he had been sleeping at the edge of Rosa's recess, although she was not sitting in her usual spot. He looked around, but she was not in the immediate vicinity.

Leaning up on one elbow, he heard voices speaking in hushed tones from along the tunnel. Curious, he climbed slowly to his feet, stretching the stiffness from his body. Walking along the tunnel, he discovered Rosa speaking with Sylwester and two other men he recognized without knowing their names. And then there was Mercedes.

As soon as she saw him, she squealed with excitement and ran toward him. To his surprise, she wrapped her arms around him, inadvertently squeezing the wound in his side. "Syl says you're going to escape the camp tonight. And you're taking us with you."

Taken aback by the sudden show of raw affection, Garrett's first thought was to ruffle her hair. He immediately realized that was a mistake as his fingers became tangled in the knotted mess. "Hey, Mercedes. That is my plan, although I'm waiting to see if Syl is going to help."

"He is. He said so. That's what he's talking to Rosa about. We've been sharing the news with the rest of the camp."

"And what do you think about that?" he asked, genuinely interested to hear her reaction.

"I want to go on a rocket ship into the sky and see other planets. I didn't even know people lived elsewhere until Rosa told me. She told me about the night sky and how stars twinkle, like tiny crystals."

"You've never seen the sky at night?" As soon as the words came out, he felt stupid. Mercedes had spent all of her life in these tunnels, venturing out one day a week for exercise and a brief opportunity to experience fresh air. She may have been lucky enough to see the sun breaking through the clouds, but she would have never been outside after dark. It was likely none of the young people had. He realized what an enormous leap of faith he was requesting of everyone. More than that, he was asking them to trust their lives in his hands.

For the first time, he wondered if Rosa was right. Was he being unreasonable and selfish, exploiting the superior numbers of the prisoners in order to save his own life? Might the cost be too high? Were his motives pure?

He was no longer completely sure he was doing the right thing for the prisoners. Perhaps he wouldn't be certain until he was safely away from Drani IV.

Mercedes' expression suddenly changed to one of sadness. "I want to see where you come from. If I can live outside and be free to choose, then I think I will be happier."

Garrett felt the need to be honest with the girl. "This will not be easy. There's a chance I will fail, or that some people will die."

"Syl says you are dead already."

He looked across at Sylwester and laughed bitterly. "That doesn't mean I have to take you all down with me. However, I want the opportunity to save you while I still can."

Rosa spun around, a concerned expression on her face. "Sylwester and about thirty others have agreed to join the escape attempt tonight."

The number was more than Garrett had hoped for. It was probably enough for his plan to succeed, but he had secretly wanted to save the entire camp. Any stragglers were likely to be punished by a vengeful Zaen.

"Do you think you can persuade many more?" he asked Sylwester.

"I think so. It is still early, and we've not shared the news on all levels. It is the older ones who are harder to convince. The young ones are more enthusiastic."

Garrett nodded. The older ones had less to lose by remaining. "What did I say to convince you?"

Sylwester shrugged. "It's the prospect of a better life. Both you and Rosa have given us hope through your descriptions of life in the Stellar Cluster. And it's the children, like Mercedes, who really deserve a life outside of these damned tunnels."

"Thank you for your belief. I cannot tell you how grateful I am."

Rosa's frown continued. "We're not off the planet yet," she said, "We shouldn't raise our hopes just now."

"What is the immediate plan?" Sylwester asked.

"This is just a normal day," Garrett replied. "We can't have the instructors being suspicious of our actions. So we dig all day, deliver the rocks to the kitchen, and get fed. In the meantime, you and your friends round up as many volunteers as you can. Tell them they can either come with us to the spaceport or they can find their way back to their old communes on this planet. They can even stay here in the camp if that's where they feel safest. No one is going to be made to do anything they don't want to."

Sylwester and his friends listened carefully to his words, nodding their understanding. "Will there be any violence? You know we are not fighters."

"Syl, I'll be honest with you. We will need to overpower the instructors. They will not simply let any of us walk out of the camp. Rosa and I will deal with most of the instructors. I know where we can get rifles. The rest of you may need to attack with whatever weapons you can lay your hands on. Tools or rocks are all you require. The more recruits you can find, the better the odds of success."

"What time are we escaping?"

"We'll make a move at the end of the second siren. Everyone can congregate at the conveyor for their regular prayers. But instead of returning to sleep, they will make their way to the kitchen. The instructors will be fast asleep; they won't know what hit them until it's too late."

"You make it sound so easy."

"It will be," Garrett assured him. "If you want to send some volunteers down to me throughout the day, I'm happy to teach some basic self-defense moves that may come in useful."

"I can do the same," added Rosa. "Rudimentary fighting skills may just save your lives."

***

Garrett stirred as soon as the first siren sounded. He had slept deeply and felt the early signs of adrenaline building inside him.

By the end of the previous day, the number of people willing to take part in the prison break had risen to a respectable seventy-four, with another ten undecided. There was no telling how many would change their minds when the escape became a reality.

He glanced across at an anxious Rosa. She had not left this tunnel for months, as she had hidden her presence from the instructors. Although she had reservations about the plan, he had absolute faith she would come through the challenge of the next few hours.

"Ready?" he asked.

"Not really," she replied, smiling weakly. "Is it normal to feel as if I'm about to throw up?"

"It's just nerves. They're good for you."

As they started the walk toward the conveyor belt, a concerned Sylwester met them. "We have a problem," he said.

"What's wrong?" Garrett asked, fearing the instructors had uncovered the plan.

"It's Maja. She refuses to be part of the escape and will not visit the instructors tonight."

Garrett's heart sank at the news. "Does she realize that the whole attempt hinges on her being able to leave the gate unlocked?"

Sylwester nodded. "She says the instructors have been good to her, and she does not want to betray them."

"Shit! The instructors will suspect something is wrong if she fails to show up. Is there anyone who can take her place?"

Sylwester looked shocked. "Do you think any of our women want to have sex with the instructors? I would not ask that of any of them. How could you even suggest it?"

"I'm sorry, Syl, I should have thought before I spoke."

"Thamsi is prepared to go, but she cannot distract the instructors and wedge the gate open."

Garrett cursed. The escape attempt was over, even before it had begun. He knew he was asking a lot of the prisoners, yet had convinced himself they would understand his point of view. He had been a fool to have raised his hopes.

"I'll do it," Rosa said, catching him off guard.

"What? No, you can't."

"Why not? You're willing to exploit the other women."

Garrett knew his actions were hypocritical as he fought to find a valid reason. "The instructors won't recognize you. They'll be expecting Maja. How will you explain that to them?"

Rosa folded her arms, looking more determined than he had ever seen her. "I've met Maja. We're of a similar build. If I dirty my face and have my hood up, they won't spot the difference."

"How will you disguise your accent?"

"I'll let Thamsi do most of the talking. After all, it's her that will distract the instructors."

He was becoming frustrated. How could Rosa have worked out her responses so quickly? "I don't like it," was the best he could manage, resigned to letting her go.

"If you have a better way, I'll take it," she said grimly.

He looked to Sylwester for support, but he merely stared blankly back at him.

"The light isn't great along that tunnel, and it will be dark outside," Rosa added, trying to offer reassurance. "The risk is slight. You've said the instructors aren't very attentive. They may not realize their mistake until it's too late."

"And if they do?" Garrett replied, unwilling to consider the consequences of Rosa being unmasked in the middle of the instructors' barracks.

"Then I know you won't be far behind, ready to save me."

"Shit!" he exclaimed, knowing he could not talk her out of her plan.

Sylwester coughed. "We're wasting time. The instructors are expecting Thamsi and Maja in the next few minutes. Rosa needs to go now."

Rosa rubbed her hands on the ground before smearing the dirt onto her face and raising the hood of her top. Garrett had to admit she looked more like a prisoner than he had expected.

"Good luck," he said as she walked toward the conveyor that would take her to the kitchen.

Rosa didn't turn as she stepped onto the conveyor and began the climb.

"How long should we wait?" Sylwester asked. He was fidgeting, stepping from one foot to the other in nervous anticipation. Garrett could only hope that he and his friends were up to the task. The pickax in Sylwester's hand would be a deadly weapon, as long as he wielded it like he did when digging for precious metals.

"Five minutes should be more than enough." Garrett had planned to allow a longer gap, ensuring the instructors and women were clear of the far end of the tunnel. But Rosa's swift intervention left him with little choice. He needed her to be close when the inevitable firefight broke out. She was the only one he trusted to fire a laser rifle.

"I will inform everyone to wait for your signal," said Sylwester, climbing onto the conveyor and quickly disappearing upward.

Alone with his thoughts, Garrett played through what had to be done in the next ten minutes. He knew that even the best strategic plans often had to be adapted as situations evolved and new intel became available. This escape was no different, as Maja's reluctance had already shown. The secret to success was to stay at least one step ahead of the opposition and anticipate their reactions.

The one element he couldn't control was how the prisoners were going to react. They weren't fighters and there had been little time to train them. He had selected twenty of the strongest men, including Sylwester, to be the first wave of attackers. They knew what they were supposed to do but would they be able to follow through?

Garrett forced the negative thoughts from his mind. He had the element of surprise on his side and numerical superiority. If he could keep that for as long as possible, he was confident the escape would succeed.

It had to work.

Mentally counting down the time, he took one final deep breath and jumped onto the conveyor, heading for the kitchen five floors above his existing level.

Chapter 45

Garrett reached the kitchen area, ready to react to any threat from waiting instructors. If the instructors were aware of his plans, he knew his lack of weapons gave him extremely limited options. To his mild relief, the large room was empty and silent. Monitoring the corridor that hopefully would lead to his escape from the camp, he waited patiently as Sylwester and the rest of the first wave of prisoners arrived in silence. These were the volunteers willing to fight against the oppression they had endured.

Garrett looked at each of the men. Only Sylwester made eye contact with him. The others had their heads down, looking nervously at one another as they ambled across the kitchen area toward the corridor. They looked nothing like fighters; Garrett only hoped they had enough courage to avoid running when things turned ugly.

He gathered them into a small group.

"Men, this is your one chance to free yourselves and your families from the tyrannies inflicted on you by the Brotherhood. I know you're all scared to death. That is a normal reaction, I promise you. Remember, we outnumber the instructors by more than two to one. When they see us, they will be more scared than you. If you do what I taught you, we will be victorious. Follow my lead. Strike hard and strike fast."

"Hard and fast," the group said in half-hearted unison, with far less enthusiasm than Garrett would have liked. He could see potential in some prisoners, but they were nothing like the elite troops he had trained when he was a gunnery sergeant on Lafayette.

He quietly made his way to the corridor in the far wall, careful to remain away from the line of sight. When he reached the wall, he counted to five before cautiously peeking around the entrance. The corridor was empty. His luck was holding out. But the heavy gate appeared to be shut.

Signaling the group to follow, he ran along the corridor, his heart beating faster. As he drew closer to the gate, it still appeared locked. This could be the shortest prison escape in history, he thought. Failure wouldn't only mean death for him in a matter of hours, Rosa was alone and defenseless on the far side.

He nervously applied pressure on the gate, letting out a sigh as it swung open with a squeak. "Good girl," he muttered, spotting a brown pebble at the bottom of the gatepost.

Wasting no time, he ran through the gate and made his way toward the rack of laser rifles, collecting two of them and hanging one over his shoulder, before stuffing a couple of spare power packs in his pocket.

Moving to the next door, he turned to check the group was still with him. He briefly considered giving the three spare rifles to Sylwester and two others but decided against it. None of them had handled weapons and were as likely to kill each other or even him as anyone else. The pickaxes and hammers were going to be more effective in close quarters.

"Is everyone ready?" he asked. A series of small, uncertain nods answered him.

Garrett pushed the external door, expecting it to swing open. It refused to move. He applied more pressure but frustratingly realized the door was locked. Cursing, he took three paces back before aiming his rifle at the lock and firing a quick burst, thankful that laser rounds were virtually silent.

The lock erupted in a shower of sparks and molten metal. Garrett tried the door once more, but it still held fast. Conscious that precious seconds were being wasted, he reached his left hand into the hole created by the laser blast. The edges of the lock were still hot, causing his artificial skin to char. Ignoring the minor discomfort registered through the nano-nerves, Garrett's fingers located the locking mechanism. Squeezing his hand around the spring and ratchet, he gave a sharp pull, removing the lock in one swift motion.

The door swung outward, although Garrett flinched as the hinges creaked loudly in the still night air.

Outside, the air was warm and humid. Puddles on the ground, reflecting the overhead spotlights, indicated there had been recent showers. He could hear animals howling and calling out to one another from the nearby jungle which was in complete darkness beyond the range of the spotlights.

Sensing no movement in the immediate vicinity, Garrett sprinted to the first building, feeling exposed as he passed below the spotlights. The group behind him sounded like a herd of elephants in the still night and he feared the instructors would discover them at any moment.

Staying close to the wall, Garrett crept forward with slow, deliberate steps, all the time listening for any alarms or other signs they had been discovered. So far, he could not believe his luck, but he was conscious the situation could change in a heartbeat.

Glancing back over his shoulder, he spotted Sylwester only a few paces behind him, mimicking his movements by staying low and close to the wall. Behind Sylwester, the rest of the group were following in single file. Above the sound of their footsteps, Garrett could hear rapid breathing from the men closest to him.

The barracks shed was now only a few meters away and seemed to be peaceful. Lights were visible through the shutters on two of the windows.

"Stay on the grass and away from the gravel path," he whispered to Sylwester, who nodded and passed on the instruction to the man behind him.

Garrett waited thirty seconds for the message to feed down the line before moving toward the entrance to the shed, crouching all the way to keep his head below the base of the windows. The entrance, a large wooden door with a glass panel in the top half, was located halfway along the side of the building, with two steps leading up to it.

Garrett paused when he reached the door, checking his rifle was still showing a full charge and the spare power packs were easily accessible. He wished he had a smaller handgun, anything less unwieldy than the rifle, which was not the ideal weapon of choice for close conflict.

"Wait here," he said to Sylwester. "I'm going inside to find Rosa and Thamsi. Make your move as soon as you hear fighting or see lights from other rooms. And remember, they will kill you if you don't kill them first."

Sylwester swallowed hard and nodded.

Garrett took two deep breaths. This was the moment of truth. He couldn't worry how the prisoners would perform. For all he knew, they might turn and run at the first sound of conflict. As he reached for the door handle, all he could hope for was to maintain the element of surprise.

Which lasted about two seconds as a woman's piercing scream shattered the silence of the night.

Chapter 46

Garrett could not tell if the scream came from Rosa or Thamsi, not that it mattered. One of them was in trouble. Yanking the door open, he ran into the barracks shed, which was still in semi-darkness.

The barracks' entrance hall was twice the width of the door, with notice boards on either side. Two meters in, corridors went left and right. Garrett peered around the corner, looking to his left where the lighted rooms were situated.

He could hear movement coming from various parts of the building but, as yet, no one had entered the corridors and there had been no more screams. Garrett didn't like not having backup. If he made his way toward where he thought Rosa and Thamsi were located, he would leave his rear exposed to a potential attack. Back when he had been training his recruits, he would have told them to always wait for support. Going into this type of scenario alone would get them killed.

Unfortunately, he had no option. All he had were the twenty scared volunteers who had never fought in their lives. He would rather not have his life depend on such an unknown quantity. At least Sylwester was crouching with one other man in the doorway, fidgeting with their weapons and glancing anxiously behind them.

With time at a premium, he crept forward, anticipating a door would open at any moment. Each door was approximately two meters from the next, roughly indicating the room dimensions for each instructor. In the darkness, he counted four doors on either side of the corridor. The second one on the left had a crack of light coming from a sizable gap at the bottom of the door.

The light flickered for a moment before the door swung open. Garrett raised his rifle, ready to fire, relaxing his trigger finger when Rosa poked her head out into the corridor. She was panting and her face had turned red. He took several steps toward her and urged her back into the room, closing the door behind him.

"Are you okay?" he whispered, controlling his joy that she was safe.

Rosa nodded and pointed to the single bunk in the middle of the room. One of Darr's instructors was lying on his back, his lifeless eyes staring at the ceiling. Garrett could not remember the man's name, not that it mattered anymore. The cause of death was obvious; a thick-handled knife was sticking out of the side of his neck as a pool of thick, crimson blood oozed from his carotid artery and congealed beneath his head, sinking through the sheet and into the thin mattress below.

Effective. He smiled at Rosa with a new sense of admiration.

She did not return the smile. "As soon as he switched on the lamp, the instructor realized I was not who he thought I was. He went for his knife but I'd already spotted it and was ready for him."

There was little sign of a struggle other than the man's fists gripping the sheet tightly. He had probably died without comprehending what was happening to him.

"So it wasn't you who screamed."

"God, no. I was about to search for Thamsi when I found you."

"She's in the last room on the left," Garrett replied, remembering the lit window.

He cracked open the door, just as an instructor ran past toward where Thamsi was.

"Damn!"

"Don't you think you should give me a rifle?" Rosa murmured.

Garrett cursed silently. In his haste, he had forgotten the spare rifle he was carrying. I'm losing my touch, he thought, handing his rifle to Rosa, along with a spare power pack.

Taking the rifle from his shoulder, he said, "I'll head for Thamsi's room. Can you watch my back? Syl and the men are by the entrance."

He didn't wait for a reply before opening the door again, checking to his right. Two instructors were at the far end of the corridor, marching toward his position. Someone had switched on the overhead lamps, giving him a clear view of the instructors, but also allowing them to see him. He fired three shots in quick succession, blue beams of light appearing blindingly bright in the gloom.

The first shot hit an instructor in the middle of his chest. He instantly dropped to the ground. The second instructor was more nimble, ducking for cover in a room. The laser bolts ricocheted off the walls before hitting the far wall in a shower of sparks.

Garrett had already turned to his left, crouching low as he aimed the rifle at the back of the instructor who had just run past. The blast hit the instructor squarely between his shoulder blades, forcing him forward so that his face hit the wooden floor with a resounding thump.

Garrett ran forward, knowing the instructor would not cause him any trouble. Even so, as he passed four closed doors, his trigger finger was ready to fire off more laser bolts should any luckless instructor appear.

Once he reached the end of the corridor, he twisted the door handle, ready to fire on anyone who threatened him from inside. At that exact moment, he was vaguely aware of movement halfway along the corridor as someone came out of another room. Glancing over his shoulder, he spotted one of Darr's men with a handgun pointing directly at him. Although not a powerful weapon, it would still inflict considerable damage from five meters away, and there was no time to raise his own rifle in self-defense.

As Garrett was about to dive for cover, an electric-blue aura momentarily surrounded the instructor. His whole body convulsed before he fell flat on his face and remained still. Garrett spotted Rosa staring at him, her rifle still pointing at the fallen instructor. He nodded his gratitude before returning to the end door.

Hearing heavy breathing within, he forced the door open, to find a naked instructor laid on top of an equally naked Thamsi who was fighting and struggling to escape. She was no match for the bulky instructor as he continued to force himself onto her, unaware of his immediate danger.

Garrett took some pleasure in cracking the rifle butt hard against the base of the man's skull. His body immediately went limp. Thamsi opened her mouth to scream until she spotted Garrett holding a finger to his lips. He rolled the unconscious instructor onto the floor and retrieved Thamsi's clothes that were strewn about the small room.

"I'm getting you out of here," he said as she dressed and wiped tears from her eyes.

"Thank you," she mumbled as she stared down at the unconscious instructor. "He was getting angry with me tonight. He knew something was wrong but I wouldn't tell him."

Garrett placed a comforting hand on her shoulder. "You're safe now. Stay behind and keep your head down."

Cautiously opening the door, he could now hear men shouting angrily from along the corridor.

That was when the alarms sounded and all the lights in the building came on.

***

With the element of surprise gone, Garrett knew they now had a limited window to make their plan work. The good news was they had already taken out four instructors. Although uncertain of the total complement of guards, he guessed there were less than ten more to deal with.

As he peered into the corridor, the door to the room opposite also swung open. Garrett was suddenly facing an instructor who regularly served the tasteless stews every night. He stared back with wide eyes and an open mouth, clearly not expecting to see sinners appearing from his colleague's room and wasting valuable fractions of a second. Garrett didn't hesitate, raising his rifle and firing two rapid shots. At this range, a single shot was lethal, the electricity from the laser blast burning every cell and nerve ending of the man's body. The power of the shots threw him back into his room and he was dead before he hit the floor.

Before Garrett could move on to his next target, wood splintered on the end wall to his left, leaving three small holes about the width of his finger. The instructors were using projectile weapons. Less effective than the laser rifle he was holding, but almost as deadly at short range.

Along the corridor, Rosa had moved toward him, finding cover in the doorway of an empty room. She was randomly firing her rifle every few seconds and, although she was not hitting any targets, she was at least keeping the instructors nailed down. However, the instructors were using their skills to advance on Rosa's position. Garrett knew it would not be long before they reached her. Time for him to provide some covering fire.

To Garrett's surprise, the shooting suddenly stopped. Several seconds later, Darr's voice rang out.

"Garrett, give yourself up. Don't make matters worse for yourself."

Garrett laughed. "How can they possibly be any worse? I'm due to be executed tomorrow."

"Do you want your friends to join you? We'll eradicate everyone in this camp. Their lives will be on your head."

"Darr, we outnumber you and your instructors. Any threats you make are empty. I suggest you drop your weapons if you want to live."

Garrett saw two of the instructors had almost reached the entrance hallway, no doubt intending to escape or retrieve more powerful weapons. He quickly fired two shots close to their position, making them think twice about moving forward any further.

He heard Darr's voice again. "You can't keep this up. There are only two of you. I would like to know your friend."

"That will not happen, Darr. This is your last chance to order your men to stand down. I'm a trained soldier. Your men stand no chance."

The reply was almost instant as a hail of gunfire sent more splinters of wood flying, forcing Garrett to take shelter behind the door frame. He knew the gunfire was a ruse to get Darr's men to the entrance, but there was nothing he could do to prevent it.

The firing paused for a moment. Garrett waited for several seconds and was ready to leap out and fire a salvo when he heard angry shouts and the distinctive sound of metal hitting metal.

In the heat of battle, Garrett had forgotten about Sylwester and the prisoners. Perhaps it was because he had not expected them to remain once they realized the jeopardy they faced. Yet here they were, surging into the hallway, their crude weapons flailing in pure rage. He could only guess at the levels of frustration and anger being released against the instructors.

The prisoners swarmed as one, quickly overpowering the instructors. Garrett edged forward, unable to fire his rifle for fear of hitting one of them. The noise was incredible yet brutal at the same time as it changed to the distinctive sound of metal crashing into bone. The instructors were becoming overwhelmed by the sheer number and ferocity of the prisoners.

Garrett reached for Rosa, who was transfixed by what she was seeing. "Who knew these people could be fighters?" she said, in awe.

Garrett nodded. "Humans! They never cease to amaze me." He had seen plenty of violence during his lifetime, but what he was witnessing now, the hand-to-hand combat, left him stunned.

The fighting ended almost as quickly as it had begun. The occasional groan from a fallen instructor was swiftly followed by the thunk of a pickax piercing a skull. Except for the heavy breathing of the prisoners, the corridor soon fell silent.

"Darr escaped through a window," Sylwester reported, walking up to Garrett. A light sheen of sweat covered his face and arms. Garrett noticed the end of his hammer was covered in blood and hair.

"Excellent work, Syl," Garrett replied. "You and your friends did an incredible job. I'm proud of you."

Sylwester grinned, sticking his chest out in pride. Garrett wondered how often in his life had anyone complimented this man. *Could this be the first time?*

Sylwester looked across at Rosa. "What Oz said," she said, her voice almost cracking with pride.

"We can celebrate later," Garrett reminded them. "We need to locate Darr, Stagg, and any other instructors before they can alert Zaen or anyone else. Rosa, stay close to me and provide supporting cover if I need it. Syl, bring your men too. We must make this camp safe."

"We're really doing this?" she asked, unable to hide the disbelief in her voice.

Garrett frowned. "That's what I said I'd do. I'm not in the habit of breaking my promises."

Without further debate, he ducked back out into the night, on the hunt for the warden and head instructor.

Chapter 47

Darr jumped through a window and fell to the ground in a panic, shocked by the level of violence directed at him and his men. He could not understand how the sinners had escaped from the tunnels. He had clearly underestimated Garrett's ingenuity. It was too late for regrets; what mattered now was survival.

Leaving the ugly sounds of the fight behind him in the darkness, he headed directly for the warden's office. He knew the siren would have alerted Stagg to the disaster. If he was as weak as Darr suspected, he would already be preparing a hasty escape. Which was fine, as long as he included Darr.

There was a look of guilt and fear in Stagg's eyes as Darr opened the door to the warden's office. "My God! I thought you were a sinner. What's happening out there?"

"Garrett's leading a riot. The sinners have escaped the camp and murdered all the instructors. Garrett is going to be coming after you and me next."

Stagg fumbled through his desk drawers, looking for his keys. "How long do we have?"

"Not long enough," Darr replied grimly. "I suggest you get your vehicle and I'll get the commodities to the loading bay."

"Can we load everything in time?"

"Only if you move your lazy ass." Darr regretted not having the stolen ore already on board a transport vehicle, but he never would have guessed the sinners had it in them to turn so violent. He shivered as he recalled seeing the hatred in their eyes. They were like a pack of wild dogs, attempting to sate their bloodlust.

With a cry of relief, Stagg found the keys he had been searching for. He dashed for the door before disappearing into the night.

Darr followed him from the room, heading in a different direction; to where they had hidden their retirement fund. Fortunately, the diverted precious metals were not too far from Stagg's office, loaded in ten sturdy crates and stored in a derelict cold room that, until twenty years earlier, had stored fresh food for the instructors.

He hurriedly began to move the crates, using a trolley jack to slide them onto the loading bay. All the time, he listened out for the rampaging sinners, grateful for every additional minute he had available. His men must be putting up a good fight in the face of such a violent attack, although he expected nothing less.

He heard the deep roar of Stagg's personal utility vehicle approach, but it seemed to take a lifetime for the warden to reverse it next to the loading bay. By then, Darr had four crates ready to slide onto the back of Stagg's vehicle, but that meant using the single trolley jack. Darr left the crates on the loading bay, instead, venturing back into the cold room to collect a fifth crate. This he then wheeled directly onto the rear flatbed of Stagg's vehicle.

It was then that Darr heard the crunching of many feet scurrying across gravel and stone. He had run out of time. The precious metal and ore would have to be abandoned, millions of credits wasted.

Stagg had a different idea. "Don't just stand there," he ordered. "Get those crates loaded now. We can still make a getaway. Those sinners don't care about us. All they want is to escape from here. They don't know they'll be rounded up in the next few hours."

Darr shook his head. "You didn't see their faces. The sinners are baying for blood. They want revenge."

"What for? We give them food and shelter. No one has ever wanted to escape from my camp."

"I've no time to argue with you," interrupted Darr. "If we don't leave now, we'll be too dead to enjoy our riches."

"You're joking. There's at least one million credits' worth of gold and other metals in every one of those crates. We cannot simply walk away from all that wealth. Especially when we're so close."

"One more and that's it," Darr replied firmly, quickly placing the trolley jack under one of the crates on the loading bay.

Stagg tried to push another crate with his bare hands, but it wouldn't move. "I never had you as a quitter," he said, straining his muscles for all he was worth.

Darr jumped from the flatbed and ran to the cab. "Get in. Now!" He went to start the engine, only to find the keys were missing.

***

Garrett was leading the band of prisoners to the compound when he heard voices and movement behind a building to his left. He stopped, raised his hand in the air, and motioned for everyone to remain still. There was still a chance there were more instructors, along with Darr, who were ready to ambush the escaped prisoners.

"Rosa," he whispered. "You're with me. Syl, remain here and wait for my signal."

"What will it be?" Sylwester asked.

"You'll know," Garrett replied, before sprinting toward the building, keeping low. He reached the corner of the building, grateful it was in shadows. Taking a deep breath, he peeked around the corner for a fraction of a second.

"What did you see?" whispered Rosa.

"Stagg and Darr. Loading a vehicle. No one else."

"Do we kill them or tie them up?"

"Rosa, I'm not a murderer. There is a third alternative."

Before she could ask what the third option was, Garrett turned the corner, staying low and moving slowly to avoid being detected. Both Stagg and Darr were too preoccupied to notice him creep closer until he was only a few meters away from the front of the vehicle, partially hidden by a bush.

He watched as Darr climbed into the vehicle, let out a series of expletives, and jump back out. "Where are the keys?" he shouted at Stagg.

"Load these crates and I'll tell you," came the response.

Garrett watched as Darr jumped up onto the loading bay and walked straight up to Stagg, snatching the warden's shirt by the collar. "We're going now."

"I don't think so," Garrett said, stepping out from the shadows with his rifle pointed at the two men.

Darr pushed Stagg away in anger. "I told you we had to leave."

Stagg stumbled and fell, slowly getting back to his feet while staring suspiciously at Garrett. Straightening his shirt and jacket, he tried to present an air of superiority, yet his eyes told an entirely different story. "Mr. Garrett. You've had your fun. Reserves are on their way and will have this camp surrounded within fifteen minutes. There is no escape for you or your fellow sinners. Only certain death."

Garrett shrugged. "I don't believe you. If that were the case, why are you attempting to escape?"

"I'm trying to save my life. Darr told me you slaughtered all of his men. I'm not waiting around to let you do the same to me. You're all barbarians."

"Yet here you are. What's in those crates that you had to take them with you?"

Stagg glanced down at the crates and then at Darr, as if giving him a signal.

"Don't do anything stupid," Rosa shouted out, stepping from the shadows and standing next to Garrett with her rifle raised.

"Who the hell are you?" Stagg asked.

"Don't you remember your own prisoners?"

Darr rubbed his chin before his eyes suddenly widened. "You're the last off-worlder we had from several years ago. The one looking for her son. We thought you were dead."

"I've been well cared for. No thanks to your instructors."

Garrett took a pace forward. "Enough of the introductions. You have a choice. Remain here or help us get on board a ship at the spaceport."

"Are you serious?" scoffed Stagg.

"I'm the one holding the laser rifle."

"I don't respond well to threats from sinners."

Garrett doubted if Stagg had any experience of prisoners questioning his orders, let alone threatening him. Not that it mattered.

To Garrett's astonishment, Darr was the one who cracked first. "Garrett, I can understand you're desperate. And I also want to stay alive. So I'm prepared to help—"

"You're a lowlife traitor," shouted Stagg, interrupting Darr. "Betray me and I'll ensure you face the death penalty along with this scum."

The head instructor spun around to face Stagg and, with surprising speed, drew a handgun from a hidden holster and fired a single shot. The projectile hit Stagg in the center of his forehead, flying out of the back of his head along with a thick spray of blood, bone, and brains.

"Drop the gun," Garrett screamed before Stagg's lifeless body had hit the ground. His trigger finger applied more pressure, ready to fire if Darr refused to comply.

Darr did as Garrett ordered, dropping the gun before slowly turning around.

"Why did you kill him?" Rosa asked.

Darr smiled. "He's pissed me off for a while. And he would never agree to help you."

"Will you?"

"Like I was saying, I want to live. Where are you planning to go if you leave this planet?"

"The only place that's safe. Back to the Stellar Cluster. We'll take as many people as want to come."

Darr nodded. "Take me with you and I'll help you get onto the space-port."

Darr's swift capitulation shocked Garrett. "Why are you really offering to help? You hate these people. You've treated them appallingly for years."

"I've also been planning with Stagg for years. These crates are an invest-ment for our future. They're full of precious metals we've held back from Em-inence Zaen. At least ten million of your credits, according to our calcula-tions. If not for you, we would soon have been making our own way to the Stellar Cluster."

Rosa stepped closer to the vehicle to get a better look at the crates. "I guess you'll now be donating this collection back to the people who dug it out of the ground."

Darr shook his head. "They can have Stagg's share. He doesn't need it anymore. That is still five million. Those sinners won't know what to do with even that much money."

"I don't think you were listening to my friend," Garrett said. "Her sug-gestion is not negotiable. You did nothing to earn any of what's inside those crates."

"Maybe not. But I expect some recompense for getting you off Drani IV."

"Isn't your life worth enough?"

Darr shrugged his shoulders. "I'll need something to start a new life. Or we can all die together here when Zaen's guards catch up with us."

Garrett turned to Rosa, who shook her head. "I think we'll take our chances."

Holding up his hands in defeat, Darr said. "How about one crate in return for valuable information?"

"What could you possibly tell us that's worth one million credits?"

Pointing a quivering finger at Rosa, he replied, "I know where her son is being kept."

Chapter 48

Garrett gathered Rosa and Sylwester in what had formerly been Warden Stagg's office. He had cleared the old wooden desk of all papers and books and replaced them with laser rifles and handguns collected from across the camp.

"Is this it?" Garrett asked, looking at the sorry haul of weapons and spare ammunition. A total of six laser rifles and fifteen antique handguns seemed little for a prison.

"We searched all the buildings and the instructors' bodies," Sylwester replied, his voice subdued.

Garrett would have preferred better weapons in case they had to fight their way onto the spaceport. Then again, he wondered if any of the prisoners could fire the handguns, let alone hit any targets.

"Head Instructor Darr provided keys to all the transports," Sylwester added, trying to sound more positive. "They are fully fueled too."

"How many of your friends are coming with us?"

"To the spaceport? Sixty-two."

That was fewer than Garrett had expected. He wanted to rescue all the prisoners.

"Did you tell the others they would likely die if they remain?"

"Yes. There are twelve who refuse the leave the camp. They are old and have been here longer than anyone can remember. But they regard this as their home. The others want to return to their communes, to be reunited with family and friends."

Garrett nodded in understanding. He would force no one to do anything they did not want. In any case, he was running out of time to argue with them. It would be daylight in a few hours, and he had to be as far away from the camp as possible by then.

"Thanks, Syl. Good work." Garrett turned to Rosa. "You're quiet. Is everything okay?"

Rosa had run away when Darr broke the news about her son. Garrett had chosen not to follow her and, when she had returned, her eyes were puffy and red. Since then, she had kept herself busy by organizing the prisoners and get-

232

ting them outside into the fresh but cold night air. She had not spoken again to Darr, who Garrett had bound tightly to a chair in the next room.

"Rosa?" he asked again.

Angrily wiping a tear from her eye, she replied. "Do you think he's telling the truth?"

"Honestly? I don't know. It could simply be a ruse to save his own miserable skin. He said he wants to speak with you."

"To play with my mind?"

"Perhaps. Although I can't see what he has to gain."

"What if he's telling the truth? I can't leave this planet if there's a chance Mikel is alive."

"I know. Which is why you have to speak with Darr."

"I'm scared."

This was a new side to Rosa that Garrett hadn't seen. The vulnerability of a loving mother breaking down the walls she had built around her in order to survive the tunnels. He understood her anguish. Darr's revelation had placed her in an impossible position. But avoiding the question would get them nowhere.

Sylwester looked on, looking embarrassed at Rosa's discomfort.

Garrett placed his arms around Rosa's shoulders. She didn't pull away. "We need to go soon. Let me sit in the room with you while you question Darr. Ask him any question you have to."

Rosa nodded and allowed herself to be led into the adjoining room. Darr was sitting in the middle of the room, staring down at the floor. The room was the camp's communications room. Two aging consoles against the far wall enabled transmission and receipt of audio messages only. Or they had done until Garrett fired laser bolts into them, frying the electronics. The surviving instructors could not contact the outside world for help.

Darr looked up as they walked in. He smirked. "I assume you have some questions for me."

"Why would you say that my son is still alive?" Rosa asked, her voice steady once more.

"I thought you should know. I remember when you first came to this camp. You cried for days, pleading for any news that your son was alive. We didn't know at the time, not that we would have told you anyway. About a year ago, I was talking with a colleague at another camp and he told me about a young off-worlder who had arrived with a group of others. They had stupidly believed they could bring their message to the people of the Bevas Sector."

"That could be anyone," Garrett said. "You specifically said it was Rosa's son."

"The off-worlder's name was Mikel. At the time it sounded familiar, but I couldn't place it. By then, Rosa had been missing for months, presumed to be another victim of the tunnels. It was only when I saw her tonight that all the pieces fitted into place."

"Have you spoken about this prisoner since then? How do you know he's still alive?"

Darr shook his head. "I'm not in the habit of checking up on sinners, whether in this camp or others."

"So you're giving me false hope?"

"I thought you'd like to know. Before you leave this planet."

"Shit!" exclaimed Rosa, pacing up and down.

Garrett leaned in close to Darr. He could feel the anger building once more inside him as Darr played with Rosa's emotions. "Where is the camp located?"

"About an hour west of here. It's another instructional camp converted into a mine, similar to this one and equally well guarded."

"I'd hardly call this place well guarded. It was relatively straightforward to overpower your instructors. They were slow and complacent."

"You took us by surprise, that's all. My instructors are some of the best."

"And yet you were quick to abandon them."

Darr fell silent at the accusation, his gaze dropping to the floor.

"Can we rescue Mikel?" Rosa asked. "Surely we can do what we did here? We have enough people with weapons."

Garrett shook his head. "These people aren't fighters. They channeled their anger against the instructors because it was personal. I don't think they would react in the same way against a fresh set of instructors."

"Even to save their own people?"

"I can see it in their eyes. The experience has already traumatized several. I can't put them through it again."

"So you're going to leave my precious son behind?"

"That's not what I'm saying, Rosa. We just need to be smarter."

The statement piqued her interest. "What do you intend to do?"

Garrett stared at Rosa and then at Darr as his brain formulated a plan. Events were changing quicker than he had expected. His commanding officers had always valued him for his ability to find solutions in the heat of battle, but this scenario was more challenging than any he had faced. He had limited resources, virtually no intel on which to base his decisions, and many civilians in his care who were anxiously following his instruction.

"We all need to get away from this camp in the next five minutes. Rosa, I want you to lead these people to the spaceport and locate a ship."

"No, if you're going to find my son then I should go too."

"That's not an option. Who else is going to guide these men, women, and children? Sylwester is a good man, but he doesn't have the necessary skills, especially if you face any resistance at the spaceport."

She gripped his arm. "Oz, you can't go on your own. It will be a suicide mission. I have to go with you."

Garrett shook his head. "I won't be alone. I'll be taking Darr with me."

Darr tensed at the sound of his name. "What? You can't be serious?"

Once more, Garrett bent over so his face was level with the man's. "You're going to take me to the camp and you're going to get us in there. They know you and will trust you. By the time they realize their error, it will be too late."

"No, it's a mistake. You'll be wasting valuable time. We need to get away before Zaen discovers what is happening. If he captures us, we will all be dead."

"What did you expect us to do when you told Rosa about her son?"

Darr glanced at Rosa. "I'm sorry. I thought you would like to know the truth. That it would make you feel better."

"Then you're a bigger fool than I thought," she replied. Turning to Garrett, she added, "I don't like this plan, but I don't have a better alternative. This had better work."

"It'll work," he replied, with more assurance than he felt. He silently hoped he was not making a grave miscalculation, but he would not leave anyone behind.

Chapter 49

Zaen awoke unusually early when it was still dark outside his bedroom windows. His room was quiet except for the heavy, rhythmic breathing of the young man lying next to him, his muscular body partly hidden by the fine silk sheets.

Usually, Zaen would have tried to sleep for another few hours, but his mind was far too active and his body restless.

It was too early for any of his servants to be awake to dress him. By the flickering light of thirty candles, he found a discarded robe and left the bedroom to roam the empty, silent corridors of his palace. He could not recall the last time he had wandered around his home with no one around. During the day, there was always the hustle and bustle of people; proctors, staff, and attendants running about their duties, looking busy and avoiding eye contact with him.

In honesty, he did not know what most of the people did. Neither did he care, as long as his daily routine ran smoothly. There must have been hundreds of people working within the palace, their only purpose to serve the eminence.

Just as it should be.

He smiled to himself. He had done pretty well for himself, rising through the ranks to become one of the most important people on the planet. His word was law. People feared him because he had the power of life and death. It felt good.

The vast palace, with its fine art, lavish furnishings, and luxurious fittings, was a just reward for his years of service to the Brotherhood. As he continued through the dim corridors, he could appreciate the grandeur of the building for what it was, without the commoners who filled its halls because of him. They were the fortunate ones; he had given them the opportunity to taste a lifestyle they never deserved. Yet none of them showed their gratitude.

He reached the cloister, going through the doors into the chilly night air. A fine layer of dew covered the paved path and plants, reflecting the moon in a silver, glistening light. Zaen wrapped his robe tightly around him, briefly fascinated by his breath forming condensed clouds of water vapor.

A fine dew covered the bench, the moisture sinking into his robe as he sat down but not leaching through the thick layers of cloth.

His arrival must have disturbed the local wildlife as Zaen heard rustling sounds coming from beneath several bushes and birds began to chirp in the trees. Being close to nature at this hour made him feel strangely alive and closer to the gods. It was perfect.

The day ahead was also going to be perfect. He knew this was the true reason he could not sleep. He wanted to live every minute of the day because it would be the fitting end to the darkest chapter in his life, allowing him to move on to the next level.

"Osiris Garrett!" he murmured.

Eminence Zaen was not a superstitious person. He didn't particularly regard himself as religious either, although he believed there were gods who had created the worlds, plants, and animals. His role as eminence was a title within the Brotherhood; a badge of honor that gave him unimaginable power. He had almost lost everything because of one individual. Osiris Garrett.

Zaen had convinced himself that Garrett had cursed him. Overnight, a common soldier from the Stellar Cluster had torn asunder his life. His existence would have been so much better if he had not crossed paths with Garrett.

Today, after years of hurt and discomfort, the curse was finally going to be lifted. Zaen was certain of it. Garrett's execution was the only way to lift the cloud of uncertainty that had haunted him for so long.

He would be there to witness Garrett's death. So many nights and days he had thought of nothing else. And now, within a matter of hours, he would stare into Garrett's eyes as his tormentor breathed his last breath. He would rejoice as he saw the life extinguished. And, although he had witnessed many deaths, Garrett's would be the most satisfying by far.

A disturbance close by made his head jerk. The pale gray sky told him he must have dozed off for a short while. Disconcerted by this lack of control, he looked around for the source of the noise and saw Chief Proctor Chan approaching, a look of concern on his face.

"Your Eminence, I was hoping I would find you here," he said, bowing in front of Zaen. "Your servants worried when they couldn't find you in your private quarters."

"I'm entitled to some privacy," Zaen replied, still feeling slightly disoriented. He had never known himself to fall asleep like that and hoped it wasn't a sign of old age creeping up on him. "Surely they didn't send you to find me. I'll have them flogged for their insolence."

"Nothing of the kind. I have received a message from the office of the Elders on Bevas Prime. They have invited you to attend their next conference in five days from now."

"Finally!" he exclaimed loudly. This was it. The recognition he had craved for so many years. They convened the Elder Conference only when an Elder was retiring, or died, and a replacement being instated into the venerable role. On rare occasions, the Elders could make an additional appointment to increase their numbers, but this was used primarily for political reasons to boost the support of the Senior Elder. With no impending elections, the invitation had to mean a replacement was to be installed.

Zaen considered who the outgoing Elder might be. To his knowledge, there were at least four candidates who were senile or close to the end of their lives. Not that it mattered which one it was. He was finally going to attain the title he deserved, affording him greater power and luxury.

I have lifted the Garrett curse, after all, he thought.

"Make plans for my craft to be ready for launch tonight. And begin packing my best robes."

"Already done," Chan replied, with no hint of self-importance.

Zaen nodded. The chief proctor may have his faults, but his ability to anticipate and execute the eminence's requirements was not one of them.

"Do you require anyone to attend to your needs on your journey?"

Chan's meaning was clear and discreet. Zaen enjoyed male entertainment and proving his virility. "Not this time, Chan. I have an acceptance speech to write and I will need all my wits about me. The conference will be the most important event of my life and I intend to make the most of it."

"As you will, Your Eminence. I have made arrangements to leave the palace at four o'clock tomorrow and will soon have confirmation of your accommodation on Bevas Prime."

"Excellent. And what about today's entertainment? When is Garrett due to arrive?"

"I advised Warden Stagg to be here no later than ten thirty. You may want to return to your quarters to let the servants prepare you."

Zaen waved him away, not enjoying being told what to do. "I shall take my breakfast first. For now, contact Stagg and confirm the arrangements. I want nothing to go wrong."

Chapter 50

The black clouds were gradually turning a dark shade of gray as Garrett slowed the large, armored transport, then stopped several hundred meters from the instruction camp where Mikel was supposedly being held. Next to him, Darr stared silently ahead, as if mesmerized by the headlights casting their twin beams of light along the road.

The trip had taken far longer than the one hour Darr had suggested, making Garrett increasingly nervous. The road had been poorly maintained over the years, with plenty of large potholes waiting to rip out a vehicle's suspension. With no such thing as streetlights, he had relied solely on the inadequate headlights and the occasional piece of advice from Darr.

Garrett didn't trust the head instructor as he had proved himself to be loyal to only himself. However, he had caught Darr looking longingly at the ore-filled crates being loaded onto the other transports before Rosa left for the spaceport. They were the insurance policy Garrett could rely on for Darr not to lead him into a trap.

Or so he hoped.

"This is where you do your bit, Darr. As we discussed."

Darr held out his bound hands with a smile. "It's also where you untie me. I still don't know why you felt the need to bind me like an animal. I gave you my word I would help you."

Garrett sliced the bindings with a small knife he had found in Stagg's office. The fifteen-centimeter blade had a sharp serrated edge that could cause significant injury and the ornamental bone handle provided the knife with a good balance that impressed Garrett. It was the only object that had impressed him since arriving on the planet.

"Make one mistake, or betray me, and I will gut you," Garrett said through gritted teeth.

Darr rubbed his wrists. "Hey, I want to live as much as you do. I'll do as I promised."

Garrett doubted the man had ever kept a promise in his whole life. He climbed over the back of his seat, into the gunner's chair. From there, he could control the twin cannons perched on top of the armored transport. He recognized the make and reckoned it had to be surplus military from before he was born. The ammunition appeared to be original too, but he had taken time to fire off a few rounds with ease.

As Darr slid into the driver's seat, Garrett said. "Remember, get us inside the camp. Persuade your friends to pass Mikel over to you, and we can avoid any bloodshed."

"This is most irregular. The instructors will be suspicious."

"All the more reason to be at your most persuasive."

"You know, I'd feel much better if I had a weapon. The two of us could wipe out the camp guards in no time at all."

"That's not going to happen," Garrett replied from his new position, convinced more than ever that the man was devious. *Who would kill his own men?* "Now drive."

"I'm on your side," Darr muttered, slamming his boot onto the accelerator.

Garrett didn't care. He was focusing on the video screen close to his head. The image was green and slightly fuzzy as it showed the view straight ahead. Within two minutes, he saw the sign for the camp on the left. A narrow track led into the jungle, quickly becoming hidden by a long, sweeping bend.

"How far?" Garrett asked.

"We're almost there. Be patient."

Several seconds later, a steel blockade came into view. Darr stopped the vehicle in front of the imposing gates and waited, the engine ticking over.

Maybe one minute later, the gates opened wide enough for one person to walk through. Garrett used the electronic sights to target the guard and was immediately convinced the man was no threat. Although he was holding a laser rifle, it was resting across his forearm, his trigger finger on the guard. Garrett reverted to scanning the immediate vicinity for any signs of an ambush.

Darr lowered his window as the man drew closer.

Garrett heard the man speak. "We weren't expecting any visitors today."

"Is that the way to address a superior officer? I am Head Instructor Darr from Instruction Camp Four. What is your name?"

"I'm sorry, I didn't recognize you," the man stammered. "My name is Bernd. How can I help you, Head Instructor Darr?"

"That's more like it. As you should be aware, the execution of an off-worlder will take place later today. He is a real nasty piece of work. One of his last requests is that a fellow off-worlder witnesses his death. We understand you have such a person and I am here to collect him."

Garrett held his breath. This was the moment of truth, determining if Darr was being honest with him. His laser rifle was close at hand, ready to kill Bernd, as well as Darr, should the need arise.

"Has this move been sanctioned? I have no records of such a request being made."

"Of course it's sanctioned," Darr replied indignantly. "Warden Stagg sent through the request late last night. I was expecting the sinner to be ready for collection. I have a long drive ahead."

"It's not in my notes. I will have to check with my warden."

"Do you really want to disturb him so early? If your warden is like mine, he's not a morning person. Perhaps you can allow the transfer and catch up with the paperwork once I'm gone. I promise you, your initiative will impress your warden. It could even help fast-track you to the position of head instructor."

"Yes, I see your point," Bernd replied slowly. "Follow me into the compound. I will see if we can locate the off-worlder and bring him to you."

"That would be appreciated. I will inform Warden Stagg of your intelligence and dedication to your job."

Through the windshield, Garrett could see the gates slowly swing open. There was no going back now, even if he wanted to. He was committed to the mission, with only two aims in mind.

Survive and reunite Rosa and Mikel.

***

The compound was almost identical to the one at Instruction Camp Four. High steel walls on each side gave the space a sense of impregnability. Garrett spotted gun emplacements and spotlights on each corner, but none were manned. He had expected as much from his previous experiences. The instructors were not expecting any trouble. In reality, they were nothing more than nursemaids, ensuring the prisoners mined and extracted the ore on the barest of rations.

All in the Brotherhood's name.

Garrett would have whipped the instructors into shape if they reported to him. But their complacency and lax standards currently played into his hands.

Bernd walked in front of the vehicle toward the rear of the compound, where a set of heavy doors built into the wall were already open.

Garrett ordered Darr to stop the vehicle just inside the compound, preventing the outer gates from closing. Darr did as instructed, cutting the engine. "What do we do now?" Darr asked.

"What would you do on a normal prisoner transfer?"

"Usually the sinner would be waiting in the compound, freshly disinfected. Instructors would lead them to the rear of the vehicle for loading. The entire process takes less than ten minutes."

"How will they find Mikel?"

"It's a similar setup to my camp. The instructors will single out any sinner and order him to bring Mikel to the kitchen. If he fails to show, more sinners will be sent to find him. After that, the instructors will descend into the tunnels and retrieve him by force."

"If they can find him. Your men lost track of Rosa."

"True. I could reprimand my men for their lack of detail. If only you hadn't killed most of them."

Ignoring the sarcasm, Garrett replied. "I suggest you go with Bernd. Remind him of the urgency of the request and the impatience of Zaen. The clock is ticking here."

Darr turned in his seat. "Do I get a weapon now?"

"What for? This is just a routine transfer. I don't want you arousing suspicions."

"I always carry my handgun. It's a lucky charm if you will."

"Do your gods believe in luck?"

"Damned if I know," Darr replied with a sour expression. "As head instructor, I'm expected to have a weapon to hand, especially when handling sinners."

"I've not seen a dangerous prisoner yet," Garrett scoffed, disliking the man more by the second.

"Tell that to my men! Stop wasting time. Pass me a handgun. I promise not to shoot you. We want the same thing here."

Garrett retrieved a handgun from a rack next to his seat, removing all except one projectile from its magazine before handing it to Darr.

"Are you serious?"

"Go!"

Darr opened the door and climbed down from the cab. "Is everything okay?" Bernd asked, staring worriedly at Darr, who slammed the door closed before Garrett could hear his response. Garrett paid close attention as Darr walked beside Bernd until the two men disappeared from view through the far gates.

Chapter 51

Garrett did his best to sit calmly while Darr was out of sight. With every passing minute, he felt more exposed, parked alone in the middle of the compound. He continually scanned the top of the surrounding wall for any sign of movement, ready to jump into the driver's seat and make his escape at the first sign of trouble.

Yet leaving without Mikel was not an option now he was so close to being rescued. Garrett had seen Rosa's reaction when she had discovered her son could still be alive and held captive. To lose her son for a second time could devastate someone whose hope had only just been restored. He knew he would struggle to face her and explain the mission had failed. And she would not leave the planet without her son. She had already endured so much for him and would suffer more if there was any opportunity of reconciling with Mikel.

He finally breathed a sigh of relief as he spotted Darr coming back through the gate. He was too far away to read Darr's expression, but his body language appeared relaxed. Several seconds later, a tall man with long, straggly black hair, a thick beard, and a tattered prison tunic appeared behind Darr, followed closely by the efficient-looking Bernd.

About time, Garrett whispered to himself. The stranger's height, some fifteen centimeters taller than Darr, identified him as an off-worlder. Surely this had to be Mikel, even if his appearance was nothing like Rosa's description. Anyone could be hiding under the unruly mop of hair and beard.

Mikel, if that's who he was, had his hands behind his back and stared continuously at the ground. His shoulders slumped, and he looked as bewildered a person as Garrett had ever seen. He could not begin to guess what the young man had been through.

Darr was halfway to the vehicle when he and the tall stranger suddenly paused. Garrett held his breath, reaching for one of the laser rifles next to his right leg.

What now?

He watched on, nerves building within him as Bernd turned back to face the gate he had recently passed through. Garrett thought he could hear raised voices, and he immediately regretted not having opened a window. Something was wrong, but he had no idea if it concerned Mikel.

As Darr's body tensed, Garrett saw movement through the far side of the gate. Men were running. He switched to the electronic gun sights to scan the walls of the compound, confirming his worst fears.

The instructors had discovered them.

Darr knew it. Garrett could see the man wanted to run. Mikel didn't have that luxury as Garrett spotted the instructors had shackled his ankles.

So much for a quiet rescue!

With no other alternatives, Garrett braced himself in his seat, took careful aim at a gun emplacement on the far corner of the compound, and pressed the trigger. The twin cannons on the vehicle's roof spat out four explosive rounds that tore through the metal wall like a knife through butter. It severed the gun emplacement from its mount, toppling it backward. Garrett swung the cannon to his left, swiftly taking aim at the second gun emplacement and firing in the same movement.

The cannons gave a satisfying whumping noise as they fired the ten-centimeter-wide projectiles at the top corner of the compound. Garrett saw two men working hard to aim and fire their weapons at him. They were too slow. Garrett's view screen erupted in a blinding light as one of the cannon's rounds hit the ammunition store. The gun emplacement exploded in a shower of sparks and molten shrapnel. He assumed he'd killed the two men in the blast but didn't wait to confirm the situation.

More instructors were coming through the far gate. But Mikel was in the way, preventing Garrett from getting a clean shot. Darr had abandoned Mikel, running for the vehicle, and climbing into the driver's seat.

"We're not leaving without Mikel," Garrett shouted, barely controlling his temper at Darr's apparent cowardice.

"I have no intention of abandoning him. But I also have no plans to get myself killed in the process. Pass me a rifle."

Garrett looked at Darr, scrutinizing the man's face for any hint of deception. Out of the corner of his eye, he saw two more instructors burst through the gate. They all appeared to have only handguns.

Cursing at his lack of options, Garrett threw a rifle to Darr. "We don't leave without the kid. Is that clear?"

Darr nodded and jumped back out onto the ground, rolling over in an over-theatrical way. Garrett grabbed a second rifle and followed Darr, crouching by the front wheel arch for cover.

Mikel was still shuffling his way across the compound like a penguin, his head down as if to ignore the surrounding mayhem.

By now, several of the instructors were firing their weapons. Garrett heard the distinctive ping of bullets ricocheting off the vehicle's bodywork. This was far from an ideal scenario, but Garrett reminded himself he had been in worse fixes. And he had lived to tell the tale.

Two meters to his side, Darr was calmly kneeling on the ground, taking aim at the onrushing instructors. "We need Mikel alive. If you kill him, I'll shoot you myself," Garrett called out before attempting to take aim. It was no good though; Mikel was too close to his line of sight.

Darr did not seem to have the same issue as he fired off a salvo of laser bolts, striking three instructors, two of whom were dead before they knew what had happened.

"Cover me," Garrett said without waiting for a reply. He sprinted toward Mikel, his rifle raised, ready to open fire at the first opportunity. Close by, the air sizzled with the electrical charge from Darr's laser bolts. He could almost touch the deadly blue light as Darr continued to fire at men coming through the gate.

Running up to Mikel, Garrett shouted, "Head to the back of the vehicle. I'm here to get you out of here." If Mikel understood the instruction, he didn't react but instead continued to shuffle slowly forward.

That was until his luck ran out. A projectile fired from an instructor's gun caught him in the right shoulder, spinning him around.

Garrett stared in dismay, first as he saw the bullet exit the front of Mikel's shoulder, with blood and sinew spraying out. Before he could react, Mikel tumbled forward. With his hands tied behind him, he could not recover his balance. Mikel landed heavily on the ground, face first.

Garrett had no time to check on the young man; four instructors were bearing down on him, their weapons drawn. He fired two shots in rapid succession, taking out an instructor. He heard the soft whine of a laser rifle behind him as he spotted another instructor being bathed in a pale blue light before collapsing to the ground.

The two remaining guards stopped, looking hesitantly at one another, and then across at Bernd, who was standing to one side, looking pale.

"Drop your weapons," Garrett commanded, hoping the men would react to his taking control of the moment. To his slight amazement, it worked. The guns hit the ground, kicking up small clouds of dust as the compound fell silent.

Garrett got to his feet and was about to check on Mikel when two more laser blasts sizzled the air. "What the—" Garrett exclaimed as the two instructors fell to the ground.

He turned to Darr. "Why did you kill them? They were unarmed."

Darr shrugged as he too stood up. "What did you plan to do with them?"

"Not murder them in cold blood. Put the weapon down." Garrett didn't want Darr to continue his killing spree; the man's blood lust had to be stopped. "Tie Bernd up."

Kneeling down, he cautiously rolled Mikel onto his back to examine the wound. The man's eyes were open and transfixed by the gray clouds above. Satisfied the wound was superficial, Garrett asked. "What is your name?"

The man didn't respond, so Garrett repeated the question.

The man blinked. "Why do you want to know my name? No one is interested in me."

Garrett offered a warm smile. "I'm from the Stellar Cluster."

The man's eyes widened. "Has my mother sent you to rescue me?"

"Possibly. What is your name? Or your mother's name?"

A shadow passed across the man's eyes as Garrett helped him sit up. "My name is Mikel Pasma," he said. His eyes darted between Garrett and Darr. "My mother is Rosa Pasma."

Garrett breathed a sigh of relief. "In that case, yes. I am taking you home."

A single tear ran down the man's cheek, quickly lost in his beard.

"Why does my shoulder hurt?"

"The instructors shot you. The good news is that it is only a flesh wound, so no lasting damage. Can you stand?"

Garrett helped Mikel to his feet and, with his knife, cut the bindings holding his hands together. He turned to ask Bernd for the keys to Mikel's shackles, only to discover the instructor writhing on the ground, a long blade sticking into the center of his chest. Darr was standing over him, a key in his hand, staring down in fascination at Bernd's last seconds. As the writhing slowed then stopped, Darr offered a silent prayer.

Garrett gave him a disapproving look, wondering at how easily Darr had murdered his fellow instructors with no sense of remorse.

"Back to the vehicle, Darr. We need to get the hell out of here."

Garrett expected Darr to comply and was therefore surprised when Darr raised his laser rifle and ran through the far gate, disappearing toward some low buildings, eerily similar to the barracks and warden's office from Instruction Camp Four. He didn't have time to chase after Darr. Instead, he unlocked the shackles and helped Mikel walk unsteadily to the passenger side of the armored vehicle.

Garrett was about to reverse out of the compound when he spotted Darr sprinting back toward him, an enormous smile on his face. A few seconds later, Garrett noticed wisps of smoke rising above the height of the compound's walls.

Mikel slid into the center seat, allowing Darr to climb into the passenger seat. As Garrett carefully reversed the large transport, he asked. "What have you done?"

"What needed to be done," was Darr's cryptic response. "You will thank me later."

Garrett rolled his eyes as he maneuvered the truck so that he was once more driving forward. "Are any instructors left alive?" he asked, already knowing the answer and hoping he was wrong."

"More than that," Darr said proudly. "I have smashed all their communications equipment. No one can warn Eminence Zaen. You're right. I already made sure the remaining instructors and the warden would never share our secret. But you can never be too careful; there may be spies among the sinners."

"Did you unlock the gates for the prisoners?"

Darr smiled. "Of course I did. I'm not inhuman, you know."

Garrett continued to have his doubts about that. But there was no mistaking the ferocity Darr had shown. He clearly wanted to escape Drani as much as anyone else.

"Mikel, how are you feeling?"

"Confused and in pain. But glad to be alive. Thank you for risking your lives to save me."

"You can thank me when we're off this planet. There are still people wanting to prevent that from happening."

Garrett accelerated the vehicle, bouncing along the uneven road. With the arrival of daylight, he could travel faster. But he couldn't shake the worry the rescue had taken longer than he had planned, and there was still a long way before they reached the spaceport. He could only hope Rosa had secured the ship.

There remained too much outside his control.

Chapter 52

Rosa and Sylwester stood together on the edge of a clearing overlooking Drani IV's only spaceport, less than three kilometers away. They had arrived shortly after dawn and parked the convoy of three trucks carrying the former prisoners under nearby trees to make them less conspicuous.

Her initial plan had been to drive straight up to the gates of the spaceport and force entry. But during the long drive from the camp, Rosa had decided she was not comfortable with that approach. She wanted to avoid bloodshed if possible; there had already been enough death for one day. Second, a direct assault might raise the alarm to the local military garrison. While she and her ragtag collection of prisoners might be able to overpower a handful of guards, they could not defend themselves against a sustained attack by a larger group of soldiers.

There was no telling how long it would take Garrett to turn up with her son. She stopped herself from thinking too much about that possibility, afraid to raise her expectations for fear of being disappointed. It was difficult, but she told herself she had to focus on her aspect of the mission. If, by some chance, Garrett found Mikel, the effort would be wasted if she did not secure a means of getting off the planet.

"What do you see?" Sylwester asked nervously.

Continuing to study the spaceport through binoculars discovered under the driver's seat, she replied. "Still not much action. Only two guards at the main gate. One delivery is being sent to a warehouse on the far side. There's an adapted freighter over near the larger hangars. I think it's probably from the Stellar Cluster from its design."

"Is that important?"

"Oh yes," she said, lowering the binoculars. "I wouldn't trust a Brotherhood ship to get us out of the Bevas Sector. Our best option is the freighter."

Sylwester accepted her analysis with a small nod. It impressed Rosa how quickly he had adapted to the situation they all now found themselves in. Unlike some of his companions who were content to hide in the back of the transports, Sylwester continued to show an interest in what was happening, and even offer suggestions of his own. "Are there any other guards?" he asked.

"It's hard to tell. There are many buildings located around the perimeter. The large gray building across from us could be a hospital or a prison, and there are smaller sheds that look like barracks or maintenance facilities. I need longer to carry out a full recon job, but we don't have the time."

"I'm scared, Rosa. We were safe where we were. Now I feel as if the Brotherhood will discover us at any moment. I don't think they will return us to the instruction camp."

"That's nonsense," Rosa whispered, placing a reassuring hand on his arm, at the same time looking around to ensure no one else was listening. "What you are all doing is courageous, and it is normal to be afraid. But you can trust me and Oz. Are the others feeling the same?"

Sylwester nodded, looking back at the group of people hovering close to the three transports that had brought them this far. "Only the children are excited about this adventure."

Rosa looked back at the entrance to the spaceport. The two guards were talking to each other near the small hut next to the main gate, their rifles leaning against the hut. One guard laughed, presumably at something his friend had said. These two were not expecting any trouble. But she knew discovery of the jailbreak was only a matter of time, and that would bring hundreds of Zaen's troops down here. The spaceport would become an impregnable fortress if they did not act soon.

"I have a plan," she said after two minutes of contemplation. Not for the first time, she wished Garrett was with them.

***

Rosa's truck led the convoy of three vehicles across the five kilometers from the spaceport's main gate to the aging freighter at the far end of the facility. In the row of seats behind her, two guards, their eyes filled with terror, sat still. On either side of them, a former prisoner pointed a handgun at their heads.

The two men had been taken by surprise when Rosa's truck had rolled up to the small wooden cabin next to the main gates. She had hidden her long hair under a cap and, as the guards had casually walked out to greet her; they had no suspicions anything was amiss. It was only when she opened the cab door that it shocked them to see a woman. One of them ran back to the hut in search of his rifle, only to see a young child running away with it around the corner of the truck.

The two men had quickly surrendered in the face of twenty people, most of them carrying a weapon of some kind. The men had not struggled as Sylwester bound their hands and forced them into the rear of the transport's cab.

Rosa didn't think they needed to know she had removed the bullets from the two handguns pointed at their heads. Removed for her safety as much as theirs.

She looked at the freighter through the windshield. As she drew closer, she could see the effects of a prolonged stay in Drani IV's humid climate on the ship's hull. Dull red patches of rust and oxidation confirmed the ship had been grounded here for at least a week. As she parked her transport less than fifty meters from the ship, she hoped it had not been abandoned.

Telling the others to remain in the cab, she stepped down onto the concrete landing pad and walked toward the ship's hatch.

"Finally!" a male voice shouted from the shadows of the hangar to her right. "I was beginning to doubt the supplies would ever arrive."

Rosa spun around, raising her gun, and pointing it at the stranger.

"Whoa lady!" said the man, raising his hands in submission. "There's no need for that."

"Who are you?" Rosa demanded.

"Captain Dreyfus. This is my ship. Who are you? Why are you aiming that gun at me?"

Rosa ignored the questions. "Does your ship fly?"

Dreyfus lowered his hands and smirked. "She may not look like much, but she's never let me down. This goddamn planet has brought out the worst in her. You ask a lot of questions, by the way."

"I need a ride off this planet."

Dreyfus shrugged. "I was waiting for you to make the request. I was asking myself why a resident from the Stellar Cluster dresses like a local peasant to force their way onto my ship. Can you answer my question?"

"Necessity! Let's just say I have to make an urgent getaway."

The captain looked at the three trucks parked in a row and raised an eyebrow. "Just you?"

"Sixty-five. Men, women, and children."

She thought Dreyfus's eyes would bulge from their sockets as he contemplated the number. "The answer has to be no, lady. I'm here to conduct a business transaction with the Brotherhood. I can't carry their cargo and act as a taxi service for your waifs and strays. There simply isn't the room."

Rosa could see the captain was serious. She raised her gun at him again. "This is a humanitarian emergency. If I don't get these people off Drani IV in the next few hours, their blood will be on your hands. You will help us."

"Now hold on. Threats won't work on me, so please stop pointing that toy gun. Second, you are the one who brought these people here. I'm just the unlucky captain who was in the wrong place when you arrived. It sounds like you have no proper plan other than hijacking a ship. Any deaths will therefore be on your head, whatever your name is. And I will continue conducting business with the locals. They may have weird ethical values, but they also have deep pockets."

"The Brotherhood only have credits because they exploit people like these."

Dreyfus shook his head. "I make a policy of not getting involved in local politics. All I care about is having enough credits to pay my crew, my bar tabs, and for repairs on this little beauty. I won't get rich by acting as a charity to someone who won't even reveal her name."

Rosa's dislike for the man was growing. Yet she realized she was at fault for getting off on the wrong foot with the captain. She should not have tried to intimidate Dreyfus, and she had been foolish to think otherwise. He was a simple captain of a freighter, with probably limited ambitions and no allegiance to anyone other than himself. She was asking a lot to think he would simply roll over and allow her to commandeer his ship. She wondered if she would react in the same way if the roles were reversed.

"My name is Rosa Pasma. I'm originally from Nesta, but the Brotherhood imprisoned me here when I came to find my son. That was over three years ago. These people with me were all locked up for disobeying the Brotherhood's laws. I promised them a better life if they came with me."

"My heart bleeds, Rosa. But you really shouldn't make promises you can't keep."

"What will it take for you to transport us back to any planet in the Stellar Cluster?"

"More than you have," scoffed Dreyfus. "Much more."

Rosa raised an eyebrow. "How much is the Brotherhood paying?"

"That's none of your business. I can tell you it is a good sum toward my retirement plan."

"One hundred thousand credits?" she asked.

"Double it and add some more," he replied, smiling wryly.

"So, let's say a quarter of a million credits. That seems very generous for transporting fruit and vegetables. It's a shame they're making you wait."

"It's still more than I make on a standard run back home."

"What if I said I could pay you one million credits?"

"I'd say you're crazier than I already think you are. And you must think I'm an idiot if you believe I'll fall for such an obvious scam. What is it? The credits will be waiting for me when we arrive at the destination."

"No tricks. I can pay up front."

"What did you do? Steal an expensive trinket from Zaen's palace?"

"Something like that. Do we have a deal?"

Dreyfus began walking slowly toward her, rubbing his hands together. "One million is a good starting number. But it doesn't really cover my costs and contingencies."

His response was not unexpected. He was a chancer, and she had already figured he would want to haggle.

"How much?" she said, folding her arms.

Dreyfus rubbed his chin, his lips moving as if he was working out the sums in his head. "What you're asking is very dangerous. If it's discovered you and your friends are on my ship, the Brotherhood's fleet may come after me."

"Your ship has more than enough weapons to defend itself."

"And there will be no more trade with the Brotherhood," he continued in an unsubtle attempt to pull at her heartstrings. "They will blacklist me forever. So I need to calculate the future loss of considerable earnings."

"Go on."

"Five million," he replied, his face deadpan.

It was Rosa's turn to scoff. "One minute ago, you thought I had nothing. Now you want five million. I don't have that much, and I wouldn't pay it even if I did."

Dreyfus returned her angry stare. "Four million. That's my best offer. Take it or leave it."

"One and a half million. That's way more than you make in five years."

"Don't go making assumptions about my earnings. Worry about how much these lives cost. Three million."

"One and three quarters," she countered.

"No," he replied, but she heard the hesitancy in his voice. "Two and a half."

She shook her head. "Two million. I think that's more than generous."

"You obviously don't place a high value on your life. Or on my retirement"

"Do we have a deal?" she said, holding his gaze and failing to be swayed by his deep blue eyes.

He reached out his hand, and she shook it. "You'd better not be playing me, Rosa."

She shook her head. "There are ten crates in the back of these trucks, each of them filled with precious metals. Two of them are yours."

"Does that mean you have ten million in total?" Dreyfus said, after spending several seconds calculating what she had just shared, his eyes glazing over for a moment. "What aren't you telling me?"

"I expect Zaen to come looking for us. Another person should arrive at any moment, and he's due to be executed today."

Dreyfus's jaw dropped. "Oz Garrett?" he murmured.

Rosa smiled. "Yeah, maybe I should have mentioned him sooner."

Chapter 53

"Is my food ready?" Zaen asked, standing and stretching his legs as Chan reentered the cloister. The cold weather was not helpful for his aging joints. At least Bevas is warmer and drier, he consoled himself.

"It is, Your Eminence," said Chan with a concerned expression. "But I could not contact Warden Stagg or anyone at Instruction Camp Four."

Zaen tensed at the news, not believing this could be happening. "Are there any reports of power outages?"

"None. We cannot connect to their comms equipment, but it is unclear why. I have dispatched an outrider. We should have confirmation within thirty minutes."

Zaen instinctively knew the communications failure was too much of a coincidence. Cursing himself for trusting the day would go as he intended, he rushed from the cloister with Chan in tow, five paces behind. "Prepare the guards. I want them ready in ten minutes," he barked.

Chan disappeared, leaving Zaen to stride back to his quarters where his two personal servants were standing, waiting to give him his daily bath.

"No time for that," he shouted, walking past them and through his bedroom to his dressing room, barely noticing his bed was now empty, the sheets and pillows straightened. His only thought was of Garrett, convinced that he had somehow escaped the instruction camp.

"Do I have to do everything myself?" He was raging at no one in particular but directing his anger specifically at Warden Stagg. If Stagg had failed him, there would be hell to pay.

The two nervous servants caught up with him and stood quivering by the door. "Find me my battle robes. I'm going on a hunt."

***

Confirmation that the instruction camp was empty, with the instructors killed or seriously injured, came through to Zaen just as he led the convoy of elite guards from the palace's main courtyard. The news that Stagg's body had been located was no consolation.

Zaen ordered the captain of the guards to head directly for the spaceport, the only logical destination for Garrett who was no doubt intent on leaving the planet and avoiding his execution.

"Mobilize the local battalion. I want no one entering or leaving the spaceport," he instructed Chan. "And ground all flights."

There was no telling how many hours head start Garrett had. For all Zaen knew, the man could already have taken a craft and be halfway back to the Stellar Cluster. After all, he had done it before.

"You may as well ready the planetary defense force," he added.

At the back of his mind, he wondered how these events would play out with the Elders. With luck, he could recapture Garrett and contain news of the escape attempt. But if the worst-case scenario occurred, it was bound to raise doubt in the minds of the Elders that he was capable of joining their ranks. The damage to his prospects did not bear contemplating.

"Go faster," he urged his driver. The armored transports behind him would simply have to keep up.

***

Zaen's car arrived at the spaceport main gate at the same time as the local battalion commander. He stared at the unguarded gates with a sense of foreboding.

"Where are your men?" he demanded.

The commander, a man he did not recognize, cowered under his intense gaze. "I would like an answer to that question as well. Two of them were assigned here. There is no sign of a struggle."

Zaen looked beyond the gates at the distant hangars and assorted spacecraft. All seemed tranquil, with nothing out of order. "Have there been any unauthorized departures in the past twenty-four hours?"

"They have brought nothing to my attention," the commander replied, without confirming one way or the other.

The answer did not satisfy Zaen. "Get your men to search all those ships and hangars. There is a fugitive loose and I have a powerful reason to suspect he's out there somewhere, looking for the means to escape Drani IV. You cannot let that happen. Do you understand me?"

The commander blanched. "Perfectly, Your Eminence. Do you want him dead or alive?"

"I don't care. But you will if he gets away."

Zaen turned to Chan. "Where is my captain?"

Chan was about to answer when he heard the roar of engines from the guards' transport vehicles.

"About time," Zaen shouted at the hapless captain. "Search the spaceport with the battalion commander's men. You're in overall command of the mission."

"Yes, Your Eminence." The captain saluted stiffly, before directing the guards to follow the commander's men toward the first set of hangars.

"And have two of your men guard my ship. That bastard will not steal it again."

Zaen climbed back into his car to keep warm but, within one minute, was outside once more, pacing up and down, waiting for a report that would recover the tranquility he had hoped this day would bring.

"Garrett must have had help to escape," Zaen said to Chan, for want of anyone else being within earshot. "I want a full investigation as soon as Garrett is recaptured or killed. Proctor Chan, do not spare anyone to discover the truth. If there's a conspiracy, I want to know everyone involved. Round them up for me."

"Of course, Your Eminence." Chan hoped these orders would be the end of Zaen's paranoia. He had seen too many times how the old man was overly suspicious of those around him. It would not surprise him to receive some accusations from Zaen before this escapade was over. The unfolding events should never have arisen. If he had any chance of remaining as Zaen's chief proctor once he became an Elder, then the complete truth, and all those who had helped Garrett, had to be uncovered.

Zaen was about to issue further instructions when the car radio burst into life with the captain's excited voice. "Your Eminence, we have him cornered in the Stellar Cluster freighter. My men have the ship surrounded."

"Excellent work, Captain," said Zaen, slamming his fist down on top of the car's roof with such force that he left a dent in the shiny black metal. "Keep him there until I arrive."

Chapter 54

Although Santiago's hold was voluminous, it was designed to carry pallets and crates stacked on top of one another to maximize the entire storage area. The shipbuilders had never anticipated it would one day carry human cargo.

As for the crew cabins? They were minimal, both in size and comfort. This was a freighter, not a luxury passenger liner. Every inch of space had to pay its way. The exception was the bridge and the crew lounge. Whoever designed this class of freighter had some appreciation of what confined spaces could do to the human psyche over a long period.

The problem for Rosa was Captain Dreyfus had a full crew compliment. With the generous fees being paid by the Brotherhood, he had spared no expense to bring along six crew members with the aim of turning the ship around as quickly as possible. It had worked well on previous missions to Drani IV; this was the first time Dreyfus had experienced such a lengthy delay.

And so the question remained; how to accommodate sixty-five additional people with limited space, supplies, and, most importantly, bathroom facilities.

"I assume none of these people have experienced space travel?" he asked Rosa, mainly out of hope.

"Look at them. What do you think?"

The crowd of people in the hold mingled like cattle, scared, and not knowing what to do as they glanced nervously around at their new surroundings. With at least seven days' travel to the closest planet in Stellar Cluster space, Dreyfus knew this was going to be a long and challenging journey ahead of him.

"Everyone is now on board," Dino-Gretz, his first officer, said over the internal comms channel. "Closing the ramp."

Rosa coughed. "That's not quite right. I'm waiting for three more."

"You're what?" Dreyfus exclaimed.

"I told you. We have to wait for Oz Garrett. He's bringing my son. And possibly one other person none of us cares for."

"Look around you, lady. You can see we're pretty full already."

"So three more individuals won't really make a difference," she replied, cutting him off.

"You said he would be here by now. Every minute we're here risks detection. Someone will miss those two guards you left tied up in the hangar soon enough. Then what?"

"We wait."

"What if Zaen's troops turn up?"

"I noticed the Santiago has plenty of firepower to protect itself," she said with a cute smile.

"You're right. My ship possesses some nasty surprises for anyone I don't like. However, it cannot fight off an army. We optimized the defense capabilities for space, not terrestrial combat. We are a sitting duck, an enormous whale waiting to be harpooned. A ponderous—"

"Yes, I get the metaphors. Hopefully, you won't need to prove how inadequate your ship's defenses are."

Dreyfus frowned. "Nothing on my Santiago is inadequate. Except maybe the cargo."

With those words echoing around the hold, Dreyfus stormed off.

"The captain is very sensitive about his ship," Sylwester said, walking up close to her. "Perhaps you need to be careful before making further criticisms."

"Noted," she replied, once more worrying about Garrett and Mikel. She knew the waiting was making her irritable. Not knowing if Garrett had been successful was excruciating. Although Garrett's rescue plan was optimistic at best, she was confident in his ability to improvise. She told herself for the millionth time that Mikel was in the best possible hands, even though she still believed she should also have gone to rescue her son.

"How long can we wait for Garrett?" asked Sylwester.

Rosa sighed. "I don't know, Syl. What I can tell you is I won't be leaving without Mikel. I made myself a promise when I came out here to take him home and I intend to honor it."

"You must wait for Oz," Mercedes pleaded as she climbed onto the gantry next to Rosa. "We all owe him our lives and the opportunity to start something new." She paused for a moment. "There won't be any more mining where we're going?"

"Only if you want to. The Stellar Cluster's constitution has thousands of pages detailing freedoms afforded to every one of its people. Of course, there are always individuals who work outside the strict codes necessary for a society. Luckily, those people are few and far between. You and your friends will have far better lives than you can imagine."

Mercedes stared up at her, smiling. Rosa wondered how much the young girl really understood about the new lives they were about to embark on. She hoped Mercedes, and everyone else who had chosen this path would have no regrets in years to come.

"Will you stay with us to show us the ways of your world?" Mercedes asked, grabbing hold of her hand.

Rosa glanced at Sylwester, surprised by the girl's question and not sure how to respond. She had not had time to think about the next steps, having focused solely on escaping alive. She only knew she wanted time with Mikel, to hold him close and tell him how much she loved him. Which was why Garrett had to succeed.

Looking into Mercedes' eyes, the magnitude of what they were attempting finally dawned on her. From now on, there could be no vagueness around setting up a new life somewhere in the Stellar Cluster. These people deserved certainty. All the credits in the galaxy could not provide that stability unless these refugees from the Brotherhood had a place they could call home and feel safe in. If they couldn't have that, what was the point of this exercise? One she had encouraged them to take part in. She couldn't break that trust now.

Gripping Mercedes' hand, she said. "Of course I will. You'll be safe with me."

"Thank you. And will Oz be there too? I want him to teach me how to fight."

"You'll have to ask Oz that question. He has his own life and responsibilities. I don't know what his plans are."

Seeing the look of disappointment on Mercedes' face, Rosa added. "He does care for you. I'm sure of that much. Anyway, you won't have to learn how to fight. The people in the Stellar Cluster are not like the Brotherhood."

"Heads-up, we have company," Captain Dreyfus announced over the internal comms system.

Rosa rushed to the bridge, leaving Mercedes and Sylwester in the hold.

Dreyfus and Dino-Gretz were studying the image on a scanner when she arrived. "Is it Garrett?" she asked hopefully.

The captain grimaced. "Only if he's brought friends."

"Those are military transports," Dino-Gretz added.

Rosa looked at the screen, dismayed by what she saw. They were military for sure; armored vehicles with forward-mounted cannons and plenty of room to carry troops. They were heading toward Santiago.

"I knew we had stayed here too long," Dreyfus said, focusing on the front transport. It suddenly veered off the road, making its way to a series of hangars.

Rosa stared closer at the screen for any sign of Garrett or her son, but all she could see were soldiers.

"They don't know we're here," she said. "Otherwise they'd be surrounding the Santiago. We still have time."

"Time for what? How will your friends get past those troops?"

"Oz is very resourceful. Don't underestimate him." She smiled.

"You're putting my ship and everyone aboard at risk. For three men."

"The Santiago can defend itself. You have cannons and lasers, so you must have a defense shield."

Dreyfus nodded. "I've told you, this ship can't withstand sustained attack from military-grade weapons. And I cannot deplete the power cores if we want to make it off this planet."

"The captain is right," said Dino-Gretz, focusing on the second military transport that was making its way toward two small spacecraft less than two kilometers away. "The reactors have been idle since we landed on Drani. We can power the shields for only thirty minutes. Any longer and we won't have sufficient reserves to make it to orbit."

"In that case, we need a distraction," Rosa said, staring at the nearby hangar.

Chapter 55

Rosa lined up in the hangar alongside Sylwester and four others from the instruction camp, together with three of Dreyfus's crew, led by Dino-Gretz. Between them, they had seven laser rifles, twenty spare power packs, a portable rocket launcher with four high explosive rounds, and six handguns.

In any other scenario, this was a decent arsenal of weapons, but she knew it would be inadequate against the trained Brotherhood military. Only she and the Santiago crew had any experience of firing weapons in anger. The five volunteers from the camp anxiously held their rifles as if the weapons were going to bite them.

"Remember what I told you," she said to them. "Simply point the rifle using the sight on the top, and press lightly on the trigger when you've found your target. It doesn't matter if you hit them, just as long as you keep the soldiers from reaching us. They don't know how good you are, only that you're firing at them."

"But they will fire back," said Sylwester, understandably nervous.

"Yes, which is why you have to stay hidden behind these containers. Don't give them a big target to aim at and you'll be safe."

Dino-Gretz shouldered the fearsome-looking rocket launcher on his shoulder, grunting under its weight.

"Have you fired one of those before?" Rosa asked.

He smiled. "Not yet. I've been waiting years for the opportunity though."

She could see the gleam of excitement in his eyes. The same went for the rest of the Santiago crew, who all seemed eager for the fight. Each of them gripped their rifles with confidence, talking casually among themselves as if it was a normal event.

Rosa wished she was so confident. She sympathized more with Sylwester and could recall the fear she had felt the first time she had gone into a war zone. And that was with two years of military training.

"Don't worry," said Dino-Gretz. "Those bastards may have the numbers, but they don't know how to fight. The captain will keep them busy."

At that moment, they could hear the steady roar of the military transports approaching. Rosa and the men ducked down into the shadows of the hangar. Through a gap between two large metal boxes, she spotted the first transport as it came into view only a few hundred meters away. It lumbered across the tarmac. Heading directly for her position.

"Oh, shit!" she whispered, looking across at Dino-Gretz for any inspiration.

He smiled back, his overoptimism getting under her skin. "The captain knows what he's doing. Wait and see."

She hoped he was right.

The transport was halfway between the Santiago and the hangar when Rosa saw two of the freighter's cannons swivel in their turrets, before firing projectiles that tore up the tarmac only meters in front of the transport. Concrete and rock flew into the air, followed by a thick cloud of brown dust.

The vehicle's driver responded quickly, applying the brakes so hard that the tires squealed in protest.

Dino-Gretz glanced at Rosa as if to say, I told you.

As she watched the transport reversing, she could not help but wonder where Garrett was. And if Mikel was with him. All of this activity would be in vain if neither of them arrived in the next thirty minutes. Was it worth putting everyone's lives at risk to satisfy her own selfish desires?

"What can you see?"

Dino-Gretz lowered the bazooka to the ground. He had a clearer view of the military transport. "They're waiting for the other two transports, by the look of it. They realize they can't do anything on their own."

Rosa felt the tension lift from her shoulders. They had a few more minutes' respite. But she knew this was the calm before the storm. The Brotherhood now knew Santiago was what they were looking for.

***

As his car raced across the tarmac toward the freighter, Zaen cursed for not searching the ship sooner. The freighter had been nothing but trouble since its arrival. Of course, it made sense for the captain to harbor a condemned criminal. Dreyfus lacked a moral compass and respect for the Brotherhood. He would need to be taught a lesson.

"Chan, mobilize the rest of the garrison. Prepare the fighter squadron. Garrett is not leaving this planet."

"Yes, Your Eminence," came the immediate response, even as the proctor opened a comms channel to the garrison.

Looking out of the front of his vehicle, Zaen spotted the cloud of dust floating in the air, close to the freighter, and even closer to the military transports. Were his men coming under attack? He ordered his driver to stop about one kilometer from the freighter.

"Captain, what is happening?"

"Your Eminence, they fired on us without warning, narrowly missing the commander's transport."

"That's an outrageous act of warfare against the Brotherhood," Zaen raged. "You have my authorization to destroy that vessel. Everyone on board is now declared a war criminal." He was not sure he had the power to make such a declaration, but he soon would as an Elder. What did a few days matter? He'd argue the matter later if he had to.

"They have raised their shields. Our weapons cannot penetrate them."

Zaen frowned. "I may have limited understanding of how the technology works, but don't the shields rely on vast energy reserves when attacked? You should be able to deplete them with continual fire."

The captain nodded. "I don't know how long that will take. We don't have enough weapons with us now."

"Which is why I have ordered reinforcements." Zaen wondered at how the man had ever risen to the rank of captain. If he maintained his negative attitude, he would soon find himself demoted back to the ranks.

"Thank you, Your Eminence."

Zaen cut the comms link and watched as the military transports spread out, circling the freighter.

"Don't you find it strange, Your Eminence?" Chan asked.

"What? That I cannot find competent people to do my bidding?"

"No. That the freighter is still here. Why would they remain to face the might of your army? They must know that their shields have limited effectiveness. Surely they should have made their escape as soon as Garrett was on board. Or at least when our troops were still on the far side of the spaceport."

Zaen knew Chan made a good point. Why was the ship still here? Was Garrett actually on board? "Contact Captain Dreyfus. Let's see what he has to say for himself."

Chan pressed a series of buttons on the comms console, before indicating that he had established a connection.

"Captain Dreyfus, you continue to be an annoyance. Stand down or I will destroy your ship."

There was a brief pause before Dreyfus's voice was heard through the loudspeaker. "Eminence Zaen, please tell me why you have ordered your soldiers to surround Santiago. It is a very aggressive move. I'm a simple trader."

"Don't play games, Dreyfus. Your ship has the most sophisticated defense capability I've seen on any freighter arriving on Drani. Did someone pay you to rescue Osiris Garrett?"

"I don't know what you mean. I'm only here because your goons still haven't delivered the supplies you promised. And isn't Garrett supposed to be executed today following his trial?"

Zaen cursed. He had forgotten about the supply fiasco. Clearly, Director Jaques was no better than his predecessor and would have to face the same fate for causing the current state of affairs. But there were other more immediate questions to resolve. "Why did you shoot at my men? That is an outrage."

"Accept my apologies. That was a technical problem with the targeting computer. I hope I didn't injure any of your men."

Zaen glared at the comms equipment. No one had ever dared lie to him in such an obvious and calculating way. Dreyfus was going to pay with his life. "Are you going to lower your shields?"

"Not while your men surround my ship and threaten to attack. I don't want to end up like Garrett."

"You'll end up dead like him if you refuse. This is your last opportunity."

"I'll take my chances," Dreyfus responded.

Zaen cut the connection, livid at the casual contempt shown by Dreyfus. There was no way he, any of the ship's crew, or Garrett, would leave Drani alive. He would soon feel the might of the Brotherhood military.

He watched with pride as two of the transports fired a salvo of rockets at the freighter. Each rocket trailed a thin black line of smoke from its exhaust before exploding against the freighter's defense shield. A faint blue hue glowed around the ship each time a rocket struck.

His pride, however, was short-lived and swiftly turned to dismay as the freighter returned fire against one of the transports. Three of its cannons fired at and scored direct hits against the transport, which erupted in a ball of flames, sending soldiers running for their lives. A moment later, a second transport also exploded, sending a mushroom cloud of flame and thick black smoke into the air. But on this occasion, the attack had come from the near-by hangar.

"That has to be Garrett," he said excitedly. "Tell the captain to target the hangar."

Zaen stayed leaning forward in his seat to get a better view. *This is the reason the ship is still on the ground,* he thought. *Garrett is trapped in the hangar. The Santiago is nothing more than a decoy.*

***

The booming sound of the rocket launcher was deafening as it echoed around the hangar. The distinctive smell of the detonator reminded Rosa of previous battles. Those memories were not her favorites. Even when battles were won, lives were lost, and she had witnessed far too much death.

"They know we're here now," shouted Dino-Gretz, unloading the used shell casing, which dropped to the floor with a mighty clang. One of his men inserted another shell and closed the rocket launcher's loading port.

Rosa looked between the crates at the burning remains of the military transport. The shell had inflicted terrible damage on both the vehicle and the unfortunate soldiers standing too close when the shell struck. She could see men writhing and screaming in agony, next to several bodies that would never move again. Taking several deep breaths, she suppressed the sudden need to vomit.

Dino-Gretz put a finger to his ear, his expression becoming vacant for a few seconds. "Confirmed," he said to an unknown person. He turned to Rosa. "The captain says he's infuriated Zaen and has detected more troops moving around the perimeter fence. But still no sign of your friend."

Yet again, Rosa wondered if she had made the wrong decision. If she had taken Dreyfus's advice, the freighter carrying the prisoners would be safely off-planet and well on its way to the Stellar Cluster. She cursed at the lack of communications devices that would have permitted her to know whether Garrett had been successful. Instead, she was relying on gut instinct that Garrett's experience and tenacity would get him through. But he was only human. No one was invincible.

She now had to face the real possibility that Garrett had failed to rescue Mikel. Perhaps the Brotherhood had killed both of them in the attempt. Maybe Darr had lied all along and Mikel was not at the camp at all. Had her uncompromising devotion to her son clouded her judgment, potentially resulting in the deaths of more innocent people?

"Come on, Oz," she whispered. "You need to get back here."

Another explosion from near Santiago interrupted her thoughts. She peered around the crates to see a fireball bellow into the air from the location of the third military transport. That was when she heard the ping of projectiles hitting the metal sides of the hangar, causing her to duck her head quickly.

"Now the fun begins," exclaimed Dino-Gretz with a mischievous grin.

Chapter 56

The rising plume of black smoke above the tree line was enough for Garrett to know not everything at the spaceport was going to plan. He was half expecting it; by now it was mid-morning and it amazed him his luck had lasted so long. He had suspected that as soon as the Brotherhood discovered his escape, Zaen would close the spaceport; it was the only logical destination.

"What's that?" Mikel asked, pointing toward the swirling smoke.

"Your mother, hopefully," Garrett replied. "I think she's settling a grudge with the Brotherhood."

"What if she has failed to find a suitable vessel?" Darr asked, not for the first time. He had been subdued for most of the journey from Instruction Camp Two, leaving Garrett to worry if the former head instructor was having second thoughts about joining the escape effort.

"Rosa won't fail. Too much is at stake." Yet, seeing the cloud of smoke, Garrett was no longer as assured as he had been. This plan relied far more on luck than he liked. He did not know how busy the spaceport was or if there were any suitable ships. For two or three people, it would be straightforward; less so for at least seventy people; few ships capable of ferrying that many would visit Drani IV regularly. The odds weren't worth contemplating.

"How accurate are you with this transport's cannons?" he asked Darr, turning a sharp bend in the road as he did so.

Darr shrugged. "I'm highly proficient. I was top of the class in the training exercises."

"Have you fired at live targets?"

Darr's silence confirmed what Garrett had suspected. He didn't push the question further.

He turned to Mikel. The young man flinched whenever the transport ran over a large rock or pothole. He looked pale and his skin was clammy—not from the humidity. "Can you drive this transport?"

"Me?" Mikel answered, surprised by the question. "You want me to drive an armored transport into the middle of a battle?"

"You can fire the laser rifle from the passenger window if you'd prefer. It will be a battle zone, so we need all the firepower available. I don't figure you as a fighter, so driving is the only option."

"Okay, if you put it that way," he replied hesitantly.

Garrett pulled over to the side of the road and jumped out of the driver's door to the ground. By the time he had run around to the passenger door, Mikel had slid across to the driver's position and Darr had slipped into the gunner's position behind the driver.

"Let's go," Garrett ordered, not wanting to give Mikel time to think. As soon as the transport began moving again, Garrett gathered the rifles and spare power packs onto the middle seat, ready to be used at the first hint of trouble.

Rounding a bend, the entrance to the spaceport came into view, less than two kilometers away. Noticing Mikel's knuckles were turning white, Garrett said. "Relax, Mikel. All you have to do is drive. Darr and I will do the rest."

"Easy for you to say."

"This cab and the windows are armor-plated and will resist gunfire. If we're hit, the sound will be incredibly loud, but we'll be secure inside here. The situation is likely to evolve quickly, so I need you to keep your wits about you. Listen to my voice and follow my instructions. I will keep you safe."

"What do I do if there are too many soldiers, or you're killed."

"We'll handle the soldiers. If I die, then listen to Darr. He may be the enemy, but he will be your best hope."

"Thanks for the recommendation," Darr said from his position in the gun turret.

"I've seen you kill plenty of your own men, so I'm still watching you. A leopard doesn't change his spots overnight."

"He does when there are millions of credits at stake."

Wealth had never been a motivating factor for Garrett. He despised mercenaries; they all had a price but when the going got tough he had known them to run, deserting colleagues to save their own miserable skins. He suspected Darr would do the same if the fighting became too intense.

"Slow down," Garrett said as they approached the empty entry gate. There was a junction with roads running to the left and right. No traffic appeared to be nearby, but he spotted the imposing gray prison hospital he had escaped from in what seemed a lifetime before. He unconsciously rubbed his left shoulder at the memories of his short time in that building, remembering how he had almost died.

"I see movement!" exclaimed Darr.

"Where?" Garrett asked, looking around but seeing nothing.

"Coming from the garrison. Three transports. The front vehicle carries the insignia of the flight squadron. They're just over six kilometers away."

Which means we have less than five minutes' head start, he guessed to himself.

"What about where the smoke is rising. Can you see what's happening?"

Darr fell silent for a few moments as he adjusted the targeting scanners. "There's a freighter, surrounded by troops. Two, possibly three, transports are burning."

"Can you tell if the freighter is damaged?"

"It appears to be intact. There's also a pale blue shimmer surrounding the ship. I don't know what that is."

"It means the freighter has activated its shields," Garrett said with a sense of relief. "Good news for us. If I'm right, it means the ship is waiting for us and Rosa was successful after all."

"Do you expect me to drive straight through those soldiers?" Mikel asked.

"No, that won't be enough," Garrett said, scanning the spaceport. "The ship can't take off with its shields activated. And as soon as it lowers the shields, it will become a sitting target. We need to do more. Head across to that small black hangar, as fast as you can," he said, pointing to his left.

Mikel floored the accelerator, speeding through the main entrance before turning toward the hangar Garrett was directing him to. The lumbering military transport was not built for high speed and lurched over the bumpy track.

Garrett smiled grimly as they drew close to the hangar. The silver insignia on its side confirmed the hangar belonged to the fighter squadron. Two guards were opening the hangar doors as he approached.

"What do you have in mind?" Darr asked.

"I've seen what these craft can do. I can't let them attack that freighter. They need to be destroyed."

Suddenly, one guard turned to face the oncoming transport. He must have realized something was wrong because Garrett saw him shouting to his colleague before raising his weapon—a laser rifle. A purple beam of light emerged from the rifle's muzzle. Almost instantly, the transport's windshield shattered.

Mikel screamed and slammed on the brakes.

"Darr, target the guard on the right," Garrett shouted, before leaning out of the passenger window and firing his rifle at the other guard. His first two shots missed, allowing the guard to fire. His shots hit the front of the transport, sending a surge of electricity through the vehicle. Garrett's third shot struck the guard in the chest, just below his left shoulder, and he fell to the ground. The second guard disappeared in a cloud of concrete and dust as a cannon shell exploded at his feet.

"Cover me," Garrett shouted, jumping from the transport and sprinting to the hangar, staying alert for signs of any further guards. Reaching the half-opened hangar doors, he briefly peered in, watching and listening for any movement.

He sucked in a deep breath as he saw four sleek attack craft, the same design he had briefly seen several years earlier when he had lost his arm and the Brotherhood had killed Colonel Lane. The hatch on the closest ship was open. Garrett ran across and looked inside at the pilot's cockpit. To his relief, the pilot interface was traditional; manual input controls with touch screens, rather than modern synaptic interfaces with faster response times.

He had used similar controls and knew he could fly this ship.

Running back to the transport, he instructed Mikel and Darr to make their way toward the freighter but to keep their distance until he had finished his attack runs. He left them with confused expressions on their faces. After opening the hangar doors to their full extent, he climbed into the cockpit of the first fighter, powered up the displays, and closed the hatch.

The cockpit was a tight fit and Garrett found he had to bend his knees at an uncomfortable angle to sit squarely in the pilot's seat.

As the touch screens and external viewers sprang to life, Garrett quickly scrolled through the control menus, familiarizing himself with the various inputs and, more importantly, reviewing the array of weapons at his disposal.

To his pleasure, he found the fighter armed with high-velocity cannons, twelve detonation missiles, and a small selection of bombs.

"Time to go!" he said to no one in particular.

His seat trembled as the powerful jet engines fired up. Deftly, he touched the screen in front of him and the fighter moved, its nose swinging around to face the hangar exit. As the aircraft moved forward, Garrett could see Mikel driving the military transport as instructed, also clearing the way for the aircraft to accelerate.

Still inside the hangar, Garrett increased the engine power to launch velocity and held on tightly to the joystick. The reaction was almost instant as the force of the acceleration pushed him into his seat. It took less than ten seconds for the speed to increase sufficiently for the fighter's stubby wings to create enough lift and he was airborne.

Within another three seconds, he had soared to one thousand meters, giving him the perfect view of the spaceport and the surrounding area. To his left, he spotted the perimeter road with the fighter squadron vehicle now less than one kilometer from the main gate. He swung the aircraft around, slowing the speed before commencing a shallow dive aimed directly at the fast-moving vehicle. The driver must have seen him because the vehicle began to swerve erratically. With a combination of the target acquisition screen and the weapons computer, Garrett fired two missiles, the second of which landed just in front of the vehicle, flipping it over onto its roof.

Satisfied with the dramatic result, Garrett flew on in search of the other military transports. The slower vehicles had fallen way behind the first vehicle, allowing him time to regain some altitude before beginning another slow dive. This time, he used the cannons, strafing the convoy with hundreds of high-velocity projectiles that ripped the vehicles and the soldiers to shreds in a matter of seconds.

With the reinforcements neutralized, it was now time to turn his attention to the troops attacking the freighter.

Chapter 57

As he glared at the burning transports in stunned disbelief, Zaen wondered if his day could get any worse. The garrison's soldiers and even his elite guards were in disarray as they fought to recover the situation that was slipping from their grasp.

"Chan, where are the reserves?" he shouted in rage.

"Your Eminence, I am assured they will be here soon."

"Not soon enough," Zaen muttered, his mind already considering what he could say to the Elders in mitigation of this unfolding disaster. At the moment, however, he could not see an option where this incident would not permanently damage his reputation, unless the Elders never found out, or his troops prevailed and recaptured Garrett. One fact was certain; he would punish all those that had allowed these events to occur.

"There goes one of our fighters now," Chan blurted out, pointing to a black dot rising sharply into the sky.

"About time," exclaimed Zaen. Maybe he could recover this day after all. He allowed himself a small smile as he continued to watch the black fighter aircraft accelerate and bank to the left. As he glanced back at the squadron's hangar, waiting for the remaining pilots to take flight, he noticed the single fighter go into an attack dive. "What's the pilot doing? He's in the wrong place. Chan, call him back."

At that moment, a stream of bright light and flame erupted from the fighter's nose. Zaen looked on in horror as several missiles tracked to the ground beyond the perimeter fence, creating several small explosions.

"What is that pilot firing at?"

Chan frowned. "I can't contact the pilot. Communications channels are being ignored."

As he watched the fighter attack another target, Zaen felt suddenly vulnerable parked in the middle of the spaceport. Whoever the pilot of the fighter was, he could not be trusted. "Get us to my hangar as quickly as possible," he instructed his driver. "Chan, tell me what is happening. Now!"

There was a look of confusion on the proctor's face. He was usually several steps ahead of anticipating Zaen's needs. But this time he was struggling to piece together the scant pieces of information he could get hold of. "I've lost contact with the garrison reserves," was all he could say, glancing worriedly across at the latest towers of smoke rising into the air from beyond the perimeter.

"Garrett?" Zaen whispered in disbelief, giving the black fighter even more attention. It was the only answer that made sense, even though the prospect seemed almost impossible. How could the man have stolen one of the Brotherhood's most sophisticated aircraft? He had a charmed life.

"Go faster," Zaen told his driver with greater urgency. There was no telling Garrett's next victim, but there was no doubt his vehicle was an easy target while it remained in the open.

***

Dino-Gretz held his hand to the comms set in his ear. "The captain has reported a small single-seat fighter has taken to the air and is flying several kilometers away."

Rosa frowned. "Will Santiago's shields be enough protection?"

"For a time. It depends on how good the fighter pilot is and what weaponry he's carrying. I'd also expect there to be additional fighters. When they attack, they will deplete the shields quicker than is happening at the moment."

"But the ship has an array of weapons. It can shoot the fighters out of the sky."

"It's not as simple as that. We designed the weapons systems for optimal performance at greater distances when the angles to the target don't vary dramatically. Whereas that fighter can traverse one hundred and eighty degrees of sky in no time at all. Operating in the planet's atmosphere also means the cannons have to contend with air friction. It may only convert into an extra millisecond or two to acquire target lock, but that can be enough to result in a miss."

"Do you have any positive news?" she asked, feeling the chances of success rapidly vanishing.

"I didn't say it was impossible," Dino-Gretz replied. "Dreyfus is a craft captain. He knows a few tricks those pilots won't be aware of."

"Let's pray you're right," she said, before venturing another glance outside from her vantage point. She counted seventeen soldiers taking cover behind remnants of their destroyed vehicles, regularly firing shots at either her position in the hangar or at the Santiago. Several of the soldiers appeared to have advanced their position on the hangar, despite random gunfire from Sylwester and his friends, who were all currently sitting with their backs to the crates being used for cover. Each of the men looked to be in a state of shock, staring at the rear wall of the hangar. There was no telling how much more action they could take.

She ducked back down and sat next to Sylwester. "How are you holding up, Syl?"

He didn't blink, all of his facial muscles taut with tension. "Will it soon be over?"

Placing a hand on his forearm, she said, "Not much longer. Garrett will be here soon."

Her soothing tone had the desired effect. Sylwester nodded, concentrating on maintaining his composure as he gripped his rifle. Rosa felt genuinely sorry for him. He was a long way outside his comfort zone, yet was continuing to perform admirably and setting an example for the others to follow.

"Dreyfus can now see a military transport approaching," Dino-Gretz shouted, breaking her train of thought.

"Reinforcements?" she asked, knowing the answer. Her heart sank further. If the Brotherhood could simply call upon more men, this was a battle of attrition her side could not win.

"That's my opinion," Dino-Gretz replied. His earlier excitement was now replaced with a more solemn demeanor that did not instill her with confidence. "Wait, the fighter aircraft has attacked some targets on the perimeter and is now circling around. The other military transport has stopped over one kilometer away."

Rosa wanted to ask Dino-Gretz what this new information meant. But before she could do so, she heard a shout from outside, followed by the thunderous staccato roar of bullets and lasers hitting the crates.

This was it. The enemy soldiers were charging on her position. She gripped her laser rifle and prepared to face the enemy. If this was the day she died, she wanted no regrets.

Other than dying and getting everyone else killed, she told herself. *Oh, and not reuniting with my son.*

As she had done regularly for the past fifteen minutes, she checked the energy levels on her laser rifle and double-checked the spare power supplies, ready to swap as soon as necessary. It would not be long before she exhausted all of her weapons.

Please, Garrett!

Chapter 58

Garrett brought the fighter around in a tight turn, pushing the aircraft's maneuverability and handling to the limit. The fighter was far too good for the Brotherhood and more sophisticated than any other vehicle he had witnessed on the planet. But Drani IV was not the first planet he had visited where the military had more than their fair share of expensive toys.

Looking across the spaceport's expanse, he briefly considered destroying the squadron's hangar to ensure there were no immediate airborne threats. He had enough bombs on board to render all the remaining aircraft useless, denying any further attacks against the population.

But a glance toward the besieged freighter confirmed that should be his priority. That spacecraft was his ticket off the planet and the surrounding soldiers were the only thing now standing in his way.

Flying directly toward the freighter, he spotted a small vehicle speeding across the runway, heading away from the battle. It was too small to be a military transport so he ignored it. His immediate target was a group of five soldiers who were using an overturned transport as cover from the freighter's weapons, leaving them exposed to his cannon fire. As he began his attack run, the targeting computer swiftly acquired them on the scanner in front of him.

The soldiers were oblivious to the threat from the sky and to their rear. Projectiles from the fighter's cannons ripped into their position, killing them instantly. The black attack craft screeched low overhead before anyone else could react.

Garrett flicked the controls to the left, searching for his next target as he passed close to the freighter. Although intent on freeing the immense vessel, it intrigued him to see a small group of soldiers attacking the adjacent hangar. He could make out gunfire coming from the open hangar doors but had flown past without identifying the source.

What was so important for the soldiers to ignore the freighter?

***

Rosa was firing her rifle at the oncoming soldiers as she spotted the sleek black fighter roar past barely fifty meters above the runway. She had heard the frightening sound of the aircraft's cannons but was too preoccupied to see if it had hit the Santiago.

As gunfire continued to rattle against the metal containers, there was a long, loud scream somewhere to her right as one of the men clutched at his shoulder and slumped to the ground. There was no time to offer any medical help as the firefight became more intense. The enemy soldiers were now on the edge of the vast hangar, using its doors as cover. They were putting their military experience to good use, firing salvos more accurately and effectively than the prisoners or the Santiago crew. It was keeping Rosa's group pinned down, allowing the soldiers to advance their position.

"Any ideas?" she shouted to Dino-Gretz

"The captain won't use the cannons at this range when we're so close to the target. Anyway, he has his own problems to contend with. Did you see that fighter?"

"Was the Santiago hit during that last run?"

"No. Captain Dreyfus says the pilot is inept. Lucky for us, although not a surprise on this backward planet. The idiot ended up killing his own men. Can you believe it?"

Rosa flinched as more bullets impacted the crates near her position. If only the pilot had been bad enough to shoot the soldiers attacking her position, she thought.

"Wait!" she exclaimed. "You said the attack craft was spotted firing at targets a long way from here. What if the attack on those soldiers was deliberate?"

"Why would he do that?" scoffed Dino-Gretz.

"Don't you see? Somehow, Garrett is piloting that aircraft. He's clearing a path so we can take off."

"I hope you're wrong. Dreyfus is about to shoot him out of the sky."

"No. Stop him," she screamed.

***

By now, Garrett was adept with the controls of the aircraft. He could almost will it to change direction and cycling the weapons was child's play. At any other time, he would be enjoying the experience. But this situation was different. Many lives were on the line, including his own, and it looked as if he had arrived not a moment too soon.

Whoever was inside the hangar was in grave danger and he suspected it was likely to be Rosa and the prisoners, trapped and unable to make the final few hundred meters to the safety of the freighter. He had to do something before the soldiers overran them.

The tightest of turns forced Garrett hard into his seat. Bright dots of light formed in front of his eyeballs, briefly impairing his vision. But then the craft leveled out, and he had the soldiers in his sight. They were paying him no attention, more intent on their prey inside the hangar. He pressed the firing button one more time.

The cannons fired a short, sharp round of projectiles, killing two of the soldiers. As he adjusted the targeting screen for the remaining soldiers, something suddenly hurled the fighter violently to the side. As the craft tumbled out of control, red warning lights flashed across all the screens in front of him. It took a fraction of a second to realize the craft had been hit but he had no idea who had fired the shot. Not that it mattered. The aircraft had lost power and the control surfaces were inoperative. He was crashing to the ground at over four hundred kilometers per hour and nothing he could do was going to prevent it.

*∗∗

Rosa's hopes rose as she saw the soldiers cut down by the aircraft's first salvo. Her confidence was short-lived as she saw the fighter fly past the open hangar door, half of its tail end missing and in flames, smoke billowing behind it.

Seconds later, she heard the unmistakable sound of metal scraping against concrete followed by a muffled explosion. She turned to Dino-Gretz, a horrified expression on her face.

Dino-Gretz listened to another message on his comms channel. "The captain says the fighter went down three hundred meters away. He expresses his condolences if your friend was piloting the fighter."

"Apologies won't bring Oz back," she snapped.

"Maybe not. But he gave us an opportunity to survive. Let's not waste it."

She begrudgingly knew he was right. And it was no use blaming Dreyfus. Events had happened so fast. She was not even sure if it had been Garrett at the controls of the fighter. Maybe he was still out there somewhere. With Mikel.

"Do you have a plan?" she asked.

Dino-Gretz smiled, his first in a while. "We now have a numerical advantage, but they know how to keep us pinned down. I'm going to fire another shell from the bazooka directly at them. There's going to be plenty of noise, dust, and confusion following the blast. We use that moment to charge, finishing anyone that survives the explosion."

Rosa sucked on her bottom lip. "The blast is damn close. Will we be safe?"

"As safe as we are now. The direction of the blast will mainly be away from the hangar. These crates will shield us from shrapnel. It's the only plan I have."

Rosa shrugged. "Let's do it."

She instructed Sylwester and his men to sit as low as possible and to cover their ears. She did the same as she watched Dino-Gretz prepare the rocket launcher. As soon as he stood up to take the shot, she held her breath.

But as Dino-Gretz took aim, he staggered backward, gasping in pain. Reflexively, his finger tightened on the trigger sufficiently for the detonator to ignite, firing the shell, although not where he had intended. The shell hit the floor approximately four meters short of the planned target, well within the confines of the hangar.

The blast was deafening, even with her hands over her ears. She watched as Dino-Gretz went flying backward, landing heavily on his back. One second later, a thick cloud of dust swept through, and she could not see a thing.

Chapter 59

Zaen whispered a silent prayer as his vehicle drove into the shelter of the hangar. His ship, the Soul of Pegasus, stood proudly in the middle of the vast space, its jet-black hull gleaming under the overhead spotlights.

Climbing out of the vehicle, he turned to watch the battle unfolding in the distance. He let out a triumphant cry when he saw the fighter aircraft crash onto the runway less than three kilometers away. A thick plume of smoke rising into the sky convinced him Garrett was now dead. He only wished he could witness Garrett's smashed body to make absolutely sure. Hopefully, his soldiers would soon prevail over those who had dared to confront him. Until then, he could not entirely relax without seeing the corpse for himself.

Yet there was still a concern that the day would not go as he intended. The remaining troops surrounding the freighter had suffered heavy losses in the last ten minutes. With supporting troops at least thirty minutes away from the spaceport and the fighter pilots incapacitated, Captain Dreyfus may get the chance to take off. To mitigate that eventuality, Zaen had ordered Chan to call up the remaining elite soldiers from the palace. It left the palace and his prized possessions unguarded, although the risk was worth it if he seized back control of the situation.

"I will await the outcome on the Pegasus," he told Chan.

His ship was always prepared for ad hoc trips at Zaen's whim. He insisted it be stocked with the finest foods and wines, with a pilot permanently assigned to live on board, ready to launch within five minutes.

As such, the Soul of Pegasus made the perfect place to sit out the rest of the battle. He could watch in luxury as his troops overcame the disreputable captain of the Santiago. He would take great pleasure as his soldiers cleared the battlefield, allowing him to see Garrett's broken body. When victorious, he could even fly directly to Bevas and receive his new honor.

But, as Zaen was about to climb the steps into the Soul of Pegasus, he heard a familiar voice from the shadows below the ship's lifting fins.

"I am surprised to see you running away, Your Eminence?"

Zaen stopped and turned, hiding his surprise as he peered into the shadows to confirm the speaker. "Andron? What are you doing here?"

"What do you think? When you evicted me from the palace, I had nowhere to live. You provided me with a roof over my head for as long as I can remember, so I decided the next best place was here. At least it means I can still feel close to you, even though you have no more use for me."

"How dare you presume to be owed so much from me," Zaen blustered, having no time to deal with Andron's latest show of disrespect. "You have no right to remain in any of my properties. I made that abundantly clear."

"You don't care if I die?"

"Don't be so dramatic, Andron. Millions of other normal citizens survive without me to take care of them. While I may have spoiled you for too many years, you're not special. I want nothing more to do with you. Reintegrate into society and remember your place."

As Andron stepped out of the shadows, Zaen could see he was shakily pointing a handgun at him.

"Put the gun down now," Zaen ordered with his most authoritative voice. There was an expression in Andron's eyes that he had never seen before. It was a mixture of fear and hatred that caused a shiver of dread to run down his spine.

"I'm tired of you telling me what to do," Andron replied, his eyes filling with tears of frustration. "You've used me for so many years, only to discard me at your finest hour. I have always shown you loyalty."

"You've shown me obedience because that is the right thing to do to an eminence. That is what everyone is born to do. It is your duty."

Andron took another step forward. "You cannot deny you treated me differently. I want you to see me as that person again. The one who takes care of your special needs."

Zaen stared steadily into the eyes of his former acolyte, no longer recognizing the young man standing before him. "Lower the gun, Andron, or I will have you killed."

Andron's aim didn't waver. "I felt dead the moment you dismissed me. I have no life if I cannot spend it in your service."

Zaen glared at him with a look that withered most others. "You're mistaken if you think you can threaten me. Drop the gun."

Andron, ignoring the command, cast a knowing glance at Chief Proctor Chan, who was standing open-mouthed by Zaen's transport. "You keep him close to you. Why not me?"

"The chief proctor performs essential duties. Things you would never understand."

With no warning, Andron swung his gun around and fired three shots in quick succession, hitting Chan in the chest. With such a short distance between him and the weapon, Chan stood no chance. Three dark crimson patches spread across his jacket, even as he fell back against the car.

As Chan slumped lifelessly to the ground, another shot rang out, echoing around the hangar. Andron turned back to face his former master with a confused expression on his face. Zaen fired a second shot from the small firearm he had kept hidden in the sleeve of his robe. The bullet created a small neat hole in the middle of the young man's forehead. His eyes glazed over as he fell, landing heavily on the concrete floor.

Zaen sighed as he looked down at Chan's body. The chief proctor had been a loyal and valued servant for many years and was going to be difficult to replace. But then again, he thought, maybe it's time for a change.

Before climbing the steps to board the Soul of Pegasus, he took a brief moment to glance at Andron's corpse. Thick crimson blood had been quick to pool behind the young man's head as his lifeless eyes looked up at the roof of the hangar. While his soul may have been tortured for the past few days, the expression on his face was strangely serene. For a second, Zaen wondered at the fragility of life, contemplating his own mortality. Quickly dismissing the thought, he finally climbed the steps to his ship and strode past the pilot who was waiting by the open hatch.

It was time to put an end to the chaos of the day.

Chapter 60

The dust and flying fragments quickly settled, allowing Rosa to see Dino-Gretz laying face up on the ground, one of his crewmates kneeling over him. She ran across to inspect him and saw to her relief that he was still breathing. A bullet had hit him above the shoulder blade, passing through the fleshy part and somehow avoiding the bone. While the wound would be incredibly painful, she knew it was not life-threatening. However, his neck and face were a bloody mess that made the injury appear worse than it actually was.

"What are you waiting for?" Dino-Gretz murmured, returning her concerned gaze.

Seeing he was okay, Rosa knew it was time to complete the mission. "Stay with him," she said to Dino-Gretz's companion, wishing she knew his name. The third member of the Santiago crew was crouching, ready for the instruction to counter-attack.

She turned to the men from the camp. "Syl, we have to do this for Oz. His death can't be in vain."

Sylwester and the men nodded. There was a steely resolve in their eyes that she had never seen inside the camp. Leaving their wounded friend on the ground, they stood as one, ready to defeat the enemy.

Rosa led the charge, hoping that none of the men accidentally shot her in the back. An odd feeling, considering she had less fear of the enemy soldiers ahead of her.

The entrance to the hangar was a chaotic mess, reminiscent of wars zones she had experienced in her distant past. A shallow crater, thirty centimeters deep and three meters wide, revealed where the shell had struck. Chunks of concrete thrown clear by the blast had peppered the hangar wall and door, leaving holes the size of melons.

She could hear moans and coughing coming from outside. Choosing not to wait to discover how many soldiers were still alive, Rosa sprinted from the hangar, her rifle raised and ready to fire at anyone who moved. To her surprise, only three soldiers could still hold their weapons. As she confronted them, their eyes bulged at the unexpected sight of Rosa and the men running straight at them. There was no time to react before Sylwester's men cut them down in a hail of gunfire. And, with that, the battle for the hangar was over.

Rosa paused to take a breath, amazed she was still alive. None of the other men had been wounded in the final push, which was a minor miracle. But the steady hum of laser fire coming from the Santiago reminded her there was still work to do. Unfortunately, there was no cover between the hangar and the remaining soldiers, who were securely protected by the wrecked shell of their former transport.

She stared at the gap between her and Santiago, frustrated by how tantalizingly close it was. Yet still so far away.

***

Garrett was vaguely aware of rough hands gripping his arms tightly and pulling him. His feet were dragging along the ground. He wanted to resist. A voice inside his head shouted that he should fight back, but his body refused to respond.

It was only as he felt himself being lifted that he could open his eyes. He found himself staring into Darr's concerned face. Glancing around, he realized he was lying on the ground next to the armored transport.

"I wasn't sure if you were dead," said Darr.

Garrett couldn't tell if it upset Darr that he was still alive. "What happened?" he asked, before coughing. The smell of acrid smoke was in his nose and throat, making him want to vomit. Twenty meters away, the once sleek fighter was now nothing more than a smoldering wreck.

"The freighter. It shot you out of the sky."

Garrett raised an eyebrow as he climbed to his feet. He had been so focused on the soldiers that he had not even noticed the freighter had weapons. It was unusual, to say the least.

"Why would it do that?" Mikel asked.

"They didn't know I was on their side. Whoever is in command of the freighter could only assume I was a Brotherhood pilot with a mission to destroy them, or at least prevent them from taking off. I would have done the same. Whoever it was is a damn fine shot."

Garrett shook out his arms and legs for any signs of injury. Other than minor abrasions and bruises, he was remarkably unscathed. The fingers on his left hand were slow to respond to commands and he wondered how much longer his arm would continue to function. He certainly could no longer use it to fire weapons.

The worst injury was a bump to his forehead, which he knew would swell up into a large lump but he was sure the ringing in his ears would soon disappear.

"We saw you crash, and Darr thought you might need our help," Mikel said proudly.

"Thank you. I guess that makes us even. But we need to get back into the battle. Those soldiers are threatening our people and preventing our escape."

Garrett allowed Darr to help him back into the cab, with Mikel taking the driver's seat once more.

"How do we know the freighter won't shoot this transport?" Darr asked, climbing back into the gunner's position in the gun turret.

Garrett looked across at the large ship, looking like a beached whale in the middle of the landing pad. He had underestimated it once and would not make the same mistake again. Yet there was no escaping the fact that the small band of Brotherhood troops still needed to be neutralized to allow the ship to take off. He wished there was a way to communicate with the ship. The best he could manage was to act in a non-aggressive way and hope the ship's captain was smart.

"Take us in, Mikel. But give that ship a very wide berth."

Garrett leaned his head out of the transport's window, allowing the cool fresh air to wash across his face and bring him to his senses. Ahead, he could see the freighter, its shield continuing to shimmer under the onslaught from Zaen's soldiers.

He could now see the cannons dotted across the freighter's hull and wondered how he had not noticed them earlier. They packed a menacing punch; more than he had seen from similar ships. The captain was clearly fond of modifications and defense. Garrett hoped there were other upgrades to the freighter that would help them all return to the Stellar Cluster.

Assuming the captain didn't shoot at his transport by mistake!

"Don't get any closer, Mikel. We don't want to give him the impression he's being threatened."

Mikel adjusted the steering wheel, altering the direction to move them away from the freighter, but still drawing closer to the enemy soldiers. He was keeping his eyes firmly on the road ahead, his breaths short and quick.

"Okay, Mikel," Garrett said. "Swing us around and head directly for those soldiers. Don't let them think anything is wrong until it's too late."

"Yes, Oz," he replied, almost in a whisper.

Garrett leaned back and glanced at the weapons section behind Mikel's seat. "Darr, are you ready up there?"

"Weapons are primed and targets almost in range," came the immediate response. Garrett could hear the excitement in Darr's voice; the man was relishing the opportunity to unleash his vindictive tendencies. In any other situation, it would concern Garrett, memories of the events from Instruction Camp Two still fresh in his memory, but Darr's blood lust was exactly what he needed now.

Garrett scanned the view ahead. From the gunfire coming from the wrecked transport, he estimated seven or eight soldiers hiding there. The transport was effective at providing cover.

"Why isn't the freighter returning fire?" Mikel asked.

Garrett shrugged. "Maybe they're saving power for the shields. Just be happy they're not shooting at us. They could quickly change their mind."

"I never thought of that." Once more, Mikel gripped the steering wheel so tightly that his knuckles turned white.

Nice one, Oz, thought Garrett, not having meant to worry Mikel. The young man was doing well under stressful circumstances, and he needed it to stay that way.

"Slow down and stop," requested Garrett. "Are we close enough, Darr?"

"Oh yes," came the response, followed by the dull but rhythmic thrump, thrump sound as the cannons fired. The heavy projectiles tore into the enemy transport with a loud explosion. The force was enough to spin the wreckage around by ninety degrees, leaving two of the soldiers exposed. Garrett raised his rifle and fired, killing one soldier. A directed laser blast from the turret above cut the other soldier in half. Darr must have cranked the power to maximum.

The remaining soldiers must have been alert to their new enemy. Two of them began firing at the transport, while their colleagues continued to attack the freighter. Garrett almost pitied them; they were fighting a lost cause and didn't even know it. At least they were putting up a valiant fight and he could not ask any more of a soldier, whoever they fought for.

By now, Darr was finding his range with the cannons. He fired salvo after salvo at the troops, as well as using the lasers to cut through the metal chassis. In less than a minute, the wrecked transport was nothing more than twisted shards of metal partially hidden in a cloud of dust. By then, the soldiers had stopped shooting, yet Darr continued to bombard them with the cannon.

"You can stop now," Garrett shouted. Darr ignored the command for another ten seconds before heeding Garrett's second request.

Garrett jumped from the cab, instructing Mikel and Darr to stay where they were while he checked for any sign of life from the enemy soldiers. He doubted anyone could have survived the hail of cannon fire from the overzealous Darr, but he had to be sure. He approached the mangled wreckage with his rifle ready. As he stepped over warped metal, fabric, and charred body parts, he soon accepted that everyone was indeed dead. It was impossible to tell how many soldiers had been present from the many dismembered limbs and scorched corpses; he hoped the Brotherhood would not force any of the relatives to identify their loved ones; it would be a gruesome task.

As the bitter, acrid smoke burned his eyes and nostrils, Garrett realized people were running toward him. Although he could hear boots on concrete, the smoke was too dense to see who it was. He raised his gun once again and shouted. "Who's there?"

"Oz?" came a voice he recognized. Rosa.

Avoiding any trip hazards, he walked toward the sound of her footsteps until she emerged through the smoke. She ran to him, throwing her arms tightly around him. "I thought you were dead," she said, a look of amazement in her eyes.

He smiled, feeling the tension ease from his body. "It takes more than a bad landing to kill a Space Marine. Before I forget, I brought you a gift," he said, looking over his shoulder.

She looked at him with a confused expression. "Mom?" came a voice from behind Garrett, causing tears to form uncontrollably in her eyes. Releasing Garrett, she ran the few steps to Mikel, squeezing him to her for thirty seconds until he flinched in pain. Stepping back, she took a moment to look at his face, brushing his hair away from his forehead before spotting his wound.

"My God, what happened to you?" she said, removing the bloody cloth from his shoulder.

"It's nothing to worry about, Mum. Oz took good care of me."

Rosa squeezed him again. "My beautiful boy. I thought I would never see you again. You look so thin." This time he returned the hug, holding her almost as tightly.

"Oz told me you came searching for me. I'm sorry for causing you so much bother. I should never have come to the Bevas Sector."

Rosa wiped the tears from her eyes. "That's not important anymore," she spluttered. "I have you back with me. That's the only thing that matters."

Garrett, conscious this was a personal moment, walked back to the transport and sat in the driver's seat as he tried to ignore the aches and pains emanating from various parts of his body.

"Can we leave now?" an anxious Darr asked as he remained seated in the weapons section.

Still unsure if the battle was over, Garrett told him to stay in position, but not to fire on anyone. In the confusion, he was no longer sure if any of the enemy were still close by, waiting to ambush the escape.

Five uneventful minutes later, Captain Dreyfus appeared in their midst. "I'm sorry to hold up the family reunion, but we do need to leave immediately. Unless any of you want to stay behind."

There was no dissension. Garrett was last to board the Santiago, following Rosa and Mikel who walked arm in arm. As soon as he sealed the outer hatch, he felt the rumble of thrusters as the freighter lifted off.

His luck was still holding.

Chapter 61

The climb out of Drani's atmosphere was uncomfortably slow and tortuous. The entire ship vibrated and rattled as its atmospheric engines accelerated close to their maximum energy outputs.

Garrett found his way to the bridge, holding onto the handrails to keep his balance and waiting for the ship to break apart. It surprised him to see how relaxed Captain Dreyfus was, sitting in his chair as he calmly watched data scrolling on a monitor in front of him.

"Doesn't this thing go any faster?" Garrett asked, scanning the view screen for any signs of pursuit.

Dreyfus sneered. "The Santiago is a venerable old lady, not a flashy speedster. You try hauling this much weight, fighting the effects of gravity."

Although Garrett appreciated the captain's sentiment, he couldn't help but feel exposed. Back in his military days, he had shot down plenty of ships during this phase of flight, when the low speed and lack of maneuverability left them at their most vulnerable.

Even the shield was offline, with the ship's computer prioritizing the propulsion system. One direct hit from a medium-sized missile would be enough to bring the freighter crashing back down. Garrett was convinced the Brotherhood had plenty of those in their arsenal.

After what felt like an eternity, the sky turned from a dark gray to black as Drani IV fell away behind them.

"A craft is approaching from the planet," Dreyfus said as Garrett was beginning to breathe easier.

"Are you sure it's not a missile?" Garrett said, feeling less nonchalant than the captain.

"I know the difference. This one is traveling too slowly." As if to prove his point, Dreyfus switched the image on the view screen to show a small craft, about twice the size of a standard shuttle, emerge from the top of the clouds and head into space less than fifty kilometers from the freighter's position. It moved quickly away, but Dreyfus kept tracking in case it changed direction.

"Can you magnify the image?" Garrett asked.

Dreyfus touched a button on the console, and the spaceship suddenly filled the screen. Garrett leaned closer to study the lines of the vessel as it sped away. From the majestic style of the ship, he suspected this was Zaen's personal shuttle, although he could not be sure. Not that it mattered. The Santiago was now picking up speed as the vacuum engines kicked in, surging the freighter forward. Toward safety.

"You look like shit," remarked Dreyfus, leaning back in his seat.

Garrett grinned. "The Brotherhood aren't the most welcoming hosts. I don't intend to return."

"You and me both. I may have to find some new trade routes though."

"Thanks for listening to Rosa. And for waiting. Few people would put their ship and life at risk. It's appreciated more than you can know."

Dreyfus shrugged as if it was nothing. "It felt like the right thing to do. Plus, your friend can be very persuasive when she wants to be."

"Rosa has put her life on the line for her son. It's difficult not to want to help people like that."

"You should go to her. Get those wounds cleaned up."

Garrett nodded, aware of the aches and pains throughout his body. He was amazed he could even walk. He stood slowly, suddenly feeling his age. "How long until we reach the border?"

"Thirty hours. Plenty of time to rest, although I apologize for the lack of comfortable bunks and private rooms. You'll have to sleep where you can find a space."

"Not for the first time," Garrett remarked, making his way back down to the hold where Rosa was treating the other patients.

***

He awoke to the sound of Dreyfus's voice over the internal comms. "We have company, Mr. Garrett, I suggest you come to the bridge."

He had slept sitting upright for four hours, wedged between two crates in a quiet part of the ship. Before falling asleep, Rosa had tended to his wounds and given him drugs for the pain. Whatever she had prescribed had quickly sent him into a deep and undisturbed sleep. But, as he pulled himself up and performed some stretching exercises, his body protested at having remained in an awkward position for too long.

No rest for the wicked, he thought as he strode to the bridge, stretching his arms and legs as he went, to free up any residual stiffness. Dino-Gretz, his arm in a sling, was standing next to Dreyfus as Garrett walked onto the bridge. "Apparently, your friends want you back. You've made quite an impression."

"I have that effect," Garrett replied, glancing at the view screen. It revealed a tactical view with five dots converging on Santiago's flight path. "The Brotherhood?"

Dreyfus nodded. "Warships. An old design that was obsolete before I was born, but still with enough firepower to destroy us."

"Can you outrun them?"

"No. I've tried every trick I know to throw them off, but they're closing in on us."

Suddenly, the comms channel crackled to life with the sound of Zaen's voice. "Captain Dreyfus. You have committed punishable crimes against my military forces. Prepare to be boarded."

Dreyfus cast a questioning look at Garrett. "Any ideas?"

Garrett asked Dino-Gretz to display the schematics of the warships on the computer screen closest to him. The aging craft lacked heavy weapons, but there were still enough armaments to crack the Santiago open like an egg. The freighter may have been able to dodge one warship, possibly even cripple it with its hull cannons, but defeating five vessels was impossible.

If he was on his own, Garrett would likely have given it a go. After all, there was nothing to lose. But the Santiago was carrying almost one hundred people, all of whom deserved to live long and fulfilling lives. He couldn't take the risk.

"Captain, how many escape pods do you have?"

Dreyfus shook his head, understanding where the conversation was heading. "Enough for the crew. The Santiago is a freighter, not a cruiser."

Garrett had suspected as much. But he hated conceding without a fight. Maybe this time had to be different.

He asked Dreyfus to open a channel. "Eminence Zaen. I was hoping to never hear from you again.'

"Osiris Garrett!" There was a tone of excitement in Zaen's voice. "So you are on board. Are you going to allow everyone to perish with you?"

"You're going to kill them anyway."

"Come now, Mr. Garrett. It is only you I want. The others may have made a mistake in believing your lies, but I'm prepared to let them live. You have my word."

Garrett knew Zaen's promises were worth nothing. He was a vindictive old man. Unfortunately, Garrett had nothing to negotiate with.

"You don't have to do this," Dreyfus whispered.

"We'll comply, Zaen," Garrett said in a resigned voice.

"A wise decision. Prepare to be boarded."

Dreyfus cut the connection, unable to make eye contact with Garrett.

"No, Oz. Zaen will kill you!" It was Mercedes. He realized she must have been eavesdropping on the conversation.

He turned and forced a smile as she rushed onto the bridge, hugging him tightly around the waist. Rubbing her hair, he noticed she had washed it. In fact, she was clean and smelled fresher than he remembered in the tunnels.

"How much did you hear?"

"Enough," she replied brazenly. "I followed you here."

"In that case, you know I have no choice. If I refuse to go, Zaen will destroy this ship. I don't want you or anyone else to die because of me."

"You can't die. You promised to teach me how to be a better fighter. I want to be a Space Marine, like you."

"Thanks, kid. I have no plans on getting myself killed today or anytime soon. And if I do, then there are plenty of other sons of bitches gunnery sergeants, who can train you nearly as well as I can."

Garrett felt the Santiago stop accelerating as Dreyfus eased the engines to standby mode. The scanner showed one warship move closer as the other four vessels took tactical positions, preventing the Santiago from making a run for it.

"Go stay with Rosa and Syl," he said softly, leaning down to look into her face. He could see she was struggling to hold back tears. He had never been good with emotions, although he had always found the right words to console relatives of soldiers lost in action. Mercedes' sadness was different. This was personal.

"Promise me you'll come back," she said, wiping away a stray tear running down her cheek.

"I'll do my best," he replied. Many people had tried and failed to kill him over the years. He was going to do his damnedest to ensure Zaen wasn't the one to succeed.

Mercedes disappeared into the corridor.

After a few seconds, Dreyfus asked. "If Zaen is going to kill you anyway, why doesn't he simply attack this ship?"

"If you saw my trial, you know why. Zaen craves an audience. My execution is a symbol of his power and a message to the politicians in the Stellar Cluster. He could kill me now, but there are few witnesses out here in deep space. Destroying this ship with me on it wins him no credits with his peers."

Dreyfus nodded in understanding. "I wish you luck, my friend. And I pray Zaen keeps his word and lets us live."

Garrett cast Dreyfus a knowing glance; they both knew Zaen would destroy the Santiago at the earliest opportunity.

"There is one favor I would ask," said Garrett. "Do you have anything for this?" he asked, pointing to a small flap on the forearm of his artificial arm.

Dreyfus smiled. "I think maybe I do. Take this."

"Godspeed, Captain. We may yet get to travel together soon." And with those words, Garrett left the bridge and made his way to the airlock.

Chapter 62

Four heavily armed soldiers met Garrett at the airlock. He stepped through onto the warship and, within seconds, one soldier placed him in handcuffs. Garrett glared at the man until he looked away.

Another soldier, with four stripes on the shoulder of his uniform, said, "No games, Garrett. Follow me."

As the soldier turned and began marching along the narrow corridor, the other three surrounded Garrett, guiding him forward.

The situation was playing out exactly as Garrett had expected. The anxious soldiers were leaving nothing to chance. In their heads, they had subdued the prisoner and had covered any escape routes. Their superiority in numbers would intimidate anyone in his position. Despite the soldiers' military physiques, Garrett towered over them by at least fifteen centimeters.

He sensed an air of complacency from them, similar to the instructors at the camp. These men were used to handling compliant individuals. Although the soldiers marched in unison and stared straight ahead, their bodies were not tense and they held their rifles too low. Minor details, but easy to spot for someone who had trained thousands of Marines.

The group walked in silence along empty narrow corridors, with only the rhythmic sound of the soldiers' boots on the steel floor echoing around them. Having evaluated the men around him, Garrett paid attention to the ship itself.

His first impression of Zaen's flagship was a musty relic. The structure looked solid enough, with reinforced bulkheads every five meters. However, the air purifiers needed upgrading to remove both the stale smell and the humidity. He could not imagine spending months on duty aboard the ship; it wasn't much better than the tunnels of Instruction Camp Four.

Eventually, the soldiers guided him onto the warship's bridge, one of the largest Garrett had seen on any spaceship, with twelve operators manning different control stations. Each operator stared intensely at a large glass screen in front of them and ignored him as the soldiers marched him in. He noticed the operators were wearing different uniforms to the soldiers, making him suspect they were civilian technicians rather than military.

Zaen was pacing up and down the middle of the room, his robe swirling behind him each time he changed direction. He grinned triumphantly at Garrett. "You've learned nothing about the reach of my power, have you?"

Garrett stared back indifferently. "I know you enjoy abusing the authority the Brotherhood gave you. That doesn't make you a powerful leader."

Zaen nodded, his grin becoming broader. "Strong words from a condemned man. Yet here you stand before me."

"How many of your men has it taken to bring me here? Surely you could use your resources in a more constructive way."

Zaen stopped walking, his grin changing to a scowl. "How dare you tell me how to behave? You're in my world now. A fact you seem to ignore. Yet you have the audacity to turn my loyal subjects against me. Where did you think you were taking your fellow escapees?"

Garrett took a moment to glance around the bridge, surprised that none of the operators were paying attention to the exchange. "Each person chose to go to a better place, where they won't face persecution and injustice."

Zaen's laughter caught him off guard. "You're so self-righteous, Mr. Garrett. What gives the inhabitants of the Stellar Cluster any right to judge the Brotherhood? Are any of your worlds an Eden of peace and harmony?"

"Nowhere is perfect. But we do value our freedom and the rights of individuals."

Garrett's peripheral vision noticed several of the operators stirring in their seats. "While there may be the occasional conflict, most people are content, free to live and work where they want and have an abundance of food. Can you say the same?"

"I say you place too much importance on those concepts. People don't know what they want. They need to be instructed."

"So they can serve the elite, like you? I saw your decadent palace and the hundreds of servants. You act as if you're a god."

Zaen's face turned a dark shade of crimson. "I am a god," his voice thundered, causing the soldiers surrounding Garrett to take a small pace back.

Garrett stared into the eminence's eyes. The man was delusional. Years of entitlement with few to challenge him had left him with untold power. How many others like Zaen were there?

Zaen took two deep breaths, his evil grin returning. "It's time for a demonstration. Are you ready to watch your friends die before I take you back for your overdue execution?"

The threat did not surprise Garrett. He was only partially paying attention to what Zaen had to say and was more intent on studying the others on the bridge. Although the four soldiers around him were standing at attention, their posture remained too relaxed. Each of them was confident they had the situation covered with their prisoner safely bound.

Since arriving on board Zaen's flagship, he had presented an air of compliant resignation. It was similar to the body language he had seen from the prisoners inside the instruction camp. The soldiers expected that type of behavior.

And that was their mistake.

Feigning anger at Zaen's betrayal, Garrett took a small pace forward. "You promised you would spare their lives."

The movement was a ruse, allowing him to grab the small knife hidden in the compartment in his left forearm. With one swift motion, he swung the blade round and up, slicing the throat of the senior soldier standing to his right, followed by a second guard behind him. The other two soldiers froze in horror, ill-prepared for what was happening in front of them.

Garrett dropped the knife and grabbed the gun from the second guard, whose hand went to his neck in a vain attempt to staunch the bleeding. Two rapid shots killed the remaining soldiers. The whole action took less than two seconds.

The gunshots had caught everyone's attention. As one, all operators turned in their seats, their duties briefly forgotten, the fear in their eyes confirming they really were nothing more than technicians. Garrett could tell they would not cause him any problems.

By now, Zaen's face had turned a deep shade of purple. "How dare you!" he raged. "This is an outrage. You will never get away with this."

"Yes, I know that, Zaen. As long as you're alive, there will be no peace for me or anyone associated with me."

"You're absolutely right." With a speed belying his age, he drew a handgun from the sleeve of his robe and pointed it at Garrett's head, barely two meters away.

All Garrett could do was stare at the deadly muzzle aimed squarely between his eyes and calculate the chances of overpowering Zaen before the gun fired. Despite the age gap, he had witnessed the old man's reflexes. He was fast, and his hand was steady.

"I know you want to kill me," said Zaen mockingly. "Go on, try it."

Garrett steadied himself, channeling his inner rage. If he was going to die anyway, he may as well die trying to save himself. But, even as he tensed his legs to leap at Zaen, he heard the gun's trigger and firing pin click. Instinctively, he closed his eyes and waited for oblivion to consume him.

It took several seconds for Garrett to register that he was still alive. He opened his eyes to see the look of disbelief on Zaen's face as he stared at his gun.

Not wanting to give Zaen a second opportunity, Garrett lunged forward, taking the old man by surprise. The eminence stepped back, but he was too slow to avoid the attack. Garrett's left hand wrapped around the old man's throat, lifting him off the ground.

"This is for everyone you have ever killed and tortured," Garrett snarled through gritted teeth, his left hand tightening as Zaen struggled to free himself, his arms and legs flailing. But Garrett's hand was like a vice, squeezing the life from the eminence.

Zaen's eyeballs rolled up into his head as his body went limp. Garrett, recovering his composure, tried to release his grip. Killing the man like this was wrong. However, his arm and hand were now locked in position, all control frozen. Garrett used his right hand to try and release his fingers but the handcuffs prevented him from reaching across. He could only watch in vain as the life ebbed from Zaen.

Too late, Garrett pulled his thumb back, dropping Zaen to the floor. He stared down at the corpse, his feelings conflicted, Although he had not intended to kill, it was no less than Zaen deserved.

Breathing heavily from the exertion, Garrett glanced around the bridge. None of the bridge operators had moved or even tried to save Zaen. Instead, they sat transfixed in anticipation of Garrett's next move, probably hoping they would not be next. But he had no argument with any of them. They had only been following orders, living under the tyranny created by the Brotherhood and Zaen. Now, without their leader, they looked lost.

"Where's your captain?" he asked the nearest technician.

The man quivered with fear as he pointed to one of the dead soldiers.

"Who is next in command?"

The man glanced anxiously around the room. "I don't know. We are all equal."

Garrett gave the man a friendly smile. "In that case, I hereby grant you a promotion. You're now captain of this vessel."

The man didn't move, instead, staring nervously at his colleagues.

"What's your name?" Garrett asked.

"Dylko," the man stammered.

"Well, Captain Dylko. Please, can you unlock these handcuffs? You'll find the key in your former captain's pocket."

Without hesitation, Dylko retrieved the key and Garrett was grateful to be free once more. With some effort, he pushed his now useless artificial arm to his side, with his left hand fixed in its deadly clawlike position.

Dylko was about to return to his station when Garrett stopped him.

"Not so fast, Captain Dylko. I need you to contact the other warships and tell them to stand down on the instruction of Eminence Zaen."

"But the eminence is dead," Dylko replied, unable to look at Zaen's body.

Garrett clapped Dylko on the shoulder. "No one knows that yet. Only the people on this bridge."

Dylko slowly nodded his understanding. He stood, his legs shaking, and walked to the command seat, watching Garrett all the time as if he was expecting a trap.

"You can do this, Captain Dylko," Garrett said. "Have faith in yourself."

Dylko pressed a button on the side of the seat. A light flashed on the screen next to him. "This is Captain..." he began, before pausing. "This is Dylko on the Punisher. Eminence Zaen has the prisoner safely on board and is instructing all ships to return to orbit around Drani IV."

"Dylko, this is Captain Crouch on the Travesty. Your request is most unusual," came the reply from one of the warships. "What is your rank and why isn't the eminence giving the order?"

Dylko looked doubtfully at Garrett, cutting the link. "I knew this wouldn't work," he said.

"Convince him," Garrett said. He knew there would not be a second chance to get this right.

Dylko opened the link again. "Eminence Zaen is interrogating the prisoner. Do you want me to inform him you are challenging his orders?"

The reply was instant. "No, of course not. There's no need to interrupt the eminence. We will comply."

"Thank you," said Dylko, breathing a sigh of relief as he closed the comms link.

"Good work," Garrett said, watching the dots on the main view screen alter course for Drani IV.

"What will you do with us?"

Garrett hadn't given that question any thought. "How many others on this ship?"

"Only two more. In engineering."

That didn't sound right. This was a warship, after all. "Where are the rest of the soldiers?"

"We left them behind at the space dock. Eminence Zaen said we didn't have time to get them on board, so we have only a minimum complement."

It must be my lucky day.

He asked Dylko to open a channel to Santiago. "Captain Dreyfus, this is Oz Garrett."

"This is a pleasant surprise. What does Zaen want now?"

"Zaen's dead. The crew is non-military, so it will be safe for you to come aboard."

There was a moment's pause. "I don't know how you did it, but congratulations. Why should we come across?"

"I was hoping Sylwester and his friends could persuade the crew to join us on the trip back to the Cluster."

"You are full of surprises. I'll be across shortly with Rosa and Sylwester."

Garrett turned his attention back to Dylko and the bridge crew. They were all looking at him as if he was going to massacre them. He supposed it did not help that Zaen and four soldiers were lying dead in their midst. Time for some reassurance. "I promise, no harm will come to any of you. There are more of your people on the freighter. I am taking them to a new life in the Stellar Cluster. It would give me great satisfaction if you joined us."

"And if we don't want to go?" a technician asked tentatively as he stared at Zaen's corpse.

"Then you'll be free to return to Drani IV. Unharmed. All I ask is that you listen to what your fellow people have to say."

None of the crew looked convinced by his words. He could not blame them; the Brotherhood had convinced them that savages populated the Stellar Cluster. It would take more than a simple speech by him to convince them otherwise.

Chapter 63

Four hours later, Captain Dreyfus called Garrett to the Santiago's bridge.

"Do you know a Levi Murphy?" he asked.

Garrett nodded, puzzled by the question. "He's a good friend. Why?"

"Damn right I am," came Levi's voice from the loudspeakers. A moment later, a hologram image of his face appeared on the comms desk in front of Dreyfus. "Oz, you had us all worried. I can't tell you how relieved Leela and Keisha will be to discover you're still alive."

Garrett grinned, unable to recall ever being happier to see his old friend. "You should know me better than that. It takes more than a death sentence to keep me down. Where are you?"

"Four hundred thousand kilometers from your location. I'm holding station because of that warship flying next to you. I don't want to be captured like you."

"No need to worry. They're friendly. In fact, the crew's coming with us, seeking asylum."

"So I'm too late to rescue you?"

"You've saved my ass more times than I can remember." Garrett laughed. "But thank you for looking out for me."

"Where are you heading?"

The question threw Garrett, having given it no thought. He turned questioningly to Dreyfus, who said. "Rosa requested we go to Nesta."

"Weren't you at war with that planet?" Levi asked.

"That was a long time ago," acknowledged Garrett. "You know that most wounds heal, given time."

Levi's brow furrowed. "I do."

Despite his words, Nesta was not an immediate destination Garrett wanted to visit. Although he had no issue with the people, nothing was waiting for him there. "As you've come all this way, maybe you can give me a lift. I have unfinished business back at Destiny Station."

"I thought you'd never ask. I've several bottles of whiskey that simply don't taste the same when drinking on my own."

***

Garrett found Rosa and Mercedes in the single spare crew cabin. Rosa was now dressed in a set of military fatigues she had found on the warship. The clothes were two sizes too large, but still an improvement on the prison garb she had worn. And better than the clothes he had found for himself, which were too small for his hulking frame.

At some point, she had cleaned herself up and now looked ten years younger than the last time he had seen her. He was taken aback by the natural beauty that had been hidden under layers of grime and dirt.

Mercedes excitedly jumped from the bunk and ran to him, hugging him once again. He was getting used to the young girl's displays of affection and no longer felt uncomfortable. However, he felt a sense of guilt knowing this was a time for goodbyes.

Rosa must have seen the concern in his eyes. "What's wrong? Are we being pursued again?"

"No, nothing like that. We're still on track to leave the Bevas Sector in several hours and there are no Brotherhood ships for millions of kilometers. We're safe. And according to Dreyfus, Syl and the other former residents of Drani IV are settling into the troops' quarters on board the warship. Even making friends with the ship's technicians."

"So why the glum expression?"

Mercedes stepped back, looking up at him with pleading eyes, doubling his angst. Unintentionally, she was making this far more difficult than he had anticipated.

"It's time for me to say goodbye," he blurted. "One of my colleagues has arrived. He's going to take me back to Destiny Station."

"No!" cried Mercedes. "You said you would stay with us all the way to Nesta."

"You did promise," Rosa reminded him, looking almost as disappointed as Mercedes.

Repressing his guilt, Garrett said, "Nesta is your home, Rosa, not mine. And you don't need me anymore. You need time alone with Mikel, and to help these refugees. I would be in the way."

"No, you wouldn't," Mercedes said. She tightened her grip on his arm. "You can keep us safe."

He shook his head. "You'll be on Nesta. It's a peaceful planet. You won't need protecting."

"What about all the wild animals? I've been told they eat full-grown humans. And the savages that kill people for fun?"

Garrett kneeled so his eyes were level with Mercedes' tear-stained face. "There are no savages. The Brotherhood made up that story to scare you. And while the occasional wild animal kills a human, it is very rare. Trust me, you and your people will be safe."

"Oz is right," said Rosa softly. Mercedes ran back to her, sinking her face into her shoulder. Rosa glanced at Garrett as she hugged the girl. "Your mind's made up?"

"It is. I'll stay close until all ships are safely inside the Stellar Cluster. After that, it will be time to take our separate paths."

"I knew this would happen," Rosa replied, rubbing her hand soothingly on Mercedes' back as the young girl sobbed silently. "I never figured it would be so soon. Or so difficult."

"We made a great team. I wouldn't be alive if it wasn't for both of you. And I'm proud of what we achieved. But I'm an outsider here. You have your son back and these people to care for. That's more than enough. Where is Mikel, by the way?"

"He's sedated in the captain's cabin. The stubborn lad refused to rest and was delaying the healing process on his wound." She paused and smiled mischievously. "As a mother, I had no other choice."

"You mean he's still not listening to you."

"I'm not sure Mikel ever will," she said with a wry smile. "Very much like his father; he didn't know what was good for him either."

Garrett nodded, suddenly lost for words. This farewell was dragging on longer than he wanted. "Anyway," he said, awkwardly shuffling his feet. "I will visit once you're all settled."

Rosa wiped a tear angrily from her eye. "You better had. It's down to you that all these people are free to begin a new life without fear of persecution or pain. You've created a new future for these men, women, and children."

He shrugged his shoulders. "I never saw it like that, but you're right." His face brightened. "Give me a few months to get my arm fixed and I'll find you."

Leaning forward, he hugged Rosa. Trapped between them, Mercedes turned to wrap her arms around him. Out of habit, he gave her hair one final rub as he realized how much he would miss both of them.

After twenty seconds, he pulled back, giving each of them a knowing look. "Take care of each other," he said, turning to leave the tiny cabin.

"Look after yourself, Oz," Rosa called out after him. "And no drinking alcohol for the next three days. It will dull the effects of the medication."

"Yes, Doc," he shouted back, smiling to himself as he headed for the airlock.

Chapter 64

Garrett was dressing as the door to his room chimed. "Who is it?" he called out.

"Levi. Who else are you expecting?"

"You're early. You're never early!" Garrett pressed a button for the door to slide open.

"There's a first time for everything." Murphy entered the room with a half-empty bottle of twenty-five-year-old whiskey and two shot glasses. "We didn't have time to finish this one," he said with a mischievous smile.

Garrett stared in dismay at the bottle. The six-day journey back to Destiny Station had been a drunken mess as the two men recounted victories and stories. There was at least one day he could not remember and it surprised him that any alcohol remained on Levi's ship.

"I thought we were heading to Hunter's Lodge. Won't the others be waiting?"

Murphy raised his eyebrows. "Don't you think they'll start without us?"

Garrett laughed. "Of course not. What was I thinking? Pour me a good measure. I've not had a drink since the operation."

Murphy placed the glasses on the black weapons cabinet and filled them to the rim with amber liquid. He waited for Garrett to finish dressing before passing him a glass. "Cheers, Oz. Here's to friendship," he said, before quickly downing his drink in one gulp.

Garrett followed Murphy's example, almost choking as the sharp-tasting whiskey hit the back of his throat. Now he remembered why they had not finished the bottle while on Murphy's ship.

Murphy ignored his discomfort, quickly refilling both glasses. "How is the new arm?" he asked.

As if to answer, Garrett raised and lowered his left arm three times, while clenching and relaxing his fist. "Dr. Cassidy is happy with my progress. The nerve endings are functional, but I need more time to get the finesse I had before with my fingers. She keeps telling me to be patient. Can you imagine?"

"Does that mean you're ready for your next mission?"

Garrett gave Murphy a shrewd look. "What do you know? Has Leela said something?"

Murphy downed his whiskey before holding up his hands in innocence. "I know nothing," he said, but his wry smile said otherwise.

The smile didn't go unnoticed. "I suppose I'll find out soon enough," Garrett said, sipping his whiskey, allowing the burning sensation to coat his taste buds before it attacked his tonsils. He slammed the empty glass down on the cabinet, making it clear he'd had enough for now. "Okay, let's get this over with."

***

Murphy enthusiastically led Garrett into a crowded and raucous Hunters' Lodge. It was rare to see so many bounty hunters in the bar so early in the afternoon. An anxious Garrett wondered if Bernardo had a special promotion running that he was unaware of. He half expected fireworks and a giant cake to appear, especially if Murphy had anything to do with the celebrations.

Leela stood in the middle of the room, holding court as she recounted the capture of one of her many bolters. Although she was nearing the end of the story, Garrett knew who she was talking about. It did not surprise him when she leaped onto a chair and swung her arms around her head.

"So there was Pascal, standing precariously on the cliff edge," she continued. Most of the people standing around smiled in friendly appreciation for a story they knew too well, but she didn't seem to care. "He waved his saber at me as he held tightly onto Jessika, shouting that, if I took one more step, he would jump and they would both plunge to their deaths. My rifle had failed and the only weapon I had left was my brain. I could hear Pascal's gang approaching from my rear. The situation was grim."

Leela paused for effect and was rewarded for her dramatics when a young man with wide eyes standing close to her chair asked, "What did you do?"

She smiled sweetly at the man and was about to respond when she saw Murphy waving at her. "I'm sorry. I'll have to finish that story another time. The hero of the hour has arrived."

Garrett sighed as everyone in the bar turned in his direction. He winced as, two seconds later, there was a unanimous cheer.

Wanting to head back out of the door, Garrett instead found himself shepherded next to Leela by Murphy. The whole situation felt more awkward than any other moment in his life.

That was until Murphy stood on a chair, looking ready to make a speech.

"You don't have to do this," Garrett whispered.

Murphy smiled back and whispered. "Of course I do. It's not very often I embarrass the great Osiris Garrett."

Before Garrett could protest further, Murphy held his hands up to quieten the room. "Thank you all for attending today to welcome back our brother in arms from the jaws of death. You all know where Oz has been over the past month. His experience is something none of us ever wishes to endure. But if anyone can survive a death sentence, it has to be this man."

A protracted round of applause drowned out Murphy's next words. He stopped until the noise had subsided as Garrett's face turned a bright shade of red. "There is no doubt in my mind that Oz exceeded the standards expected of bounty hunters across the Stellar Cluster. His values and determination are characteristics to be admired. And let's not forget Oz not only saved himself, he rescued almost one hundred civilians from the Brotherhood's depravity. So let's hear three cheers for Osiris Garrett, the most famous bounty hunter of all time."

Once more, the room erupted in loud celebrations. Someone forced a drink into Garrett's hand as he stiffly accepted the praise. He was ill-prepared for the event or Murphy's over-the-top words. His nightmare became worse as Leela called him up to say a few words.

Replacing Murphy on the chair, Garrett took several seconds to look around Hunters' Lodge, stunned at how many people had packed the main bar area. Until that moment, he had not appreciated how many people he knew. So many faces he recognized were smiling up at him, waiting to hear his words. Bounty hunters were a close-knit family, but today's gathering took that to an entirely new level.

"Friends," he began. "This is a humbling experience for me. Knowing that you are here for me seems unreal. When Colonel Lane recruited me to be a bounty hunter, I never knew how rewarding it could be. Until that point, I'd spent my adult life in the Space Marines where comradeship was a large part of the military DNA. Seeing you here today is as close to that sense of comradeship as I've felt in a long time. So, thank you. It's incredible to be back."

For fear of getting overly sentimental, Garrett stepped down onto the floor, only to receive multiple pats on his broad shoulders.

"Gracious speech," Murphy muttered into his ear.

"I'm still going to kill you," said Garrett.

***

The bar had largely emptied after three hours. Garrett had done his best to circulate, speaking to many of his friends and graciously accepting free drinks, which he asked Bernardo to keep behind the bar for later.

Eventually, he reached Leela's table. By now, she was more subdued as she spoke with Keisha, Toru, and a heavily bandaged Naoki.

"I didn't know you were back at Destiny Station," said Garrett.

Naoki pointed to her torso, which was encased in a carbon-fiber medical casing. "I arrived six hours ago, against the doctors' advice. This casing keeps all my organs in place and aids the healing process. I wanted to be here to thank you for saving my life. Leela told me what you did."

Garrett blushed. He'd had enough compliments for one day. "Like I said earlier, comradeship means we don't leave people behind."

He noticed Leela briefly look away, but he didn't comment.

"Even so," Naoki persisted. "I'm more than grateful and hope we can work together again soon."

At that moment, Murphy joined the group carrying a tray of drinks. Glancing at Leela, he said. "Has he agreed?"

This time, it was Leela's turn to blush as she scowled at Murphy. "I've not spoken to him yet, Levi," she snapped.

"Agreed to what?" Garrett asked, staring directly at Leela.

Keisha laughed out loud. "Now you've done it, Levi. Your timing is impeccable."

Toru also laughed, although his confused expression confirmed he had no clue where the conversation was going.

"Leela?" Garrett asked again.

Leela fidgeted in her seat. "Well, after the successful mission on Lafayette, we now have a bucketful of credits, as well as an enhanced reputation."

"Yes, I know. And I still don't feel comfortable you used a portion of those credits to fund my new arm."

Leela shrugged unapologetically. "You were entitled to it. Seth said you should have his share, considering it was his information that allowed us to track down and capture the bolters moments before they were due to leave the planet."

Garrett grunted. Seth's act of charity didn't sit well with him. He would have to pay his brother back at the earliest opportunity. It didn't matter that Seth was wealthy. It was the principle.

"Anyway," Leela continued. "The way I see it, we work well as a team. If we combine the skills of the six of us, we could target bigger and more profitable jobs."

"No." Garrett's sharp response caught everyone by surprise, but Leela wasn't finished.

"Wait, hear me out. It's like you said in your speech. You feel part of a big family. One that supports each other through thick and thin. Together we can achieve some amazing outcomes."

Garrett nodded. "I get all that, Leela. Thanks for the offer, but the answer is no. I operated as part of a team for many years until they got ripped apart because one person wanted to chase the big credits. I'm not ready to do that again. It's too painful."

Leela's brow furrowed in confusion. "I don't understand. We made a good team."

"We had one mission, where Naoki nearly died. Leela, thanks for the offer. I'll let you know if I change my mind."

"But—"

"Leela, you need to respect Oz's decision," Murphy interrupted. "The man has been through a lot. Give him some space. You've already signed up the rest of us."

"You never begged me to join," Keisha said, slamming her empty glass angrily onto the table.

"Remember, I'm only joining you for one last mission," said Toru.

Garrett glanced around at the group. It would be too easy to accept Leela's invitation. These were all good people with a professional attitude to bounty hunting. He imagined it could be fun working with them. But, for now, he needed some space to consider his future. This decision had to be made on his own.

Chapter 65

It was a spring morning as Garrett rode along the path meandering between golden cornfields. The mid-morning sun felt hot on the back of his neck. Watching a flock of birds swooping across the hedgerow, he felt more relaxed than he had in a long time. The steady trot of his steed was soothing in its own way, reminding him of his younger days on his father's ranch back on Lafayette.

Rounding a bend, he heard the raucous sound of children laughing and playing. He passed a sign that read 'Drani Freedom School', before seeing a newly erected building with fifteen children in the playground, many of them chasing a ball without a care in the world. One of them he instantly recognized as Mercedes. She had a beaming smile as she played a game with two friends who appeared to be a few years older than her. Despite the age gap, she was telling her friends what to do.

He rode past, not wishing to interrupt what she was doing though finding it difficult to resist the urge to race up and surprise her with his presence. But he knew there would be plenty of time for that later.

Three hundred meters along the road, he stopped and dismounted, tying the horse up next to three small electric vehicles that were parked outside the civic center for the village.

He was about to enter the building when Rosa and Mikel appeared, running down the steps as soon as they saw him.

"Oz!" said Rosa. "I only just received your message. You could have given us more notice. I would have prepared a proper reception."

Garrett grinned as she came up to hug him. "You know that's the last thing I want. You're the one who deserves all the credit for this."

"That's what I keep telling Mom," said Mikel, coming forward to shake Garrett's hand. "Great to see you again. You never said goodbye when you left the Santiago."

Garrett took a moment to take a proper look at the young man. Now cleanly shaved with a neat haircut, he could see Mikel's resemblance to his mother. He also looked as though he'd put some weight on. Life must be treating him well.

Pointing to the buildings, he said, "It's impressive what you've achieved in only six months."

Rosa shrugged her shoulders. "I would have liked to have done so much more. Damn government bureaucracy has been a hindrance while the politicians decide the status of everyone we brought back with us."

The news came as no surprise. Garrett had a long-standing distrust of almost all politicians. His experience of them was that they were either out of touch with reality, incompetent or corrupt. The few honest politicians, like his brother, had little chance of success when dealing with those individuals. As a consequence, they rarely made positive decisions in a timely manner, leaving normal citizens to suffer.

"Do you know if the Brotherhood made a complaint?"

"Not that I know of," said Rosa. "Perhaps losing almost one hundred of their citizens, an eminence and a warship, was too embarrassing. Or they fear an uprising if it becomes common knowledge that their army could not contain the prison break. Can you imagine the hope it would give to communes across the sector?"

Garrett could picture that scenario. He hoped he would see it happen in his lifetime.

"Anyway," Rosa added. "We do our best with what is available to us and trust the process will support us."

"Even without help, you've still been able to create a school and a small community. Pretty impressive, if you ask me. I knew these people were safe in your hands."

She nodded. "Having almost ten million credits helped. Those ore crates were worth far more than Darr estimated. Even after paying Captain Dreyfus for his services, we had more than enough to purchase twenty thousand hectares of land. The construction droids finished the dwellings almost one month ago."

"What about Darr's share?"

"Miraculously, he reconsidered his position somewhere between your escape and arriving on Nesta," said Mikel. "Maybe it was speaking with his companions and understanding the suffering they had endured at his hands. Or perhaps he wanted to be accepted. Whatever the reason, he donated his entire share of the credits to this project."

"Incredible!" remarked Garrett.

"People are still wary of him," said Rosa. "He has a lot of bridges to build. So far, things appear to be working out. We've set him on several construction projects and he's not afraid of getting his hands dirty."

"What about everyone we rescued? Are there any regrets?"

"They are all thrilled," interrupted Sylwester as he descended the steps of the civic building. Garrett hardly recognized him. It wasn't just the clean-cut look, tanned skin, and smart suit. He now had an air of quiet confidence that began with a glint in his eyes and a warm smile.

"Syl! What have they done to you?"

"You like the look?" he said, cheerfully spinning around to give Garrett a full view of his suit. "Rosa has made me civilized. I am now the elected mayor of this village," he added proudly.

"Congratulations. I can't think of anyone more deserving."

"Thank you, Oz. None of this could have happened without you. You led us from darkness to this bright new life."

"You have it all wrong," Garrett replied. "Each of you achieved this for yourselves by making the brave step to a better existence. Your future is entirely in your hands. And from where I stand, it looks bright."

Sylwester's smile turned into a beaming grin, revealing a new set of pristine teeth. "It was still your bravery that ignited the spark in us. And for that, we will be eternally grateful."

Garrett felt his cheeks flushing at the compliment, feeling unworthy of the praise. "I was hoping someone would give me a grand tour of the village. Maybe the mayor could spare me an hour?"

"It will be my absolute pleasure," Sylwester replied.

"How long are you staying for?" Rosa asked. "Is this one of your flying visits? Mercedes will be so disappointed if it is."

Garrett pointed to the leather bag tied to the rear of his horse's saddle. "I'm here as long as you can put up with me. I figured it was time I contributed to the relocation. Although I'm not sure you need me now." He winked.

Rosa grabbed his hand. "Don't worry. I have a long list of jobs for you."

For the first time in many years, Garrett felt at peace. Not knowing or caring how long the feeling would last, he vowed to embrace the moment.

<<<THE END>>>

IF YOU ENJOYED TWISTED JUSTICE

My Mars Frontier series charts the progress of human colonization on Mars. The series is available on Amazon now.

DISCOVERY sees Mission specialist Georgia Pyke arrive on Mars with bold intentions to establish a legacy, unaware one of her colleagues has been holding a grudge for six years. How far is that person prepared to go to exact their revenge?

The mission quickly becomes a matter of life and death for the twelve astronauts as they struggle to establish a foothold on Mars. While Georgia and her crewmates fight the elements as well as their personal demons, something is lurking out of sight. Something that will change them forever.

WHAT READERS ARE SAYING:

"This book is an easy read. It's well paced and sets the scene for the next books in the series. The characters are well formed, believable and very human. There is just enough technical talk to make it all seem real without turning the reader off. This is the first book I've read by this author and am looking forward to finding out what happens next! Highly recommended" – J. Bee

If you're looking for a fast-paced action adventure, get your copy of Discovery on Amazon today!

GET EXCLUSIVE CONTENT

Building a relationship with my readers is the very best thing about writing. I occasionally send newsletters with details on my current projects, new releases and special offers.

And if you sign up to the mailing list, I will send you a copy of Deception, my prequel to the Mars Frontier series. You can receive this novella, for free, by signing up at www.paulrixauthor.com[1]

---

1.   http://www.paulrixauthor.com

ABOUT THE AUTHOR

Paul Rix is the author of the Mars Frontier human colonization series. His online home is at www.paulrixauthor.com[2]. You can connect with Paul:

on Twitter at www.twitter.com/PaulRix8[3]

on Facebook at www.facebook.com/paulrixauthor[4]

or email at paul@paulrixauthor.com if the mood takes you.

---

2. http://www.paulrixauthor.com

3. http://www.twitter.com/PaulRix8

4. http://www.facebook.com/paulrixauthor

Made in United States
Orlando, FL
21 February 2022

15031653R00178